AFTER YOU WERE GONE

Praise for *After You Were Gone*

'Gripping, propulsive, and unbearably tense – the best psychological thriller I've read in years' – **Mark Brandi, author of *The Others***

'An elegant, powerful and utterly compelling thriller. The best book I have read all year' – **Lucy Christopher, author of *Release***

'An expertly crafted psychological thriller… need-to-know addictive propulsion… The ending felt just right' – ***InDaily***

'An original thriller full of empathy' – **Sarah Bailey, author of *The Housemate***

'*After You Were Gone* is the very best kind of thriller: tender and wise as well as pulse-poundingly tense' – **Anna Downes, author of *The Safe Place***

AFTER YOU WERE GONE

VIKKI WAKEFIELD

NO EXIT PRESS

First published in 2022 by Text Publishing, Melbourne, Australia
First published in the UK in 2023 by No Exit Press,
an imprint of Bedford Square Publishers Ltd,
London, UK

noexit.co.uk
@noexitpress

ISBN
978-1-915798-02-2 (Paperback)
978-1-915798-03-9 (eBook)

2 4 6 8 10 9 7 5 3 1

Typeset in 11.4 on 14.6pt Garamond MT Pro
by Avocet Typeset, Bideford, Devon, EX39 2BP
Printed and bound in Great Britain by
CPI Group (UK) Ltd, Croydon CR0 4YY

MIX
Paper | Supporting
responsible forestry
FSC® C171272

BEFORE

When I was a child I believed there was a place where lost things collected, the way sea-drift found its way ashore to the same sheltered cove on our beach. I never knew if it was a story I'd heard or one I had made up, but I could picture it clearly: a black hole where time stood still and the lost things lingered – socks, shoes, purses, keys, missing pets – until people stopped looking for them and they faded from memory.

After Sarah was gone, I imagined her in that place. Suspended, sleeping.

Not knowing was like living inside a well with slippery sides and the occasional crack between stones, a foothold, a scrabbling place. I yearned for answers; I tortured myself, going over the things I could have changed if only I had been paying attention.

After Sarah was gone, I moved on, but I built my house around the well. While I was busy living, it sank deeper; the distance was greater, the light dimmer. This time the climb might be impossible, but I had no choice – I let myself fall.

My life is a story in two parts.

Before.

After.

The day my daughter went missing, we were at war.

Our two-bedroom, ground-floor unit in the outer suburbs was one of twelve, close to a busy main road. I wanted to go to a weekend street market. At the time I didn't have a car, but the buses ran hourly and our stop was only a ten-minute walk away. The bus I wanted to catch arrived in fifteen minutes, but Sarah was still standing in the hallway, facing the wall, arms folded.

'It's going to rain,' I said. 'You'll be cold. Put on some long pants and a jacket.'

She shook her head and stamped her bejewelled flip-flops.

I tugged at her dress – pink with a leotard bodice and a tulle skirt, more suitable for a fairy-themed party than an unseasonably cool day. I'd taken her to see the fireworks at the beach the night before and she was overtired and bad-tempered.

'We'll miss the bus. Quickly – get changed.'

She slapped my hand. 'You can't make me!'

I stepped away lest I slap her in return. 'We're not going until you do as I ask.'

'I don't want to go. It's too far. The market is just stupid people and weird fruit.'

She flounced to her bedroom. Seconds later, I heard the chime of her jewellery box and the clack of beads.

I followed, taking deep breaths, and watched her from the doorway.

Sarah didn't look much like me except for her skin tone and build: golden and quick to tan, slim but muscular. She could hold a handstand against a wall for five minutes and turn eight cartwheels in a row, but her hair was straight and dark, unlike my tight blonde curls, and so silky it slipped from a hair tie. She had fuller lips, inscrutable expressions, and eyebrows that threatened to meet. Fierce, independent and intelligent in a way that was spooky in a child, Sarah delighted in pushing me past logic and into pure reaction. If I lost my temper, she would smile.

'Sarah, let's go!'

I should have given in. If there was ever a moment in my life I could change, it was then.

But I listened to that infuriating chime, let my frustration build and peak, and by the time I'd dragged her from her bedroom, her graceful neck weighed down by a string of beads, she was crying. She grabbed her ever-present drawing supplies from the dining table – a leather briefcase that made her look like a tiny office worker – and tried to stuff her doll Annie inside. The catch wouldn't close.

I wrenched the doll away and flung it on the couch. 'I'll just end up carrying her around. Leave Annie here.'

The police would ask me later if I saw anyone parked outside our block of units, if it was possible we were followed. I told the truth when I said I didn't see anyone, but I was in no frame of mind to notice details. Even hypnotherapy only gave sharper, more painful focus to the things I'd done: squeezing Sarah's hand too tightly, barking words I meant at the time and regretted later. The time I was trying to make up with long strides, pulling her along the footpath, was counteracted by her dragging weight. Sarah retaliated by plonking herself down, but I hauled her up by the armpits and recommenced our slow progress, unwilling to give her what she wanted – to go back home, and also, I suspected, to win.

We missed the bus.

The next one came after an hour of stony silence – Sarah scribbling furiously in her scrapbook, only breaking concentration to glare at me, covering her work with her arm so I couldn't see. Another portrait of her monstrous mother, no doubt. Sometimes she gave me a ball gown and wings; more often it was bulging eyes, claws and sharp teeth. Her mutinous expression had softened, but it had been replaced by a resoluteness that made me fear she was building towards a humiliating public tantrum.

But I won.

We got off the bus and trudged the last five hundred metres to the market in Buskers Lane, a cobbled street flanked by the kind of narrow-fronted shops that relabelled and resold imported goods as designer fashion and homewares. It was a busy, crazy maze: outside the shopfronts, stalls flanked a pedestrian walkway just wide enough for four people abreast. It was mostly junk jewellery, deep-fried food, homemade crafts and cheap souvenirs, but Sarah loved the snow cones and I always headed for the fresh produce.

Despite my insistence that Sarah should wear appropriate clothes, I'd worn ridiculous shoes: wedge heels that made walking on the uneven cobblestones difficult. My ankles ached, but I was determined not to go home until I'd filled my shopping bag with weird fruit and taught my daughter a lesson.

'Look, they have those crane kites you always wanted.' Sarah was subdued.

'No.'

'Raspberry snow cone or Coke?'

She glared. 'They make my teeth hurt.'

I pointed to a man making balloon animals, but Sarah was having none of it.

'No.'

'If you don't snap out of it soon, miss, you'll be going to bed at six o'clock for a week.'

It started to rain, a fine, floating mist that turned the cobblestones shiny and slick, enough to send people scurrying for cover.

I stopped at a stall to feel and smell the produce. The vendor held an umbrella over my head.

Sarah tugged at my arm. 'I want to go home *now*.'

'Then you'd better start walking.' I said it without thinking, and picked up a spiky fruit. 'What are these?'

'Ritlee rambutan,' the woman said. 'They're grown in North Queensland.'

'Fresh?'

'Came down yesterday. The jackfruit are from the Northern Territory. Very fresh.'

After choosing six rambutan and two jackfruit, I unfolded a canvas shopping bag and carefully placed the fruit inside. When I turned to speak to Sarah, she was gone.

'Did you see my little girl?' The vendor shook her head. 'She was right here.'

I checked under the table. I looked up and down the street. No Sarah.

My temper flared again; instead of the expected tantrum, she'd pulled a disappearing act.

'You saw her, though, right?'

She shook her head again. 'No.'

'She's wearing a pink dress. If she comes back, can you tell her to wait here?' I picked up my bag and ducked into a side street where I had a decent view of the area.

The rain was heavier now. My hair was sticking flat to my head and my arms were covered with goosebumps, but my primary concern – and I would later admit this to the police – was that Sarah was hiding somewhere, watching. I suspected she had witnessed my rising panic and found another way to punish me.

So I hid.

I stayed there for at least five minutes, hoping Sarah would blow her cover when she realised I had gone. I wanted her to be the lost child standing in the middle of the street, crying because she couldn't find her mother. People would stop to help her. Still I'd wait, until her panic matched mine and she was inconsolable. I know I wasn't the first parent to think about pulling this trick, but maybe I was the first to actually do it, and to have the stunt backfire in such a spectacularly devastating way.

Ten minutes later, I'd abandoned my shopping bag and my ridiculous shoes under a table. I never found them again.

I worked my way from stall to stall. 'Have you seen a little girl?' I described her hair, her beads, her dress. Held my hand waist-high. Told them her name. My feet were bleeding, my left big toe stubbed and shredded.

A crowd began to gather.

'How long has she been missing?'

'Could she have run off?'

'Should I call the police?' a woman asked.

'I don't know!' I wailed. 'No. Yes!'

Somewhere, an accordion was playing the 'Beer Barrel Polka' in an endless loop. I'd never get the tune out of my head. I watched a blue helium balloon detach itself from a bunch and sail away – I remembered that, but I couldn't recall the faces of the people who tried to help.

It didn't occur to me that she wouldn't come back, or that we wouldn't find her. My panic was still laced with guilt and, if I am honest, anger.

Despair came later.

Over the following hours the search spread from the laneway to nearby streets and parks; the police knocked on doors and searched shops, warehouses, roofs, even drains, anywhere a child might have been hurt or become lost. The sky darkened. More rain fell. There were baying sniffer dogs, portable spotlights that hurt my eyes, and faceless people who asked the same questions over and over, as if I might remember things differently.

It was that evening, when the sun had set and the only people left were those directly involved in the search, when I first heard the word 'abduction'. Until then, it had been 'lost', 'missing' and 'misadventure'. I was sitting on the rear step of a police van, a scratchy blanket wrapped around my shaking shoulders, feeling numb and alone. There were calls to be made, but first I had to accept that Sarah was really gone.

A tall, middle-aged man wearing a dark suit approached, holding out his hand.

'My name is Inspector James Hooper. I've been brought in as the specialist investigator on your daughter's disappearance.'

He had a warm handshake and gentle eyes. After the repeated questioning and blunt manner of the other officers, it was too much. I broke down.

He gave me a packet of tissues and sat next to me. 'Ms Morgan, we have to consider that this might be an abduction.'

'A *what?*'

'Is there anyone who might have taken your daughter? Anyone she'd go with willingly?'

I shook my head. There was nobody, unless someone from her school happened to be in Buskers Lane and thought it was a good idea to convince Sarah to go with them. It seemed like long odds.

'My parents live in Athena Bay. Jess – my sister – is in Greece.'

He checked his notepad. 'You're a single parent. What about her father? Is there a custody arrangement?'

'He's not in her life,' I said. 'You'd be wasting time looking in that direction. I couldn't even tell you where to find him.'

'Regardless, we'll need names – anyone you can think of, any details, no matter how small or insignificant they might seem.'

'No, no, it's nothing like that. This is my fault – she wanted to go home. I told her to start walking, but I didn't mean it.'

'We're checking all possible routes.' He closed his notepad and tucked it in his shirt pocket. 'Do you think she might have tried to make her way home, alone?'

I pictured Sarah's habitual scowl, the stubborn set of her chin. 'It's possible,' I admitted.

'There's some footage coming in. We'll see what that shows us. I know you must have been over things a dozen times, but –'

I started telling him about the argument.

He interrupted. 'I know those things. Tell me about *her*.'

She's bright and wilful – we argue all the time – but she can be so sweet. She has a chickenpox scar on her right shoulder. Her bottom two teeth have just cut through. She believes in ghosts and fairies – she thinks she was a princess in a past life. She swims like a fish. Her earliest memory is of playing at the beach, and she likes hiding in small spaces but hates the dark.

We spoke for nearly an hour. I showed him photos of Sarah on my phone, and sobbed.

'I won't stop until we find her,' he promised.

At seven o'clock an officer told me she'd been instructed to drive me home. I didn't want to leave, but by then it was no longer a busy market – just a wet and lonely street, cordoned off from onlookers at each end. I clung to the possibility that Sarah had got lost. Perhaps someone had thought they were doing the right thing by taking her home. She might be waiting for me there, so I didn't argue.

I sat in the back of the police car, shaking so hard my teeth felt loose. I chewed my nails and the cuticles bled. Until then I had ricocheted from one fraught moment to the next, but now reality hauled me down so heavily I felt the shocking need to crawl into bed and sleep.

I made a mental list. It was a short one: call my parents, and call Jess in Greece. I had no idea what time it was there.

Back at the unit, there were other officers waiting, some already inside. They took my phone. They bagged Sarah's hairbrush. They questioned me relentlessly, through the night and into the early morning, until I could barely form a coherent sentence, let alone recall what I'd said before. They also gave me updates on their investigation, which were not reassuring.

Footage from the cameras in the laneway proved inconclusive. It was difficult to find a clear view of the street and the pedestrians because every angle was obscured by vendors' awnings and umbrellas. Every vehicle registration matched locals, vendors or visitors. No witnesses had come forward.

Sarah had simply vanished, as if she'd never been there.

The one thing the footage *did* prove was that I had spent roughly five minutes waiting in the side street, playing cat and mouse with my missing child, which at least gave police an approximate time for her possible abduction. Five minutes, waiting for her when I could have been looking. I should have remembered more: the exact time she disappeared, faces of passing people, cars in the parking lanes. But I simply waited, thinking she'd be back at any moment. I'd dragged Sarah all the way there, clenching her tiny hand in my fist, and then I'd let go.

Five minutes, wasted.

I won and I lost.

By midmorning the questions had ceased and an officer had returned my phone. I was encouraged to rest. Instead I spent hours in my bedroom making desperate calls, while a revolving shift of police officers crowded the unit. My neighbours had been woken during the night and questioned. Jess had promised she would be on the first flight home and my parents were on their way. Each conversation only made Sarah's absence more painful and real, and I couldn't help but replay, over and over, what my mother had said when I managed to choke out that Sarah was missing.

What are you saying, Abbie? Are you telling me you lost her?

That she was distraught, but not shocked, was another twist of the knife.

My phone battery eventually died. I put it on charge and picked up a book from my bedside table. I'd read the first half, about a woman, an amnesiac, who woke each morning with no memory of her life. How awful, I'd thought, to forget everything while you slept. My bookmark was one of Sarah's drawings, given to me the day before. Now, when I unfolded the paper and looked more closely at her characteristic bobble-headed figures and fussy colouring in, the drawing seemed like an omen.

Sarah: smiling and dancing.

Me: standing over her, faintly menacing, hands on hips.

When I finished that book almost a year later, I knew intimately how terrible it was to wake each morning and remember.

NOW

Twenty minutes before we were married, Murray and I had sex behind the box hedge separating the backyard from the winter creek that ran behind our house. I pondered whether it was bad luck to screw before the wedding, but shrugged it off – I should be living in the moment, not dwelling on the past or thinking about what might lie ahead. It was 2010, the year of the Haiti earthquake, the Deepwater Horizon oil spill, WikiLeaks, the Chilean mining accident, the Times Square bomber, and Lady Gaga's meat dress.

Sarah had been missing for almost six years. It didn't make the papers.

On the other side of the hedge there were seventy-two white chairs, two blocks of six by six; in the middle, an aisle strung with fake ivy and real roses; at the end of the aisle, a wrought-iron gazebo, still tacky after two coats of white enamel paint. Seventy-odd people – it wasn't many for a second wedding and a combined family, but we invited people we liked, plus a few we didn't. Blood was blood. Our guests were seated and waiting. Not my mother, Martine, who'd staked out her chair front left-of-centre and announced, since we were taking so long to get started, she was going inside to open a second bottle of champagne.

The sex wasn't sexy and we gave up after a few minutes, laughing.

'Be seeing you,' Murray said.

We kissed.

Murray dashed around to the front door and sneaked into the spare room.

I entered the house through the sliding door on our bedroom deck, switching on the ensuite lights to check myself in the mirror. The heavier-than-usual make-up was making me sweat. My curly blonde hair had been slicked down and pulled back, my body waxed, tweezed and squeezed into a sage-green halter-neck dress that made my swimmer's shoulders seem gargantuan. I looked stiff and unnatural, like a tomboy who'd had a makeover.

I plucked a fistful of tissues to blot my nose and cleavage, counting down from a hundred until my breathing steadied. At the last moment, I switched the matching green heels for well-worn flats, to give me a better chance of staying on my feet.

Jess was waiting in the kitchen, ready to walk me down the aisle. Four years younger and two inches taller, she was just shy of six feet when she drew herself to full height, which was always. Her hair fell in loose ringlets to the middle of her back and she wore a sleeveless linen shift the colour of milky tea. The dress was already wrinkled, but Jess wouldn't care. My twin in looks but not in temperament, she stood with her hands on her hips and her feet apart, as if braced for a tackle.

'Morning glory?' Jess smirked.

'It's almost three in the afternoon.'

She reached behind my ear. A leaf materialised. 'You have hedge in your hair.'

I patted the twist at the nape of my neck. 'It must be from the bouquet.'

'He's a good guy, Abbie.' A bold statement from Jess, who didn't believe there were good men, only those who hadn't been caught. 'Relationship goals.'

'My last relationship goal was to have a musician who looked

16

a bit like Rick Springfield write a song that sounded a lot like "Jessie's Girl", for me,' I said. 'I'm punching way above.'

Murray and I had planned a simple wedding, which meant we'd hardly planned at all. I booked the celebrant, Deirdre, and the cake and chairs online. I sent invitations by email and organised a cheap caterer. Murray repainted the gazebo, set up the chairs and filled an old bathtub with bottles of wine and champagne. There would be drinking, dancing and insulting speeches, and after everyone had gone we'd fall into the same bed, watch a late movie we'd seen before, make love missionary-style and fall asleep straight after, the way we'd been doing it for four years.

Nothing would change, especially not my last name. Morgan, not Lucas – so Sarah could find me.

Jess checked her watch. 'How fashionably late are you planning on being?'

I glanced outside. Our guests were fanning themselves: it was over thirty degrees despite being midway through autumn.

'Let's get this over with,' I said.

Jess's expression darkened: on cue, Martine stood in the doorway, mirroring my sister's stance. Her mother-of-the-bride outfit was the same beige lace-trimmed suit she'd worn to my father's funeral two years ago. Her cheeks were stained raspberry and wisps of greying blonde hair had slipped loose from her bun. Even ageing and tipsy, she was formidable.

People said that about the three of us, that we were women of strong bearing, big bones. But I didn't feel strong today – I felt as if, with the right pitch and frequency, I might shatter.

Martine raised her glass. 'What are you standing around for? Are you ready?'

I nodded. I took my mother's half-glass from her and threw it back, partly for show, partly to keep her from drinking more.

'Where's Murray?' Jess asked. I shrugged. 'He's coming.'

Martine cackled. 'Maybe he's changed his mind.'

'Maybe he's changing his pants,' Jess said under her breath. She made an obscene gesture with her tongue. 'Come on, we're all adults here.'

In any exchange, even a good-natured one like this, Martine tended to hit below the belt, Jess aimed for shock value and I tried to distance myself from the indignity of it all. Martine always said I wasn't invested, that there was a picture of me under the word 'egocentric'. She said I was careless with people.

I didn't think that was true. Not anymore.

'Where's my wife?' Murray boomed. He grabbed Jess by the waist and spun her around. 'Wait. Wrong sister.'

I smiled and waited. Martine would say something cruel and Murray would shoot her down. I depended on it. *Three, two, one...*

'Your *second* wife,' she said. 'And almost young enough to be your daughter.'

'My last wife, if she'll have me,' Murray said. 'Count me blessed.'

Martine huffed and went outside to take her seat.

'Marry him before I do,' Jess said, knocking me with her elbow.

Edie opened the sliding door. 'Dad? We're melting out here. Cam has already taken off his shirt.' She blew me a kiss. 'Abbie, you look beautiful.'

'Don't you make me cry, kid.'

I did anyway.

Deirdre was at least seventy, twenty years older than the picture on her website, but she was professional and expressionless and perfect. She beckoned Murray to stand next to her under the gazebo. He took his time, shaking hands and kissing cheeks on his way down the aisle.

Jess held me back in the kitchen for longer than I wanted.

'Wait,' she said. 'Let everyone sit back down.'

I stood by the door, fiddling with the fine gold chain around my neck. My hands jerked and shook. If I waited too long and something went wrong, it would be my fault. I was constantly looking for ways to avert disaster – not obsessively, just countless minute calculations and adjustments that made my worries bearable, like making sure Edie and Cam were safely home before I went to sleep. Vigilance.

Jess stilled my hands. 'Abbie, stop.'

'I'm fine.'

'It's okay to be happy.'

'I know.'

'Do you?'

I'd asked Jess to give me away. I hated being the centre of attention, and my sister commanded it. She walked beside me, her arm hooked through mine. I held her hand so tightly I squeezed the blood from her fingers, but she neither flinched nor complained.

I half-registered the many faces on my way down the aisle, most of them Murray's family and friends. Sherri, Murray's ex-wife, was sitting with Edie and Cam, and I wouldn't have had it any other way. My own guests probably totalled fifteen: aunts and uncles, a couple of cousins, and Tara, another instructor from the swim centre where I worked, who had brought her partner, Cleo. I noted the unoccupied seat next to Martine, and assumed she was displaying uncharacteristic sentimentality by reserving it for the ghost of Dad.

It was then that I saw her, Cassandra Albright, second row from the front. I knew the familiar slant of her posture, her determined chin. She was alone. She must have come all the way from Sydney – I'd sent an invitation to be polite, but I didn't think she'd turn up. We had spoken just once in the past twelve years, the day after my father's funeral, two years ago.

Cass brought everything back. Cass was there when my life switched tracks; she was not there when it completely derailed.

I returned her tentative smile.

Jess gave me a moment to recover and gently pulled me along. I stumbled up the steps, glad I'd taken off the heels. Deirdre took our hands and crossed them over each other. Rather than the usual *we are gathered here today she said welcome to this most glorious union*, and I stifled a hysterical giggle.

I focused on Murray. As he fumbled for the rings in his pocket, I felt the awful weight of knowing that, if we were fortunate enough to reach old age, and given women tend to outlive men by seven years, I might spend up to thirty years of my life without him. The thought had no place here, but I was intimate with foreboding. Now it was a guest at my wedding.

We'd written our own vows. Mine were heartfelt, delivered in a low, tremulous tone that had everybody straining forward to hear. Murray spoke loudly and with conviction but, as always, he made it sound as if a punchline was coming.

'Second time lucky for this old man,' he said, and there was a rumble of laughter.

We exchanged rings. Murray slid the band over my knuckle.

I glanced at the chair where my father should have been. The seat was now taken: Sarah's doll Annie, arms and legs akimbo, head drooping like a sleeping child. She had loved that doll – fed it, slept with it, carried it everywhere, except the day I'd made her leave it behind.

Jess and I locked eyes. Her hands flew to cover her mouth.

Deirdre cleared her throat. 'Should I repeat the last bit?' she said through her teeth.

I shook my head.

She pronounced us man and wife. I don't remember how we

kissed, probably close-mouthed and passionless. My lips were dry, my body stiff with anxiety.

Martine went inside with the doll straight after the ceremony. She'd made her point. My mother was my constant reminder that my child was still missing, that my time hadn't been served.

I barely remember accepting congratulations from our guests – at least not until Sherri approached. We were opposites: she was fifteen years older, olive-skinned, dark-haired, small-boned, always impeccable in her manner and dress. We shared an easy friendship because Sherri made it easy.

Murray's arm tightened around my waist and he swung Sherri around with the other. Was it wrong that he still looked at her like that? Was it strange that I didn't mind?

Sherri pecked his forehead. 'You lucky man.' She cupped my cheeks. 'You look gorgeous, Abbie. But what happened up there?'

'I had a moment,' I said. 'I'm fine now.'

Murray sighed. 'Martine.'

Sherri nodded. 'What can I do?'

'Nothing,' I told her. 'Eat. Drink. Be Sherri.'

She smiled. 'I have an early flight, but I'll do my best.'

Murray wandered away to speak to a work colleague, and I took a flute of champagne from the tray Edie was holding. She was the image of Sherri, but like her father in personality, with grand plans to take over Murray's veterinary practice when he retired. I envied her drive and focus at only nineteen. Her brother, Cam, two years older, somehow managed to juggle a thriving social life, football, tennis, more than one girlfriend and an engineering degree.

Blinking away tears, I surveyed the garden, our guests, the way everything glowed a sunny yellow. At Edie and Cam's ages I had been a pregnant teen and a single parent on welfare.

'Abbie.'

My heart skipped – I wasn't sure if it was gladness or nerves. 'Cass. Thanks for coming. It's good to see you.'

'Of course,' she said. 'Wouldn't have missed it.'

'Did you fly down?'

'I drove. I'll head to Athena Bay tomorrow to visit Mum and Dad.' She laughed. 'Funny how I still think of it as home – I haven't lived there for almost half my life.' She took in my bright eyes. 'You look happy.'

'I am.'

She gave me an awkward hug and I returned it, knowing how precarious these moments of friendship could be.

'I've missed you,' I said.

'Same.'

'I'm sorry it's been so long.'

'Me too.'

Someone turned up the music.

'Where should I put this?' She held an envelope. 'It's a gift card. I know you said no gifts, but seriously, nobody ever means that.'

We laughed.

'Thank you. There's a wishing well on the bridal table.' I looked down at my not-wedding dress. 'I'm a bride. Who'd have thought?'

Cass grinned and looked twenty again. 'I've been close a couple of times but you beat me to it.'

'Where are you staying? I want to hear all about – you know, we've missed so much.'

'Oh.' She seemed embarrassed. 'I was going to sleep in my car.'

'We have a sofa bed.'

'But it's your wedding night.'

I shrugged. 'We've been living together for years. Nothing is going to change.'

*

It was midnight. Many of our guests had stayed longer than expected and I was disappointingly sober, still doing the goodbye dance at the door.

Jess was taking Martine back to her room at a nearby hotel. It was her gift to me, she said, and we hugged long and tight as they were leaving. I moved to hug my mother too, but she swooped in and out of my embrace, our bodies barely touching. Her outfit had wilted; her cheeks were dry as paper. She looked old. I felt sorry for her, which would probably upset her far more than me thinking she looked old.

'Congratulations, Abbie,' she said.

'Thanks for coming.' I watched her snake sideways down the steps, gripping the balustrade for balance. 'Why does she hate me so much?' I whispered to Jess.

'Because you pretend you don't need her,' she said.

'*You* don't need her.'

'But I pretend that I do.' Jess squeezed my hand. 'I'll take the gorgon now. You take your husband to bed.'

'I haven't seen him for a while. He's probably already there.'

Jess smiled. 'I love you.'

'Love you too.'

I locked the door behind them, checking it three times before glancing into our bedroom. As suspected, Murray was flat on his back, snoring. I took a spare pillow and a quilt from the linen cupboard in the hallway and carried them to the lounge room.

Cass was sitting on the couch, nursing a cup of tea. She'd cleared away the last of the wine glasses and brought the wishing well inside.

I dropped the pillow and quilt on the sofa bed opposite and sat next to her. 'I feel terrible. Was I supposed to open the cards in front of the guests?'

Cass sipped and shrugged. 'I'm not up with wedding etiquette, but feel free to ask me anything about debt collection.' She pulled the wishing well across the table. 'You could open them now.'

'Sure. Help?'

She chose an envelope, broke the seal with her fingernail, drew the card and placed it on my lap, open. 'There's a hundred bucks.' *Rip.* 'Another hundred here.'

'People have been so generous. We don't need anything.'

'I know. I mean, look at this place.'

Murray's home – *our* home – was beautiful: a restored 1920s villa set on a wide street in the kind of leafy, affluent suburb that didn't brown off in summer. It had a wide return verandah and a rambling quarter-acre garden, and our neighbours were hidden behind wrought-iron gates, tall brick walls and high hedges. Sherri's classy touch was evident everywhere, which should have been uncomfortable but wasn't.

'What does he do, your man?' she asked.

'He's a vet. A very good one.'

'We wanted to be flight attendants, remember?'

'Until I realised I was afraid of flying.'

Cass reached for another envelope. After a pause, she said, 'You were afraid of everything, Abbie.'

I tensed. 'Because we took so many risks.'

'We were young.'

'We were stupid.'

'We had fun.'

We had sex with strangers and played Russian roulette with pills. I had a baby. My child was abducted. I was little more than a child myself when it happened. None of it was fun.

But I just said, 'Well, that depends on who's telling the story.'

Cass held up a card and another couple of fifty-dollar notes. 'It was nearly thirteen years ago. You're still angry.'

'I'm not angry. I'm scared. It never stops.'

It was like having a floater in my eye – I could see beauty all around, but this thing was *there,* clouding my vision, making everything ugly.

Cass leaned close and slung her arm around my shoulder. 'I don't know what to say except I'm sorry. This was meant to be a happy day.'

'I *am* happy. That's why I feel like shit.' I gave a strained laugh and wiped my eyes. 'Clearly I haven't consumed enough alcohol.' I chose the next envelope because it was small, plain, and it seemed lost among the bulk of the rest. It was tucked, not sealed, nothing written on the front. Inside was a piece of A4 copy paper, folded twice. I unfolded the paper and smoothed the creases.

My breath caught in my throat.

Over the years, I had become used to Sarah's drawings turning up when I least expected – in drawers, tucked between the pages of books, among her old toys and games. Each one was a cursed reminder, and a gift. In this drawing we were wearing bell-shaped gowns, holding hands. I had something approaching a smile on my face, and Sarah had accurately portrayed her own features, with her direct stare and Frida Kahlo-esque brows.

Along the top of the page were the words: *Happy Wedding Day, Mummy.*

Written by an adult hand, made to look childish? Sarah had never called me Mummy. She was born a hundred years old. How typical of Martine to keep this precious thing from me until now, and to ruin it by scribbling all over it.

'What is it?'

'It's nothing.' I shuffled the paper and envelope with the rest and gathered them to my chest. 'Help yourself to anything you need. I'll see you in the morning.'

Cass reached out to grab my hand. 'Will you visit? Come to Sydney?'

Like touching a hot stove, my first reflex was to snatch my hand away. I had the sensation of falling down the familiar rabbit hole. None of what happened to Sarah was Cass's fault, but I had developed irrational ways of coping.

I made a noncommittal sound.

I wouldn't visit Cass in Sydney. For my own survival, some doors had to stay closed. I was a veteran of disaster, used to life-changing events. Hypervigilant, jumpy, prone to overreaction in a crisis. I knew tragedy could arrive with a bang, but I forgot to pay attention to the hairline cracks and seismic creaks.

You think death is the worst thing – your whole life coming for you. But it's not the worst.

BEFORE

For six months of the year, the tourists in Athena Bay outnumbered the locals. The rest of the time it was the usual people, too-familiar faces, and the class divide between the business and beachfront property owners, like the Albrights, and the back-street blue-collar locals like us.

What kind of family were we? Sometimes I only knew what we were not – not a family who ate together, like the Rowneys next door, who had six kids and held barbecues every weekend, who played beach cricket and slept in tents in the backyard during summer. Unlike my friends' houses, ours was never filled with the sound of music and television. We didn't have people over unless it was a big occasion, like Christmas, Easter, or somebody had died. Our mother read the daily death notices because she didn't trust any mode of communication that wasn't in print. She was a committee person: she got things done. I started calling her Martine when I was twelve and she didn't stop me. Dad was a plumber: he worked six days a week, came home at five, ate sitting in his recliner and fell asleep after dinner with a beer in his hand. We lived two streets back from the postcard-pretty beach, but our parents rarely went there. We had books and rules and timetables, and we had enough freedom, but that, I suspected, was because our parents wanted quiet in the house.

Jess and I were the kind of kids who preferred to be at other people's houses. That's who we were.

Cass and I went to the same school; I had sleepovers at her place almost every weekend, slept head-to-toe with her. High school was a breeze. We were decent students, popular, always busy with our local boyfriends, as well as the transient boys of summer. Our weekends were spent defending our hard-earned corner booth at the kiosk and the best spot on the surf beach, and in turn I was protected by my friends – by the town itself – from the world.

Our last summer together in Athena Bay ended in February 1997. Cass went away to university. Everything familiar was suddenly strange; I burned with impatience for the next stage of my life to begin.

Cass had been gone three months when she called late on a Friday night. I'd been out at the surf club, but had left early. We were asleep when the phone rang; my parents stumbled out of bed, clearly assuming the worst, and Jess followed. I grabbed the receiver and pulled the phone cord along the hallway until it was at full stretch. I had to leave the base in the hall and wind the receiver coil underneath the door, so I could close it. I sat on the floor with my back against the wall. Two streets away, the waves slapped the shore.

Jess, just turned fourteen, snuffled at the base of the door like a puppy. 'Who is it?' she whined through the gap.

'Go back to bed.'

To Cass I said, 'It's really late.'

She sounded drunk. 'My flatmate is moving out. I miss you. Will you come?'

'Come there?' I lowered my voice. 'You mean live with you?'

When I opened my bedroom door, Jess was slumped against the wall, staring at me with a look of betrayal. My mother stood with the other end of the cord wrapped around her wrist; she was strung so tight I could have drawn a perfectly straight line along her back.

'You're leaving,' she said.

'I'm eighteen. I'll get a job. It'll be fine.'

'I give it three months.'

'I'm eighteen,' I repeated. 'You can't stop me.'

Jess cried.

Cass was as lean and muscled as a dancer, with short, dark hair worn in a bob, pale skin, pierced nose, perfect legs. She met me at the train station. We hauled my two battered suitcases onto a bus and sat on the rear seat, elbows and thighs touching, smiling like idiots.

'You're here,' she said. 'Things will be okay now. It's been hell.'

'What happened with your flatmate?'

Cass shrugged. 'She had a problem with the house rules.'

Our unit was close to a main road. The kitchen was little more than a kitchenette; any more than four people and the lounge room was overcrowded. There was an enclosed yard, barely big enough for two deckchairs and a wall-mounted washing line, and a mould-ridden showerbath combo in the bathroom. Rising damp had lifted tiles and curled vinyl, but when Cass had complained the landlord threatened to raise the rent.

It was a shithole, but it came semi-furnished and now it was ours.

Cass had the main bedroom. Mine was three by three metres with a draughty window that played like a flute and a ceiling hatch above my double bed. There were dirty handprints around the edge, as if someone lifted the cover at night and looked down at me while I slept. When I had trouble falling asleep, I counted the sounds of gear changes instead of sheep.

Here we were, fresh out of home, leaving behind bedrooms with posters of Kurt Cobain on the walls, and drawers half-full of cheap cotton underwear and pharmacy brand make-up. Cass had started her Bachelor of Business. Against my parents' wishes, I'd deferred my place at teachers' college because I wasn't sure it was what I wanted. Ten years in a surf lifesaving club and six months as a checkout operator were my only qualifications, but within a week I'd found a casual job as a junior swim-school teacher.

Ambition seemed like something I could leave in my pocket for later.

I borrowed Cass's clothing and emulated her style. I cut my hair into a bob like hers, dyed it dark, blow-dried it straight, pierced my nose and lost nine kilos. We looked so alike people took us for sisters. With practice I even danced like Cass, but the nineties club scene wasn't kind to me. I was beach-born. I needed a solid month of sun to look healthy and waves up to my waist to hide my wide hips. Living like nocturnal creatures turned my skin yellow; the undyed roots of my hair showed green. I missed my rent payments to pay for drugs I rarely took, to earn membership to a scene that didn't fit, to keep up with a friend who'd outgrown me so fast she seemed like a changeling.

Cass received top-up money from her parents.

Mine were watching me paddle from afar, hoping I'd sink.

Cass kept a glass jar filled with loose change in a kitchen cupboard – sometimes I took a few dollars. Not too much for her to notice, but enough to afford a pack of cigarettes or to pay for bread and milk if it was my turn. She brought home guys who smoked weed inside and wandered around half-naked. She ignored the dishes in the sink until we either ran out of plates or I gave in. I'd go to wash my clothes and find hers twisted in the basin, stale and stinking.

'What *are* the house rules?' I asked.

I knew the answer. There weren't any.

'No guys we don't know, okay?'

She agreed, but did as she wanted.

In the beginning, I only had Cass. Home was over two hundred kilometres away and, apart from Michael Tate, another instructor from the swim school, I was too shy to make new friends of my own. Cass had fallen in with a group from uni – Karla, Reno, Fiona and Brent. Others came and went, but the six of us hung out a lot.

Fiona and Brent were an on-again-off-again couple, both still living with their parents. Brent disappeared for hours at the clubs, and when he returned they'd fight. Fiona cried a lot. Cass and I counselled. They always ended up together again, making up on our couch, and we forgave them for the drama.

Karla was on exchange from Berlin. She was living on campus and appeared mysterious and terminally bored. While we danced, she watched, repelling the boys with her cold stare, sneaking glances at the girls. Cass admitted they'd kissed one boozy night, but to my knowledge Karla never showed any other sign of being a sexual being. She ate our food, slept on our couch and used our toiletries, but she was the perfect house guest: she'd slink away quietly leaving the dishes washed, the couch cushions plumped, and intricate doodles of the solar system on the notepad next to our phone, which she used frequently to call home. She always left money to pay for the calls.

Reno was even more of a mystery than Karla. Cass found him fascinating – she said he looked like Marilyn Manson without the make-up, and she suspected he had the IQ of a genius. He also had the best drugs and a seemingly endless supply of cash. He was the one with the contacts and a free pass into every club, and the only one of us with a car, a red 1976 BMW 5-series with ripped leather seats and a machine-gun exhaust.

'Reno fancies you,' Cass told me one morning. 'We have to pay extra this week for the gas bill. And we're out of milk. Do you want Lucy or Molly for the weekend?'

'Molly,' I said. 'How do you know?'

'Reno told Brent. Brent told Fiona. I'm telling you. It would be so great if you two got together.'

'I don't think we have much in common,' I said. 'He's not really my type.'

I gave Cass my last hundred and was lucky enough to get Michael's classes while he was sick. I made it through the next week by offering to clean our elderly neighbour's unit, the following week by cashing in stolen empty bottles and cans. I pawned a gold chain my parents had given me for my eighteenth, but when I went to get it back it had been sold.

During the day, I reassured new mothers while I held their squirming toddlers in the pool. I blew in the kids' faces and dunked them, dodging tiny fists as they hit and kicked and paddled like frightened puppies. At night I followed Cass: to bars and clubs, to share houses filled with loud music and overheated bodies, along quiet streets as we found our way home in the morning.

Work, watch TV, sleep, dance, work, sleep – it was freedom and independence of a sort, as Cass had promised when she summoned me to the city. Here was the world, ready to explore, but it turned out my greatest ambition was to deliver a lie convincing enough to stay home, to have the unit and the TV to myself.

They were my friends, and they were not. I hardly knew them, I didn't trust them, but Cass included them in everything. I complained that we never did anything together anymore, just us, the way it used to be.

Cass bloomed. I began to fade.

One afternoon, a few months after I'd moved in, Cass was outside watering the pot plants when Michael dropped me home after work. We had been taking classes in adjacent lanes for a couple of months. When he noticed I caught the bus after our shift he started offering me rides.

I found him shy but harmless. He reminded me of Lenny from *Of Mice and Men*: huge, shaggy and lumbering – not exactly slow, but not a quick thinker. The kids loved him. Cass thought he was weird.

I sat in the car for a few minutes making polite conversation – I couldn't invite him in, not with Cass eyeing us from the porch, semi-naked and openly hostile.

'She mustn't feel the cold,' Michael said, and he wasn't trying to be sarcastic.

'Probably.'

'I don't think she likes me.'

'Oh, she just doesn't know you.'

I got out, slammed the door and tapped the roof twice in thanks. Cass watched Michael drive away. 'He's one strange cat, Abigail.'

'No stranger than half the guys you bring home, Cassandra.'

'You must give off weird pheromones. You always did attract the losers.'

It was the first time I realised that my version of events and Cass's weren't quite the same – like going to your high school reunion and finding out your perceived popularity was an illusion. It wasn't the losers I attracted, it was the loners. Guys who didn't hang in packs, who broke the rules. Or were they the same thing?

'Don't encourage him,' Cass said. 'You're too nice.'

'Encourage what? He just gave me a ride home.'

She pinched off the hose and aimed the nozzle at me. 'Don't even.'

'Is that a dare?'

Cass came after me and I ran until the hose reached its full length. She kept me standing out on the street, dripping, while she laughed and laughed.

I took a few days' leave and travelled home to visit, once.

I went to my old haunts and caught up with friends, but I'd lost my sense of belonging. Everyone had slipped seamlessly into adulthood while I was stuck in between. Jess was still mad: she barely spoke except to announce she'd taken over my bedroom as her study room – I'd have to sleep on the couch. Dad was either at work or drinking beer in his shed, and my mother served her regular hot meals but maintained her cold distance, slopping food onto my plate and furiously shifting my belongings from the couch to a corner of the lounge room, where they wouldn't offend her.

'Why does everyone hate me?' I whined to Dad. 'Jess is being such a brat. It's like you don't want me here.'

He said, 'Do you mean we should all stop what we're doing and treat you like you're on holiday?'

'Martine isn't even speaking to me.'

'You're as stubborn as she is.' He smiled wryly. 'It'll pass. It started when you told her she couldn't control you and it'll stop when you realise that to her it isn't control, it's love.'

At dinner that night, Dad asked pleasantly, 'So how are you and Cass finding life in the big city, Abbie?'

Before I could answer, Martine said, 'They're probably doing hard drugs and having unprotected sex all over the place.'

Jess burst into laughter.

Dad left the table.

The next morning I packed my bag and went back to Cass.

When Reno and I eventually hooked up, it was a classic case of peer pressure and the euphoria of Reno's pills. Disorienting, awkward and unpleasant, both times. He wasn't the first guy I'd had sex with, but he would be the one I'd never forget.

The second time he stayed the night, I woke early, hungover and overwhelmed with regret. I decided I found him repulsive: his long, pale, almost hairless body, and the way he ground his teeth in his sleep. I lay there unmoving for an hour, facing away and feigning sleep. I sensed he was awake too.

A hand slid across to cup my hip, and I sprang from the bed. I couldn't cover my nakedness fast enough.

'You don't have to stay.'

He uncurled from my sheets like a lazy cat. 'What do you mean?'

'I mean, it's okay to go. I won't be upset.'

I went to the kitchen to make coffee. A minute later I heard the shower running.

By the time the kettle had boiled, he was dressed and standing too close behind me in the small kitchen. I found his height and presence intimidating, his blown pupils unsettling. I felt his breath on my neck. Cass wandered in, smirking.

I sighed in relief but didn't turn around.

Reno read the room and left.

He had used my toothbrush and towel and left them both in the sink, wet. For four days straight he called the landline two or three times a day, until I unplugged it and signed up for my first mobile phone plan. Another expense I couldn't afford. He called Cass instead, and she translated his increasingly aggressive messages to the whiteboard.

'Did something happen?' she asked.

'No. Not really.'

'He likes you.'

'I can tell that.'

'You're harsh, Abbie.'

'God, I'm too nice, I'm too harsh – which is it? I don't fancy him.'

'Then why did you hook up?'

Why did I sleep with anybody? To fulfil other people's expectations. Out of boredom. For comfort. Never because I was in love. Because, when I felt the heat of another's skin, I wasn't invisible and I wasn't alone.

NOW

Two days after our wedding, Murray was called in to cover the emergency shift at the animal hospital until the regular night vet returned, and we postponed our honeymoon.

We settled into the familiar and frustrating night-shift routine – meeting briefly between the sheets in the early morning, like a couple having an affair. It was the only time I felt truly safe: curled into his heat, feeling his big hands on my body, smelling the hint of antiseptic that clung to his skin even after he'd showered.

It was his second week of night shift, eight days after the wedding. We had made love, and he was already slipping away into exhaustion and sleep. I lifted his heavy arm from my waist and tried to slide from the bed without disturbing him.

He stirred and pulled me closer. 'Stay.'

'I'm driving Edie to uni,' I said. 'She has a meeting first thing.'

'Edie can catch the bus.'

'I promised.'

Murray groaned and rolled onto his back. 'You're a disgrace to wicked stepmothers everywhere.'

'I'll come back after,' I lied.

Murray stared at the ceiling. He seemed lost in reflection.

'Bad night?' I asked.

He nodded. 'Some Pentecostal twit brought in his dachshund. Said he thought she'd eaten rat bait, but when I wanted to put in an IV and keep her overnight he said he'd take her home and pray for divine healing.'

'What did you do?'

'Nothing I could do. No one will ever thank you for telling them how to look after their animals or their children.' He checked his phone. 'What day is it? Do you have classes?'

'It's Monday. I have Nippers and Dolphins in the afternoon.'

'Driving across town for two classes?' he said. 'You don't need to work. You could quit.'

'I love teaching kids to swim. You know that.'

I smiled to hide my annoyance and slid out of bed. I took a quick shower and started getting dressed. Out of habit, I popped a contraceptive pill from the packet and put it under my tongue. At the same time, I pulled on a clean pair of underwear, one-handed.

'Multitasking, like clockwork,' he said.

I smiled. 'Go to sleep.'

'Speaking of clocks – what if you stopped taking them?'

I froze. 'What are you saying?'

He patted the bed. 'I'm sorry, that was clumsy.'

I went over to him and he caught my hand.

'Am I too old to be a father again?'

I slumped on the edge of the mattress. His arm curled around my waist and a lump rose in my throat.

'Say something.'

An ache started in my lower belly and spread. This was how it was meant to be: loving each other, taking another step forward, making plans together. But I was terrified to open my mouth in case something awful came out.

'You're not too old,' was all I could manage.

'Is it too soon?' He said it gently, but his arm tensed.

'Too soon,' I parroted.

'Can you give me some indication of when might be the right time? Give me something to look forward to?'

I made a noncommittal sound, peeled his arm away and continued dressing.

Murray lay on his side, watching. He looked about as far from sleep as I was from engaging in conversation.

How could I explain? He trusted I'd told him everything. He knew about the boxes stacked in the storage space in the roof, holding Sarah's clothes, toys and drawings, and bulging with photos and newspaper clippings. But there was another box – I carried it in my mind. It was only for putting things in, never for taking them out. I'd shove my worst thoughts inside and let the lid slam shut, as if it was a box of snakes. I could not tell him that the thought of having another baby made me feel hollow when I should be filled with joy.

Mothering Edie and Cam was easy: they came to me whole and perfect, without a shaky foundation of guilt and past mistakes. How they turned out was neither my fault nor to my credit.

But Sarah – I'd failed her in countless ways. Another child would only feel like a fill-in for the one I'd lost.

My afternoon classes at the pool ended up being cancelled due to low numbers. I spent the day tiptoeing around the house while Murray slept, slow-cooking a roast and freezing meals for the kids in case they were hungry when they got home from uni over the weeks to come.

I was stirring a saucepan of gravy when the landline rang. I turned the gas burner to low and rested the wooden spoon across the top, wiped my hands on a tea towel and flung it over my shoulder. Cam had left a pair of dirty football socks in the hallway – I threw those over my shoulder too, and reached for the phone.

Hardly anyone called our home number. Murray was old-school:

he insisted we keep it in case there was ever a network conspiracy or an alien invasion. I lifted the receiver and listened, waiting for the line to connect and the telltale sound of a call centre to come through, so I could hang up. There was only a faint background hum.

'Hello?' I said.

Nothing.

'Hello?'

'Abbie.'

A male voice: deep.

'This is Abbie Morgan.'

'You didn't change your name?'

My skin prickled. 'Look, it's not a survey, is it?'

'No.'

'You have about thirty seconds before my gravy burns.'

'This might take a while.'

I assumed he was a telemarketer and hung up, swearing under my breath.

A text from an unknown caller came through on my mobile immediately after – *don't hang up this time* – and the landline rang again. I turned off the gas. The old adrenaline raced through my veins; bile burned my throat.

Three rings. Four.

During the months and years after Sarah was taken, the trolls and the liars came for me regularly. Sitting in the police station – listening to recorded calls and trawling through false leads and fake evidence – gave me something to do when I couldn't bear to be alone with my thoughts, lest I pick and pull and unravel completely. Hope and despair coexisted until I could breathe on my own.

In a way, the trolls had kept me alive.

I took a step closer. The display read *No Caller ID*. Why, if he had my mobile number, was he calling the landline?

Five rings. Six.

I was blindsided by a flashback: my hand, a bony claw around the receiver, dirty plates stacked in the kitchen sink like the spine of a child with scoliosis, the darkened shapes of furniture. I remembered how I'd felt my way around my silent house because I couldn't bear to open the curtains, how loud noises made me plug my fingers in my ears. Back then my daily survival depended on the rituals: preparing pots of tea, waiting for the leaves to steep, doing thousand-piece puzzles and tenderly filing my bitten nails. With careful planning I could fill hours and days. Fifteen minutes until I checked the letterbox; forty-five minutes until my next cigarette. Though I'd since stopped smoking, many of those same rituals still carried me from one moment to the next.

But this was a new number, a different house. There had been nothing for years. How did they always find me?

Eight. Nine. I worried Murray would wake. I closed the hallway door and moved to the lounge room. Ten rings.

I picked up on the eleventh and pressed the receiver to my ear without speaking.

'You got the drawing,' the voice said. 'Your wedding card.'

'Who is this? Why are you calling me?' I whispered.

'She was quite the little artist.'

Beats of silence. The drawing was in a box with Sarah's other pictures, where it belonged.

A shudder crawled along my spine. 'I'm sorry – I don't understand.'

But I did. *Martine hadn't put it in the wishing well.*

'It was you?'

'Yes.'

'Who are you? How did you get it?' I stammered.

'I have more.'

I said, 'I don't believe you. I get these calls all the time.'

'Not like this.'

40

Don't give the crazies your pain was the wisest thing my mother had ever said. 'I'm hanging up now.' But I didn't hang up. I cracked. 'What do you want from me?'

'I want you to listen.'

'Have we met?'

He paused. There were a thousand miles of silence; I sensed he wasn't close.

'Are we going to keep playing this game? I wasn't quite ready, but you've forced my hand.'

'What –'

'Your marriage.' A sharp exhale. 'It really was unexpected – and unseemly, considering how close we are to our sixth anniversary.'

It took me a moment to catch up. In two months, Sarah would have been gone six years. A tear dripped onto the open palm of my hand, held stiffly on my lap.

'You're insane. Filth,' I spat. 'Monster. You're a liar.'

'*You* know what you did.'

He spoke as if he knew me. Why didn't I recognise his voice?

'I kept her things – her bag and dress. Her shoes.'

In desperation, I hissed, 'This call is being traced.'

'Stop wasting time. Stop crying.'

I shot to the window. I pulled back the curtain and pressed my palm to the cold glass. In seconds, it fogged up like an aquarium.

'What am I doing right now?'

He took a sighing breath. 'There are no cameras. I can hear it in your voice.'

'How will you know if I go to the police?'

'I know everything about you. Your husband will be home at six. You'll pick up his daughter from work at ten.'

His voice was crisp, clipped, as if he was reading from notes. *Your husband. His daughter.* Not *Murray* or *Edie* or *your stepdaughter.*

41

It was true. I always drove to pick up Edie after her late shifts at Pasta Joe's on Mondays and Thursdays. My life was predictable, but I didn't document everything the way Jess did. I never shared pictures of my family or updates on my whereabouts. And he was wrong about Murray being home at six. He was still in bed, asleep.

He didn't know everything. But he was the one who took Sarah – I *felt* it. My mind scrambled to make connections; my body vibrated with rage and fear. Was he at our wedding? Impossible. Close friends and relatives – that was all. I picked up my mobile. Could he be tracking my location?

'What's your name?'

He grunted.

'Why are you calling me now?'

'I took what I'm owed. Now it's time –'

'You took my child's *life*! You can't hurt me any more than you have already!'

'I can take more,' he said.

'What do you want from me?'

'I want you to dismantle the placeholder life you have built for yourself. Piece by piece.'

A burst of static. Did he chuckle? Did he have no conscience, no feelings? If he was one of the crazies, he was calm and methodical in his insanity, and it was terrifying.

'I'll do anything.'

'Good,' he said. 'But there's only one way, otherwise this all falls apart.'

'I understand.'

'It will take some time. You have to be patient.'

Time was all I had. Too much of it – endlessly waiting, hoping, praying to a god I didn't believe in, for six years.

'How much time?'

'Weeks, maybe.'

I barked a hysterical laugh. *Weeks.* Was that all?

'Why are you laughing?' For the first time he seemed uncertain.

I heard Martine's voice again. *Don't be careless, Abbie. How can you be so careless when there's so much at stake?*

'I'm sorry. It's just… I've waited for so long.'

Down the hall, a toilet flushed. Murray was awake. I wanted the call to end, so I could tell him. Together we would call the police.

'Listen carefully.'

'I'm listening.'

Murray's footsteps in the hall.

I looked around the lounge room, as if any crack, vent or knick-knack could conceal a pinhole camera.

The hallway door, opening.

'I'll call again soon. I'll be switching phones and changing numbers – you cannot return my calls or messages unless I allow it. If you tell anyone, I'll know. If you alert the police, I'll know. If you speak to your husband or your sister or your friends, I'll know. If you deviate from the plan or you take too long to achieve the objectives I set, I'll know. I'll disappear, and you'll never know.'

'You're in another world,' Murray said.

We were stretched out on the couch, top to tail, watching the late news before he left for the night shift. Dinner hadn't worked out: the roast beef was dry, the vegetables undercooked, the gravy congealed in the saucepan. Murray had tried multiple ways to get my attention, asking inane questions about my day, telling me stories about his animal patients, pulling my body closer when I broke contact.

I wanted to tell him: *everything is wrong except for you.* But that wasn't true anymore. I felt it the moment I hung up the phone – the need to float away by myself, to retreat, to disengage. One phone call and a matter of hours had already set me back years in terms of trust and intimacy.

I needed Murray to go away so I could resume trying to send the same pointless message to the unknown caller — *Where is she???* — though every time the message had failed to send.

My mind was in chaos. *Tell him. Tell him. You can't. If you tell him, you'll never know.*

Murray's voice came at me like an annoying whine. 'What's wrong?'

'I'm just tired.'

'*You're* tired.'

'Okay, you're more tired. You win,' I said.

I didn't have to see his face to know he rolled his eyes.

'Is it about this morning?'

This morning? I tried to rewind the day, like walking backwards through a doorway, poking my mind into remembering. *Sex. Pills. Clocks.*

'Oh, the baby thing.' I sounded offhand. I didn't mean to.

A news story came on. I watched the banner fly across the bottom of the screen. *Breaking: seven-year-old boy fights off abductor outside school.*

I sat up, curling my legs underneath me, transfixed. Sarah had fought me on everything: what she wore, what she ate, what time she had to go to bed, everything. But she didn't fight back when he took her. She couldn't have. Someone would have noticed.

The screen flickered and went black.

'What happened?'

'I turned it off. You don't need to watch that.'

'But I need to know what happened!' I snatched the remote and tried to turn the TV back on.

Murray grabbed my wrist. 'Abbie, stop.'

44

The front door opened and we froze. Cam, home from football training.

'What's up?' he said, looking from his father to me.

Murray let go of my wrist. 'Hey, mate.'

I got up. 'I made dinner. I'll reheat it for you.'

'No, thanks. I ate already.'

Cam slung his sports bag in a corner and went to his room. I willed him to come back and put it away, but he didn't. A moment later, loud rap music echoed down the hallway. I got off the couch and started washing the dishes by hand for something to do other than talk.

Murray put on his shoes and picked up his keys. 'I'm going to work. Don't forget to pick up Edie.'

'Have I ever?' I snapped.

'You can talk to me about anything, you know.'

'I know.' *Not this.*

He waited, with one foot out the door. 'Is it your friend? The one at the wedding? I feel like whatever is going on with you right now, it started with her.'

In response, I turned the TV on and stared at the screen. I gripped the phone with one hand and the remote in the other, flicking between channels, trying to find out what had happened to the boy, but my thoughts drifted to the voice on the phone.

I want you to dismantle the placeholder life you seem to have built for yourself.

Murray swore and slammed the door. The dismantling had begun.

I pictured Cass. Did it start with her? Where does anything really begin?

You were afraid of everything, Abbie.

The fear – its shape and shadow were familiar, the same. It was still with me. Maybe it had never left.

BEFORE

Cass and I were going to a twenty-first birthday party at a share house, guys we didn't really know, friends of friends. Usually I dreaded Saturday nights – I worried about what to wear, how to get home, what I owed for drinks and drugs, was I dancing the right way, was I pretty enough, was I *fun*? I suffered social burnout, bone-deep tiredness, sore feet and brutal hangovers. A house party seemed quaint. Safe. Fiona, Brent, Karla and Reno weren't invited, and I was feeling upbeat.

We caught the bus from our unit and walked the rest of the way in high heels, sharing a cigarette, passing a half-bottle of vodka between us. We left the empty bottle standing on a brick pillar outside a block of flats, and Cass stopped behind a tree for a delicate spew – a waste of good vodka, but expected. She'd swallowed two Es half an hour earlier. Mine were still in my purse.

The house was old, built in the twenties or thirties, bungalow-style with a deep verandah and sandstone bricks. The kind of place that would fetch a fortune after renovation, but at the time it looked like a serial rental. There was a broken concrete path, a gravel driveway and a Commodore wagon on bricks on the front lawn.

I suspected we were overdressed in our little black dresses. Cass wore a red poncho she'd found in a second-hand designer-clothing shop; I wrapped my arms around my waist and shivered, wishing I'd brought a coat.

We knocked on the front door. Nobody came.

'I guess we just go in,' Cass said.

The pills had hit her hard. I wished I'd taken mine earlier, but now it was too late. At the time, I'd opted to fake a high and sell the tabs to Fiona later to make my money back. Cass and the others were in sync when they took drugs, but I either outlasted the club hours and couldn't sleep when everyone else had crashed, or I was the first to slump in a corner. There was no in between – I was an abject failure as a recreational drug user, like I was with everything else, or at least that's how it felt at the time.

Cass opened the door. The entrance and front bedrooms had stained-glass windows; the sinking sun poured through the glass, making rainbow prisms on the scarred floorboards. There was a stain on the welcome mat in the shape of Portugal. Cass tottered down the hallway, running a hand over the 1970s wallpaper as she passed, puncturing the bubbles with her sharp nails. The hall was long and narrow, and led to a filthy kitchen with sticky vinyl floor tiles.

The house appeared empty.

We heard music coming from outside, but not the kind we were used to. We found an exit through a laundry where an old stone basin was filled with ice and beer. The music got louder: a male voice singing a reggae song, accompanied by an acoustic guitar and what sounded like somebody thumping a plastic bucket with a wooden spoon.

Cass smacked the screen door with the flat of her hand. She missed a step, stumbled and disappeared from view. The music stopped. I caught the slamming door as a short guy with dark, coarse-haired arms helped Cass up.

She put her hands on her hips and surveyed the group. 'Have we got the wrong party?'

Seven guys, sitting on rough-cut tree stumps around a smoking kettle barbecue, a moat of empty beer cans on the dirt underneath.

No other girls. The guys were average-looking, dressed in loose jeans and T-shirts to cover gamer guts, long-haired, greasy-skinned, and none met my eye. They looked like a bunch of perpetual IT students who still lived at home.

I relaxed. Here was a group of people less cool and more socially awkward than me.

'Whose birthday is it?' Cass asked.

She took a beer from a guy with fine blond hair and a patchy beard, swigged, gave it back. She took a half-smoked cigarette from someone else.

'Andy's.'

'Who's Andy?'

There was a roll call of introductions – Mike, Leroy, Andy, Carl, Scott, two Daves – each putting their hands up as if they were in class.

I let go of the railing and picked my way carefully over the cracked concrete. 'Wrong place. Let's go.'

Someone said, 'Stay.'

Cass pouted. 'One beer?'

'I want to go,' I said.

'Chill out. It's fine.'

The guy with the guitar started singing again. Now he was self-conscious – stumbling fingers, pitchy voice, half-closed eyes. He sounded better before we came outside. And I noticed something else: they were *excited*. They didn't want us to leave.

There was a casual shifting of seats until two guys were standing. A couple of spare stumps appeared.

'Are you sisters?' the guy with the beard asked. 'I can't tell you apart. What's your name?'

Cass nodded and chose a lap, randomly it seemed, until I realised she was transfixed by the tassels on his jacket. 'Abbie,' she said. 'And Cass.' She slipped her red poncho over her head and whizzed it around on her finger, until it flew off and hooked over the Hills hoist. 'You should sing,' she said to me. 'She's got a great voice,' she told everyone else.

'Just one beer,' I said.

Did I sing? I think I did. It was later, after not one beer but so many I lost count.

I woke early the next morning on the sofa in the lounge room, head pounding, stomach churning. There was a red bucket sitting on the carpet within throwing-up distance – on inspection it was empty. My skin itched and burned. I discovered a trail of insect bites travelling up my inner arms, between my breasts, down along my torso and thighs. Cass's poncho was spread over my lower legs – I vaguely remembered putting it on when the night had turned colder and the fire went out.

But where was Cass?

After fifteen disoriented minutes of opening various doors, I found her, asleep in a back room, naked and uncovered, next to a male body shrouded in a sheet. One of her arms hung over the side, her fingers lying gracefully against the carpet. A black and white cat was curled in the crook of her leg.

I woke her gently. I found her bag, wrapped in her dress like a parcel on the floor, and I managed to get her clothed and out of the room. As we tiptoed into the lounge room, she stopped to pick up her poncho and pointed to her bare feet.

'Wait here. I'll get them,' I said, and went back to the bedroom.

The guy in the bed was awake.

I hooked the straps of Cass's stilettos under my fingers and turned to leave. He hadn't moved, but his accusing eyes followed and I prickled all over with embarrassment. Since we'd crashed their party and drank their beer, I felt I should say something.

'Thanks for everything. It's been lovely.'

Cass forgot her poncho but took the red bucket, which she

carried all the way home. She'd go on to re-enact the morning escape scene to Karla and Fi, making fun of it all: the squalor of the house, our deeply uncool hosts, my drunken singing and my incredibly stupid parting words. She made up events I wasn't convinced had happened – each time the story would get funnier, the girls would laugh harder and I, going along with it all, could only laugh about it too.

Another Saturday. I hadn't seen Reno for a couple of weeks, but I knew I couldn't avoid him forever.

I was sitting on the carpet wearing my pyjamas, sipping tea. My hair had grown out of its dark bob, fading to a drab brown, and the daily straightening and constant exposure to pool chemicals had left it dry and split. Cass had washed and blow-dried hers – now cut in a pixie style, and dyed deep red. I felt betrayed.

'You owe two hundred and twelve for the electricity bill,' Cass said. 'Where do you want to go tonight?'

'Are the others coming?'

'Yes.'

'Everyone?'

'Of course.'

'We could stay home?' I said.

Cass laughed as if I'd said the funniest thing. She dipped into her purse and waved a tab under my nose, pinched between her fingernails. 'So have you decided where we're going?'

'Planet,' I said.

It was within walking distance. I could sneak away quietly if things got too intense.

'Planet is mainstream,' Cass said.

'You asked where I wanted to go.'

'Fine, whatever.'

Cass didn't want the rain to ruin her hair, so we caught a cab at eleven. She paid for the fare and my first drink – after the money for the electricity bill, I had only nineteen dollars to last the rest of the week.

The club was packed. I'd swallowed a quarter tab in the taxi and half an hour later felt next to nothing, as intended. Karla and Fiona met us there, but Reno and Brent weren't around.

I relaxed. I danced with Karla, who managed to be both intimidating and reassuring. Fiona paid for my second drink and we bitched about Brent in a quiet corner, where we could hear each other above the bass.

We spotted Reno at the same time and Fiona gave me a nudge. He sauntered past without looking in our direction. 'Cass said Reno said you used him?'

It was such a high-school word. *Used.* It implied I'd taken what I wanted from Reno without any consideration. That's not how it had felt to me. *I* felt used. In my mind, Reno got exactly what he wanted. I felt manipulated, exposed, dirty.

'That's not it.' I shrugged. 'It's hard to explain.'

Near the front stage, just above head height, a giant cage was suspended over the dance floor. Every couple of tracks the cage was lowered and the previous dancer would tag the next, like an extreme version of choosing a sports team in school. It worked the same way and in the same descending order: the most beautiful faces and athletic bodies first.

None of us had ever made it to the cage.

'Look!' Fiona's attention had turned to the stage. Her face split in a wide smile.

Cass was going up. She fluttered her hands through the bars, beckoning us closer, and I had to go because this was her moment and she was my best friend.

It must have been a challenge to dance gracefully in a giant metal birdcage that tipped and spun without warning, while

51

people threw drinks at you and bass throbbed through your body. Cass was amazing, and when the second track ended and the cage was lowered, she dodged the other girls coming at her and lunged towards me. Her body was slick with sweat. Blue glitter winked on her scalp.

'Tag!' she yelled, grabbing my hand and dragging me across the floor.

'I can't,' I said. 'Cass, no!'

Cass was in one of her moods. If we didn't dance enthusiastically enough, or participate in one of her scene-stealing acts, the night would go from pleasant to unbearable in a blink. Still, I resisted, but, like a swooping black bird, Reno was suddenly there to help her. They shoved me inside and closed the door. Cass twirled her finger at the DJ.

Up I went.

The cage rotated as it rose. I planted my feet wide, gripping the bars for balance, and didn't let go. I didn't move for an entire song. I stood there, until the lights and the spinning got the better of me and I threw up two vodka limes and a decent amount of penne carbonara. When the cage came down, Reno opened the door, smirking, and Karla and Fi helped me climb out. Cass had fallen back with the crowd, arm in arm with another girl, their hands covering their noses.

'That was spectacular,' Reno said, and the cruel twist to his lips confirmed everything I'd suspected about him.

Karla gave him the finger.

'That's it! The group is breaking up!' Fiona wailed and threw up her hands, while the crowd chanted, 'Tag, tag, tag.'

I reached for the nearest body but the wave retreated. Hoots of disgust followed as I staggered past the bar to the foyer, gasping for air. I needed to be away from the lights and the noise and the smells. No one followed me outside. I wiped my mouth with the back of my hand and straightened my skirt, unable to decide whether I wanted to laugh, throw up again or burst into tears.

I walked home. Alone, or so I thought, until three streets from the unit a brittle awareness cut through the nausea and fatigue: the echo of my footsteps wasn't an echo at all but measured, matching steps behind me.

I paused, panting but trying to be quiet, hypersensitive to every movement. If instinct had a sound, mine was screeching like a car alarm. I hovered, listening, at the end of a driveway leading to a house with its porch light on, ready to bash on the door and call for help.

A few minutes passed. Nothing.

By the time I reached home, I had myself convinced it was my own paranoia, the edges of a bad trip.

Fiona was right: the group was breaking up.

After the cage incident I'd made efforts to redeem myself, but my presence was tolerated, not encouraged. On a hot, airless night after one of Brent and Fiona's more brutal arguments, we left the clubs early, almost sober. In what was becoming a monotonous pattern, Karla went back to her dorm, Cass threw a tantrum and Fiona cried herself to sleep on the couch.

Unsettled and sleepless, I got up around two to get a glass of water. Fiona had moved from the couch to the floor, closer to the creaky fan. I ran the tap for a minute, trailing my fingers under the stream, waiting for cool water to run through.

Our kitchen window overlooked the yard, which backed onto a separate group of units; the neighbour's cat often walked the fence like a tightrope, squalling for a fight or a mate. I looked up. There was no moon; the shapes and shadows were familiar. But something was different. I heard a thud, as if someone or something had dropped to the ground.

I backed away from the sink, heart pounding.

'Fi.'

I crouched and spidered across the floor. Fiona was hard asleep on the spare mattress, her arm thrown across her face.

'Fi, wake up!'

I shook her, but she groaned and rolled onto her side.

I tiptoed to Cass's room. She was sleeping with her head where her feet should have been, trying to catch whatever faint breeze might drift through the open window. I peeled back the curtain to check the front porch – nothing, nobody – then closed the window.

Cass stirred. 'What are you doing?'

'There's someone in the backyard.'

'It's probably Brent,' she mumbled. 'Ignore him and he'll go away.'

'You shouldn't sleep with the window open.'

She huffed and rolled over again.

I crept back to my bedroom.

Shortly after, I heard a grating sound from Cass's room. I dashed to the kitchen, took the biggest knife from the drawer and ran back to her room, but it was only Cass opening the window again.

'Jesus Christ, Abbie! Go to bed!'

I sat on the end of my bed for the rest of the night, clutching the knife, swinging my attention from the window, to the door, to the ceiling hatch.

A week later, Cass and I had our first real fight.

Cass had gone out with a new group of friends the night before. I'd spent the evening wrapped in a blanket, nursing a head cold, watching old black-and-white movies until I crawled into bed. I didn't hear Cass come home.

At around six, I got up to use the toilet but the bathroom door was closed. I heard someone pissing from a height. I knocked and the door opened to reveal a guy, about thirty, half-shaven and wearing nothing but tight boxers.

He slammed the door. Seconds later the shower was running.

'Cass,' I said, as I tapped on her open bedroom door.

'What?' she muttered.

'There's someone in our bathroom.'

Cass opened one eye. 'It's Eric.' She flipped her body in one smooth motion to face the window.

'Who's Eric?'

Beneath the tangled sheets, she shrugged.

'How do you know he's not a psychopath?'

She turned her head to me, sighing. 'Check his wallet. It's right there.' She flung out a bare arm and pointed.

'I don't think they list that on your driver's licence.'

'He's not a serial killer. Okay?'

'We agreed – nobody we don't know, right?'

She groaned. 'I do know him.'

'Since *when?*'

'Since last night. And please stop yelling. I've got a headache.' I lowered my voice. 'I think there's someone in our roof.'

Cass laughed. 'What the fuck?'

'Watching us – like maybe there are cameras in here and we don't know. If you go up through the ceiling hatch it leads to the roof space above all the other units.'

'We'll check the roof.' Cass glanced at the bathroom. 'I'll ask Eric to check the roof.'

'What's he doing in there?' I shrieked.

Cass flopped straight up as if a puppeteer had yanked her strings. 'Why are you so paranoid?' She stood, wrapping the sheet around her naked body. 'I can't do this anymore. I seriously can't.'

'I can't either.' I said dazedly. 'I haven't slept properly in months.'

'So go, Abbie. Who's stopping you?'

'I will. Anywhere but here.'

'I hate you right now,' she said.

NOW

Soon, he'd said, but the second call didn't come until a week later. Seven days was long enough for me to start to unravel. Murray had switched back to day shifts, and it became easier to hide that I was slipping back into old habits. I was having trouble sleeping. I forgot to eat, lost track of time and avoided contact with people. I carried the home phone and my mobile around in my pocket and left the house only when necessary. I took a week's leave from work and cancelled my Friday lunch date with Jess. I snapped at Edie and Cam for being lazy and leaving mess around, or for simply being around. On Thursday night, I forgot to pick up Edie from work; when she called to remind me, I asked her to get a ride with someone else. She walked home alone in the dark. And when Jess announced she was coming to visit, I lied and told her Murray and I were having a romantic weekend to make up for the indefinite postponement of our honeymoon.

It was like before, when Sarah disappeared: the walls closed in around me. I was in limbo.

Monday, midafternoon. I was alone in the house when Sherri arrived without warning. Her furtive knock made me jump.

Heart banging, I went to the door and peered through the glass panel. She stood on the step with her overnight bag and a huge box of doughnuts.

'It's only me,' she mouthed.

Since I'd moved in with Murray, Sherri continued to waft in and out like a fragrant breeze. She was a relieving branch manager for a bank, travelling countrywide for up to a month at a time. Her employer provided her accommodation and she'd felt no need to settle into her own place after the separation and divorce. There was never any question of her staying in a hotel when she was in town; Edie and Cam adored her, and Murray remained her biggest fan. The way they were with each other – easy and affectionate – hurt me in the beginning, but the spite that often laced relationships between mothers and stepmothers, first wives and second, wasn't there. Certainly not on Sherri's part, and it didn't take her long to win me over. The small fourth bedroom at the rear of the house held a collection of her clothes, her favourite books and the faint smell of her perfume.

Sherri had asked for the divorce. The initial separation had been hard – Murray was bitter. Sherri responded by moving out and taking the kids with her, but the juggle became impossible. The amicable part came, she said, when she apologised and brought the kids home.

'She wanted it all,' Murray told me. 'She couldn't be a wife and mother and keep her job at the same time.'

'You were a husband and father,' I said. 'You kept your job.'

Murray shook his head as if I couldn't possibly understand. 'She travels a lot. You've seen how often she's away. We couldn't make it work.'

'Did you try?'

'But then I wouldn't have married you.'

When I broached the subject with Sherri, she said, 'Murray is the best man I know.' She smiled wryly and added, 'As long as he's the centre of your life.'

I released the deadbolt and opened the door.

'Murray's on night shift?' she whispered. 'I was trying to be quiet.'

'No, he's back on days now.'

'Oh. No need then.' She resumed her usual cheerful tone. 'Let me in?'

Reluctantly, I stepped aside.

She bustled past me into the kitchen, put the doughnut box on the counter and headed down the hallway to the spare room. When she came back she whirled around the lounge room like a small tornado, flinging the curtains wide and opening windows. 'It's so dark in here.'

I stood motionless, pinching the bridge of my nose.

She stopped. 'I'm sorry – is this okay? Do you have a migraine?'

I shook my head.

'Abbie, you look like hell.'

Acutely aware that she was whole and perfect and I was fast becoming a collection of broken pieces, I burst into tears.

'Is it Murray? Has he... I know he can be –'

'Murray is fine. Murray is great. I just haven't been sleeping.'

I went to the kitchen to find something to do with my shaking hands.

Sherri followed. 'I can stay at a hotel if you like. I know this arrangement isn't ideal. It's selfish of me to expect you to go along with it.'

'No, no,' I said. 'You want to be near the kids. That's not selfish at all. Make yourself at home.'

Our eyes met and she laughed.

'I'll cook dinner for me and the kids tonight,' she said. 'You two should go out. Can I borrow your car?'

I pulled a face. She was so unfailingly polite. When they were together she and Murray had bought matching Audis, but he mainly used the clinic's four-wheel drive for work. Technically my car was hers, another thing she'd left behind and only 'borrowed' when she needed to.

'That's a nice idea. Thank you.'

Sherri seemed to understand I wasn't in the mood for our usual tea and conversation. She encouraged me to do something relaxing while she went grocery shopping.

I had a shower – washed my hair, shaved my legs, plucked a few stray eyebrows – with both phones sitting on the vanity next to me. I'd taken to showering with a towel slung over the glass; I couldn't shake the sense that I was being watched, though I'd gone over the entire house, inch by inch, checking for any evidence of cameras or microphones.

I dried off and dressed in the shower cubicle, then used a hand towel to wipe the condensation from the vanity mirror. My hair was losing its chemical green tint from the pool, but it was long overdue for a cut. My eyes were bloodshot and bruised-looking – I'd have to wear more than my usual make-up to hide the puffiness before dinner tonight.

It was five-fifteen. Murray would be home at six. I needed to book dinner somewhere, make it look like it was my idea and not Sherri's. Make a goddamn effort. I picked up my phone to search for the number for a local Vietnamese restaurant – and that was when it rang.

'Yes,' I said.

'Abbie.'

'You said *soon*. It's been a week.'

'I'm busy,' he said. 'I've been moving house. You know how it is – all those boxes.'

The blood left my extremities. 'Moving? Moving where?'

'Closer.'

I shuddered. 'To here?'

'To you. Of course, that depends what you're willing to do.'

'I haven't said anything to anyone.'

'I know.' He seemed pleased.

'*How* do you know?'

'That's not important. All you have to do is follow instructions.'

'I am. I have been, I will.' I hated the sound of my voice – so needy, desperate. 'But – I just – how would you know if I didn't?'

'If you tell one person, the game will change,' he said. 'Tell your husband, he'll involve the police. You know it. If you tell your sister, she'll talk. Everyone wants someone with authority to tell them what to do. Right now it's just you and me – what you want and what I want.'

'You haven't told me what you want!' I said, my voice echoing in the tiled space.

'But I will, Abbie.'

The steamy bathroom was too hot. I threw open the door and strode into the kitchen.

'Tell me where she is. I need to know.'

'Then let's begin,' he said.

'Yes, let's, you goddamn fucking *motherfucker*.' Spit flew from my mouth. I clawed at my hair.

Sherri was back, frozen, the front door ajar. 'What – ?' She raised her eyebrows. 'Abbie?'

'Someone is there with you,' he said.

'No.'

'I heard a voice.'

I pointed to the phone against my ear and pressed my finger to my lips.

Sherri's mouth snapped shut. Her eyes darkened. Quietly, she put the shopping bag and the car keys on the counter.

'No. It's just me.'

Sherri made herself scarce but I could tell she was lingering in the hall. I went to our bedroom and closed the door.

'It was the TV. I'm alone. Are you still there?'

No reply.

'Please. I'm listening. Please.'

He breathed out. 'I'm here.'

His voice was calm, but I sensed now that there was as much at stake for him as there was for me. I'd give him what he wanted, whatever the cost, I knew that. Knowing the worst and living with it would be better than imagining the worst and having the story change, daily, like a never-ending twisted fairytale.

'If I suspect you're not taking this seriously, it's over,' he said. 'I'm doing this for you, not myself. I ask nothing of you except your trust and your honesty – if you can't give me that, it's all over.'

'Yes.'

'What are your plans tonight?' he asked pleasantly.

I thought about lying, but didn't. 'We're going out for dinner.'

'Everyone?'

'Just me and my husband.'

'Perfect.' His voice was tight. 'You'll have an argument, and when the fighting is over I want you to move your things to the spare room. I want you sleeping apart.'

'But we just got married – we don't argue. There's nothing to fight about!'

'No relationship is perfect, Abbie. Stop pretending. Tell the truth and everything will be as it should be.'

When the call ended I stayed lying on the bed, completely still.

A knock at the bedroom door. It opened an inch.

'Abbie, is everything okay?'

I sat up. 'I'm fine. I'm sorry about before – it was an important phone call I couldn't miss.'

'Oh. What was it that got you so upset?'

I could have stopped it right then, but every terrible thing took me closer to knowing. I felt so completely alone.

'Insurance,' I said flatly.

'Insurance?' She was obviously suspicious.

'Yes.' I brushed past her without making eye contact. 'Goddamn motherfucking insurance.'

I wore a simple black dress with a knee-length split skirt and heels. Murray was late arriving home. While Sherri made dinner and chatted with Edie, he changed out of his uniform into the T-shirt and jeans he'd flung over the chair in the corner of our bedroom.

In the car, I said, 'Would it kill you to wear a shirt and pants from this decade?'

Murray gave a bemused smile. 'Are we going somewhere special?'

'Thanh Thanh,' I said.

'Where the decor hasn't changed since the eighties. I'll fit right in.'

'I know, but –' I gestured to my dress. 'I made an effort.'

'You did. And I appreciate that.' He parked the car and turned off the ignition. He slid his hand between the split in my skirt. 'This is how much I appreciate it.'

Resignation had left me feeling empty. Resolve was a tight knot in my gut.

I opened the door. 'I'm starving,' I said and slid smoothly out of reach.

We were seated at our usual table by the fish tank. I liked to watch the eel coiled in its hole, the way its eyes followed movement, seemingly nonplussed by the goings-on of humans. Shy, but deadly.

We ordered. The waitress brought our bottle of wine, and I drank my first glass before Murray had touched his. I immediately poured another.

'Sherri said you were upset earlier,' Murray said. 'Something about insurance?'

I looked away. This was going to be easy. She shouldn't have got involved.

'About Sherri.' I couldn't meet his stare. 'I'm not comfortable

63

with her turning up whenever she feels like it. I'm not happy about having her put her spin on things when I'm perfectly capable of telling you myself.'

He kept his tone even. 'What were you going to tell me?'

'It doesn't matter now.'

'You haven't been right since the wedding.' He reached across the table and held my cold hand. 'Is this all something to do with Sarah? Is it what your mother did with the doll?'

The wine was acid in my stomach, but I swallowed another large mouthful. I couldn't let kindness break me – we might not survive this, but I couldn't survive a lifetime of not knowing.

'No, it's about your ex-wife,' I said. 'You were right, she wants it all. She abandons her children and thinks it's fine to stroll in every few weeks, throwing glitter and trailing rainbows. Bringing doughnuts. She gets the best of them and you – I get late-night pickups and dirty washing, I get the bad attitudes and the –'

'If the kids aren't pulling their weight, I'll talk to them,' Murray said.

'The kids are fine!' I yelled. 'It's us. It's everything.'

'Keep your voice down.'

'Don't tell me what to do,' I hissed.

He sighed. 'I didn't know it was a problem. Obviously I know now and we need to talk about it.'

Don't make this harder for me.

There was some truth to everything I'd said, enough to make it seem real, but none of it was worth attacking Murray over. I loved him, but now I had no choice but to distance myself. I knew the twenty-year age difference was the way to do it.

'I'm on strike,' I said. 'I'm not cooking, I'm not cleaning, and I'm sure as hell not playing hostess to your ex-wife anymore. Maybe your sexist attitude and caveman tendencies ended your first marriage – did you ever think of that?'

He let go of my hand. His were probably white-knuckled under the table.

'Funny, I didn't,' he said. 'I know it's hard for you when I'm on nights, but I thought we were happy. We just got married, for Christ's sake.'

'I'm not happy.'

'That's obvious.'

The food came. Murray loaded his plate and stabbed pieces of pork like a robot, barely chewing.

I leaned back in my chair and drank. The wine hit my empty stomach and my bloodstream with equal force: I felt queasy, but I couldn't stop – not my vicious mouth, nor the sickening momentum that was building.

'Do you still think about sex with Sherri?'

Murray coughed. He wiped his mouth with a napkin and crossed his knife and fork on the still half-full plate. 'Where is this all coming from?'

'She still looks at you that way. When was the last time you two had sex?'

'That's *sick*,' he said.

But there was a split second when his eyes slid away before he dragged them back.

'Murray?'

He changed the subject. 'Did you go to work today, Abbie?'

The layers of guilt that had been accumulating over the previous week flattened and merged. I wanted to apologise for letting a psychopathic stranger into our lives, our bed; I wanted to tell him about the phone calls – anything to stop him looking at me this way. Above all, I wanted to tell him it was different this time. I was different. It wasn't hope I clung to but rage, and it was more powerful than hope had ever been.

'No. I did not.'

'I called Jess,' he said. 'I told her how you've been.'

I slammed the wine glass on the table and leaned forward. 'You did what? How have I been, Murray?'

'You know, wandering the house at night. Not seeing anyone. You left a teenage girl to walk home alone in the dark!' He rubbed his hand over his face. 'Edie didn't want to tell me. She told Sherri and Sherri told me. She thought you were negligent...' he hesitated. 'And I tend to agree, given you, of all people, know what's at stake.'

It hit me like a slap. I struggled to breathe. I'd backed him into a corner, but what he said was true.

'I'll move out,' I said, after long seconds of silence. It came out impassive, though my body was racked with emotion. 'That solves all our problems.'

He flinched. 'That's not what I want. Jess said you've been like this before – we can work through it. You can get help. I'll take time off. *I'll* help.'

'I don't need your help.'

'You can't keep running from everything, Abbie,' he said gently. 'Maybe that's why you're where you are now.'

I stood, gathered my coat and went outside to wait by the car while he paid for the food and wine we had wasted.

The fresh air made my head spin and I shook all over as if I was coming down with the flu.

It was done, and it was hard, but it wasn't the hardest thing I'd ever been through. Murray was right about me being careless – he didn't use that word, but the sentiment was the same. And he was wrong – I wasn't running away. I was running towards the answers I needed. I just had to find the courage to see it through.

BEFORE

Cass and I still lived together but we were falling apart. She stayed out for two, three, sometimes four nights in a row, and I took on as many classes as I could manage, in order to avoid conflict and to save enough money to pay what I owed for the rent and bills.

SwimSmart Pool Centre had a fifty-metre pool and a shallower twenty-five-metre pool. Michael and Trent usually took the older kids in the deeper pool, and Merrilyn and I took the babies and toddlers in the other one. Classes went for forty-five minutes with a fifteen-minute break in between, but after we'd gathered floaties, paddleboards and diving rings and high-fived the kids, we rarely had time for a break.

I had just finished my fifth class and had twenty minutes for lunch – just enough time to eat an apple and a suspicious yoghurt from the fridge in the staff room. Merrilyn and Trent had clocked off. Michael was printing certificates in the office and Carol, the manager, was getting ready to kick out the stragglers and close up.

I decided to take a shower at the centre before I went home, something I rarely did in the beginning because the change room showers were never particularly clean. But Cass said we had to take shorter showers to save on bills, and it made good sense to use the centre's water on days when I needed to wash my hair.

I took my towels, dry clothes and toiletry bag from my locker, and stripped off in the last of the six cubicles. I waited for the water to run hot, shaved my armpits and lower legs, and stepped under the spray to shampoo my hair.

I'm not sure what made me call out – a noise maybe, or simply the feeling that I wasn't alone.

'Is that you, Carol?'

I bent down to look under the cubicle door. A pair of dirty sneakers, white with blue stripes, shuffled backwards and out of sight.

'Hello?'

I turned off the taps and listened, but the only sound was the *splat, splat, splat* from the dripping tap. I wrapped one towel around my midriff and twisted the other around my wet hair.

'Carol?'

The women's change rooms were at the far end of the centre, close to the filtration room; the vibration from the pumps drowned out any sound that might reach the office.

Beads of sweat broke out all over me. The steam made my head spin. Still dripping, I pulled on clean underwear, track pants and a T-shirt.

I stepped onto the shelf to peer over the top of the cubicle, but it wasn't strong enough to take my weight. It gave way. I slipped, smashing my chin on the partition, and fell.

My last memory was the sensation of hitting cold, wet tiles.

I couldn't account for any of the time that passed between hitting my head and coming to on the change room floor, two paramedics leaning over me.

Michael had heard somebody yelling in the women's change room and called Carol to investigate. Carol found me lying on the floor and dialled triple zero. She said the shower cubicle was unlocked and the door was open. I must have crawled halfway to the exit. With all the blood and water, she said it looked like a crime scene.

I was taken to hospital in an ambulance, nauseous and panicky because I knew the bill would tip the balance: I wouldn't be able to catch up the last month's rent.

'It's a nasty cut to your chin but we're more concerned about the bump on your head,' the nurse said. 'We'd like to do an MRI to make sure there's no fracture. Do you think you're able to complete this form?'

I sat up, wincing from the throbbing pain in the base of my skull. 'I'll try.'

Blood from my chin had soaked the front of my T-shirt and run in rivers between my breasts, but it was already congealing. I found the lump on the back of my head with my fingers. They came away watery red.

The nurse looked up. 'You'll need stitches in the chin and the scalp. I have to shave your hair around the cut. Do you need help with the form?'

The questions were mainly about my medical history, and there were boxes to check if I had any metal in my body – a pacemaker, implants, braces or retainers. I removed my earrings and unclasped my necklace.

The next section made me pause. The pen hovered for a moment, then I checked the YES box.

I handed the form to the nurse, who scanned my responses.

'You might be pregnant?'

'I'm not sure.'

'When was your last period?'

'I don't know. Nine weeks? Maybe ten?'

She smiled gently. 'Okay. I'll advise the doctor. He might opt for an X-ray or CT scan instead. Is your bladder full? I can arrange a test?'

She went to leave the room but I stopped her.

'Please. If it's positive… the thing is, I've been drinking and I've possibly taken some drugs.'

'Possibly?'

'Probably.'

She nodded. 'One thing at a time. Let's do the test while we're waiting for the doctor.'

I thanked her and, when she had gone, I cried, curled on my side.

Later, I peed in a cup in the bathroom. It wasn't one of those stick tests that give you an immediate and private result; they took the cup away and made me wait for almost an hour. It didn't matter how long it took – I knew.

In that time, the blood on my T-shirt turned brown. I used my new mobile to call Cass on hers: it went straight to voicemail. I called the landline too, but it rang out and the machine picked up. 'I'm at the hospital. I've had an accident – I hit my head. They're keeping me in overnight. Call me?'

Four stitches in my chin and two in my scalp. A mild concussion, but the CT scan revealed there was no fracture. Overnight my left knee blew up to twice its size – I must have twisted it when I fell.

I'd barely slept, woken regularly by either the nurses checking my vital signs, or the thoughts screaming inside my aching head.

I was sure now that there had been someone else in the change room. Had I somehow managed to open the cubicle door? I couldn't remember. Between falling and waking, there was nothing.

And the test result: *positive*.

Reno. Both times he had used a condom – or so I believed. What if he hadn't? Or one broke? I hadn't refilled my pill prescription in the past month, but I was taking it at the time – wasn't I?

70

My fault. *Stupid, stupid.* I hit my forehead with the flat of my hand and only succeeded in exacerbating my headache. I already knew my life was about to change – even if I chose not to go through with the pregnancy, I'd need help and money.

At nine o'clock a doctor checked me over for the last time and said I could go home. Cass had not returned my calls or responded to my text messages.

I discharged myself, caught a bus to the city, then another one back to the unit. My clothes were bloodstained and damp, but a nurse had given me a jumper to wear over the top of my T-shirt. The other passengers stared at the dressing covering my chin and the dried blood in my hair.

On the ride home I called Cass again and again. No answer. I started to panic – had something happened to her too?

I hobbled painfully from the bus stop back to the unit. The blinds were down, the curtains drawn. It looked as if Cass wasn't home. On the front porch, behind the pot plant, there was a large arrangement of orange tulips wrapped with a yellow bow.

I bent and read the card tucked inside.

Sorry about what happened to you. I will see you tomorrow. C

There was no name, but I presumed the flowers were for me. From Carol, or from Cass?

I unlocked the door and took them inside. The unit was dark and quiet. Dirty dishes from the days before were still piled on the sink, and the stale smell of wet washing emanated from the laundry.

The flat was a mess. That was normal.

More disconcerting was the immaculate state of my room: my bed was made, the pillows and cushions arranged perfectly, the cover smooth, and I noticed a subtle symmetry to the make-up and perfumes on my bedside table. I rarely wore perfume, but I knew the scents of those individual bottles – the smell in my room was unfamiliar and overpowering, as if each bottle had been tested, the scents mingled. I opened the top drawer. I had a bad habit of shoving bills and letters in there, unopened, to avoid facing my accumulating debt. But the pile was neat and, although it was nothing I could put my finger on, I suspected envelopes were missing.

If Cass had been there I might have confronted her. *Somebody has been sleeping in my bed. Someone is wearing my perfume.*

I threw my furious energy into packing two suitcases. Apart from my clothes, shoes and personal items, nothing else would fit. I found the notepad by the phone: the top sheet was covered with Karla's doodles and a cryptic note for me – *Abbie, call back,* followed by a mobile number, and the words *staying at Jeff's.* I had no idea who Jeff was. I took money from Cass's jar, wrote a short message and an itemised IOU, and tucked it among the tulip stems, leaving them on the kitchen counter. I couldn't carry them with me. Cass would see the flowers as soon as she walked through the door and assume they were for her – that way she wouldn't miss my note.

It was the coward's way out, but I felt so unbearably lonely and fragile, as if I could fall apart or disappear and no one would notice for months. And though it was too soon and likely impossible, I was sure I felt the baby's heartbeat in my blood. I had to keep it safe – my only option was to swallow my pride and go home.

NOW

It had been over a week since I had been to work or taken so much as a walk around the block. The instructions were clear: I was not to leave the house except to do the things the caller asked me to do. I was not to invite company, nor accept it. I should not engage in conversation by phone or in person unless necessary. I should behave as if I was extremely agoraphobic, as if my world had shrunk to the limits of the house, its windows and walls, the patches of sunlight that streamed through the glass in the afternoon. I was not allowed to ask questions.

I wasn't stupid. I knew what he was trying to do, but I didn't know why. Step one: withdrawal and alienation. The irony was that I had withdrawn from the world before and it had saved my life; now the house was a prison.

After our fight and for the next three nights, Murray lay close enough for me to feel his heat, but we did not touch.

'You need fresh air,' he said.

A day later, 'You need to see a doctor.'

The morning after that, 'You're depressed. You need medication.'

Edie said, 'We need you.'

Sherri only stayed half the time she'd planned to. 'You need space. I should go.'

She left on Thursday and I moved into her room. I packed her things away in the wardrobe and locked the door.

Murray tried to draw me out of the room, but I sensed he was afraid to push too hard. Edie and Cam crept around like ghosts. When Edie tried to cook dinner that evening and the smell of burning meat seeped under the bedroom door, it was all I could do not to dash into the kitchen and take over.

Jess called, but I didn't speak to her. I knew it was only a matter of time before she turned up on our doorstep, and I was terrified. Jess would know something about this was different – instead of being flat and miserable, I was overstimulated, jittery and vicious. But it wasn't difficult to keep up the farce of being unreachable – I was just that. Murray struggled to cope with the long work hours and the backlog of household chores. The fridge and pantry were bare. Dirty washing piled up. The wooden floors grew sticky; dust and clutter accumulated on surfaces and in corners.

Part of me was satisfied: here was Sherri's warning coming into play. Murray was not the centre of my attention and he didn't like it at all.

On Friday morning I waited until he left for work and climbed into our bed. The sheets were rumpled and starting to smell – he could probably go for months without making the bed or changing the linen – and the space on his side was still warm. I curled on my side and turned on the television to watch the morning news, all bad, and a weather reporter forecasting hail.

A light knock on the open door. Cam was holding up a fistful of damp clothes.

'I'm sorry. I rang Dad first. Do you know why the dryer smells like it's on fire?'

'You have to clean the lint filter,' I said.

'Where's that?'

I sighed, got out of bed and squeezed past him. Cam stepped aside as if sadness was catching. I had the urge to take his gangly body in my arms and tell him it would be okay, I wasn't going through with this – what I had was more important than what I'd lost.

That wasn't true. I loved my stepchildren, but sometimes I resented watching them grow. They weren't mine.

In the laundry I showed Cam how to peel the wad of lint from the filter. I handed it to him, a perfect circle of purple fluff – why was lint always purple? – and Cam took it, pressing it to his cheek.

'It smells like my socks,' he said.

I laughed before I could stop it. It was true. The whole room stank like his socks. I'd changed the washing detergent to my own brand when I moved in because the odour of the previous one had made the clothes smell unfamiliar, other. It was the first thing Sherri had noticed, and I often wondered if she resented me for that.

My smile disappeared.

Cam said carefully, 'Is this about Sarah?'

My eyes shot to the window. I looked up into the corner nearest the back door where a few cobwebs dotted with tiny insect carcasses floated in strands. I checked behind me along the dark hallway.

'What are you doing?'

'Nothing.'

'Should I call Dad again?'

'No. I'm fine.'

'You're acting really weird, Abbie.'

Good, I thought.

The following Monday, after Murray had left and I'd taken a quick shower and dried off, I stopped in front of the full-length mirror in the bedroom.

I dropped the towel.

It had been a while since I'd looked at myself like this: lingering over the details. My body had always been strong, utilitarian – broad shoulders, wide hips, long legs, taut quads and calves. Now

I noticed my jutting clavicle, defined shins, the clefts between my ribs. It wasn't that I'd lost a lot of weight – it was as if the relentless stress had made my body turn on itself. My muscles were wasting, leaving fat and bone.

I stood on my toes and my calves bunched painfully. I dropped to a squat and stretched my right leg to the side; the abductors strained and my hip popped. I turned slowly, lifting my arms and lowering them, but my lats remained slack and soft. I spun back around to avoid looking too closely at the dark spread of ink across my upper back.

Whatever was in store for me, I wouldn't be able to fight. And I wanted to fight – more than anything I wanted him to reveal himself so I could find him and kill him – but not at the expense of losing Sarah all over again. If I didn't play my part, he might disappear and I would never know.

The colossal pile of washing in the laundry had been building for weeks, while I ignored it. Edie and Cam only seemed to wash what they needed, and several times Murray had taken his uniform and scrubs to the drycleaner in a fit of pique.

I put a load of towels through the quick cycle so I had a legitimate reason to venture outside. When I'd finished hanging them on the washing line, I streaked across the lawn to Murray's shed and unlocked it using the key he kept in the gutter above the door.

I spotted what I needed: Cam's weightlifting equipment and stretch bands.

I dragged them to the door and checked the backyard. If I was going to get caught doing something that didn't fit the brief, it would be now. He could be holed up in one of the townhouses behind us, or rooming in one of the neighbours' substantial homes. Despite what he'd said, there could be cameras installed in the house.

It took three trips to carry the equipment inside. I hid the weights under the bed in my new room. I might not be able to leave the house, but I could stretch my weakened muscles, build them back to strength.

Immediately I felt calmer, more in control. I found myself waiting for the next call with something approaching pleasant if nervous anticipation, and emailed work to tell them I was taking another week's leave.

Days passed. I watched Hitchcock films back-to-back – they carried me through hours on end, suspended in a viewer's catatonic state of fear and suspense, which was so like my inner state I could almost convince myself none of it was real. Murray arrived home to find me glazed and unresponsive in front of the TV. I refused to turn it off until the credits rolled. The lounge room became my dark domain; the flickering screen was a portal to a dimension not unlike the one I was in.

I didn't watch to escape – I watched because I needed to feed my rage.

He had taken Sarah, but I wouldn't be a passive victim. I would not let it stop until he was dead too. My body might have been confined to the chair, but my mind veered off into violent, full-colour fantasies where I fought back – I poisoned, tortured, stabbed, burned, smothered, violated and killed him in a hundred different ways.

All those women – and they were always women and girls – stalked and manipulated and murdered by men.

But sometimes they fought back and sometimes they won.

BEFORE

Martine, Dad and Jess didn't know I was coming home. On the train, I tried to remember the best way to begin a conversation with my parents and couldn't. Should I gather them together, ask them to sit down? *There's something I have to tell you.* And – *I'm sorry.*

It was midafternoon when I arrived. The pain in my head and jaw had intensified, but the ache in my knee had subsided. I took a deep breath of sea air and headed along the backstreets to the main path through the dunes, straight to the beach.

It was the tail end of the off-season and the car park was nearly empty – only a couple of diehard surfers and the distant figure of a woman walking her dog. I left my suitcases outside the kiosk and sat on the hard, damp sand, burying my toes. I sat there for so long my shadow crept behind me and the sea turned grey. A huge swell built and the wind swung around, cutting westerly across the beach, whipping dry seaweed into my legs. I eyed the deceptively calm section of shore where the hidden undertow was strongest, thinking it was a pretty good metaphor for what was about to happen.

There would be no shouting, I knew, so why did I feel so afraid? I had an intuition, but I did not, at that moment, know she was a girl, only that she was mine. Not for a second did I think of the baby as part of Reno; I didn't want to think of him at all. Telling my parents was unavoidable, but getting rid of her was unimaginable – several hours alone with my thoughts had only made that revelation clearer.

A sand-crusted tennis ball landed near my feet. The dog I'd seen earlier bolted after it, eyes only for the ball. When the kelpie skidded to a halt, sand flew into my mouth.

I turned to the side and spat.

'Abbie Morgan? I thought that was you. What have you done to yourself?'

Ange Fletcher: seventy-something, tough as an old boot, and mouthy. She'd run the local newsagent for forty years – still did, as far as I knew. At first I thought she was talking about being pregnant, but then I realised she was staring at the dressing on my chin.

'You've been sitting here awhile. We've done a whole lap.' She held a flattened hand to her eyes, shielding them from the sinking sun. 'You're home, then? Your mum'll be pleased. She said you'd be back.'

'I'm just visiting.'

Ange shrugged. 'My car's in the park. You want a ride?'

'My bags are at the kiosk. I'll walk.'

'Suit yourself.'

With a stiff back, I struggled to my feet. It wasn't that I was showing yet – just a smooth tightening of my belly and slightly fuller breasts – but Ange cocked her head and gave me a shrewd squint.

If I didn't hurry, my news would arrive home before I did.

'What happened to Sam?' I asked, remembering her other dog. He used to lie outside the shop all day, waiting for treats and pats. This one looked like him, but he was young and fast, still a pup.

'Went missing. Ran off. Maybe went home with another family. I like to think that.' She pried the ball from the dog's jaws and threw it towards the shoreline. 'This one is Sam too.'

The kelpie took off.

'Sam Two. That's funny,' I said, and burst into tears.

I had a set of keys, but I rang the doorbell. It seemed the right thing to do. Nothing had changed: our small front garden looked tidy but unloved, and I still felt the familiar teenage dread of only going home because I'd run out of options.

Jess came to the door and threw it wide open. 'Martine!' she yelled over her shoulder.

'Seriously,' I said. 'You don't have to shout.'

Jess put her hand on her hip. She was wearing make-up — eyeliner, caked foundation, blush and lip gloss — all inexpertly applied. Tight blue jeans and a halterneck top, in this cold. At fifteen going on twenty, she looked like what Martine would call a handful.

'What happened to your face?'

'I had an accident,' I said. 'Is Dad home?'

'Not yet.'

I tried to hug her but she pushed me away. 'What's wrong with you?' I asked.

'I haven't forgiven you for leaving me here.'

'Well, how long will it take? I need you on my side.'

She stood back and regarded me for a moment. 'Okay. I'm over it.'

'Good.'

She let me in and skipped down the hallway.

My bedroom was no longer mine and it wasn't Jess's either. The posters were gone, the walls repainted white. In the corner where my desk used to be stood a locked steel cabinet, and on my single bed was a plain white coverlet and two plump pillows; a hand towel in the shape of a swan lay at the foot of the mattress. It looked like a hotel room.

'Auntie Lira is coming to stay,' Jess said, peering over my shoulder.

'Why? For how long?'

'Uncle Nev has been fucking around.'

I heaved my suitcase onto the bed, obliterating the swan. 'Since when do you swear like that?'

She shrugged. 'Since nobody pays any attention to me anyway.'

'Nothing's changed, then.'

Martine's younger sister was coming – I'd be on the couch again, or an air mattress on the floor of Jess's room. It wasn't the first time our uncle had cheated on her, but the timing was terrible. A double crisis might tip Martine over the edge.

'When is she arriving?'

'Tomorrow, I think.'

If I left telling them until after she arrived, Martine would choke down whatever she had to say and bring it up again later with extra bile. Whether she was cleaning the house, organising an event or preparing a meal, Martine worked with a forensic intensity that might have appeared efficient to everyone else, but I always thought bordered on violent. Meals were the worst: her brisk steps, the crashing of plates and the clattering of cutlery, and God help us if we weren't seated when the food was hot and ready, or if Jess and I didn't immediately clear the table after we'd eaten.

But my coming-home dinner was a mostly silent affair.

Roast beef, mashed potato, carrots, pumpkin, beans – everything in shades of grey, including the conversation. Jess chattered about school and her part-time job at the supermarket, but shut up when nobody appeared interested. Dad chewed and made the requisite appreciative noises without actually saying anything. And Martine pushed food around on her plate, plainly waiting for me to explain my injuries and apologise for turning up unannounced.

Our parents rarely offered life advice apart from *don't take drugs,* or relationship advice like *don't get pregnant*. I grew up thinking mutual tolerance was a state long-term couples aspired to, if they weren't cheating on or beating up each other. If that was the only criteria, our parents had a perfect marriage.

We were about to enter the after-dinner clean-up phase, which meant we wouldn't all be in the same room.

I blurted it out. 'I have something to tell you.' Three heads swung my way. 'I'm pregnant.'

Martine didn't miss a beat. 'I figured.'

Dad kept chewing, his mouth so slack I could see the grey meat inside. 'I didn't figure,' he said.

Jess jerked back in her seat, her arms flopping to her sides. 'Holy shit.'

'Watch your mouth,' Martine snapped.

'I don't know what I'm going to do yet,' I said. 'I need to consider my options.'

'Your options?' Martine said. 'Seems to me your options just multiplied by one and divided by two.'

Jess screwed up her nose, apparently trying to work out the equation.

'How far gone?' Martine asked.

I noted her choice of words but opted to de-escalate. 'Maybe ten weeks.'

'You're going to need a job, and you can hardly go back to being a lifeguard.'

I shrugged. 'I'll look for something.'

She raised her eyebrows. 'The same way you went looking for freedom and got a life sentence?'

I had no answer for that.

Auntie Lira stayed three days. She went back to her husband and I moved back into my old room. Martine made an appointment for me with the local GP, where I had a second test to confirm the pregnancy; from there the news spread like a summer cold and any choices I had left grew heavy with the weight of public opinion. In a way it worked in my favour: it only took one well-meaning busybody to congratulate Martine on becoming a grandmother for her to stop mentioning termination. I moved into the second trimester, hardly noticing the time that had passed, and before I knew it the lack of a decision meant the decision had been made.

During the first few weeks at home, before I started to show, I pretended it wasn't happening. I caught up with friends, went surfing a couple of times, even had a few drinks. The caravan park needed an extra cleaner on weekends so I picked up a few hours' work there, and Ange gave me Mondays and Tuesdays in the newsagency so she could spend more time looking after her grandkids.

I heard on the grapevine that Fiona had moved in with Cass, but I was doing everything I could to avoid unpleasantness, so I didn't call. My name was mud. Cass's mum ignored me on the street.

Being a pregnant teenager in a small town drew the kind of attention I hated. I couldn't walk to the supermarket without copping sympathetic smiles, unsolicited advice and sly comments about babies being hard work. People loved a good fuck-up, and Martine had a shit-tonne of judgement coming back her way.

Martine drove me to the medical centre for the first ultrasound. She followed me into the imaging room and together we watched as the grainy image of my baby took shape in the screen: a perfect heartbeat, the slope of a nose, the arch of the spine. My belly rippled in time with a kick from a tiny foot.

'Would you like to know your baby's sex?'

'No,' Martine said.

I nodded. 'Yes.'

'I'll write it down. You can decide later.'

My mind was made up. I looked at the paper while we were waiting for the images, and experienced a rush of wonder and relief. Another step further from Reno. In time I would erase him completely, not by wishing him gone but simply by forgetting.

On the ride home I waited for Martine's curiosity to get the better of her, but she didn't ask.

I stuck the piece of paper on the fridge along with the ultrasound image under a magnet that read: *Athena Bay – where life's a beach.*

One day Martine took me to pick up a garbage bag filled with second-hand baby clothes. Someone she knew was giving them away. She'd hated doing it – she was the giver of charity, not the recipient – and didn't get out of the car.

As we drove home I pawed through the layers of clothes, disappointed to find most of them were stained and stretched out of shape. They smelled like someone else's baby.

'I don't need this stuff.'

'You'll need them, trust me,' Martine said.

'I'm saving all my money. I'll buy new things.'

'Have you seen how much nappies cost? You're living in a dream world, Abbie.'

'You were only a couple of years older when you had me.'

She pulled the car over and let me have it, emphasising her words with hard smacks on the steering wheel.

'I was *married*. Your father and I had been together for *five years*. You have no idea how much this affects our family, do you? You made a mistake and now we're all paying for it, but don't you *dare* sit there and turn your nose up. You're lucky you're not living in a shelter or out on the street. You're *lucky*.' She sat back, breathing heavily. 'You don't even know who the father is, do you?'

It was the first time she'd mentioned him. 'Oh, now you're asking me?'

She fixed me with a stare. 'Well?'

I shrugged. 'Of course I know who he is. He doesn't want her. Okay?'

I said *her* every chance I could. The ultrasound image and the scrap of paper – *congratulations, it's a girl!* – were still stuck to the fridge, and I knew Martine must have seen it, but I noticed she only said *the baby* or *your pregnancy*, as if she was keeping herself a step removed.

'Let me guess – he's not exactly father material?'

'Jesus, why are you so angry all the time?'

'Do you know what, Abbie? I'm not angry. I'm afraid.' She sighed.

'Of what?'

She seemed to push the words from cheek to cheek with her tongue before she let them out. 'I'm scared for the baby. You're still behaving like a child yourself – you're in no fit state to bring one up.'

'I'll learn.'

'I won't help you more than I already have, you do realise that? It's going to be hard.'

I closed the bag and heaved it onto the back seat. 'So everyone keeps telling me.'

I glanced at her profile. It was as if she was carved from rock. The lines around her mouth made her look like a sixty-year-old smoker, but she had never smoked and she was not quite forty-one. I couldn't remember the last time we'd laughed together. About anything. Her disapproval was relentless – she could no longer fight with me about breaking curfew or my tight jeans or my laziness, so I decided she just loved a fight.

Martine lowered her voice. 'I know what you're thinking. You think your child will love you, but it won't. They aren't capable of love yet – they want, they need, they demand and take – that's what they do, and all you can do is hang onto a rope that never slackens. It *always* pulls in the opposite direction.'

I wanted to ask her if we were talking about the baby or me and Jess.

When we arrived home, Martine got out of the car and stormed into the house. I dragged the bag up the driveway, where it promptly split open, spilling baby clothes all over the oil-stained concrete.

Standing in the doorway, my mother watched me as I picked up every item.

'Thanks for your help.'

She pursed her lips. 'This baby will force you to grow up. And if you're ever faced with a terrible choice, I hope you'll do the right thing even if she hates you for it.'

'What are you talking about?'

'Selflessness, Abbie,' she said.

NOW

Jess. Wearing those ridiculous platform sneakers of hers, the ones that made her high-step like a draught horse because the soles were so rigid she couldn't flex her feet, striding up the path as if she had something on her mind and wouldn't stop until she'd given me a piece of it.

Everything was finally going right in my sister's life: she'd landed her dream job in event management, she had an enviable social life, and she'd recently moved into her own high-rise apartment not far from where we lived. I'd been counting on her busyness to divert her attention, but I knew Murray had been in touch, maybe more than a couple of times. She was always going turn up. Jess liked her confrontations face to face, but I didn't have a plan. There was no procedure manual when it came to my little sister.

I experienced relief that she was near, and dread that I'd have to send her away.

She hammered on the door.

I opened it and stood back.

'Oh good, you're alive.' She gave me a dirty look and swept inside, dumping her handbag on the couch and taking an overripe banana from the fruit bowl. 'Fuck's sake, Abbie.'

I've been avoiding you, I know. I'm sorry. 'What?'

She half-peeled the banana, inspected it, then tossed it uneaten into the bin under the sink. 'Do you want to tell me what's going on?'

I can't talk to you. He's watching. Still hovering near the door, I said, 'I don't know what you mean.'

'Right. You've been married for barely three weeks and already you're headed for divorce.'

Murray looks at me like he doesn't know me. 'We're fine.'

'Then why do I speak to your husband twice a day but you can't pick up the phone?'

He's listening. 'I spoke to you yesterday.'

'You basically hung up on me. What's happening – did I do something wrong?'

'Of course not. I was just busy.'

'Busy doing what?' She looked around at the mess. 'Murray says you're not leaving the house. He said you don't go to work and you're sure as shit not doing housework all day.'

'I've taken some time off. I've been a bit down.'

'I'm sorry,' Jess said, softening her tone. 'But why won't you talk to me?'

'I just needed to wallow for a while.'

Because if I tell you one thing, I'll tell you everything. And if he finds out he'll give me nothing.

I closed the door and headed to the kitchen.

Jess wasn't leaving without tea and conversation, so I filled the kettle and switched it on. I put teabags in two mugs, when what I really wanted was to open a bottle of something harder. If I could just get through this without her pressing so hard I cracked, I could go back to killing time watching TV and waiting for phone calls in the dark.

'I can't remember if you're doing sugar these days.'

'One sugar.' Jess came up behind me, picked up a hank of my greasy hair and let it fall heavily on my shoulder. 'There's something you're not saying.'

'I'm fine. Tell me what's happening with you.' I jiggled the bags.

'I'm not buying, Abbie.'

I sighed. 'You're only making me feel worse.'

She spun me around and squinted shrewdly. 'Why now? What set you off?'

'Just *stop*.' I pushed her, harder than I meant to, and she stumbled backwards. Mortified, I reached out to her. 'Look, I'll be okay if everyone would just back off.'

'You can't look at me when you lie.'

'I'm not lying.'

She frowned. 'The last time you wallowed I thought I'd find you in the bath with slit wrists. Tell me this is not like that time, Abbie.'

At last, a question I could answer honestly. 'It's not like that.'

'Look at me.'

I held eye contact. 'It's not.'

'I don't have the energy to save you this time.' Her eyes filled with tears. 'I can't check on you every day and drag you kicking and screaming back to life again, not without giving up my own. And I *resent* you for making me feel that way – I hate *myself* for feeling that way.'

'I don't need you to save me.' I would save myself – if it meant doing this alone, then so be it. Telling Jess would only complicate her life further.

She lowered her voice. 'When you're like this I – no.' Shaking her head. 'No.'

'Say what you need to say, Jess.'

'What if you did end it?'

Shocked, I echoed, '*End it?*'

'Sometimes I think about that.' Her eyes were bright. 'I mean, if you did, it would probably kill me too, but at least it would be over, right? This is horrible. It goes on and on and I keep thinking one day we'll all arrive at a fresh place to start again, but that's never going to happen, is it?' She gave a helpless shrug. 'It's like you're a vortex – when you start spinning, we all get sucked down with you. And I'm not saying I blame you for any of it, but every time you go off into your own little world, you forget we're all connected.' She grabbed my hand and laced her fingers through mine. 'We're tied together, even when we're falling apart. *Abbie's in the black hole again – everybody hang on, otherwise we're all going down with her.*'

'Oh, Jess.'

She dropped my hand. 'I'm sorry. I'm just telling you the truth. This is what we think, how we feel.'

I didn't want her to let go – not my hand now, or later, when I needed her to be there if I managed to scrabble my way back to something resembling a life.

'It's a well,' I said.

'What?'

'It's not a black hole. It's a well. That's what it looks like in here.' I tapped my head.

'Well,' Jess said. 'It's still a fucking hole.'

We laughed.

'We're a miserable family, aren't we?' I said.

She blinked. 'What are you talking about?'

'Remember the Rowneys next door? I always wanted us to be like them – hanging out, doing things together, like going fishing and camping and having barbecues.'

'You hate camping.'

'But they always looked as if they were having such a blast. They actually *liked* each other.'

Jess frowned. 'Did you know Kim Rowney was always jealous of us because we didn't have to share a room? Darren Rowney is a meth addict. The youngest one, Chad, is doing six years for armed robbery. And I never told you because you weren't there, but when

I was fifteen, the old man pulled me onto his lap and put his hand down my shorts.'

'Oh, Jess.'

'If you say that one more time, I swear – but is that seriously what you believe? We're a miserable family?'

'Okay, so tell me what *you* think.'

She stuck out her chin. 'I think we had a safe home with everything we needed and a decent amount of the things we wanted. Our dad was a nice man who always came home to his family and never stuck his hand down anyone's shorts. I think we're real and we love each other.'

'And Martine?' My tone was loaded with resentment.

'I think she's a good mother.'

'Well, that makes one of us.'

Jess looked down her nose. 'God, Abbie. You're so much more alike than you know.'

'How so?'

'You're both stubborn and secretive. You play the long game to get what you want. You can hold a grudge *forever*, and you both would have changed places with Sarah in a heartbeat, am I right?'

I flinched, but nodded. That much was true.

'You both struggle to be happy. It's like you're always waiting for the fall.'

I had to flip her off, otherwise I'd burst into tears. 'How'd you get so smart growing up on a diet of meat and three vegetables is my question.'

'You need professional help,' Jess said. 'I don't want you to fuck up what you have now over things you can't change.' She gave me a shaky smile. 'Sometimes I just have to tell you shit so it doesn't sit inside my brain, okay?'

'Okay.'

Jess picked up her bag. 'You know, I never saw Martine happier than when there were three generations of us in the same room. Sarah brought us together – but she's gone, Abbie. We can't let it tear us apart.'

'We won't.' I gave her a grim smile.

She swung her bag over her shoulder. 'Now I'll go, but only if you tell me we're not going back to that place.'

'We're not going back.' I ushered her towards the door. 'I won't put you through it again. I promise.'

'I want to believe you,' she said. 'But I think you're just telling me what I want to hear.'

BEFORE

Sarah entered the world blue and silent. She'd stopped moving on the way out. There was no medical reason for it, and soon enough her robust wails would be heard by Dad and Jess in the waiting room, but for a moment I experienced a strange euphoria. It was something I'd never forgive myself for – the floaty relief that I'd followed through, but that if she were to die it was out of my hands. Everything until then had been my responsibility, but her blueness and silence were not.

In the birthing suite, Martine let me squeeze her hand and talked me through the labour –

everything will be okay no going back now

women have been doing this forever

think what could have happened if you didn't come home

you got yourself into this, now get yourself out of it

you'll forget the pain – we all do

stop whining and push

now you'll think twice about consequences

I can't do this part for you

Oh, she's coming

push

push

push

– but she didn't speak to me after Sarah was born and I'd stopped pushing.

When Sarah took her first breath and cried, I sat up and held out my arms, but she was whisked away. She needed oxygen. I took seven stitches in my perineum – at just over four hours it had been a quick labour for a first baby, and they told me she was a good size at eight pounds and one ounce. It would have meant something if they'd let me hold her.

Martine held her first. It was easy to blame the moments we'd missed for the connection we lacked; in hindsight, I was young and scared and my mother was *there*, which was more than I could have expected. But in the lingering haze of the drugs and euphoria, all I could think was that, for most of my pregnancy, Martine didn't want her. Now she was looking at my baby as if she would never let go. I had wanted her more than anything – now she was here, part of me wished there was a way to go back in time.

I wasn't ready.

The nurses took Sarah to the nursery for a stint in a humidicrib. Martine went with her, and I was left alone. I slept.

Four hours after her birth, I put on my dressing-gown and went looking for my baby. I was loose in my hips, unsteady on my feet and, although she was no longer inside me, there was a dragging heaviness in my pelvis, a phantom weight. I wondered if it would go away or stay, likewise for the livid stretch marks across my back and thighs.

A midwife pointed me in the right direction: one floor up. The mirrored walls of the lift reflected my pale, swollen face. I appeared shell-shocked.

'You need to sign in and there's only one visitor allowed at a time,' said the nurse at the station. 'Check in with the neonatal nurse, too.'

'My baby is in there.'

She checked the log. 'Who is Martine Morgan?'

'My mother.'

'She signed in hours ago.'

I peered through the glass slats. Martine was sitting on a chair next to a humidicrib. She had her hand pressed to the side, fingers spread as if she was trying to make contact.

'So it's my turn? I'm the mother, right? I can go in.'

The nurse sighed. 'Let her know you're here and you can swap.'

I watched for a moment longer before tapping on the glass. Martine looked up, smiling at first, then scowling. Reluctantly, she stood. We squeezed past each other without touching and she took a seat outside the door.

Martine had been staring at Sarah as if she was utterly familiar, but when I saw her wrinkled little face I was sure there'd been a mix-up. She was blue-tinged, dark-haired, with pursed lips and deep creases in her brow. In my imagination she had been blonde and tiny; in the real world she looked nothing like me.

Martine was right. I'd created a Hallmark fantasy world. In it, my baby was perfect, sleeping in a gently-swinging white cradle, dressed in beautiful clothes, and she loved me completely. In reality, Sarah would spend a couple of months sleeping in a porta-cot Dad had picked up from hard waste. It smelled like cat pee and sick, even after I'd scrubbed it with antiseptic and hosed it down in the backyard. The few clothes I'd managed to buy were too big for her, so she came home wearing a hideous green knitted jumpsuit I'd found in the second-hand bag of clothes. She barely opened her eyes during the first few weeks – they were scrunched shut, either in sleep or anger. When they did open, her expression was one of extreme disappointment in the world.

She didn't love me. It wasn't her job to love me.

Two days after Sarah and I came home from the hospital, I was suffering from lack of sleep and stuck in a relentless cycle of feeding, changing and washing. To avoid the conflict and crying, Jess had spent the previous couple of nights at a friend's house. When Dad got home from work, he whiled away hours in his shed. Martine was a silent, hovering presence – her only concession to having a new baby and an exhausted teenage mother in the house was to prepare meals a little more quietly than usual. Occasionally she would bring me a cup of tea.

It was almost dinnertime. I had spent an hour pacing the backyard, rocking Sarah to sleep. I put her down in her cot and sneaked out of my room, closing the door behind me, and leaned against the wall in the hallway. My dressing-gown reeked of vomit and sweat. My milk had come in with a vengeance and my entire body ached. All I wanted was to curl up in a dark room and close my eyes, but I had an hour or two at best before she'd be awake and crying again, and there was washing to hang and bottles to sterilise.

Martine peered around the doorway to the kitchen. 'Is she asleep?'

'Yes. Finally.'

'Having second thoughts?' She sounded tired. And was that sadness I detected?

'It's a bit late for that,' I said.

'Well, yes. She's here now and you have to do the best you can.'

'I *am* doing the best I can,' I muttered. 'Why do I feel like you're always punishing me?'

'I'm not. You just have to accept the reality of the situation.'

Frustrated, I banged my head against the wall. The noise woke Sarah, who started crying again, and Martine rolled her eyes and disappeared back into the kitchen. She put something on the counter with an unnecessarily loud bang.

'Thanks a lot! What would I do without you?' I yelled sweetly. 'You'd be on the stree-eet!' she sing-songed in response.

I opened the door and scooped Sarah from her cot, jiggling her against my shoulder. Her tiny body was tense, her cries vibrating through my back. I slung her across one arm and turned slow circles until her eyes popped open, flicking from side to side. She immediately stopped crying.

Martine returned. She stared at me in horror. 'What on earth are you doing?'

'We're spinning,' I said. 'She likes it. See? She stopped.'

'She's dizzy, that's why. You'll make her throw up.'

'What's new?' I turned faster. 'She's always throwing up.'

Martine held out her arms. 'I'll take her.'

'No.'

'Give her to me.'

I stopped. 'You want me to handle things by myself? Well, I'm handling it!' I gave Martine a push towards the door.

She pushed back, reaching for the baby. We tussled half-heartedly until she turned red in the face and dropped her arms to her sides, as if realising I'd dragged her down to my level.

'You're not helping,' I said.

'You're out of control,' she replied.

She left.

Martine insisted that Sarah would never learn to settle by herself if I picked her up every time she squawked; that she wouldn't stay sleeping if the last thing she felt was the warmth of my body, and then woke up alone. But how did she manage to doze through my mother and me yelling at each other, and yet the slightest sound or even a change in the wind's direction could wake her and send her into hysterics?

I looked down at Sarah's face. Her eyes were closed, her tiny hands relaxed. She was a mystery, a puzzle I needed to solve on my own.

*

I breastfed Sarah for six weeks, but she fed too frequently and took too little, always leaving me half-full and aching. She would eventually fall asleep in my arms. I'd juggle her weight with one arm and express with the other – *pump, jiggle, rock, switch* – which took twice the amount of time and meant I produced double the milk. I'd be feeding in the middle of the night while my family slept, imagining the milk flowing from my breast to Sarah's body, tainted with resentment like poison.

The books had told me pregnancy was a sublime experience; the magazines said motherhood made you glow. But my body was a caricature of itself: bloated, leaking, exhausted in a way I'd never experienced before. Pride and shame kept me from asking my mother for help. If she noticed my struggle, she didn't acknowledge it. And when the pain of recurring mastitis and the worry about Sarah's slow weight gain made me give up breastfeeding, Martine said switching to formula was proof of my selfishness.

For me it was sweet relief. Sarah finally started sleeping. I could focus on making plans for the future.

I couldn't shake the feeling that Martine was holding back her joy at being a grandmother, and that made me sad. It wasn't that she was punishing me – it was more like she saw it as a test I had to pass on my own. I wasn't sure I ever passed.

I caught her once, standing over the cot, holding Sarah's hand, whispering nonsense under her breath and making exaggerated faces, the things we do to elicit those early smiles. She got one – I could tell by the wonder in her expression. Minutes later Sarah was hungry and started to cry, and when Martine realised I was standing there she seemed embarrassed.

'You can pick her up,' I said, meaning to prolong the sweet moment.

Martine immediately stepped back, her mouth set in a thin line.

'She's your responsibility. I'm not going to help you by making it easy.'

Sarah's crying hit the exact note that triggered my milk let-down reflex. As we held our ground, the baby squalled and the milk spread into dinner plate-sized patches on my T-shirt.

Martine resolutely ignored both.

I grabbed a towel to soak up the mess. 'You're right. You're always right.'

'You'll thank me one day.'

I said the most vicious thing I could. 'I should have listened to you. Maybe it's not too late to put her up for adoption. She's still small and cute enough, right?' I picked up Sarah and held her thrashing body against my shoulder.

Martine stared in horror at the dribbles of milk on the floor.

I didn't mean it, and I did. Some days I yearned to hand Sarah to a kind-faced stranger on the street and walk away. I didn't know if these feelings were normal because I couldn't talk about them. I understood that withholding support was Martine's way of forcing me to take responsibility, of making me strong, but surely there was another way. I just didn't know what it was, or how to make it happen.

Supposedly it took a village to raise a child. My village was like a ghost town with locked doors, boarded-up windows and me parading around with a scarlet letter on my chest. I had to leave, for Sarah's sake and my own.

255 Bentley Rd, Rosewood: fully furnished one-bedroom flat with a small private garden. No pets. Close to transport and shopping. Cheap rent in exchange for cleaning duties. $120 p/w.

I agreed to the lease for the Rosewood flat over the phone after a five-minute call with the owner, who said it was in a desirable area and would go quickly. It needed some work, he said, but he was willing to negotiate. The way he described it, I imagined the flat to be a cosy, sunny space with a small rambling garden and a street view from the balcony. My savings from cleaning and working at the newsagency would just cover the bond plus four weeks' rent in advance.

I started packing late that night while my parents were sleeping. Sarah and I still hadn't settled into a routine – she was awake, lying between two pillows on the bed, snuffling and fretting. I didn't hear Martine coming. She opened the door, taking in the piles of baby clothes, the open suitcase on the floor.

'What's all this?' She picked up Sarah, soothing her by letting her suck on her knuckle.

'I've found us a place.'

Her face was white. 'You're taking her?'

'I'm taking responsibility, like you said.'

'This is not responsibility. It's madness. How will you support yourself?'

'I'll find a part-time job and I've got the single-mother payment. We'll be fine.' I kept folding. 'Anyway, I don't understand why you're upset. This is what you wanted. Now you can have your life back.'

Sarah had fallen asleep in the crook of my mother's elbow.

Martine gently smoothed her sweaty hair. 'You could leave her here with me.'

She said it so quietly I pretended not to hear.

NOW

I sat by the lounge-room window, peering past the curtain, a mug of cold tea beside me. Waiting. Ever since Jess had left yesterday, I'd sensed I was being watched.

The feeling was with me when I lived with Cass. I recognised it when I moved away from home for the second time, and it was there on and off during the years that followed. It came again when Sarah disappeared – I hid inside, while mail stacked up in the letterbox and reeking bags of rubbish piled outside the front door. I avoided contact with strangers. No one could be trusted, nowhere was safe. I could not understand how someone could take my child and never think of me, her mother, again. I would not accept that it had been random, that she was gone. I could not accept that it was over.

Others said I was paranoid. I called it intuition. The difference between the two was that when people thought you were paranoid, it was because they didn't believe you.

Movement on the street. I jumped and let the curtain fall back, but it was only the postman.

Murray's circle of friends did not include our neighbours; what little I knew of them came from observation. The block was large enough and the fences high enough that we didn't often run into each other, unless it was a polite nod and a wave from inside passing cars. A retired couple lived on one side. A family with three teenage boys on the other. To the rear, one old home had been demolished to make way for eight modern townhouses. They were a constant source of anxiety for me, especially in winter when the maples lost their leaves and the bedroom and bathroom windows of four townhouses looked into our backyard.

There had been a Christmas party invitation a year ago, a deckchairs-on-the-footpath and share-plate thing organised by the Bell family, who were new to the street. Murray was away at the time and I didn't want to be the first to arrive, so I waited inside, holding a plate of sausage rolls that cooled and turned soggy, while the family of five looked more and more despondent. Nobody turned up.

I'd always felt bad about that. But the Bells were not under suspicion.

The man directly across the road, however, made me uncomfortable. Murray said he'd moved in around the same time I had. He was around Murray's age, out of shape and with a hacking cough, and he lived alone. I called him the Hitcher, but I didn't know his real name. Most of the house was hidden behind a rambling hedge – I imagined it was as unkempt as he looked. Each morning he came out to check his letterbox, his pants falling down, gut trembling like half-set jelly. He'd pull out his mail, launch a glob of spit into the gutter, and hitch his pants before going back inside.

It was half-past nine and the Hitcher was due at any moment. I didn't want to miss him. What if my child's murderer had been living right across the street for four years, feeding his sick fantasies?

The moment he came into view, I dashed outside, fast-walking down the driveway. I was dressed in a loose T-shirt, pyjama bottoms, no bra. I didn't think about what I was doing, why I was doing it or what I'd say.

We reached for our mail at the same time.

I let the letterbox door go and the *clang* made him look up. He coughed, spat, hitched his pants, and I tutted.

My reaction seemed to enrage him. He looked both ways and shuffled across the street, his mail in one hand, the waistband of his pants bunched in the other. He'd always seemed old to me but there was a bullish strength about him: thick neck, wide shoulders, broad chest. He halted about a metre from the kerb. His eyes were freakishly blank; they flickered over my body, settling on my bra-less chest.

As he drew close, I had to stop myself from backing away. I crossed my arms. 'What do you want?'

He grunted and waved the hand clutching the mail.

I would have launched myself at him and scratched those empty eyes out if I wasn't so terribly afraid, and if a car hadn't turned down the street, travelling too fast.

He tilted his head. His mouth twisted and he lurched forward, stubbing his foot against the kerb.

Instinctively I reached out to catch him as he fell. We landed on the concrete, his heavy body on top of mine. I screamed in shock and pushed him off me as he rolled limply away.

The car pulled up where the man had been standing seconds before.

Edie jumped out. 'Are you okay?'

The Hitcher groaned and tried to sit up.

'Let me help,' she said, taking his elbow.

Edie's friend Jase got out of the driver's seat. 'I didn't see him. He was on the road.'

'Don't touch him,' I said. 'Don't *touch* him!'

Edie nodded. 'You're right. He might be hurt. Should I call an ambulance?'

'Too fast,' the man muttered. He batted at Edie's hand but allowed Jase to help him up.

I was frozen. Why were they helping him? *He* had attacked *me*.

Edie put her hand on my arm. 'Abbie, you look like you're going to pass out. I'll call Dad.'

'Don't bother calling him. I'm going inside.'

Wearing a dumbstruck expression, Edie watched me leave. She shook her head and turned to Jase, shrugging. She seemed more afraid of me than the Hitcher, who was white as a sheet and swaying like a circus elephant.

I went in the house, collapsed in a chair and turned on the TV.

Shortly after, Jase drove away and Edie came in.

'He's fine. I managed to get some sense out of him. We took him home and he called his daughter. She's coming to check on him. Are you okay?'

I nodded. 'I'm fine. I'm watching TV.'

'I can see that.' She frowned. 'He wanted to ask you to check his mail – apparently he's been getting letters for number seventy-six and he was worried they'd be sitting there awhile because he can't read them.'

'What?' I said.

'He's recovering from a stroke. He has blurred vision.'

She waited for me to say something and when I didn't, she sighed and started to walk away. How could I defend my behaviour?

'Edie?'

She stopped. 'Yes.'

'What's his name?'

Edie stared.

'Did you get his name?'

She shook her head. 'It's Robert McLean.'

'Do you know for sure?'

'I read the letters for him.'

'Okay. Thank you.'

She gave me a parting look of disgust.

I took up my position by the window again.

Whatever the feeling was – paranoia or intuition – it made me abandon reason and empathy. It made me see bad people everywhere. But it was stronger this time, and welcome, like an old friend.

I felt vindicated. Sarah's disappearance hadn't been a single, vile act – there was more to come. The senselessness of tragedy had begun to make sense, and I trusted my own conviction that my past life and present circumstances were somehow connected.

BEFORE

We arrived at the Rosewood flat during a late afternoon rainstorm. Sarah, eight weeks old, was strapped to my chest in a swaddle. I towed a single large suitcase crammed with baby gear and the medicines Martine had bought, plus a few changes of my own clothes and a new set of queen-sized sheets.

Sarah's forehead was beaded with raindrops and I was wet through.

I had been told to ask for Boston at the shop below the flat, which turned out to be a tattoo parlour called the Snakepit. It was the last building in a row of seven sad-looking narrow-fronted shops in what felt like an undesirable area. Boston had been quiet and well-spoken on the phone; in person he was emaciated, shifty-looking, about forty years old and clean-skinned as far as I could tell, but with enough piercings to set off a metal detector at a hundred paces.

'You never mentioned a baby,' he said, looking me over. He called out to someone behind a beaded curtain. 'She has a baby.'

'The ad said no pets. It didn't say no babies,' I said, sticking out my chin.

He smiled, all pointed teeth. 'Around the side. I'll get the key.'

I jiggled Sarah, who was quiet but restless; soon she'd be hungry and not quiet.

Boston handed me a set of keys.

He watched from the shelter of the verandah as I dragged my suitcase into the alley, lined with council bins, scattered with cigarette butts and upended milk crates. Above, the windows to the flat were dark. There was a long, shallow balcony at the front, but even in the grey light I could see it was close to falling down. Struggling to hold the keys, the baby and the suitcase, I abandoned the case at the foot of the steep stairs. I opened the door, clutching Sarah to my chest, and felt along the wall for a switch.

A single fluorescent strip light flickered on to reveal a cramped, filthy room that passed for a kitchen, lounge and dining room all in one. A porch at the rear had been enclosed to make a small bedroom. The bathroom had a broken window and a shallow bath, but no shower or laundry facilities. 'Fully furnished' meant a single bed with a mattress like a hammock, a stained three-drawer dresser and a black vinyl couch, spilling its springs and stuffing. From the doorway it looked like a gored animal. There was a pallet on bricks for a table and a Formica dining setting from the fifties, no fridge. An external door in the bedroom opened onto another flight of stairs, which I assumed led to the garden.

Feeling deflated but hopeful, I lay Sarah on the couch and went back for the suitcase.

So it wasn't as delightful as the ad had made it sound. What I had imagined didn't match what I could afford. All we needed was a space to call our own, a place for Sarah and me to be independent, to be our own little family.

That first night, I toasted bread over the stove-top flame and boiled water for Sarah's formula using an empty peach can I found in one of the cupboards. I doubled over our sheets to fit the mattress. Scared I'd roll on top of Sarah if she slept with me, I took the bottom drawer from the dresser and set up a makeshift bassinet on the floor.

The rain came in through the bathroom window; the wind whistled in the eaves and the rickety balcony groaned. I left all the lights on. Sarah bawled most of the night.

I did too.

The next day, I rummaged through local second-hand shops, looking for cheap items to brighten up the place: a threadbare set of Moroccan cushions, daisy-print curtains, a vase of artificial tulips and a red chequered tablecloth like they had in Italian restaurants. I found a pram for twenty-five dollars in Vinnies and a kettle that, when I plugged it in, immediately blew the fuse.

I spent the afternoon learning how to clean the shop, which involved sterilising the equipment and disinfecting surfaces. The process took about two hours when Boston looked on, half an hour less when he wasn't there. When I realised I was expected to clean every day, not weekly, I fronted Boston and demanded another fifty off the rent – to which he agreed, as long as that damned baby didn't scare off the clients.

'I'm not yer sugar daddy,' he said.

I met Tansy, Steve and Dev, the artists, and Antonella, who sat at the front desk constantly filing nails that never seemed to get any shorter. She only lasted a couple of weeks after we arrived.

Tansy was a few years older than me, a rough-talking, sweet-faced girl whose boyfriend picked her up every afternoon and whisked her away on a motorbike. With his beer gut, leather vest and biker beard, Dev looked like the opposite of a family man, but he left at two-thirty sharp every day to pick up his four kids from school. Steve was about fifty – single, quiet and intense, with the most incredible gift for inking detailed portraits on difficult canvases: calves, shoulders, ankles.

On breaks they congregated in the alley, sitting on the milk crates, smoking, talking. Their laughter drifted up and carried through the kitchen window until I couldn't stand it anymore.

Whenever Sarah was sleeping, I'd tiptoe down the steps to join them.

'Did Boston give you his sugar-daddy line yet?' Dev asked, smirking.

'He's a bit of a loner,' Tansy agreed. 'But his heart's in the right place.'

None of them could tell me anything about Boston. We had no idea where he went after he locked up every night – presumably somewhere nicer than the flat. He didn't talk much and I never asked. But Tansy was right about his heart: a few weeks after we moved in, he left a second-hand bar fridge on my doorstep, and one Sunday I came home from a weekend visit to Athena Bay to find the overgrown garden had been cleared of weeds, and there was a new swing set in a box by the gate.

On the day Antonella quit, Boston offered me her job.

I tried to thank him, but he shied away like a stray dog. I bought him a bottle of bourbon – it stayed on the shelf in the office for the two years I was there, gathering dust, still wrapped with cellophane and curling ribbon. And when Sarah was old enough to toddle around the studio, latching onto legs for balance, he'd sidestep her and dodge her reaching hands.

A month or so after we moved into the flat, Martine turned up unannounced. Jess had given her the address – under duress. Even though I'd called home weekly since we'd left, it wasn't enough for Martine. She had to see for herself.

Tansy brought her up. 'Your mum is here!' she said, smiling, and presented my mother as if she was personally responsible for the surprise.

'Oh,' I said.

Tansy went back down.

Sarah was squalling in the bedroom. She'd just woken up and the flat was a mess. I had the radio blaring to drown out the sound of the air conditioning units in the alley, and to get Sarah accustomed to noise. I had tried being quiet when she slept and it didn't work – she woke at the slightest sound regardless, so I did the opposite.

'Those steps are lethal,' Martine said, puffing.

'Come in.' I yanked the radio cord from the wall socket and opened the door wider, sweeping toys and clothes with my foot to clear a path.

Martine strode to the middle of the room and surveyed the chaos.

I knew what she was thinking.

She gestured to the mess. 'A baby could choke on all this stuff.'

'She's three months old,' I said. 'She can't even roll over, let alone pick things up.'

'Still, you should start how you mean to finish.' She sat gingerly on the couch, avoiding the sharp springs at one end, and crossed her legs. 'Did you just put her down or did she just wake up?' She jerked her head in the direction of the crying.

I scurried off. Sarah gave me her best groggy smile when I picked her up. Her nappy had burst: one side of her growsuit was soaked.

'I'm just changing her!' I yelled.

She needed a bath, but I didn't want Martine to see the state of the bathroom. Even after I'd scrubbed it with bleach, the bath was still stained green and the tiles were ingrained with dirt. I spread a towel on the floor of our bedroom and stripped off her suit.

'You don't have a cot?' Martine stood in the doorway, pointing at the dresser drawer.

'She sleeps with me at night.'

It was the wrong thing to say.

'You have no business trying to bring up her up like this. No business taking her from a stable home and dragging her here.'

'You didn't really give me a choice,' I said, so tired I couldn't be bothered telling her to get out. 'She's happy.' I shrugged. 'I'm happy.'

I zipped Sarah's clean suit and whizzed her into the air. I flipped her around to face Martine, letting her go for barely half a second, but Martine went to grab her. As if I'd let her fall.

'Do you want to hold her?'

She nodded.

'She's smiling now. Not those cross-eyed windy smiles,' I said. 'Real ones.'

Martine held Sarah close and nuzzled her neck. 'She's a good weight.'

'It's the formula.' I pointed to my breasts. 'My milk has gone.'

She pursed her lips. 'As long as she's gaining.'

I made mugs of tea, staying out of the way so Martine could spend some time with Sarah. I watched her cooing and gurgling, wondering if she'd ever been that affectionate with me and Jess. I couldn't remember it if she had. In my mind, she'd always been stern, prickly.

'We'll go shopping,' Martine said. 'Make a list of everything you need.'

'We don't need anything,' I said. 'We're fine.'

'Don't be so stubborn. She's sleeping in a drawer, for God's sake.'

I bit my tongue.

'What if I said you could come home?' She wouldn't meet my eye, focusing instead on Sarah's starfish hands as she patted them together.

'I'd say no,' I said. 'Thank you.'

Her head snapped up. 'Why not?'

Because you make me feel like a child.

Because at home I can't breathe.

111

Because it's easier to fail when you're not around.
Because right now I hate myself a little bit less every day.
Because you're capable and you know what you're doing, and I don't.
Because I'm scared she might end up loving you more.
'Just because.'
'Right then,' she said.

The night I came home to find the Rosewood flat burning, I'd taken Sarah to see a kids' film at the outdoor cinema in the park, using free tickets I'd found in my letterbox. She was just over two years old, walking, talking a blue streak, a handful. It was late, past nine o'clock. She fell asleep on my shoulder, so I carried her the four blocks home, my arms numb with fatigue.

It was a hot, breezeless night. I smelled the smoke two streets away, but I assumed it had blown over from somewhere else — if you listened to the news reports that summer it seemed like the whole country was burning.

When I saw the people, hundreds of them, lined up along the opposite side of the street, and two fire trucks parked in the middle of the road, my first reaction was disbelief. We must have turned onto the wrong street.

Hugging Sarah close, I weaved my way through the bodies, their upturned faces glowing in the eerie light. One man was taking photos with a long zoom-lens camera; another had climbed a tree for a better vantage point.

From the bottle shop on the corner across the street, I could see there were temporary barricades and dozens of police to keep the crowd back. Plumes of black smoke billowed from the windows of our flat and the sky above was a deep orange-red; the balcony had collapsed under the weight of the water and lay warped and steaming on the footpath. Clumps of sodden ash clogged the gutter. The flat was still ablaze, but the Snakepit was no longer burning, just smoking, its ceiling caved in and the windows blown out.

The shock of it made me squeeze Sarah too tightly and she woke, rubbing her eyes.

'Fire,' she said. 'Gone.'

Until that moment every new word had seemed like a beautiful miracle.

A charred scrap of daisy-print curtain drifted past and caught on a tree branch. I saw the bright flames reflected in Sarah's sleepy eyes, as my own streamed from the smoke.

Everything we owned was inside. It wasn't much, but it was all we had.

Statistics say one-third of arsonists either stay for the fire or return to the scene, but it didn't occur to me to look for familiar faces in the crowd. The only person I recognised was Boston – he had breached the barricades and was on the road behind the fire trucks, alternately pacing and shouting, or down on his haunches, muttering, his head in his hands.

'Boston!' I yelled.

He didn't hear me. He was distraught. It was understandable: if I'd lost everything, he'd lost more.

'Boston!'

He turned bloodshot eyes in our direction. His agonised expression slackened into relief and he grabbed the arm of the nearest firefighter, gesturing at us.

The firefighter came over. 'You're the tenant?'

'Yes.'

'Thank God. The owner thought you were still in there,' he said. 'Is there likely to be anyone else inside?'

I shook my head. 'No. I don't think so. How did it happen?'

'Can't say.'

'Well, where did it start?' I insisted. 'Was it upstairs?'

I pictured my movements from earlier in the evening, before we'd gone out. I had heated tinned spaghetti on the stove, but I was sure I'd turned off the gas flame. I'd definitely blown out the lemongrass candle I burned in the bedroom to mask the smell of damp and mould. One light switch in the lounge sparked whenever I flicked it off – was it faulty wiring?

'We'll know more later, when the fire is out. Excuse me.' He left to consult with a police officer.

Twenty minutes later the wreckage was smouldering. Boston was sitting inside a police car, speaking with another officer.

Sarah started to grizzle and the hopelessness hit me: what would we do? Where would we go? It was almost ten o'clock; I had less than twenty dollars in my purse and, although the night was still warm, Sarah was underdressed and shivering.

I refused to cry. I was too busy trying to work out our next move. I put Sarah down, just for a few minutes, as I struggled to find my phone in my bag. It was almost flat – the battery had been losing charge for months. I dialled Jess. It went to voicemail and I didn't leave a message. Desperate, I called my parents' landline, feeling the familiar guilt. They'd be asleep.

Martine answered on the fourth ring. 'Abbie,' she said, before I could speak, as if she had been expecting me to call. 'What's wrong?'

'Sorry to wake you.'

'No, no,' she said.

'There's been an accident. A fire. Everything's gone.' My voice cracked. 'We're okay but there's nothing left.'

'I'll come and get you,' she said. 'Tell me where you are.'

I checked along the street. 'There's a twenty-four-hour Mobil on the corner, about a kilometre down.'

'I'm coming.' She hung up.

One minute Sarah was grasping my leg, trying to climb it. The next, she'd let go. I looked around frantically. The crowd had begun to break up, but I couldn't see her anywhere.

It was less than thirty seconds later, but it felt like a lifetime – a man lifted Sarah above his head like an auction item and called out, 'Anyone lost a kid?'

You'd think I would have learned from that.

NOW

The weekend passed without contact and on Monday morning I woke late and alone. It was a pattern I was growing used to, but today the loneliness was acute, tinged with anger. I composed increasingly vicious texts to the no-caller-ID number, then deleted them, knowing the messages would not send. It helped to imagine him reading them, to pretend that the connection wasn't one-way – I could voice the things I was too afraid to say in case he carried out his threat and disappeared. But, for my own sanity, I couldn't play his twisted game of advance and retreat much longer.

While I made my bed, the home phone beeped in my pocket: it was out of charge. I placed it in its cradle in the kitchen and, out of habit, checked the pinboard on the wall.

Murray had left messages for the kids:

Edie: please clean the coffee machine (there's something growing in there)
Cam: mow the front and back lawns

The guilt returned. These were the kinds of jobs I usually took care of. It was as if the family was reverting to the old order – I was disappearing. I had no one to blame but myself.

When they were younger, Edie and Cam had drawn ugly caricatures of each other in one corner of the board, and Sherri had preserved them by sticking clear adhesive over the top. Martine had done something similar, spraying Sarah's chalk drawings on her driveway with fixative.

116

I thought of the boxes in the roof. Before I knew what I was doing, I had pulled down the folding stairs in the hallway.

I went up.

To call the room an attic was a stretch: it was a large, dim and dusty space clad with marine plywood panels, high enough to stand in the areas beneath the tallest pitch of the roof. Murray said the idea was to make it an extra living room for the kids when they hit their teens, but he forgot about the extremes in temperature: in summer it was unbearable, and in winter the added insulation didn't stop the wind and cold from creeping through the cracks.

On the day I moved in, he'd carried Sarah's belongings up the stairs while I stood shivering at the bottom. It didn't feel right to pack her things away up there. *Old houses*, Murray had said, shrugging, as if it was the icy draught that made me reluctant to follow.

Now I froze at the top of the steps, unsure whether I was in the right state of mind to continue. Every time I went looking for memories of Sarah, it was like willingly sticking my hand into a beehive, waiting to get stung.

I switched on the single bulb. Sarah's clothes were kept in vacuum-packed quilt bags, her toys in a large suitcase. The box containing the clippings, letters and cards was where I'd left it after the wedding – on a collapsible card table near the only window. A rectangle of golden midmorning light spilled through the glass, dust motes drifting in the beams like a swarm of lazy insects.

I bent down to look outside. Our next-door neighbour was raking leaves and I heard snatches of song from a radio. Three towels and a single sock hung on her clothesline, whipped by the breeze. Her upstairs window faced ours, lined up like a mirror image.

Again I wondered if he was close, perhaps living in the same street. I shook off the feeling and opened the box.

The last two police sketches of Sarah – aged ten and eleven – were on top. Just underneath were the originals of the two photos I'd provided to the police. They had both been taken minutes apart on her school's athletics day, a few days before her sixth birthday. She wore her house colours: a green T-shirt and shorts, a green headband, and her long, dark hair in a high ponytail tied with a green ribbon. I'd bought everything new because she had nothing in the violent, fluorescent shade of lime she wanted, but I couldn't afford a new pair of shoes. We'd coloured an old pair of white sneakers with green highlighter.

The police had chosen the first photo of Sarah, smiling widely, showing a dimple in her left cheek and missing her two bottom teeth, her head to one side in victory. Moments before, she had finished first in the fifty-metre hurdles race.

See? her eyes said. *I won.*

But Sarah had knocked over the first hurdle, and the adjudicating teacher made the decision to award joint first place to the runner-up. The second photo was taken soon after I'd delivered a lecture on sportsmanship and humility, right when Sarah was awarded her blue ribbon. She was glaring at it as if she had been handed a dirty sock. Her eyes were dark and furious and her bottom lip stuck out, swollen, as if she'd been punched.

'You should use this photo,' I'd told Inspector James Hooper that night. 'It's more like her.'

What I meant was that, if she had been abducted and if she was to be recognised by a member of the public, she would most likely be distraught, not smiling and showing her dimple and the gaps between her teeth.

But there's an art to choosing photos of missing children, and I understood on some level that the cuter the picture, the more her face might capture the hearts and the imagination of TV news viewers. Her smiling photo was reproduced tens of thousands of times – online, in the newspapers, on the missing posters. After a while I grew to accept that this would be the face of my child forever, if she was not found, despite what I knew to be true: the second photo was a far more accurate representation of Sarah's complicated personality. It wasn't that she was never smiling or sweet, it's that she was *more* than that. The first photo didn't capture her essence.

I compared the sketches with the photos, and experienced the usual dizzying sensation. Every year the sketches were updated, that childlike innocence and sweetness carried forward. It always felt like losing her all over again. This changeling was not my child. She was a computer-generated version: imaginary, altered, bearing little resemblance to the original. I feared that I could pass Sarah on the street and fail to recognise her.

I thought of James Hooper again. His kindness, his commitment. *I won't stop until we find her*, he'd said.

But he did stop. He had retired. I often wondered what he was doing now – probably playing golf, or writing a memoir. No, that was unfair. He'd worked tirelessly on Sarah's case for almost a year; I had seen grief in his eyes when a lead came to nothing, genuine grief, as if he'd known her. I hoped he was living a good life. I hoped he'd forgotten Sarah and the other children he couldn't save. It was better that way.

Only once did James put me before a camera; after that he never asked again. By reporters, yes, all the time, but not by the police. During the first press conference, I stammered and fidgeted. I was not at all photogenic; I couldn't cry. In private, my grief was loud and ugly, but in front of the cameras I appeared aloof and secretive, as if I was holding something back. I got plenty of letters of support, but I received an equal share of accusations, hate mail and conspiracy theories.

Martine once told me society couldn't trust a woman who didn't cry for them.

The rest of the photos of Sarah were at the bottom. I had printed every photo I'd ever taken of her – premium five-by-eight prints, in sets of fifty, in order from the day she was born until three days before she disappeared. I used to shuffle through each bundle, like a flip-book animation, until they were as well-worn as a kid's collection of football cards.

Sarah smiling, scowling, running, playing, hanging upside down, her face screwed up in concentration. She was often the sole subject: I was the one behind the lens.

Jess had watched me do it one too many times. 'You need to stop. She won't get any older, Abbie.'

She didn't mean to be cruel. She said it offhandedly, the same way she'd point out a bad habit. *Stop biting your nails. You left the lid off the milk again. You weren't born in a barn.*

I rummaged through the contents of the box and found the folder of Sarah's drawings. The wedding card was on top. I unfolded the paper. Glitter from some of her other drawings had caught in the creases; I ran my hand across the surface, blowing gently, and the pieces drifted and fell like the glitter inside a snow globe.

I scrutinised the drawing.

Us, dressed in our bell-shaped gowns, mine purple, hers pink.

Us, holding hands.

Us, smiling.

I felt the burn of tears when I saw my half-smile, my wolfish teeth. It was like Edie and Cam's caricatures – exaggerated, grotesque. Sarah's teeth were fully-formed, white and straight as a celebrity's.

I looked closer: there was a steady pressure to the marks of the drawing; the colouring stayed inside the lines.

Sarah had been impatient, exuberant, often sloppy.

The words: *Happy Wedding Day, Mummy.* Sarah was left-handed, though she'd used her right for random things like untwisting lids and untying shoelaces. Her writing had been childlike and blockish, slanted to the left – this writing was almost cursive but not quite, the script flamboyant and looping.

The letters were perfectly upright.

Sarah used to sign everything. A giant S with hugs and kisses. S*XOX*.

On the card there were none.

Something wasn't right. I spread a dozen of her drawings over the floor, like a pentagram, me in the centre. I shuffled the papers, until a pattern of similarities and differences emerged.

I didn't know how I had missed it. I wanted to curl into a ball and howl.

But if he was the one who had taken her, if he had her briefcase and scrapbook, why was the drawing not hers?

That evening I prepared dinner. I showered, dressed, set the formal dining table with the good crockery and the best glasses, and chilled an expensive bottle of white wine.

For the past few hours I had been rehearsing what I'd say to Murray about the phone calls, the drawing, the reasons for my aberrant behaviour. I waited in the seat adjacent to his at the head of the table.

By seven, I had eaten a bowl of pappadums and drunk most of the wine. Edie came home and went straight to her room. At eight-thirty, when Cam arrived but Murray still hadn't, I let him loose on the congealed Thai red curry and clumped rice.

He ate two-thirds of it, watching me warily. 'Have you called Dad?'

'Not yet.'

He picked up his phone. 'I'll do it.'

'No!' I barked. 'He'll get here when he gets here.'

'Fine, whatever.' He got up. 'Thanks for dinner.'

He left his dirty plate on the table, stains on the tablecloth, his shoes and socks on the floor.

I waited for another hour, biting my nails, moving my loosening wedding ring from finger to finger, trying to find one it fitted. I finished the bottle of wine alone.

NOW

When I woke the next morning, I found a message from Murray: *An emergency case came in. I'm sleeping here at the clinic.* He'd sent it after midnight.

The kids had gone already, leaving their breakfast dishes in the sink. With a dry mouth and queasy stomach, I stacked the dishwasher and cleaned up the dishes from the night before. It wasn't the first time Murray had stayed at the clinic overnight, but it was the first time it felt personal. If he was avoiding coming home, I understood, but in order for me to undo what I had done, we needed time alone to talk.

I baked chocolate chip cookies and took a bagful across the street to Robert McLean. When he didn't answer the door, I left them on the step. I checked the addressees on his mail to make sure the postman had got it right, and spent half an hour on my hands and knees weeding the nature strip in front of his house.

When I finished, I went inside, determined to get the house in order before Murray came home.

My mobile was ringing.

Fuck you.

I let it ring out. Almost straightaway *No Caller ID* flashed up again.

Languidly, I cleaned underneath my dirt-caked fingernails with a nail file. I moved on to scrubbing the baking trays, listening to the ringing. Was it getting shriller?

The third time I let it ring nine rings before I picked up. I made my voice sound both sharp and bored.

'What.'

'What are you doing?' he asked.

'I've been baking.'

'And?'

'Weeding.'

He grunted, as if satisfied I had told the truth, but I wasn't convinced he knew what I'd been doing.

Test him.

'My husband is home,' I lied. 'You should know that. Apparently.'

'Why is he home?' He was rattled.

'He lives here.'

Then, an odd question. 'Do you love him?'

'I married him, didn't I?' Light. Breezy.

'That's not what I asked.'

'It's not your business.'

'Are you still sleeping with him?'

I hesitated. We were sleeping apart, but I didn't want him to know things had gone exactly as he had planned. A faint clunk and a rustling sound, as if he'd dropped the phone. I let the silence build, sensing he was struggling to keep his emotions in check.

'He's my husband and I love him,' I said eventually. 'Whatever you're trying to do, nothing will change that.'

It was like poking my finger in a wound I'd inflicted. It felt *good*.

His tone grew hard. 'On the contrary, it changes everything. I had plans for you, Abbie, but I can adjust those plans.'

I slammed a cupboard door. 'Here's the thing – I think the drawing is fake. I think you're a clever manipulative liar, but that's all you've got.'

'I'm the only person who knows what happened to her,' he said. 'And you're willing to risk me disappearing again?'

I rattled some cutlery. 'Like I said, I don't believe you. I need *proof.*'

'And I need a gesture of faith!' he snapped. 'You have to finish what you've started. You're close, but you're not all the way yet.'

'I've done everything you've asked,' I said. 'My life is falling apart.'

'It's not enough for it to fall apart – you have to tear it down.' A bird trilled. I couldn't tell if it was here, outside, or there, wherever he was. 'Next, you'll see several doctors. I want you to ask for painkillers, sleeping pills, antidepressants – anything you can get. Fill the prescriptions. Leave the bottles where anyone can see you're taking them.'

They were all medications I'd taken at various times after Sarah disappeared. How did he know?

'But I don't need any of those things.'

'Evade. Manipulate. Lie,' he said. 'You're good at it.'

A sob burst from my chest.

When he spoke, his voice was hideously gentle. 'I want to get to the end too.'

'What happens at the end?'

'That will be up to you.'

'You make it sound as if I have a *choice*!'

'All of this is about your choices, Abbie. Why can't you admit it?'

In the background, a chair scraped. I heard footsteps crossing a floor.

'I have to go now. If you're thinking of telling anyone, don't. You can't have it all – you can't have truth without sacrifice. You have to choose.'

'And if I do this?' I whispered.

'I'll give you the proof you want. You have a choice right now, Abbie. A good mother would do anything to know, wouldn't she? Are you a good mother?'

He hung up.

*

I had wanted to be one of them: the good mothers, pushing top-of-the-range prams in shopping centres, towing their children by the hand and not letting go, taking their kids to school and seeing them safely inside. They made packed lunches and prepared hot dinners with just the right amount from each food group on the pyramid. They never took their eyes off their children at the playground, wiping their tiny hands and faces before they ate, changing their clothes when they were dirty. Their children were monitored, assessed, vaccinated on time, enrolled in school before they could walk; they were adored, protected from bad things and bad people.

Before we left Rosewood, Sarah had learned to crawl on the vinyl floor; she took her first steps in the backyard where I'd sunbathe on warm days while she played in her paddling pool. She'd said her first word riding Tansy's bouncing knee, while I wiped and dusted around them. Dev taught her to dance and she never lost her mimicry of his swaying, like a lumbering bear. Over the course of a few weeks, without Boston knowing, Steve had stayed late to ink my back: a cherub with Sarah's baby-face, its finely detailed wings spread across my scapula.

The tattoo had been a private, rebellious act. I thought no one but Jess and my few brief lovers knew it existed, until Martine brought it up. I'd regret it one day, she said, this desecration of my flesh. It was time I stopped behaving like a teenager and put my energies into being a good mother.

And I did regret it. After Sarah disappeared, I couldn't bear to look. I dressed without checking my appearance; it became a habit not to turn around when I got out of the shower, for fear of glimpsing myself in the mirror. I imagined the tattoo fading, like invisible ink, and over time my habit became a deep superstition.

After the fire, Sarah and I spent several weeks with my parents, before we found another place. I kept to the outer suburbs, as close to the city as I could afford and far enough away from the coast that Martine couldn't visit unannounced. A new place gave me a sense of strangeness and possibility, similar to the feeling I got as a kid when I moved the furniture in my bedroom. It made things bearable, until I ran out of configurations and grew bored. I moved often, dragging Sarah from place to place, switching kindergartens and schools.

One day when I was moving house yet again, I found Sarah's infant health record book, given to new parents when a child was born. Apart from her birth weight and length – eight pounds and one ounce, fifty-one centimetres – the circumference of her head and the signature of the midwife, there were no further entries. I was invited to join a new mothers' group, but I never went. I took her for her first vaccinations. Beyond that, it was only when she visited the doctor for various illnesses, like an ear infection or persistent nappy rash, that I was reminded she was due for boosters. The years passed and we made do, but we didn't thrive; I grew older, but I didn't grow up.

Around the age of two or three, Sarah progressed from simple needs to complex wants, and I cherished the hours when she was asleep while I was awake. From the moment she woke she was wired, swinging from manic activity to inconsolable tiredness, and the relentlessness of single parenthood made me hate myself on a daily basis. Martine visited regularly. She took Sarah to the park, the shopping centre, the beach. While they were gone I tried to enjoy the time out – have a nap, read a book, take a long shower – but I found myself watching the hands on the clock moving, the time ticking away, torn between missing her and wishing her gone a little longer.

I thought I was a good mother, but it turned out I was the other kind: a mother who left her baby in a car seat and the keys in the ignition, engine running, while she dashed inside a service station for bread and milk. A mother who made a coffee before going to her toddler screaming in her cot, because God only knew when I'd get another chance to drink it while it was still hot. A mother who let her two-year-old crawl into her bed at night and stay there until morning, because it was the only way to guarantee more than forty-five minutes of straight sleep. A mother who let her baby walk around with a soaked nappy drooping past her chubby knees, because nappies weren't cheap and another hour in the soggy one wouldn't hurt. A mother who yelled, who said horrible things, because I was so tired I could barely function and some days it was all too much.

After Sarah was taken, I questioned the decisions I'd made, and I blamed myself.

If only I hadn't forced her to come to the market when she was tired; if only I hadn't tried to teach her a lesson. If only I hadn't moved again. If only.

First I visited my usual GP. He had a decent-sized file on my history with anxiety and depression, dating back five years – he was quick to suggest a short course of sleeping tablets for the insomnia, and a course of antidepressant medication for the longer term. In under twenty minutes I walked out with two prescriptions.

The second doctor was similarly disengaged. He also gave me two prescriptions, one for sleeping tablets and the other for a relaxant, and told me to make a follow-up appointment in three weeks. I filled the prescriptions at two different pharmacies and ate a late lunch in a cafe, feeling jittery and exposed but grateful to be out of the house.

The last doctor was a female GP in a bulk-billing practice. I had made an appointment for two o'clock; by the time the receptionist called my name it was almost three. I expected to be in and out quickly since the doctor was running behind and my needs were clear, but she blindsided me with her steely thoroughness and direct gaze. Youngish, maybe early thirties, with gentle hands and kind eyes, she insisted on taking my blood pressure and probed me about unrelated things, like the dates of my last Pap smear and breast check.

'I'm here about the insomnia, anxiety and agoraphobia,' I said. 'Not that.'

She nodded, but fired off so many questions I grew agitated and tried to leave.

'Abbie, please sit down.'

I sat. 'It shouldn't be this hard.'

'I'm going to help you, but I need more information.' She typed a few notes. 'Is there a reason you haven't seen your regular practitioner?'

'He's on holiday.'

'Okay. Tell me more about your medication history. What was effective? What wasn't?'

I gave her the names of medications I'd been prescribed previously. The doctor raised her eyebrows, but said nothing.

'I've done this before,' I reassured her. 'I'm careful.'

'Then you know it can take some time to find the right combination of medication and support. Have you seen a psychologist or had any type of counselling?' she asked kindly. 'I like to offer a combined approach.'

I shook my head. 'I'll be fine once I catch up on some sleep.'

'Your reasons for not sleeping will still be there when the pills run out.'

Her pen had been poised above the prescription pad for over ten minutes.

I *had* been to a group counselling session for grieving parents once. Something another mother said had stuck with me. She likened the morbid fascination other parents exhibited when they found out her child had been murdered to the way people reacted to watching a horror film. They *took solace* from their horror; the rebound emotions they experienced from knowing their child was safe – gratitude, relief, a rush of exquisite love – were heightened and addictive.

My mind made rapid calculations. What kind of person did she think I was? How hard could I push before I went too far and she put the pen down? I was familiar with the response people gave when I told them about Sarah, but as a general rule I avoided it: the aggressive sympathy, downcast eyes, the way a conversation either ended abruptly or, worse, turned to ghoulish interrogation. It was often me who ended up consoling them.

'I just need to reset my clock,' I said, repeating what my usual GP had said.

'Are you looking for answers, Abbie? Or is it oblivion you're after?'

I sputtered, 'You can't ask that!'

I think she knew I was putting on an act, but she didn't know why. I felt a grudging admiration for her acuity, but my own frustration was mounting.

'I lost my child,' I said.

Her gaze didn't waver. 'I lost one too. I'm very sorry. I'm here to help you.'

I like you, I thought. *But you can't help me.* I stared back at her, my expression impassive, even as an involuntary tear rolled down my cheek. Sympathy I could handle; empathy I could not.

'This is a short-term solution.'

I nodded.

'I'd like to see you again next week.'

Finally, the pen started moving. I breathed out.

'I'm not convinced you're telling me the whole story, but I'm willing to take one small step forward at a time if you are.'

I took the prescription and bolted, flushed with shame.

Five hours after I'd left the house, I'd seen three doctors, been to three different pharmacies. I carried a rattling bag stuffed with pills. As instructed, I left a packet on the kitchen counter, one on the bedside table and another in the medicine cupboard. I put the rest inside the bathroom cabinet in plain view, and popped several sleeping tablets from their blisters.

I stared at the pills in my hand, then flushed them down the toilet.

The doctor had been wrong. It wasn't oblivion I was after. It was answers. I recognised the truth: I *wanted* him to be real. I had the chance to sever the connection, but to do that would be to lose hope. I knew what that felt like, and I didn't think I could survive it again.

AFTER

Sarah's disappearance was headline news and at first the police were a near-constant presence. But after several weeks and no leads or sightings, I found myself alone except when my parents or Jess came to stay, and the articles became shorter, relegated to pages where the advertisements for furniture or skin care were larger than her picture.

If Martine and I were ever to meet on common ground, it should have been in the midst of shared grief. She missed Sarah as much as I did; she knew how it felt not to be able to get out of bed some days, or pick herself up off the floor. We both kept our emotions so tightly packed, I worried we'd tear open and our pain would become one giant amorphous blob, but at least then we'd stop hurting each other. But soon enough I would say something cruel, and Martine would go out to buy milk. We retreated to our separate corners. Martine attended candlelight vigils with strangers. I withdrew. She found God, and I lost hope.

Weeks turned into months, months turned into a year. My lease ran out, but I refused to leave the unit in case Sarah was alive and trying to find her way home. I didn't bother to open my mail because most of it was correspondence from weirdos and letters of demand. I turned people away, quit my job, stopped paying rent and bills, and I got away with it. People felt sorry for me. It wasn't that I didn't have money – I'd been saving every spare cent since Sarah was born. I just couldn't manage anything beyond the fundamentals. I ate to stay alive and I drank to keep from losing my mind.

I remember the day I accepted that Sarah wasn't coming home. That Sunday morning was bad. Jess was there with me when the police came. She had made the trip from Athena Bay every weekend except three since Sarah had disappeared, arriving late on Friday night and leaving again on Sunday afternoon. She paid my bills, washed my sheets, went shopping and filled my pantry with food. Sometimes she was successful in dragging me outside and leading me on a shambling lap of the block, but it was soon apparent that the act of holding a person's hand was another trigger for breath-stealing anxiety, along with crowds, loud music and crying children.

We were up early. Jess was planning a full day of distractions before it was time for her to leave.

'We could go to the zoo? Or just get on a train and see where we end up?'

'Oh no,' I said. 'I couldn't.'

'What about the beach? How long since you've been in the water?'

'I'd probably drown.'

She shook her head. 'You're a human cork.'

'Bloat makes you float.'

Jess smiled. 'You float because you are a mermaid queen.'

I leaned my head into her chest as she finger-combed my hair. It had grown to my waist and the first strands of grey were showing.

Jess heard the cars and peered through the blinds. 'It's that detective, Jodi Barnes,' she said. 'Actually, there are more.'

I felt it then. Hope. I wanted to tell Jess it was funny – it didn't matter if you were sixteen and waiting for a boy to call or you were twenty-seven and waiting for the news that they'd found your child's bones in a suitcase at the bottom of a lake, the feeling was similar. A lift, like a bird taking flight in your chest.

'What do they want?' I started my usual pacing and flapping, which prompted Jess to pin my hands and push me into the nearest chair.

'Maybe they know something. Stay there.'

Jess opened the door and they came inside, four of them, taking up too much space in their uniforms and suits.

Detective Jodi Barnes had been assigned Sarah's case when James Hooper retired. I hadn't had much contact with Jodi – not like I did with James, who had called weekly to check in, whether there was news or not. Her brusqueness rubbed me the wrong way. She was a tall woman with the stance of a tall man, and I translated her manner to mean she didn't like or trust me. Jess said it just seemed like she was always in a hurry, but I sensed the antagonism between us each time we met, a connection like a fraying rope.

Jodi had reinterviewed me when she took over the case, pressing me to recall my original statement in minute detail, pouncing on any inconsistencies. As I was leaving, she said, 'One thing is bugging me, Ms Morgan – there is no hard evidence your daughter ever arrived at the street market that day. If there's anything you would like to tell me regarding her disappearance, now is the time.' And when I told her to go fuck herself, she seemed pleased, as if her interrogation had revealed a crack that wasn't already there.

She was talking now – something about a fresh lead and an anonymous tip-off.

'Did you hear me, Ms Morgan?' She was watching me closely. 'The caller said we needed to look to the mother.'

'What?'

Jess stood. 'That's insane.'

'*Look to the mother.* Why would he say that?' Jodi leaned closer.

I should have been curious about the caller, or even angry about the accusations, but all I felt was crushing sadness.

'Because I was a bad mother.'

'Abbie, *no*,' Jess said. 'The question is, why are there three cars and four of you to tell us about another crank call?'

'We are on our way to interview a suspect.'

'About Sarah?' I asked.

'Different case. A break and enter.'

'Right,' I said flatly. 'A break and enter.'

'I just thought you needed to know.'

Jess saw them to the door. I followed and stood on the step. Three cars, lights flashing, blocking the main residents' driveway and my curious neighbours all coming outside to watch.

'Don't send so many next time,' Jess hissed. 'Only send this many if you've found her.'

Jodi frowned. 'We'll be in touch.'

'If you want me, I'll be at the beach,' I said.

We made it to the beach. The closest one to where I lived was more of a gentle cove than the kind of wave-pounding expanse we were used to growing up, but the smell of salt and the texture of sand was comforting and familiar. We sat on a shared towel, watching kids building castles and playing in the shallows. Jess lay on her back and took photos of the clouds with her new digital SLR, showing me clear and beautiful replicas of a perfect sky.

'We have to talk about money,' Jess said. 'Or the lack of it, to be precise.'

'I have savings,' I said.

'Gone. Months ago.'

'So how –'

'I've been using mine. Martine and Dad have put money in your account too.'

I squirmed. 'Why didn't you tell me?'

She sat up. 'We didn't want to push you. Why don't you come home? Let us take care of you, get back on your feet.'

But they were already taking care of me. The very things I was afraid of, the outcomes I had avoided since I was a teenage mother leaving home for the second time with Sarah in my arms, had come to pass anyway. I needed Martine to be wrong about me; I wanted to be brave and strong on my own, yet here I was, utterly dependent.

I had been terrified of losing my child to my mother. Instead, I lost her to a stranger.

'I'm going to swim,' I said.

I walked along the shore for ten minutes, digging seashells from the sand with my toes. Something about being on the edge of land and by the ocean used to make me feel powerful. This was always where I was the bravest, the strongest. Nobody could outlast me in the water. Now I realised I was in danger of being afraid of the ocean, too.

Fear is a disease that attacks every cell in your body if you let it.

I discovered a bird, washed up against a mound of seaweed: a bar-tailed godwit, emaciated and freshly dead. I picked it up and cradled its limp body, stroking its fine feathers. Even in death it was beautiful.

I'd known about the godwits – their epic migration, travelling thousands of kilometres to this place. And for what? To die alone on a beach? Why didn't they just stay in their breeding grounds in Alaska or Siberia, where it was safe? But I didn't understand then how primitive instinct can drive an animal to risk its own life in order to do what it was born to do.

I forgot about my fear and waded into the water. The cool sand sucked and shifted between my toes, and I let the body of the bird be carried away by a retreating wave. When it had floated far enough offshore, I looked back at Jess sitting on the towel and felt blistering shame. She was twenty-two – how could I have allowed my sister to become my parent, my caregiver?

Jess raised her camera and took a photo of me then, standing in waist-high waves, fully clothed, looking back towards the shore. Head tilted, holding my dress bunched up to keep it clear of the water, in a way that made it look as if I was cupping a pregnant belly. Later I'd carry that picture in my purse because there weren't any photos of me pregnant – there were hundreds of Sarah, as a baby, a toddler, a child, but none of her still inside me, safe.

I wasn't thinking of that, though, standing in the ocean. I was focused on the way hope leaves a body: like lifeblood, slowly at first and then with a rush. I'd remained in the unit because I thought that if I stayed there, Sarah might find her way back to me.

But she wasn't coming home. It was time to accept it.

It was the day life began again – which made no sense at the time, but hope had been nothing more than a mirage that kept me putting one foot in front of the other until I woke up and realised it wasn't real.

I headed back to Jess.

'Water's cold,' I said.

'You didn't exactly swim,' Jess accused. 'I'd call it paddling.'

'Baby steps.'

Jess nodded. 'So what next?'

'I think it's time I jumped back in,' I said, but it felt like coming up for air.

NOW

'Things are almost ready. We can move forward,' he said. 'How is the situation at your end?'

His pleasant tone threw me: it was like speaking with a concerned friend.

I hadn't showered or dressed. The acid curdling in my stomach was so constant, I chewed Rennies for breakfast. I barely knew what day it was – it could have been night-time, the house was so dark and still.

I checked my phone: Friday, 10 o'clock.

'I did what you asked,' I said. 'I got the pills.'

'Good, it's time to celebrate – have a few drinks, leave the house, go for a little drive.'

'Drinks?' I looked down at my stained dressing-gown, my shaking hands. I was in no fit state to drive anywhere.

As I listened to his instructions, it became clear that was exactly the point.

'More than a few drinks, Abbie. Enough to put you well over the limit.'

'I don't understand. What if I get caught?'

He laughed. 'That's the objective. An accident, a drink-driving charge – I'll leave the details up to you.'

'Please, I can't do this,' I begged. 'It's too much. Somebody could get hurt.'

'Hurting people never stopped you before, has it?'

There was a scratching sound, as if he'd put a line through an item on a list.

'But –'

'Think of it as a trade,' he cut in. 'You'll send me proof of the charge, and I'll give you the proof you want. You're so close now, Abbie.'

I chose my poison: a bottle of Pinot Noir left over from the wedding, and a bottle of Chivas for good measure. I lined up the bottles and two glasses on the dining-room table, a heavy antique number with – according to family legend – Sherri's teeth marks on the legs, from when she was two.

Another thing she'd left behind.

Drinking alone was a habit I'd acquired after Sarah went missing. I quit before I met Murray, but now the emotions attached to it held me close like an old lover. Alcohol supposedly smoothed the edges, but I always thought it brought pain into sharper focus; I felt those weak spots in my psyche, the cracks nobody else could see but I knew were there.

I'd broken an heirloom vase of Martine's once by slamming the front door when I was chasing Jess. We had slammed that door a thousand times. Martine was always yelling at us about it. But for whatever reason – a gust of wind, an inch too far to the left or right – that day the vase toppled to the floor and smashed into twelve pieces. Martine had made me sit at the kitchen table and glue the vase back together, painstakingly, piece by piece, until she couldn't see where the cracks had been. It took hours.

When I was finished and the glue had dried, she placed the vase back on the table near the door.

'I fixed it,' I told Jess.

'It looks perfect,' Jess said, marvelling at my work.

Martine stood back with a critical eye and said, 'It's not the same.'

Two days later, Jess slammed the door and the vase broke a second time. Twelve pieces again. This time Martine wrapped them in newspaper and put them in the bin.

I finished the second glass of wine and poured a third. I got dressed, put on shoes and tied my hair in a ponytail, carrying the glass with me and taking frequent sips.

A fourth glass. A shot of whisky. My vision started to blur and my false sense of wellbeing was overtaken by a very real sense of dread. If I stopped drinking now, I could fail the task; on the other hand, I couldn't afford to pass out.

One last shot.

As a child, I thought Martine making me fix the vase was about punishment and accountability. As a teenager, I suspected she was trying to teach me patience. Now, as an adult, I understood that mending the vase had been a lesson in stupidity: she had placed the vase at risk by putting it back on the table near the door. And it was an exercise in futility, because a thing will always break in the places it has been broken before.

Half an hour later, I could barely stand.

On the way to the garage, the nausea hit – I threw up in the daisy bushes near the roller door, worried I'd have to drink more to replace what I'd brought up. But no, the alcohol was well into my bloodstream, and I was confident I was at double the limit or higher.

I took Murray's Audi, not Sherri's, and reversed out of the driveway, moving at a snail's pace in case there were pedestrians on the footpath. I was being careful, but I still managed to scrape the mirror along the letterbox on the way out.

Where to go? Not near a school or a shopping centre. On the freeway I might kill myself, not to mention others. Somewhere quiet, local, but also where there'd be witnesses.

I'd never driven drunk before – trying to judge the gaps between parked cars was like playing a video game with the controller on delayed reaction. I eased the car along a few backstreets until I reached the main road. At the T-junction I turned left and merged with light traffic. Too slow. The driver behind beeped and overtook, looking over his shoulder as he passed, waving his fist. I jerked the wheel too far to the left and brushed the kerb.

I indicated and pulled over in a bus lane. The nausea was back. I leaned my thumping head on the steering wheel and took deep breaths. Every minute I spent on the road I risked hurting innocent people; too long driving around like a lunatic and the level of alcohol in my blood would start to drop.

He'd promised: if I came through on this, things could progress.

I indicated and pulled into traffic. Again, too slowly, but getting caught was the aim of this game, so why was I behaving as if traffic laws mattered?

I passed the side street leading to the local shops and, instead of doing a legal U-turn, I took the next break in oncoming traffic, steering right across the median strip and causing the car to seesaw.

For a moment I lost focus. I had no idea which way the car was facing.

Horns blared and a driver yelled obscenities. The car bunny-hopped off the median strip. Tyres squealing, I turned sharply into the road leading to the shops. At the end of the road I braked and veered into the car park, hoping there were no pedestrians between me and my target: the tower of crates stacked at the rear of the fruit and vegetable shop.

Nothing and nobody in my way.

I didn't stop to think about it. I accelerated and the car hit the crates doing about twenty-five. I guess I thought the obstacles would bring the car to a stop, but of course they didn't – the car kept going, through a fence and into a neighbouring backyard, taking out a washing line and the rear of a shed, coming to rest with a deployed airbag and a white shirt draped across the windscreen as if a person had dematerialised on impact.

I wasn't hurt. Just disoriented, drunk and tearful. People were kind, even the owner of the shed and fence.

The police arrived. I was breathalysed, booked and taken to the station for a second test. Following that, I was charged with high-range PCA and reckless driving, court date pending, and released. The car would be towed and impounded.

Too ashamed to call Murray to collect me, I assured the officer I'd be fine to walk. I caught a taxi from the nearest shopping centre and rode in the back seat, my head hanging out the window, gulping fresh air. I already had a crushing hangover, and it was only early afternoon. And a criminal charge to boot.

I let myself in the house. It was blessedly cool and dark. I took off my foul-smelling clothes, brushed my teeth and crawled into the spare bed to sleep it off. I had the proof he wanted in the form of a blue sheet listing my offences and a period of licence suspension. What I didn't have was a logical or admissible reason for what I had done.

Everyone dreams of flying. Naked dreams, dreams about being chased, losing teeth, falling, infidelity, dying – supposedly they are manifestations of common fears and anxieties, a safe way for the subconscious mind to deal with challenging situations. My most common dream wasn't of dying, but of living. In the dream I wandered the empty lane, calling for Sarah, aware of a threat in the shadows, a malevolent presence. I couldn't fly. I didn't fall. I was always grounded – utterly human and terribly alone. In the dream, my fear didn't chase me, I hunted *it*. Except I didn't know what I was hunting because my enemy never showed his face.

Maybe it was the concentration of alcohol in my blood, but the dream I had the day I drove through the fence was different.

In it, I was buried alive. It was dark but I could feel the suffocating dimensions of a wooden box, the sharp splinters of wood. I touched my hair and clumps of it came away stuck to my fingers; when I pinched my skin it split and slid from the muscle like the skin of a boiled tomato. I smelled rot and ammonia: I had soiled myself.

In desperation, I pressed against the sides of the box – they stretched easily to give me more space, more air to breathe, but dirt began to pour between the boards like sand into a tomb. Light poured in too, coloured pink as blood in water. I kicked and pushed until the box became a room and I could stand. The light spread, filling the darkness. No longer a tomb, but a workshop – timber-slatted walls hung with tools, arranged like matching puzzle pieces, the handles and blades encrusted with black.

In a corner, a man squatting, hunched over, his back turned, his hands busy with something I couldn't see.

Turn around.

The light kept spreading and the dirt continued to sift between the cracks. The last of my hair fell out and drifted to the floor. My hands were bony claws. Dirt caked my raw body where the skin had peeled, and my skeletal frame shuddered and twitched.

I had become a horrific thing.

The man stood. At his feet, a crumpled pile of rags with a spill of thick, dark hair pooling on the floor, like a skein of tangled yarn.

I didn't want to know what it was. At that moment I only cared who *he* was.

Turn around. Turn around so I can see you.

I took jerky steps towards him and grabbed a thin-bladed chisel from the wall. His neck was hairy, pale, with knobs of spine visible above his collar. The chisel handle throbbed in time with the pulse in his throat; the vulnerable spaces between his vertebrae beckoned, but my hands and my fingertips were crumbling away by the second, turning to grey powder.

I raised the chisel. 'Turn around.'

He froze.

I wanted him to turn so he could see what had become of me – what he had *made* me – but he only raised his arms above his head and waited.

Kill him or know him. You can't have both.

The memory would have disappeared like smoke, the way dreams do, if I hadn't been woken.

'Abbie.' A voice from far away.

The man started to turn. I remember him laughing as the chisel clattered to the floor and what was left of me dissolved into ash.

Pressure on my shoulder. A blast of cold air.

'*Abbie!*' Murray was standing over me.

The quilt lay on the floor. I was curled into a ball. My hair was plastered to my cheeks; underneath my body the sheets were wet. For painful seconds I hovered between the real world and the loosening tentacles of the dream.

'What the hell is going on? The car has been impounded?' He waved his fist.

I'd never seen him like this: puffed up, mouth twisted with disgust. He looked as if he was trying to decide how we had ended up here, and how he was going to escape.

I struggled to sit up, head spinning. I couldn't speak. I wasn't afraid, but furious that he'd brought the dream to an abrupt end when something important was about to be revealed.

'I need...'

I pushed past him and shot out of the room. In the bathroom, I sank to my knees and crawled to the toilet in time to throw up.

Murray knocked on the door.

'Please, just give me a minute.'

He went away, muttering.

The spasms eventually stopped. I was left weak and gasping, clammy with sweat, the dream hovering close enough to touch. I lay on the cool tiles, trying to think of a way to justify my behaviour without conceding that I was having some sort of breakdown.

The car was registered in Murray's name – of course he was notified. There was nothing I could say to him about what I'd done and how he'd found me: lying in my own piss and fear, completely unrecognisable from the woman he'd married.

The caller's plan was going extraordinarily well.

'We need to talk,' Murray said.

I'd taken a scalding shower and washed my hair. Hunger and dehydration drove me to the kitchen, where I was making some toast and a pot of tea.

Sherri had called an hour earlier, leaving a diplomatic message on the answering machine. I heard her voice through the fog of a hangover: *Hello, my favourite people. Just calling to see how you're all doing? I'll be in town tomorrow morning. A pause. I'm staying at the hotel but I'd like to come over if that's okay. Call me back. Love!*

Jess had been ringing my mobile repeatedly. I'd stuffed it under a pile of pillows.

'Did you return Sherri's call?' I asked dully.

'Abbie, we really need to talk,' Murray repeated, ignoring my question. He took the teaspoon from my hand and switched off the noisy kettle.

'Let me finish making the tea,' I said.

'I've taken three days' leave,' he announced. 'Starting now.'

I bit my lip. Anything I said would be cruel, or a lie. Worse, I was terrified I'd open my mouth and tell him everything, the way

I'd planned to do over the Thai dinner I made the night he didn't come home.

'I've booked us into a nice hotel for two nights. We'll have a nice dinner and a few... we'll take some time for us. I've been working too much, I know that.'

I nodded, but my overwhelming response to his promise of *a nice hotel* and *a nice dinner* was the not-very-nice feeling of rage and desperation – I was like an addict whose next fix had been flushed down the toilet.

'Say something.'

'You didn't have to do that. We don't need to go anywhere. We can talk now.'

'It's done,' he said. 'Sherri needs to spend time with the kids and it'll be better if we aren't here.'

He said *we*, but I knew he meant *you*.

I popped the toast. It was burnt. 'What, I don't have a say?'

'I've packed some things for you.'

'I'm not a *child*,' I spat. 'Anyway, I can't just take time off work.'

'You're in no state to drive anywhere, Abbie, even if you did have classes, which you don't.'

I didn't bother arguing. I was well past the point where I could hide anything or explain it away.

He sighed. 'Tell me what happened.'

'I was drinking.'

'In the morning? And you *drove*?'

Shrugging, I dropped the burnt toast in the bin. 'I go to court in two months. We can get the car back next week.' My tone was flat. I didn't show an ounce of shame or contrition, but there was a logjam of emotion in my throat.

'That's it? That's all you have to say?'

'I didn't want this.'

'What did you think would happen?' he yelled. 'I'm struggling to make sense of it. This isn't like you.'

His expression changed – I knew he was probably recalling a conversation with Jess, thinking maybe it did sound like me after all.

He lowered his voice. 'Get dressed.'

'I'm not feeling up to it.'

'I don't care how you're feeling. It's all self-inflicted.'

'I'm not going to a hotel.'

'You're going if I have to drag you there.'

I raised an eyebrow.

Murray put up a hand to call a ceasefire.

I was sure he'd already decided how it would go: a *nice* dinner, civilised conversation, a neat resolution followed by make-up sex and a continental breakfast in the morning. He told me once that he and Sherri had different fighting styles: she was hot-headed and hysterical, while he was controlled and logical. He fixed things. Except he couldn't fix his first marriage, and sometimes I wondered whether he was not controlled but controlling, not logical but unyielding.

AFTER

After the day at the beach with Jess, I left isolation and entered a phase of frenzied activity, trawling through online images of violent offenders and child predators, trying to jog my brain into remembering faces I might have forgotten. I researched and assembled newspaper articles in a timeline, hoping for clues. I carried a copy of her Missing poster around with me and thrust it into the faces of strangers, who looked at me with the same expression: alarm, followed by pity. I stuck the posters to light poles and park benches, shop windows and trees. I wandered the streets surrounding Buskers Lane to search for details the police might have missed, only to head home defeated with scraped knees from kneeling to peer into drains.

Everyone I knew had been interviewed, even those from my past. People I hadn't seen or heard from in years. There were no reliable witnesses, no leads, no evidence. A spur-of-the-moment crime of opportunity, the papers said, as if someone had taken a yoghurt from the office fridge, and, as time passed, increasingly one of the most difficult crimes to solve.

Sometimes I let my mind go to the worst places; I thought about what could have happened to her. These were the only times I stopped hoping she was alive and wished her dead.

One afternoon I went to the old neighbourhood and walked past the local playground, a shared community space bordering the primary school Sarah had attended. I'd been avoiding both places because they dredged up too many memories. Here was the slide where she had come down head-first and chipped a tooth; there were the monkey bars where she had hung upside-down for so long her lunch had come up. Somewhere, lost among the pine chips around the equipment, was the gold charm bracelet I had given her on her fifth birthday.

I sat on a wooden bench set in the shade under a row of plane trees. I watched the children play. Their high-pitched screams forced liquid panic through my veins and my heart squeezed violently, but I forced myself to stay there, counting down – *five-four-three-two-one* – until it passed.

I saw: five mothers congregated on a picnic rug nearby.

I felt: the worn smoothness of the bench, the brittle texture of my hair when I tucked it behind my ear, dryness at the corners of my mouth, a stone in my shoe.

I heard: birds, a ride-on lawnmower, children screaming screaming screaming.

I smelled: freshly cut lawn and something sweet, like fairy floss.

I tasted: rot from an infected tooth.

I pulled a bottle of water from my bag, unscrewed the top, rinsed my mouth and spat discreetly into the dirt.

There were eight children, preschool age and too young for the flying fox and spider-web climbing frame – always Sarah's favourites. The mothers were sharing platters of bright fruit and pouring from a bottle of what looked like champagne. They laughed and chatted together easily, hiking up their skirts and arranging their bare legs to catch bands of sunshine peeping through the leaves.

A blonde woman glanced my way and smiled.

I returned her smile and checked my phone: the only message was a calendar reminder for a dentist appointment the following day. Jess had made the appointment in frustration – I'd been complaining about my infected molar for weeks.

Maybe I'd go. Maybe I wouldn't.

A little boy exited the public toilets and ran towards the playground. A man came out shortly after – about sixty, wearing a green jumper, greasy denim overalls and a Chicago Bulls cap pulled low. He wandered over to the opposite side of the playground, leaned against the trunk of a plane tree and casually rolled a cigarette.

I counted again: five champagne glasses, four deep grooves in the bench like claw marks, three magpies warbling, the scent of pine chips and eucalyptus –

I looked up.

– one man. Staring at the children.

He stood, cupping an elbow with one hand, his fingers splayed to cover his face while he smoked. When he finished the cigarette he pinched off the end, stomped on it with the toe of his boot, tucked the butt in his overall pocket and pulled out a phone. His gaze swung from right to left without his head moving. He stabbed at the screen, let the hand holding the phone fall, then slowly raised the phone again.

He was taking pictures of the children. No, not all of them. Just one. The boy from the toilets, who was hanging by one arm on the monkey bars, trying to swing to the next rung.

I uncrossed my legs and turned slightly. Sweat built on my palms and behind my knees; my temples throbbed. The mothers were oblivious, occasionally checking the children or responding to requests for food and drinks, but from where I was sitting I didn't think they could see the man behind the tree.

I stood abruptly. We made eye contact: mine hostile, his appeasing.

He immediately dropped his hand and put the phone in his

pocket. Taking an inordinately large breath, he shuffled to an empty bench and sat, legs splayed, staring at the ground and twiddling his thumbs in circles.

Had I seen him before? I didn't think so, though he seemed familiar. Had he *followed* me? Was he following the *child*?

He waved his hand, calling for the little boy to come to him. A surreptitious movement. The boy stuck out his lower lip, shook his head and returned to the monkey bars.

What if someone had been watching when Sarah was taken? What if they'd noticed small exchanges that weren't quite right? Had she cried? Did she try to get away? Did people notice, but assume she was misbehaving? If someone had done something at the time, things might have been different.

I approached the group of mothers at a low, crab-like run, startling them.

'The boy, the one with the blue T-shirt, is he with you?'

The woman who'd smiled at me earlier turned to look, frowning. 'Do you mean the one on the monkey bars? Why?'

'He's not yours?'

'No,' she said. 'What's wrong?'

I pointed. 'That man was taking photos of the children.'

'Are you sure?'

'I'm very sure.'

The women got up and stood with their feet wide, lips tight, hands on hips, in a smooth, synchronised movement. I turned too, mirroring their stance.

He saw us staring and stood, shifting his weight from foot to foot as if he couldn't decide whether to attack or flee.

'He's coming over,' I said. 'What should we do?'

One woman reached into her bag and pulled out her phone.

'Wait,' said another.

The man approached, his complexion flushed a deep red.

Fear fluttered in my chest. I held my own phone like a weapon. But there were more of us. What could he do?

'Ladies,' he said, touching the brim of his cap.

We were a silent, condemning group of women. Formidable.

He gestured in the direction of the boy in the playground and addressed me. 'That's my youngest grandson, Thomas,' he said. 'I have four children and nine grandchildren.' He held up a palm in a placatory gesture. 'I know why you're all looking at me this way and I hate it – I hate that I can't go to a playground and take photos of my own grandchild because this is what I get. I'm not a bad person. I'm a grandfather. This happens more often than you think and I'm tired of it. I know you mean well and you're not a bad person either, but I'm sick of it, okay? I haven't done anything wrong.'

Shame coursed through my body. My legs were weak.

The boy, Thomas, ran over. He wrapped his arm around the man's leg and looked up at him for reassurance.

'It's okay, mate. The lady was just looking out for you.'

'I don't know her,' Thomas said.

'I know, but it's okay.'

The mothers turned their attention to me.

I took a step back. 'I'm sorry,' I said. 'I'm so sorry.'

The man softened. He smiled. 'Where is your child?'

'I'm not a mother,' I said too harshly.

Their expressions ranged from confusion to outright suspicion. 'I'm sorry,' I repeated.

I wandered away, as if in a dream, and crossed the road without looking. Cars swerved and horns blared; my fingers brushed cold steel but, of all the things that scared me, death was the least frightening. In a way I felt invincible – the worst had already happened and I was still here, still breathing.

Where *was* my child?

Sarah was everywhere I looked, and nowhere to be found. I was the mother of a murdered child and that was a whole different club. *I* was the outsider, the interloper, the freak.

NOW

Murray had booked a suite at the Intercontinental and dinner at the teppanyaki restaurant on the twentieth floor. We didn't speak during the forty-minute drive to the city. After we'd checked in and unpacked, Murray sneaked an illicit cigar on the balcony while I had another shower and went through the motions of putting on make-up.

Even under the flattering bathroom lights I looked washed-out. My eyes were puffy. Toothpaste couldn't get rid of the bitter coating on my tongue, and paracetamol had only taken the edge off my headache. The thought of food made my mouth water and not because I was hungry – the hangover was one thing, but the worry that I'd get caught having a romantic weekend with my husband made my stomach churn.

The caller couldn't know. Could he?

'Dinner is at seven,' Murray called. 'That's in twenty minutes.'

He had packed two dresses: one a short, backless red number I'd worn to last year's work Christmas party, and the other a black, knee-length halter neck. Neither was particularly appropriate – they both felt like dresses a younger, thinner, more confident woman would wear.

I chose the black one and stuffed my feet into a pair of heels. Murray had brought my make-up bag but forgotten my deodorant; I used his aerosol, making myself sneeze so hard my mascara smeared. Round two with the concealer and mascara and I looked

154

at least presentable, although I smelled distinctly masculine.

I only had to get through the next couple of days, to appease Murray and let him feel as if he could *fix* me, in order to buy myself time until the caller made contact again.

I picked up my bag. Out of habit I went to check my phone, but the moment I touched the inside pocket of the bag I knew I'd left it behind, stuffed under the cushions.

Murray held the door open, waiting. 'What's wrong?'

'I forgot my phone.'

He made a dismissive sound, and I was irrationally convinced he'd orchestrated my leaving the phone behind as well as guilting me into coming here.

'I *need* it.'

'Who's going to call, Abbie?' He waved a hand. 'Jess has my number. So does your mother and the kids are with Sherri. It's fine.' He fished his phone out of his pocket. 'Here.'

'I don't want your phone.'

He sighed and slipped it in my bag. 'Take it. You know the pin. I've got nothing to hide,' he said, implying I did. 'Let's go.'

I followed him down the corridor and into the lift. He grabbed my hand and it was all I could do not to snatch it away. Irrational, yes, but I couldn't repress my escalating anxiety.

We took our seat at the teppanyaki bar with four others, an older pair who told us they were celebrating their fortieth wedding anniversary, and a younger couple who were on a second date. Not exactly conducive to a private – and possibly heated – conversation, but Murray introduced us and turned to me anyway.

'So.'

'Not here,' I said. 'I don't want a scene.'

'I don't either. I do want an explanation, however. If not now, before the night is over.'

'Fine.'

I had six courses plus dessert to think of something to say.

Murray ordered a bottle of wine. I shook my head when it came and asked for mineral water, and we ate in silence while the others chattered. After the first course, my appetite returned and the headache subsided. Murray drank the entire bottle of wine and ordered a glass of port.

'How long have you two been married?' asked the older woman. She had been glancing at us curiously since we'd arrived.

'Only a couple of months,' I said. 'We met late.'

'Second marriage?'

'First for me.'

Murray gave me a look and said, 'I'm twice married and twenty years older, as I'm sure you've noticed.'

I kicked him under the table. The woman persisted. 'Kids?'

'Two,' Murray said. 'Not together.' He waited for me to reply and when I didn't, he added, 'Abbie had a daughter.' I tensed and he reached for my hand.

'How many courses are there to go?' I asked.

The woman turned back to her husband, frowning.

When we finished the last main course we were ushered outside to a setting for two on the balcony. We ordered dessert and Murray asked for another glass of port.

'I think you've had enough to drink,' I said.

'That's rich coming from you.'

'I know, but two wrongs don't make a right.'

I stared out over the city lights. We were so far up it made my head spin. I remembered going to the Royal Show: Jess always went on every ride and I had to go with her, even though I hated heights, the sick spinning, the blood-rush of being upside down.

Murray leaned back in his seat, swirling his port glass. Half of it went down his shirt. 'So.'

'Just say what's on your mind,' I said.

156

I don't know what I expected, but it was not what came next.

'I knew you came with some baggage, Abbie, but Jesus Christ.'

'Baggage?' I squeaked.

'Maybe that's the wrong word –'

'Maybe?'

We were supposed to be fighting. It was part of the plan. But estrangement after a couple of months, an almost complete reversal of how we felt about each other, in such a short time – it was a new record, even for me.

'Tell me one thing,' he said. 'One thing that's true. Because I feel like everything is a lie right now and I can't believe I got it so wrong.'

'You mean us? It wasn't wrong,' I said. 'I know I'm hard to live with right now, but I promise one day I'll be able to explain.'

'The time is now. We have two days to work through this.' He swilled the glass again, drank, and set it on the table. 'I've got my kids to think about.'

'I have mine to think about,' I said quietly. 'I haven't stopped. Nobody is looking for her anymore. Do you know how that *feels*?'

'I don't, because you won't talk about it.' He dipped his napkin in my mineral water and dabbed at his shirt. 'I've left you alone. I've tried not to intrude. But you've been drinking too much and now you've crashed the car.'

Deliberately, I wanted to add.

'I've seen the pills. *Three* different kinds, Abbie?'

I waved a hand. 'All prescribed.'

'Prescribed by three different doctors.'

But I'm not taking them. I need a clear head.

'You know, you didn't once ask me if I was okay after the accident,' I said.

'I could see you were okay physically. It's your mental state I'm worried about.' He reached across the table for my hand.

This time I withdrew.

157

I knew it then: if I told him about the phone calls, about my conviction that this was real, Murray wouldn't believe me. Even if I somehow managed to convince him not to involve the police, he would make it his personal responsibility to keep me from self-destructing. I was running on pure emotion and gut instinct; Murray needed logic and order, and this situation was anything but.

This was the only way. I had to keep the distance between me and my family so they wouldn't get dragged into the vortex. The way back was convoluted and messy and painful; it involved lengthy discussion, explanations, justification, admission of guilt. The way forward was simple: do what the caller asked and I'd get what I wanted.

What did I want?

The truth. Peace. I wanted to know what happened to Sarah.

Our desserts arrived. Murray's was green-tea ice cream with red-bean sauce; I had ordered seasonal fruits. I picked at a chunk of kiwi while Murray watched his ice cream melt into a viscous puddle.

We were so far from each other.

My love for my husband was a veneer, easily cracked. Right now I wouldn't give my life for his. I wouldn't die for Edie or Cam. Maybe I'd take a bullet for Jess; it would depend on the circumstances. But my love for Murray and the kids had grown over the years – maybe it would continue to grow and one day I'd reach the point where I couldn't do what I was doing. That realisation terrified me. Because right now my love for my child was fierce, animal, self-sacrificing; my need to know what happened to her was all-consuming. I had been a bad mother, but the belief I had now, that I was following a true path, felt right and good.

'I need to know what the hell is going on,' Murray said. 'No more lies.'

It was a clear, still night. From the twentieth floor the city lights were brilliant, flickering all the way to the coast on one side, meandering up the hills on the other to fade and flicker off. It was beautiful.

But my eyes weren't drawn to the lights. Dotted here and there were the black holes, parts of suburbia where the light didn't reach: backyards, reserves, gullies, abandoned places. Wastelands. Over the hills there were vast acres of dry scrub, deep dams, mine shafts and quarries; further inland there were rivers, backwaters, mudflats and estuaries. There were houses, homes, families and human beings with secrets and vile compulsions.

Those were the places where the lost things collected.

It could be years or even decades before her bones were discovered by some freak coincidence, or never, if he didn't want her to be found. For some reason he did, and that reason didn't matter anymore. I only knew I couldn't live with myself if I didn't follow his instructions.

I couldn't trust anybody, but I would give Murray something without being specific. He deserved to know, even if it hurt, even if it meant there was no way back for us. So I pointed to the lights. I showed him the dark places. I gave him one true thing.

'If I had to give up everything – you, the kids, my sister, everyone – to find out what happened to Sarah, and if I had to die ten seconds after I knew, I'd do it,' I said. 'No question.'

Murray was quiet for a long time. Eventually he asked, 'What do you need, Abbie? What do you want?'

'I need to know the truth. I need peace. I have to know what happened to Sarah.'

But the moment I said them aloud, those words ceased to mean anything. The truth now was that my wants and needs had changed. Now I needed justice. Vengeance. I wanted to find the man who murdered my daughter and kill him.

He shook his head. 'Nobody can give you an answer.'

'No one except the person who took her.'

He gave me a shrewd look. 'At what point do you decide to start living again, Abbie?'

I snorted. 'I tried.'

'So keep trying.'

I reminded him of a conversation we'd had about purpose and ambition.

'You told me you have known what you wanted to be since you were ten years old,' I said, and Murray nodded. 'You said something happened to you, but you never told me what it was.'

He thought for a moment. 'It's not exactly a secret, but I don't like talking about it.'

'Because it hurts?'

'Because I'm still ashamed.'

The admission made me feel closer to him. 'Tell me.'

His face took on a sweaty pallor. 'When I was around nine my parents fell into financial difficulty. They had to take me out of private school and send me to a public one, and I struggled. I was scrawny and studious and I immediately became a target.' He gave me a self-conscious smile. 'I can't tell you how many times I got beaten up, but I kept taking it and eventually my compliance and silence seemed to pay off. When I was twelve, I was invited to a camp-out with a few of the boys near the creek behind the school. So I packed my gear and I lied to my parents, telling them I was sleeping over at a friend's house. They were thrilled I'd apparently made a friend.'

The waiter approached and I waved him away. It seemed as if the slightest interruption would make Murray clam up.

'When I arrived at the creek they were there, all five of them. Davey, Todd, Paul, Steve and Jason. Jason Bell was the unofficial leader. Not the biggest, but he wasn't afraid of anything or anyone. The atmosphere was strange – the boys were acting like they were waiting for something to happen. I set up my sleeping bag and offered to share the bags of lollies I'd brought with me. It got dark and we lit a small campfire. Jason went off somewhere and the other boys kept looking at each other – I got the sense that they didn't really want me there, but Jason had been especially friendly and kind. So I stayed.'

He reached for his glass, but it was empty. I registered the tenseness in his shoulders, the straining tendons of his neck as he hunched forward.

'Jason came back carrying a sack. He threw it onto my sleeping bag. The sack was moving – there was something inside it. I knew a terrible thing was about to take place but I didn't want to be on the outside again.'

'What was it?'

'Jason's family cat had had kittens and his old man told him to get rid of them. He said if I wanted to be part of the gang, I had to do it.'

'But you couldn't,' I said.

'I could.'

'You didn't.'

'I did. I put the sack in the creek water with a heavy rock on top to weigh it down. We sat there until the sack stopped moving. That was the price of entry to the gang, and I paid it.'

I'd seen how Murray was with animals – the way he handled them, the commitment and care he brought to the job. I couldn't picture him drowning kittens.

'But you didn't stay in the gang, not after what they made you do,' I said.

His words came out in a rush. 'Paul Edison is my insurance broker and Davey Finch coached Cam's under-twelve football team and Steve Kennett and Jason Bell were groomsmen at my and Sherri's wedding.' He paused. 'Do you see?'

'See what?' I mumbled, trying to mask my horror.

'The cost – how if you want something bad enough and you can justify your reasons, it can make you a monster.'

'But you were only a child.'

'Old enough to tell the difference between right and wrong.' He sighed and leaned back in his chair. 'So now you know.'

'One awful experience changed you forever – that's why you are who you are today,' I said. 'That's why you're a wonderful vet.'

He shook his head. 'You don't see at all. There is no justification for what I did. The moment I put that sack in the creek I became a different person. There is no taking it back.'

'What are you saying?'

'I'm saying be careful which parts of yourself you're willing to give up, and which parts you're willing to let in. Don't kid yourself about not being in control. I'd give anything to go back and choose a short term in exile over a lifetime of practising atonement.'

He didn't seem drunk anymore, just exhausted and miserable. I knew my behaviour was taking its toll on everyone around me, but there was nothing anyone could say to change my mind.

'I never knew what I was meant to be. Not until now. I've always been afraid, but I'm not anymore,' I told him.

'Tell me, what's your *purpose* if it's not to be my wife and partner?'

He spoke aggressively. The other diners on the balcony spun around in their seats.

He lowered his voice. 'I need you, too.'

Every bone in my body was tuned to the same frequency. 'I have to bring her home,' I said. 'I won't stop until I do.'

Murray stood. 'Purpose or penance – make sure you know the difference, Abbie.' He pulled his credit card from his wallet and went to pay the bill.

I followed on shaking legs. I needed sleep but I knew there would be more talk when we got back to the room.

I had to meet him somewhere in the middle, at least for these next two days. After all, this was our proxy honeymoon. We could go upstairs, take a spa bath, make love and fall asleep together. The caller couldn't possibly know if we shared a bed.

Something else had changed – it was just a feeling, but I felt sure the caller wouldn't disappear. The stakes were high for him, too.

He wanted me to find her.

AFTER

Following the incident at the playground, I gave up wandering the streets and putting up posters; I stopped smoking and drinking alone. I laughed more easily and the outside world seemed less threatening. New rituals were needed, ones that weren't about punishing myself, so I packed Sarah's clothes and toys into boxes, sorted through photos, curated the newspaper clippings, and every night before bed I switched on the nightlight in her room.

Eighteen months after she disappeared, I put my things into storage and moved out, staying with Jess at a friend's house for a while until I could find a new place. It wasn't leaving the cramped unit that made me uneasy – it was the nagging sense that I was closing the portal, leaving Sarah with the lost things forever. Sometimes, when it was quiet, I was convinced I could hear her voice coming from far away.

A few weeks later I answered an ad for a live-in carer, and moved Sarah's boxes and my own belongings to a converted barn on a rural property owned by Kelly Wilkes, a fifty-four-year-old accountant living with advancing multiple sclerosis. It was easy to find peace on her twenty acres, set in a deep and green valley about an hour north of Athena Bay. The barn had raked ceilings and double-thick sandstone walls – prettier than the more modern house, but harder to heat and cool. A flagstone patio overlooked the neighbours' vineyard. There was a cosy lounge, a kitchenette/laundry, a small bathroom and – my favourite – a loft bedroom with a tiny rectangle window that, depending on where I stood, offered a slideshow of the changing seasons. In autumn, when the harsh gold of summer gave way to softer reds and greens, I could imagine I was living in a village in Tuscany. In the mornings, whatever the weather, I'd eat my breakfast on the patio, listening to the waking calls of the birds.

Nights were still bad, but a new place meant fewer reminders, and extreme physical tiredness took care of the insomnia. I was kept busy with cleaning, preparing meals, household maintenance and, occasionally, personal care when Kelly had a bad day. The part I loved the most was helping take care of her menagerie of rescue animals: two horses, four dogs, a moody alpaca named Fred and several aviaries filled with galahs, magpies and corellas in various stages of recovery, before they were returned to the wild.

On the day Kelly first showed me around the property, she was able to walk with a frame; under two years later she would be using a wheelchair. She was exceptionally tall and thin, built like an Olympic high jumper, but her posture was poor; she slouched and shuffled like a woman thirty years older. The commute to the city accountants' office had become impossible, but she was able to work from home most of the time.

'I've interviewed eleven applicants for this position,' Kelly said. 'I've re-advertised twice. You wouldn't think it would be this hard.'

'Why me?' I asked, curious.

'Desperation,' she said. 'Why did you accept?'

I could tell the truth without giving too much away. 'Desperation, too.'

She laughed. 'My first thought when you walked up the driveway was that you looked strong. Here.' She gestured to her own frail body. 'And here.' She tapped her forehead. 'You seemed determined. I need somebody who won't give up on me.'

'I won't,' I promised.

In many ways I remembered these times as some of the best: I was me without Cass, without my family being too close, without being judged as a pregnant teen, a single mother or the careless parent of a missing child. I was just me, and Kelly seemed to like who I was. Hers was the sort of life I hoped to build by the time I turned fifty: independence, philanthropy, a stunning home, nice things and a humble generosity towards everyone she met.

Kelly liked to talk. She was highly intelligent and engaging. If she spoke of her MS, she said *this damned disease*; if she spoke of her ex-husband, she referred to him as *that damned man*, who'd left her four years before when she was at her lowest point – except it wasn't her lowest, she admitted wryly, because she continued to break that record on a daily basis.

She made me laugh.

Kelly knew nothing about my past and I kept it that way for as long as I could. It was easier to forget if I didn't have to make conversation with people who didn't know what to say. But one evening as we sipped wine and gazed out across the fields, I told her everything.

It had rained earlier. The sunset had taken on the colours of a rainbow.

'Look at this.' Kelly waved her hand. 'When Rob left me, all I said was, fine, take all the money, take our friends, take my superannuation, and this damned disease will take me eventually and then you can bloody well have this, but right now you can't take it.'

It was like listening to a poet. She always got a bit sentimental after a few drinks, but she never stopped making sense.

'The thing is, when death sidles up next to you and asks for the last dance, instead of enjoying the dance you look around wondering who's going to inherit all the shit you've worked so hard for.'

166

Kelly refilled our glasses and tipped more crackers onto the cheese plate. I'd never eaten so well as in the past year, developing a taste for all kinds of local produce I would usually have regarded with suspicion.

'Listen, listen.' She took on a pompous tone. 'I, Kelly Anne Wilkes, leave my worldly possessions to – *dun-dun-duun* – Fred the alpaca. Holy shit, I'd give up six months to have a pass-out for the recently departed so I could attend the reading of my own will.'

I laughed, but then she added, 'You know, I've never regretted my decision not to have kids until now.'

I was pretty good at dodging unsteady ground during our conversations, but Kelly must have noticed my tension.

'Abbie, whenever I ask you anything about your family you pucker up tighter than a cat's arse. I figure you don't talk much so you must be happy to listen, but if you get sick of my prattling, I trust you'll tell me when to shut up.'

I shook my head. 'It's not that.'

'What is it?'

I looked at her walker, parked next to the chair. Her doctor had recently recommended a double hip replacement. She had been putting it off because she was afraid of going under anaesthetic, scared she wouldn't come out of it. Sometimes the spasticity in her legs made her cry out at night, but she told me never to come unless she pressed the alarm. If the screaming stopped, that's when I should worry.

'Nothing,' I said. 'It just makes me sad when bad things happen to good people.'

Gently, she said, 'What bad things happened to you?'

'Oh, I'm not a good person,' I said.

'I don't believe that, Abbie.'

'It's true. I was a bad mother.'

167

Kelly fell quiet. There was only the sound of crickets nearby and night birds calling to each other across the valley. Her silence felt like a safe space, so I started talking. Nothing came out in the right order and I could tell her questions were mounting, but she didn't say a word until I'd finished.

My voice was raspy, the wine was nearly gone, and I thought this was the moment things would change. I couldn't take it back. She would always see me differently.

I said as much, and she finally spoke.

'I know what it's like when people treat you as if you're damaged. It's exhausting enough trying to live your life without having to convince others you're fine, just to make *them* feel better.'

Oh God, she was right. It was the reason I had thrived here, away from people who made it impossible for me to forgive myself.

'I'm sorry you have to live with not knowing what happened to your daughter. I admire you for still being here.'

I remember feeling relief.

Kelly lit a second cigarette. She only smoked in the evenings. She said three cigarettes a day wouldn't kill her. *Get in line, cancer.*

She took a deep drag and slowly exhaled. 'I've had fifteen years since my diagnosis to think about what-ifs. What-if I hadn't eaten processed food, drank too much, smoked things I shouldn't? What if bottling up toxic emotions made my body think it was its own enemy? What if I didn't marry the kind of man who made me feel those toxic emotions? Shit, what if my parents had conceived a month later and I was a completely different batch of cells?'

'Then you wouldn't be you,' I said.

She took another thoughtful drag. 'You know what? I've come to the conclusion you can play the odds if you believe the science, or you can put your faith in a higher power if that's your thing, but in the end it doesn't matter. Life really is that random and cruel.'

We stayed until the sunset had faded away and we were drowsy from too much wine.

I slept that night as if I'd been to confession and found absolution – the new day felt like a clean slate. For the time being, I'd found the peace I'd been searching for.

I convinced myself Kelly was right: life was random and cruel. But I was naive to believe I wasn't singled out, that there was nothing I could have done to change what happened to Sarah. Everything was connected. Kelly was the reason I found Murray, and Murray would be the reason I left Kelly. Each link could be traced back, and if I had done so I would have arrived back at the beginning.

In putting it all behind me and starting over, I stopped looking for those connections. I broke the chain.

NOW

For the remainder of our stay at the hotel, Murray and I reached a truce. The next night's dinner was a more relaxed and civilised affair – we stuck to neutral topics of conversation and avoided drinking too much. At night we made love and slept close, but his lovemaking had a rough intensity to it that left me unsettled, and my body ached in a way it hadn't since those early days when we couldn't get enough of each other.

Murray was subdued during the drive home. He said he had a headache – despite the early night and a late checkout, he hadn't got much sleep. I knew that wasn't true: I had been lying unsettled and awake for most of the night, listening to him snore.

We pulled up in the driveway around lunchtime. I took off my sunglasses and put them in their case with exaggerated slowness. It took every ounce of restraint not to rush into the house.

Murray sensed my agitation. 'Go,' he said. 'I'll get the bags.'

Sherri's perfume was the first thing I smelled when I stepped inside. The second was furniture polish – every surface gleamed. I headed down the hall and glanced into the laundry: the mountain of dirty clothes was gone. Through the back door I could see the washing line was full and Edie's underwear hung in neat rows on a rack outside the laundry.

In the spare room, the bed linen had been washed. I caught a whiff of her perfume there, too. Annoyed by the fastidious arrangement of the pillows on the bed, I gathered them up and threw them in the corner, before checking the side-table drawers and under the bed. My phone wasn't there.

I strode to the kitchen. Edie was there, still in her pyjamas, her eyes creased with sleep.

'Have you seen my phone? I left it behind.'

'Good morning, Abbie,' she said, aloof.

'I can't find my phone.'

She nodded and took it from the cupboard above the fridge. 'Mum turned it off. It kept ringing. She answered it one time in case it was an emergency, but the person hung up.'

'It was probably Jess.' I tried to snatch the phone but she held it behind her back.

Edie gave me a curious look. 'Then why didn't she just say so?'

'I don't know. Can I have it, please?'

She held eye contact, accusing.

I glared back.

When Murray came through the door carrying our bags, Edie raised an eyebrow at him and smiled sweetly. 'How was your weekend?'

'Great. Good.' He tossed my bag on the couch. 'Where's Sherri?'

'She left first thing this morning. She said she'll be back next weekend.'

'What about Cam?'

'Still in bed.' Edie glanced between us. 'So you had a nice time?'

'Yes.' I waved my hand. 'It was fine and the house looks beautiful. I appreciate everything you've done,' I said, knowing full well neither Edie nor Cam had lifted a finger to do any of it. 'Can I have my phone now, please?'

Still, Edie held the phone out of reach.

'What's going on?' Murray asked, carrying his bag to the bedroom.

'Edie won't give me my phone,' I said.

She stuck out her chin. 'Abbie won't say who's been calling her, like, a hundred times.'

'Well, I can't answer the question until you give me *the goddamn phone*!' I snapped.

Murray paused mid-stride without turning around. 'Edie, just give Abbie the goddamn phone and maybe try helping out more around the goddamn house.' He disappeared down the hall.

Edie's jaw dropped. She teared up. Murray never spoke to her that way.

I wanted to tell her it wasn't her fault, that it was mine.

She tossed my phone on the counter and went to her room. Seconds later, the door slammed.

I tried to get control of my breathing but it was getting away from me. On principle I left my phone lying there for a while longer, switched off, while I looked for things to do to distract myself.

But everything was done. Everything was perfect.

Murray came back to find me deep breathing, my hands braced on the counter, my head ducked down.

'You didn't have to speak to her like that,' I said, raising my head. 'She's upset.'

'She'll get over it.'

'I think she thinks I'm having an affair.' I made a sound between a laugh and a sob.

Murray sat at the dining-room table and picked up the newspaper. His expression was glacial. 'Are you?'

'No!' I shook my head. 'God, no.'

'You said you wanted more help around the house.' He looked around. 'You got it. What else?'

'Sure, but not from your ex-wife,' I said bitterly.

He threw up his hands. 'Sorry I asked her.'

'You asked her to clean the whole house? Jesus.'

172

'I requested Sherri's help. I wasn't specific.'

There it was again: a shifty look, a catch in his voice when he said her name.

'Murray?'

'I'm tired, Abbie,' he said.

I knew. And he knew that I knew.

'Tell me the truth – when was the last time you and Sherri slept together?'

He turned another page. I could tell he wasn't reading, just moving his eyes over the words.

'I need to know.'

'It was one time,' he said in a low voice. 'Sherri wanted to tell you but I didn't see the point. It was ages ago.'

'How long?'

He shrugged.

'*How long?*'

He snapped the paper with a sharp *crack*. 'Before you moved in. It was years ago. Let it go.'

'But we *were* together?'

He sighed. 'Yes.'

A breath-stealing revelation hit, something I had sensed but never confronted: Sherri's presence often coincided with Murray's heightened desire for me. Did it turn him on to have her sleeping down the hall? Did he instigate sex *on our wedding day* because his ex-wife was sitting not ten metres away, on the other side of the hedge?

I was cut off, adrift. I wanted to cry, but I had reached a level that didn't leave room for more. Maybe there was only so much sadness a person could hold – anything extra was overflow.

Cam wandered in wearing his usual sleeping attire, his football shorts. He rubbed his eyes and yawned. 'Why's everyone yelling?'

'Stay out of it, mate,' Murray said. 'Better for all involved.'

Cam turned hostile eyes to me. He pulled a box of cereal from the cupboard and poured bran flakes into a bowl. Every crash and clatter made my head ring.

I smiled at him. 'Is that breakfast or lunch?'

'Breakfast,' he said. 'Lunch is at four.'

'And how was your weekend?'

'Pretty uneventful and stress-free,' he answered.

I caught Cam and Murray exchanging a look and I felt it, the closing of ranks.

I blinked tears away and picked up my phone, holding it loosely in one hand below the counter edge, surreptitiously switching it on with the volume turned down. Straight away it vibrated with missed-call alerts.

I grabbed my bag and a coat from the rack near the front door.

'I'm going for a walk,' I announced.

'Do what you have to do,' Murray said without looking up.

The dog park at the far end of our street was the closest shady place to sit, but on weekends it was too busy, the dog owners too chatty, the dog-park etiquette too complex to understand. People assumed I came to play with their dogs, since I never brought one of my own, and conversations were inevitably an exercise in avoiding the black hole of information I didn't want to share.

I headed in the opposite direction, towards the primary school two blocks away, scrolling through the missed calls. The last one had been an hour earlier; prior to that there were six calls that morning alone. On *Sunday*?

I passed a young couple holding hands.

Sometimes I wondered how I would have turned out if none of this had happened. Could I have been a calmer, better functioning, more meaningfully employed adult, a more *fun* person to be around? Would I be less afraid? I couldn't remember a time when

I wasn't afraid. How would my family have turned out? Because it didn't only happen to Sarah and to me, it happened to all of us.

My curse was guilt – similar to feeling bad for experiencing joy soon after a person had died, except for me it was all the time. I never stopped feeling guilty for experiencing life, the good and the bad, and now I had brought the curse to another family. No wonder Murray had been less than apologetic about Sherri. I hated that he'd done it, but I could understand why. She was perfect.

I bought a double-shot cappuccino from a nearby cafe and found a shaded bench seat by the playground at the school. Scared I'd say more things I couldn't take back, I was prepared to spend the whole afternoon on the bench in order to avoid more conflict at home. To Edie and Cam, I was an outsider – Sherri would always be first choice and that was understandable. But why was it so hard for Murray to accept that Sarah would always be *my* first choice? Because she was dead and gone?

I watched families come and go. Midafternoon became late afternoon; the light grew intense, the prelude to a storm. A few heavy spots of rain fell.

I tossed my empty cup in the rubbish bin and got up to head home just as my phone vibrated in my pocket.

I picked up. 'Hello?'

'You haven't been answering.'

'It's Sunday. You don't call on weekends,' I said.

'You were meant to send proof. I've been waiting.'

With all the conflict with Murray, I'd forgotten.

'I did what you said. I got caught drink driving. I crashed the car and now I'm officially enemy number one.' I said it with sass, the way a teenager might to a parent. 'Are you happy?'

'Where have you been?'

I decided to tell the truth. 'To a hotel. We spent a couple of days together, but I haven't told him anything.'

'That wasn't part of the plan.'

'I have to keep up appearances. Otherwise Murray will know something is going on.'

'That's the —' he stopped. 'Did anything happen?' A strange note.

'Well, we fought —'

'Was there only *one bed*, Abbie?'

The rain fell harder. I ducked under someone's carport and plugged my left ear with my finger. 'It's raining. It's hard to hear.'

A brisk change of tone. 'How much money do you have access to?'

'I… I don't know. I'd have to check.'

'Best estimate.'

'Why?'

'Whatever is accessible from your account right now,' he said. 'Think.'

I had deposited several cheques for Murray a few weeks ago. The balance of the working account didn't fluctuate much but, at the end of the month, half our quarterly savings would be transferred to Sherri to repay her share of equity in the house. It was a longstanding arrangement — when they separated, Sherri didn't want Murray to have to refinance under pressure to pay her in a lump sum.

'Eleven thousand,' I said.

'Do you need to co-sign to make a withdrawal?'

'No,' I replied, confused. 'Wait. Are you asking me for money?'

The dynamic changed in that instant. It wasn't as if he'd been acting with any kind of integrity all along, but this cheapened everything. It was an erosion of trust.

'This was about money,' I said flatly.

'So eleven thousand is around the number?'

I could get more. There was a redraw facility on the housing loan – easy access to at least a couple of hundred thousand. He'd know that too, if he knew everything. Perhaps it was another test.

'I can get whatever –'

'All of it. Take all of it.'

'What is this?' I asked. 'I don't know what you're asking.'

But I was beginning to understand. Not a ransom. Not blackmail either. A simple transaction: money, in exchange for information. Eleven grand. Eleven thousand dollars was the price to bring her home. I'd have paid a hundred thousand – a million, if I had it – and I realised it was probably for the best. He wanted something from me; I needed something from him. It was that basic.

The rain stopped; the fear dribbled away.

'Why didn't you just say you wanted money?' I said. 'There was no need to play these vindictive games.'

'I'm not vindictive. I have been endlessly patient while you figure out what's most important to you.'

I raised my voice. 'I *never* had to figure that out! I've always known. You've manipulated me and destroyed what life I had.'

I was sure I heard him smile – the wet sound lips made when they peeled away from teeth. 'You did that to yourself. You had a choice.'

'Like I said before, it was not a choice.'

'We're even,' he said. 'Almost.'

A woman came outside, arms folded. I had been pacing under her carport – five or six stiff-legged steps, spin around, another six steps, waving my hand. *Sorry*, I mouthed, and stepped onto the footpath.

'Look, can we get this done? People are starting to think I'm going mad.'

Again, the smile. 'Withdraw the money. First thing tomorrow when the banks open.'

'I don't trust you,' I said. 'You'll take the cash and disappear.'

'Would it kill you to have a little faith, Abbie?'

'I won't transfer the money unless you give me proof.'

'I don't want you to send it,' he said. 'You'll bring it to me.'

AFTER

Jess was visiting me at Kelly's property for my birthday. She'd planned to stay for a couple of weeks. Like me, she hadn't found her path: flitting from place to place, job to job, living from day to day, and her relationships were brief and unfulfilling. A case of it's not you, it's me, she said. At the time she was working as a supermarket merchandiser, couch-surfing with friends. All her belongings were crammed in the back of her car. Kelly said she could stay as long as she needed, but I knew that, by the end of the two weeks, Jess would be gone. We were alike in that way, too.

We were trying to make dough for pizza. So far we'd made glue and managed to talk about everything but my missing child and our increasingly distant mother.

'Do you remember when you and Cass were supposed to be babysitting, and you tried to hold a seance?' Jess said out of the blue. 'You got a message saying *kill them all* and you both ran into my bedroom screaming. As if a ten-year-old could save you.'

'I remember.'

'Cass told me there was a girl who haunted my room. She said she could see her sitting on the end of my bed. I couldn't sleep for months after that.'

'When?' I said, horrified. It sounded exactly like something Cass would do.

'That same night.'

179

I shook my head. 'I'm sorry. She could be cruel like that. Anyway, Cass pushed the glass. I just let myself get caught up in her hysteria. I always did.'

'How do you know she pushed it?'

'She never admitted it, but I knew.'

'Oh. So nothing really happened.' She looked disappointed.

'Nothing happened because there's nothing out there,' I said.

'What if there is and you're just not open to it?' Jess leaned close. 'How do you feel about having a reading?'

'You mean like the Tarot?'

She rummaged in her handbag and pulled out a card. 'I got the name of a psychic – Rose DeCamillo. She comes highly recommended.'

'I bet. You don't believe that shit, Jess, do you?'

'She helps with real missing-persons cases.' Jess gave me a beseeching look. 'Look, at the very least it'll be good for a laugh. I need a good laugh.'

'At my expense. She'll know all about us from the newspapers. She'll have a research team and a thing in her ear feeding her information.'

Jess shook her head. 'I'll book under a fake name. It can't hurt, right?'

She was wrong – hope hurt. More than letting go.

If I thought about psychic phenomena it was to feel mild disgust that there were people who built empires on a foundation of grief. I had no faith in a god who had created the universe, controlling the fates of billions. I didn't believe there was anything after death, just life, then nothing – no reckoning, no higher consciousness, no light. Punishment for sin took place here on earth, or else the sinner got away with it. But at my lowest, I didn't care how I found answers, only that they came. I went along with it because part of me so badly wanted an explanation that I was willing to look to the unexplained.

*

Three days later, we went to Rose DeCamillo's apartment. The stale odour of fast food clung to my clothes after the long drive in Jess's car – it brought back memories of Martine fishing out plates and cutlery from beneath Jess's bed back at home.

She wasn't looking after herself. I decided to invite her to stay with me a little longer, until she could find a decent place.

We took the lift to the apartment on the thirteenth floor. *The thirteenth floor. Seriously?* I braced myself for a whole lot of hokey: dimmed light and candles, hoop earrings, too much make-up.

The woman who answered the door looked like somebody's grandmother. Her hair was white, twisted in a tight bun. She wore a shapeless, grey linen dress that fell to her ankles, and had battered pink slippers on her feet. Her eyes were a bloodshot blue, deep-set and tired-looking.

'Please, welcome.' She stood back and waved us through.

The tiny, beige apartment was as clinical as a surgery. She shooed a belligerent tabby from a two-seater couch and spread a sheet across the cushions.

'In case you're allergic,' she said. 'I don't do many private readings these days. Which one of you called?'

Jess put up her hand as if she was in a classroom. 'Me, but it's for my sister.'

Rose's watery eyes turned to me. 'You are…?'

My skin crawled. It was as if, rather than a human being, she was seeing a curious specimen. In a glance she took me in – after that she didn't look directly at me again but somewhere over my left shoulder.

I opened my mouth to reply.

Jess butted in. 'Elizabeth James.'

She'd given me the name of one of our old high-school teachers. Suddenly I wanted to tell the truth – what was the point of this

181

if I couldn't give myself up to the experience? It was too late for research anyway.

'It's Abbie. Abbie Morgan.'

Rose nodded and huffed. She pulled a three-legged stool out from under a coffee table and sat directly in front of me, knees up, elbows tucked, as if positioning herself to milk a cow.

Her proximity made me self-conscious and I sank back.

She held out her hands, palms upturned. 'I'll hold you for a moment to establish a connection. Then I'll let go.'

A moment didn't seem long enough. What could she see in a moment?

I reached out, but Rose batted my hands away and leaned forward, pulling me into a tight embrace. I felt crushing pressure on one shoulder and on the back of my skull; her fingers twisted in my hair and she pressed my face hard against her collarbone.

Shocked, I resisted.

Rose muttered in my ear, 'Stop.'

Next to me, Jess reared away in alarm.

I turned my head to get more air. My heartbeat sped up and a maddening whine started in my head. It felt as if she was squeezing the life out of me and my only instinct was to fight back – I brought my hands up between us and tried to push her away.

'*Stop!*' Rose screeched.

I allowed my body to go loose. Still she didn't let go. Then her hand on my shoulder released and moved to my back, tracing concentric circles, starting small and moving outwards, faster and faster, until all contact and pressure was suddenly gone. I flopped back.

'Okay,' Rose said. 'Okay.'

I stayed where I was, breathing hard.

'*Shit*,' Jess muttered, and apologised. 'Sorry.'

Rose got up and pushed the stool away with her foot. She moved to an armchair and lowered herself into it, crossing one leg over the other. 'As I receive images I will ask you a question. You will answer only yes or no.'

Now that Rose had moved away from my body, my heartbeat returned to normal and I felt awkward, foolish. I sneaked a look at Jess, who was uncharacteristically sombre. A laugh rose in my throat. I coughed to cover it up, and Jess gave me a sharp jab with her elbow.

Rose closed her eyes. I was transfixed by the movement of her eyes under the lids, flicking rapidly left to right, right to left, as if she was in another place, anxiously waiting for someone to arrive.

Here comes the hokey, I thought.

'I see a woman.'

I waited. I didn't want her to see a woman. I wanted her to see a child.

Rose opened one eye and glared over my shoulder.

'What's the question?' I said.

Jess elbowed me again.

'This woman – is it your mother?'

'I don't know. What does she look like?'

'Yes or no answers, please.'

I sighed. 'Fine – yes?'

Jess gasped.

Rose nodded and settled back in her chair. 'She is strong.' Her hand shot up, the palm flat and her fingers rigid. 'Straight, like this.'

Jess and I raised our eyebrows at each other.

'You have unresolved issues?'

'Yes,' I said, still bordering on nervous laughter.

Rose clenched her fists and ground them against each other in a twisting motion. 'She controls. Won't let go.'

'Yes.'

'There's something she wants to confess.'

'Really.'

'She is sorry. But she can't tell you. You hate her enough already.' More flickering of her eyelids.

'I don't hate her.' I stood.

'As you wish.' Rose opened her eyes. 'I'll stop now.'

'But you'll still take our money, right?'

'There is more than what you can see,' Rose said.

'Abbie, wait.' Jess motioned me to sit.

'I didn't say my only connection was to the spirits,' Rose muttered. 'Images aren't always clear.'

'Jess, I want to go *now*.'

'When you open the door I have shown you, others will open too. Maybe you should come back another time.' Rose got up, whipped the sheet out from under Jess and started folding it.

'What about a girl?' Jess begged. 'Did you see a girl?'

'Jess, no.' I picked up my bag from the floor. 'Let's go.'

'No girl,' Rose said. 'If there is a girl, she doesn't wish to communicate with you.'

A surge of violent energy came from nowhere and I was suddenly, irrationally convinced that the knowing was somewhere inside Rose's head. She was holding out on me. I wanted to grab her frail shoulders, shake it out of her. This wasn't funny anymore.

I strode to the door and flung it open. I didn't look back to see if Jess was following. I had to get out of there before I lost it, away from the cat hair and beige walls and Rose's unnerving, distant stare.

I waited by the lift, but it took ages to arrive. Jess caught up. The doors opened and we got in without acknowledging each other. I stabbed at the ground floor button with a trembling finger. We didn't speak on the five-minute walk to the parked car.

Jess was despondent. She put the key in the ignition, but before she turned it, her hand dropped. 'She didn't ask for the money. I didn't pay her.'

'Good. Seriously, what the fuck was that?'

'She wasn't wrong,' Jess said. 'It just wasn't what you – we – wanted to hear.'

I fastened my seatbelt. 'We shouldn't have come here. I feel worse, not better.'

'What she said about the door... what if we came back –'

'I'm *not* going back,' I hissed.

Jess hung her head. 'I'm sorry.'

'Drive,' I said. 'Or I'll start walking.'

By the time we'd left the car park we were laughing.

'"*As you wish*,"' Jess intoned. '"*There is more than what you can see.*" Jesus.'

'That was straight out of a B-grade movie.'

Jess nodded, wiping her eyes.

'I don't hate Martine,' I said. 'You know that, right? I see why people do this, though. If they're desperate enough, I mean –'

I stopped. Who was I kidding? *We* were the desperate people. I didn't need to see Jess's expression to know she was thinking the same thing.

No, faith didn't come to me easily. I couldn't see it, hold it, touch it. I had no desire to conjure Sarah's spirit or commune with her ghost – I needed facts and evidence and options: *here are her bones, this is what happened to her, pick a casket, choose the flowers, dedicate a song.*

I wanted to be able to say goodbye.

NOW

On Tuesday I woke to grey light, blustery winds, heavy clouds threatening rain. The weather matched my mood. I had withdrawn the money from the bank the day before, and the bundle of cash stuffed under the spare-room mattress beat like Poe's telltale heart.

I stood by the lounge-room window, watching Murray's four-wheel drive reverse down the driveway. Edie was in the passenger seat. Cam had stayed overnight at a friend's house – presumably he'd gone straight to uni from there.

I had become accustomed to Murray leaving without saying goodbye. Alone in bed the night before, I'd played through scenes imagining Murray and Sherri together, sadistically probing my wounds to gauge their depth. His confession had hurt at the time, but now I just felt a disconnection followed by a surge of self-pity. It held a flicker of a promise that it might boil over into something useful, like rage.

I did an hour of weight-training, showered, pulled on clean clothes and took my contraceptive. *Like clockwork.* I collected the pills I *wasn't* taking and threw them in the bin.

Martine called. I didn't answer.

Jess called. I hung up on her after telling her I was fine, I couldn't talk right now, and would she please stop worrying about me.

My mobile rang again.

'Jess, stop calling me.'

'How is your little sister?'

He sounded amused. I heard a new note: excitement. He was building up to something. Each time I heard him speak, another piece slotted into place, like building an identikit image but using only sound. I might not know his face, but out of a thousand people I would know his voice.

'I don't know,' I said. 'You tell me how she is.'

'You seem upset.'

'Fuck you,' I said. 'Do you have a family? Do you have to hide what you are, what you're doing?' In the background I heard a musical *ding*, like the sound of an elevator. 'Are you in a hotel?'

'Maybe!' Bright. Interested.

'So you do have a family?' I spat. 'Then you have something to lose, you bastard, but I don't. Not anymore.'

'I'm sure your new family would be appalled to hear you say that,' he drawled.

'You're a psychopath.'

He sighed. 'When you get to know me, Abbie, you'll discover I'm not. Everything I do, I do because I have a conscience. It's all for good reason.'

'I don't want to get to know you. I *hate* you.'

'Abbie, I want –'

Things weren't moving quickly enough – I couldn't keep living in limbo.

'Game over. I'm not playing anymore,' I said, and pressed *end call*.

Feeling dizzy and sick, I threw the phone across the room where it bounced off a cushion and slid under the couch.

I put on my shoes, grabbed my winter coat and ran outside. If he was watching he would have seen me standing motionless in the middle of the driveway, sleet rain coming in sideways, my coat hanging uselessly over my arm. No bag, no keys, nowhere to go, and the sound of my mobile, ringing, ringing.

If I went back inside I'd pick it up.

The old panic took control of my body and I let it: breathlessness, shaking, dread in my veins, pulse rate in the hundreds, and a feeling of absolute certainty that I was going to die. Deep down I knew I wouldn't. I had leaned into it before, willing my heart to stop, but it was a false promise the body made in times of stress — it didn't matter if I fought it or gave in, the outcome was always the same.

My heart gradually returned to a normal rate. I stopped shaking and slowly became aware of the rain and the cold seeping through my clothes, of passing traffic and chirping birds and people going about their business. And I registered the silence inside the house.

The phone had stopped ringing.

This was it. The end.

I went inside and hung my coat back on the hook. I took off my shoes, changed out of my wet clothes and put on a clean pair of jeans and a T-shirt. I opened the curtains. In a daze, I diced some chicken and stirred the pieces into a packet mix in the slow cooker, added some vegetables, switched it on. I made a pot of tea. Lit a cheerful fire in the lounge room. Burned scented candles. Paced and fretted.

Now there were twin heartbeats: the cash under the mattress and the phone under the couch. I would take the money to the bank and deposit it back into the account this afternoon; I'd ignore the phone. Over dinner I'd tell Murray and the kids about the calls. I would explain my behaviour, show that I wasn't losing my mind.

I'd call Jess.

And Martine.

Finally, I would notify the police. After that it would be out of my hands.

But my mobile started ringing again.

I ignored it at first, but *what if?* What ifs became if onlys. I reached under the couch and picked up my phone as if it was a hot brick. In total I'd missed six calls from the no caller ID number. Following the calls, he'd sent a text:

In the shed. Bottom drawer of the teak cabinet. Once you've found it, reply to this message immediately. Bring the money with you.

There was an address.

I left in a rush, pausing only to stuff the money in my bag and slip on my damp sneakers, leaving the house unlocked, the woodfire and candles burning, the slow cooker on high. Murray's car was still impounded; I took Sherri's and zigzagged through the mid-morning traffic, driving too fast, even though I was anxious I'd get pulled over for speeding or cause an accident on a suspended licence and without insurance. The need to know was as forceful as anything I'd ever felt. I couldn't turn back.

An hour into the drive the rain hit, a vast black band of it stretching along the coastline in the distance. On either side of the road, the fields of wheat were flattened by wind and rain, the ditches filled with water.

Fifty kilometres out, the fuel warning light came on. The rain was easing, but the wind had picked up and I struggled to keep the car on the road. I pulled over at the next service station to fill up, in case I got stranded before the final stop.

'You card has been declined,' the attendant said, when I went inside to pay. 'Would you like me to try it again?'

'That's not possible.'

She swiped again and waited. 'I'm sorry. Declined.'

'Shit. Give me a moment.'

I stood aside to let the other customers through. I rummaged in my bag for cash and came up with fifty dollars. Still twenty-five short. Had Murray noticed the money was missing? Had he put a stop on the card? Flustered and sweating, I ran out to check in the car but there were only a few dollars in change.

I went back inside.

'I don't have quite enough. What do we do?' I said helplessly.

'I'll ask my manager,' the girl said.

I waited for ten minutes.

Eventually an older woman came to the counter. 'You can't leave without paying. Can you call someone? I can process a payment over the phone.'

I shook my head. 'Please, it's an emergency. Can we take some fuel out?'

She gave me a bored smile. 'No, we can't do that.'

'I'll come in this afternoon? On my way back through?'

She took in my panicked expression and pulled me aside. 'Look, I'm not supposed to do this – if you leave your credit card and driver's licence with me, I'll make an exception.'

Gratefully, I handed them over. 'Thank you. I'll come back later, I promise.'

She nodded and took the cards. 'I hope everything is okay.'

Everything was not okay. But I was back in the game – or maybe I never wanted to be out of it. I had moved from a standstill to intoxicating momentum in a matter of hours.

My head was pounding. I reached for a packet of paracetamol in the zip pocket of my handbag and found the money – I couldn't pay twenty-five bucks for the fuel, yet I had eleven thousand dollars in cash in my bag. *Stupid*.

I pulled out of the service station and drove the last stretch of highway on autopilot, registering the usual landmarks that told me I was coming home: the animal park, the crumbling haystack castle just before the turnoff, the cheerful faded sign: *Welcome to Athena Bay*. Someone had drawn shark fins in the water painted around the words.

Main Street was almost empty – the rotten weather kept people inside. I passed the new community centre and had a thought: it was Friday. Martine would be doing her volunteer work in the adult-learning space.

I did a U-turn and drove through the car park, looking for her car. There it was, parked as usual without a permit in a disabled space near the entrance. I cruised back out onto the street, careful to keep my head down. It wouldn't take much for someone to recognise me, and I didn't want to be seen.

What the hell was in my parents' shed?

During my worst nights, in my most graphic imaginings, I pictured Sarah buried in bushland, burned in a backyard, or her bones sunk deep in the mud at the bottom of a lake. That was what happened to kids who had gone missing and were never found. Or they were discovered years later, long after the people who loved them were gone too. It was a sad fact: when all leads came to a dead end and too much time had passed, people gave up.

Not knowing was like living inside a cage of bones.

Wherever this was leading, I would go.

I left the car outside the old YMCA building, a street away from my parents' house.

Most of the houses here were investment properties and summer rentals, with rows of Norfolk pines and jaunty signs swinging in the breeze: *Seaside Bliss, Beach Haven, Bikinis & Martinis, Footprints in the Sand.* Gates were locked, curtains were drawn, weeds sprang from cracks in the pavement. An icy wind blew straight from the sea, smelling of effluent and rotting seaweed.

I shrugged on one of Murray's coats I'd found on the back seat of Sherri's car, pulling the hood tight around my face. I followed the uneven footpath around the block and jogged straight down the driveway of my parents' home to the battered green shed at the rear.

Opening the swing door was like cracking open a time capsule. This was where my father had stored furniture, toys, clothes, books, tools and plumbing supplies for over thirty years. Jess and I had rarely gone inside; the clutter left little room to move and the rank odour of sewerage still emanated from the machine Dad had used to clear blocked pipes. It looked as if Martine hadn't got rid of anything.

The teak cabinet was right at the back. I knew it from childhood – some hulking, turn-of-the-century monstrosity Martine had inherited from her parents, my grandparents, who'd died before I was born. She'd hated it, said it was ugly and too big for the house. Dad had used the cabinet as a workbench and a place to store tools.

I pinched my nose and breathed through my mouth, feeling my way along the narrow space between boxes and pyramids of pipe. Weak light filtered through the small windows on either side, but not enough for me to see well. I reached for the switch hanging overhead and turned on the fluorescent lights. One was blown; the other plinked on and off.

I moved forward, heart pounding, and looked down. My sneakers left clear footprints in the dust, but mine were the only fresh marks. Nobody had been in here for some time, probably not since Jess and I had dragged Dad's old chair in here on the day of his funeral. There it was, empty, coated with dust, the shape of him pressed into the leather.

I pushed a trolley aside and moved several boxes out the way. At the far end of the shed the teak cabinet loomed, three metres long, covered with a dirty blue tarpaulin and tied with rope.

To protect the cabinet? Or to hide it?

My cold fingers struggled to untie a complicated knot in the rope, engrained with dirt and grease. There was no evidence it had been tampered with, at least not recently. Whatever was inside the cabinet had been there for years. But the knot wouldn't give and I couldn't wait – I took a sharp chisel hanging on the wall and slashed through the tarp, leaving a ragged tear. I ripped it further using my bodyweight, until the tarp shrugged down. The rope loosened and fell slack onto the floor.

I sat cross-legged and grabbed the carved bone handle of the bottom drawer. As I tugged hard, it grated and jammed, only moving a few inches. Inside were various screwdrivers and Allen key sets, along with rolls of electrical tape. I pulled harder until the drawer fell out of the cabinet, slamming into my shins, almost landing in my lap. I ran my hands through the contents, sifting them through my fingers.

Nothing. Underneath, perhaps.

I tipped the drawer upside down, letting everything inside clatter onto the floor. Again, nothing of interest, only a faded and torn scrap of paper stuck to the bottom. I peered closer. It looked like an old label from the manufacturer.

Frustrated, I kicked the drawer away and turned onto my side, pressing my cheek to the floor. Too dark to see. I reached my hand underneath, cringing at the thought of spiders and rat droppings, but my fingers only found more dirt. I stretched further until my shoulder popped and the tendons in my neck burned.

There: plastic. A ziplock bag. Something weighty inside it. I scissored my fingers to grab a corner and slowly drew it out, closing my eyes as I did so. I couldn't look. Not yet. I grasped the bag and sat up, cradling it in my lap.

I knew what they were before I opened my eyes: Sarah's beads. A crucial detail I'd forgotten to tell the police the day she was taken.

I shouldn't have opened the bag but, crouched in the shed, my heart pounding, I didn't recognise the beads as evidence. They were simply proof I was headed in the right direction, exoneration for the things I'd done, and justification for what I was about to do.

*

I was confident there was no way he could know the exact minute I found the beads, not unless he was nearby and watching my every move. It was a risk I was willing to take – I had to talk to Martine.

I drove back to the community centre and sat in the car park. I stared at the automatic doors and waited for her to come out, watching familiar faces come and go, shaking so violently I bit my tongue, until I couldn't wait any longer.

I was supposed to message him immediately, but I'd never been able to reply before. I picked up my phone.

I have the beads.

I expected the usual message failure alert, but it sent with a *whoosh*. The unblocked number appeared briefly on the screen, before my mobile rang and the number disappeared.

'Hello?'

'Are you listening?'

'Yes.'

'Do not speak to anyone. Do not go home. Drive to Maidenvale – it's around three hundred kilometres north-west. There's an auto-wrecking yard about two kilometres before the town. Drive to the big shed at the rear of the lot, pay cash for three months' storage and leave the car there. Walk into town. There will be a large dam on your left – dump your phone, keys and any identification in the dam, but take the money with you. Nothing else. Check into the Maiden Motel. Room twelve, cash only and a fake name.'

'Wait,' I said, panicking. 'I need to write this down.'

'Don't write *anything* down, Abbie.'

'Then what?'

'Rest.'

'*Rest?*' I shrieked.

'Get some rest. In the morning you'll have breakfast. There will be a beige Toyota Land Cruiser in the car park – the keys will be in a magnetic box under the rear passenger-side wheel arch. Leave at eight and drive about two hours north-east to Mount Aramus. Go to the lookout and wait there. Follow my instructions and I'll see you on the other side.'

The other side of what?

'Don't waste time. Don't mess up. And don't think you can tell anyone where you're going without me knowing.'

'I can't leave. My family will be worried. I can't just *disappear*.'

He smiled, I was sure of it. 'You're unstable, Abbie. You're a drunk, a thief and a liar. Everything has been leading to this. It will come as no surprise to anyone that you cracked.'

It's not enough for it to fall – you have to tear it down. And I had, spectacularly.

'Without my phone you won't be able to reach me.'

'I'll find you. I always find you.'

He hung up.

I was terrified I'd forget something. I scrabbled for a pen and paper in the console but all I could find was a napkin. *Maidenvale. Auto wreckers. Maiden Motel, room 12, lush. 8am beige Toyota. Mt Aramus lookout.*

It was almost two o'clock. If I didn't leave now I'd be walking the highway into Maidenvale in the dark. I was already lightheaded from lack of sleep – I needed to eat and drink something soon, but not in Athena Bay. I would stop along the way. I'd buy another phone. And a weapon of some kind. I'd be stupid to trust him.

I started the engine and checked the rear-view mirror before I reversed.

At that moment Martine exited the community centre, walking fast, her handbag slung over her shoulder. I ducked my head and counted to thirty, hoping it was enough time for her to get in her car and leave, but when I looked up she was frozen, gripping the door handle of her car.

I recognised the look in her eyes: confusion, and fear.

An exchange took place through a rectangle of mirrored glass, in a split second, without words. Martine's expression hardened. My heart did the same. She was a woman who, whenever I'd asked a tough question, would put on a load of washing or scrub a plate until the enamel wore through. She'd be on the phone to Murray and Jess the minute I left, but the important thing right now was not to let her stop me from leaving.

I took off, tyres squealing, along Main Street and onto the highway, past the reverse of the welcome sign: *You're leaving Athena Bay. Come back soon!* It was the first time I'd been back since the day of my father's funeral, the day Martine cracked.

There were never any answers here, only secrets.

AFTER

My father died from a heart attack. He had been sitting in his chair with his feet up for several hours before Martine realised he was dead. That morning she'd hung out a load of washing, diced two kilos of old vegetables to make soup and, ironically, spent an hour trying to get their old printer to work so she could print a copy of an Advanced Care Directive form. He'd been ill for some weeks, complaining about breathlessness and fatigue. My mother forced him to take time off work. And so his plumber's van sat in the driveway and he sat in his chair, refusing to see a doctor.

When she found him, his hand was inside his shirt, fingers splayed across his chest, bleeding scratches on his skin. On a notepad on the armrest, he'd written a local address followed by *leaky valve & blocked pipes*, as if that explained everything.

I remember answering Jess's call, putting my hand in the air to silence Edie, who was chattering loudly, raising my stricken face to Murray. I recall the shame I felt when I realised my first thought was that I was fatherless, not that my mother was a widow.

'My dad died,' I said when I hung up, and it was Edie who cried.

The funeral was held at St John's in Athena Bay.

Murray couldn't take time off at such short notice. I made the trip alone, driving my unreliable Seca over six hundred kilometres there and back, despite Murray saying I should take one of the

197

other cars. I could not imagine turning up to my father's funeral driving an Audi.

Jess met me at the kiosk by the beach before we went to see Martine. She'd arrived the day before but stayed overnight with an old schoolfriend. We talked about how to handle our mother and one coffee turned into three, plus lunch – neither of us could bear to face the house without Dad in it, or our mother without him.

When we finally arrived at the house, Martine was tearful but aloof. All our good intentions were snuffed out. Like Jess said, hugging Martine was an extreme sport.

A graveside service would have suited my father better, but church funerals were all my family had ever known. St John's was a low-slung contemporary chapel built in the seventies, Besser-block walls, narrow windows and piss-yellow glass. No majestic stained windows, soaring ceilings or solemnity there – only the steel cross outside distinguished the church from the football club or the bowling green.

Even now I can picture every detail of the service. The chapel, with its stained brown carpet and creaking pews. The sign – *Joseph Morgan 1954–2008* – made using coloured pushpins on a black felt board. Martine, regal and fragile in her beige, lace-trimmed suit. Auntie Lira, attached to Martine throughout like a conjoined twin. People speaking with hushed voices. People saying nice things, because who wouldn't at a funeral? Kids, caterpillaring under the pews, copping warnings and smacks. Black, with pops of colour.

Me: ushering and seating people, hugging them, thanking them for coming, inviting them back to the house, gathering the flowers, crawling under the pews to pick up chips, lollies and toys left behind.

Jess: silent, sad.

Yes, I remember the details. My emotions, not so much. I was very good at placing unpleasant things inside the box. I experienced it all with an odd feeling of detachment, which prompted old friends and family members to remark on my composure.

'Lovely service. Your dad would have been proud.'

'You're so *capable*, Abbie.'

'You've been such a rock for your mother.'

'I don't know what she would do without you.'

Back at the house I arranged the flowers on the mantelpiece around the photo of Dad from the service. I offered trays of party pies and sausage rolls to our guests, and opened bottles of wine. I made sandwiches. I made small talk. I made sure to squeeze Martine's shoulder when I passed.

Meanwhile, Jess stayed slumped in Dad's chair, pressing her fingers into the cracks worn by his elbows.

When the food and wine ran out, I sat cross-legged on the carpet in the lounge room with the kids. All the seats were taken. This was how to survey a wake: at ground level, among the black stockings and polished shoes, creased trousers and pressed skirts. My cheap heels had given me blisters; my face ached from turning on polite smiles. And now that I was sitting still, the edges of grief grew sharper, threatening to sever my resolve to do all the right things. Something I'd never managed to do before.

This was how it was meant to be: a short, sharp celebration of a life, ashes in an urn, guilt-free laughter and permission to heal. No wondering. No long goodbyes.

I bludged a cigarette from a distant cousin whose name I couldn't remember, and went outside. The sun was bright but a chilly breeze blew in from the south. I sat out of sight on the concrete ledge behind the rainwater tank, legs crossed, bouncing one foot, thinking of the times I'd done exactly the same thing as a teenager, only then it was night-time and my parents were asleep. There were still old butts jammed between the cracks in the pavers. Perhaps they were more recent. Jess's.

'I tried to get him to see a doctor.'

Martine had taken off her shoes. Her stockinged feet were squashed; it made her look vulnerable. She took me in: illicit cigarette, smudged lipstick, messy hair.

'I know you did,' I said.

'He wouldn't go.' A helpless shrug.

'There's nothing more you could have done.'

'His heart just couldn't take any more.'

She seemed to stop short of saying I was the one who broke it, and ran out of air. Her chest caved and she bent over, wrapping her arms around her knees.

For a moment, I froze. I had been about to cry, but seeing my mother in that state jolted me out of it. I wobbled off the ledge and came up behind her, wrapping my arms around her, taking her full weight, and we fell backwards onto the lawn. She lurched away, but I held her as tightly as I could until she gave up.

'Breathe,' I said.

'I can't.'

Her heart beat against my fists, stubborn as ever. 'You can.'

A couple of guests came outside and saw us there. They whispered to each other and discreetly went back inside.

Martine stiffened and struggled to her feet. She straightened her skirt and patted her hair. 'You had no business taking the baby away. Everything went bad after that.'

I braced myself for a flurry of generalisations. *Everything bad. You always. You never.* I bit my lip to keep from telling her why I took Sarah away.

'We were okay. We were fine. We were happy.'

'You were in no state to take care of her. I told you so, and look what happened.'

I stood and picked up the cigarette butt. Our entire relationship had been a game of *I told you so*, but I wouldn't be drawn into a reckoning. Not now, not on this day.

'I'm going in to clean up.'

'Wait.' Her hand reached out like a claw to grab my upper arm. 'I protected you too, you know. I never told him you were having the baby.'

I pulled away. 'Told who? What are you talking about?'

Her eyes were slits, like a cat about to pounce. 'The father. Sarah's father. He came here looking for you. Your dad always said I needed to tell you, so I'm telling you.'

Shock sent adrenaline rushing, but I gave her a hard look. 'I don't understand.'

'What's so hard to understand, Abbie? He came here looking for you and the baby. I told him we didn't know where you were and he should leave.'

'When?' I wanted to slap it out of her. '*When?*'

She shrugged. 'When you were about six months pregnant.'

'How did you know he was her father?'

She gave a tight-lipped smile and her eyes drifted somewhere beyond the clouds. 'I wasn't sure until later. Then it was obvious. She looked more like him than she looked like you.'

Cass. Cass must have told Reno I was pregnant, and Reno came looking for me. For *us*.

Her gaze snapped back. 'You said the father didn't want her. I'd say he wanted her very much.'

This was new, important information. *How could they have kept this from me?*

'We need to tell the police,' I said. 'You have to tell them what happened.'

I had the sensation of shaky ground beneath my feet. This was not protection – it was manipulation, and my mother was a master at it. But it broke my heart that my father had been involved too.

'It's okay, Abbie. I told him you didn't have the baby and he believed me.'

'Why did you say that?'

I didn't want Reno in my life, but if he knew about Sarah and he had tried to be a part of hers, I would have made it work somehow. Wouldn't I?

'It wasn't him who took her.'

'How would you know?'

'I know,' Martine said. 'He won't be coming back. Let it go, Abbie. I'm only telling you now because it's what your father would have wanted.'

At that she crumpled again, but I couldn't bring myself to touch her.

'Come inside,' I said. 'You have guests.'

She waved her hand. 'Tell them it's time to leave.'

And in the middle of the backyard, in plain view of the window in the kitchen where people were gathered to pay their respects, my mother pulled up her skirt, rolled down her pantyhose and slung them over the washing line. She wasn't hysterical. She wasn't intoxicated. I believe the thing that held her spine so straight for all those years just snapped then like a weak ligament, and I wasn't sure if it was my father's death or her own confession that did it.

His dying didn't affect me the way it should have. I felt deep sadness, but not despair. Life would go on, altered but not destroyed. The same thing had snapped in me when Sarah disappeared – the painful irony was that, without it, you were left with the strength to bend, but not to break.

'I know how it feels,' I threw over my shoulder as I went inside. 'You think you can't survive this. You think it'll kill you, but it won't.'

We were like small, inhospitable planets orbiting each other.

*

Jess and I spent the evening at the Athena Bay pub, attempting to hold a conversation while a terrible eighties tribute band played and a steady stream of locals offered condolences and free drinks. We had coerced Martine into taking a long bath and prepared a plate of leftovers for her dinner. While she was soaking, we dragged Dad's chair into the shed, concealing it with an old tarpaulin, and rearranged the furniture in the lounge to disguise its absence. By the time we left, Martine had fallen asleep on Dad's side of the bed.

At nine o'clock, the dining area closed and the publican ushered the stragglers to the front bar. He moved us to the empty room, and set shot glasses and a full bottle of Chivas on the table.

'I'm sorry about Joe,' he said. 'He'll be missed.'

'Thanks, Matt,' we said in unison.

Jess poured two shots but sat there, spinning her glass, not drinking.

I was conflicted about telling Jess what Martine had revealed – I needed to come to terms on my own with what to do next.

'I'm moving in with Murray,' I said instead.

He'd been asking me to move in with him for months, but something always held me back – a feeling. Perhaps it was guilt over leaving Kelly. Whatever it was, I decided it no longer had a say in the matter.

'That's good,' Jess said. 'He's a good guy.'

'He is.'

She looked washed-out and unkempt. Her hands shook when she picked up her glass.

'What's wrong? Apart from the obvious, I mean.'

'I resent looking after everyone,' she blurted. 'I can't seem to get any traction in my life.'

Her honesty broke my heart. Old guilt resurfaced.

'It's my turn,' I said. 'I'll take care of her.'

'Good. Great. Hallelujah.'

'It would probably help if you agreed with her occasionally.'

'What do you mean?'

'I mean we're always united against her.'

Jess appeared hurt. 'What's wrong with that?'

'It just might be good if you chose her side once in a while. You know… get together, talk about me behind my back.'

She laughed. 'Did you hit your head?'

'I'm serious.'

'Abbie, please don't be…' She broke off.

'Selfish? Careless?' I finished.

I watched as a range of emotions passed across my sister's face.

'I was going to say don't be a martyr.'

I left the next day. I had over three hours of solitude on the way home to think about the next phase of my life – moving my things out of Kelly's place, adjusting to living with Murray and the kids, figuring out how to look after Martine despite being so far away.

But the first thing I needed to do was to clean up after what Martine had told me. I pulled over in a rest stop and parked under the shade of a tree. My hand shook as I searched for Cass's number, wondering if it was still connected.

She picked up on the third ring.

'Cass, it's Abbie.'

'Oh, Abbie,' she said in a rush. 'I heard about your dad. My parents called about the funeral but I couldn't get away. It's weird being back home, isn't it? I was there a few months ago and nothing changes. I'm so sorry. What's happening? How is your mum? How are *you*?'

I was taken aback by her warmth and sincerity – we hadn't

spoken in years and I, at least, was still unsure about where we stood in our friendship.

'I'm fine,' I said. 'Sad, but okay. Where are you living?'

'I'm in Sydney. Three years now. I got a transfer within the company. It's expensive living here but I'm in line for a promotion – if I can stick it out for another couple of years I might be back to head up the office there.'

'Cass,' I interrupted. 'I know this might seem like an odd question, but did you stay in contact with Reno? Did you ever tell him why I left? Did you say where I went?'

'No, never,' she replied, sounding confused. 'I might have said something to my parents about him being the father, but I lost touch with him after you left.'

'Do you still have his number?'

'Well, possibly, but –'

'I need to contact him. He came to my parents' house. He knew about Sarah. Someone must have said something.'

'Well, I didn't, and it doesn't matter now,' Cass said sharply.

'It matters. What if the police need to –'

She cut me off. 'I told them everything I knew when they interviewed me – you know, back when she disappeared. You must have given the police his name, Abbie, because I didn't.'

'I did, but – please, just give me the number.'

Silence on the line.

'Please.'

'Abbie, stop.' She sighed heavily. 'Reno was in a car accident years ago. He's been dead for a long time. I'm sorry.'

NOW

The further I drove inland, the more alone I felt. The highway narrowed to a single lane and the earth turned to the colour of rust; I passed the wrecks of cars in paddocks, the ruins of old buildings, and when I saw a sign advertising the last fuel stop for sixty kilometres it was all I could do not to turn around.

Jess believed a person could be drawn to a place, called to it, because of something that had happened in a past life – a happy home, a great love or an epic victory on a battlefield somewhere. I wondered if the opposite was true, if a person could be repelled by a place to which they had never been. I felt it now – a force, pulling me back to the sea. I rarely travelled far from home; I thought they would stop looking for Sarah if I ventured away. Like staying to guard an abandoned keep.

I drove on, window down, radio off, and finished the last mouthfuls of tepid water from my bottle. The landscape was changing again, becoming drier and more sparsely populated. No sign of rain clouds, or any clouds at all. To my right, a series of shallow, interconnected lakes dried to a brilliant white crust; to my left, windmills, hay sheds and distant yellow hills dotted with sheep. On this stretch of road there were kilometres between each driveway, and only a few passing cars headed in the other direction.

I had been on the road for two hours.

When we were kids, Jess used to bring baby birds into the

house. Once it was a fledgling wood pigeon with a deformed leg she'd found in the street; I wanted to leave the bird to nature and chance, but Jess was convinced it would die without her care. She'd nestled it in a box and tried to force-feed it worms from the vegetable garden, water from an eye-dropper. She'd put the box in the linen cupboard to hide it from Martine, and I had stayed awake all night, while Jess slept like the dead. The bird's fragility was too much – I could see its heart beating through its skin.

I'd felt the same when Sarah was born. Once I brought her home from the hospital, everything after that was up to me – not nature's way, not left to chance, but my responsibility.

Everything was my fault.

Do something. Bring her home.

At the next town I pulled over – it was barely a town at all but for a couple of tall, white silos and a single row of huddled buildings. There were signs out on the street in front of the bakery, but it looked as if it was closed, and the few houses were haggard. An overweight kelpie glanced both ways before crossing the road to rummage in a bin fallen on its side in the gutter.

When I spotted a public toilet block set back from the road, I moved the car into a parking space and got out. The wind had picked up, stirring dust and dead grass, whipping my hair into my mouth. I had thought the place completely deserted, but an older man wearing a baseball cap popped his head over a nearby fence and called out.

'Passing through?'

'Just stretching my legs. Is everything closed?'

He muttered something and disappeared, only to materialise on my side of the fence. 'Bianca will open up if you press the doorbell.' He jerked his head towards the bakery across the street. 'If you need anything.'

'I'm fine, thank you.'

I wasn't looking for conversation, but then I thought, *no, let him get a good look at me.*

'Abbie Morgan.' I stuck out my hand.

'Pete.' We shook. 'Where're you headed?'

'Maidenvale. I'm going to find my daughter.'

'She run off? Bloody kids.'

I nodded. 'Something like that.'

'Maiden's in a nice spot. Near the river.' He kicked a tyre. 'Your pressure's a bit low in the back. If you bring it 'round I'll put a few pounds in for you.'

'I appreciate that. Thank you.'

I reversed the car down his driveway, right up to the shed. Any other time I'd have been leery of trusting a stranger in such an isolated place, but honestly, what were the odds of running into *two* psychopaths in such a short period of time?

While Pete got his air compressor going, I used the public toilet and washed my hands. When I got back he'd checked all four tyres, cleaned the windscreen and refilled my water bottle.

'Good old-fashioned country service.' He slapped the bonnet twice. 'Anything else I can do for you, Abbie?'

Remember my name.

'There is something.'

I opened the glove box and peeled off a fifty-dollar note from the bundle inside. I read through the list of instructions on the napkin one more time and added my name and address. On the blank side I wrote Murray's mobile number.

'This will seem like a very strange request,' I began. 'Would you call my husband's number in… three days?' I showed him the number. 'This is him. Murray. Just tell him I was here and I've gone looking for my daughter. Tell him this.' I tapped the napkin again. 'It's all I know.'

His smile dropped. 'Are you in some kind of trouble?'

'I'm not sure yet.'

'Three days, you say?' Pete frowned. 'A lot can happen in three days. What if I can't hold out that long?'

'Any sooner and he might come looking for me before I'm ready to be found.' I handed him the list and the fifty-dollar note. 'I know it doesn't make much sense but you'd be doing me a good turn.'

He nodded. 'Okay. I can do this, but I don't want your money.'

'Please take it.' I shook his hand again. 'Just call and ask if I made it home safe.'

Perplexed, he stood scratching his head under the cap. 'Safe journey, Abbie. Hope you find her.'

I gave him a wave, started the car, and drove slowly through the gate. Before I pulled out onto the highway, I took my phone off silent and checked for a signal: there was none. I had two missed calls and a voice message from Martine: *Call me as soon as you get this.*

I deleted the message and put the phone back into the charging cradle. Soon I'd be without it, with no way of contacting anyone. Until now I had felt that as long as there were people, I'd be safe.

The sun was sinking. I'd finished half the bottle of water Pete had refilled, saving the rest out of some misguided instinct for survival.

Was I hungry? I honestly didn't know. I hadn't been truly hungry in six years – I ate to live, poked the food down, chewed, swallowed, gained a few kilos here, lost a few there, and like most people I sometimes ate and drank too much, but rarely for pleasure. The last thing I'd eaten was cereal that morning.

Apart from the hazy shape of hills to the east and the occasional rocky outcrop, the colourless landscape stretched forever, a seemingly endless plain. The only point of interest was a rough flat-topped peak that rose from the earth, as if a small mountain had got lost on the way to another place. *Wyatt's Lookout*, said the signpost at a corrugated dirt road that wound its way to the top. Not the lookout I was headed for, but I wondered if there'd be a signal there.

I indicated and turned off.

At the top there were four parking spaces and just enough room for a turning circle. A wooden viewing platform jutted from the edge and extended over the steep drop, with a waist-high safety barrier around the perimeter. Flat, brown land spread in all directions like a dirty patchwork quilt, mini tornadoes of dust rising from the dry paddocks like coils of smoke. In the far distance, a dense band of trees snaked across the landscape, a hint of deepest green.

The river.

I left the engine running and got out of the car. I held up my phone. Two bars of signal. It dinged: another text from Martine.

Abbie please call me RIGHT NOW.

If Martine had something to say, she would have to wait. If she had other secrets, I didn't want to hear them right now. Every time I'd tried to break away, she had drawn me back, twisted and pulled until my own thoughts became a tangle. *Careless. Irresponsible. Selfish. Reckless. Madness.* Now was not the time to let her words get in my head.

I deleted the message and called Jess.

'Hello?'

She sounded out of breath. I heard music and laughter in the background.

'It's me.' The wind snatched my voice away.

'I can't hear you!' Jess yelled. 'Speak up.'

'It's me – Abbie.'

'Hey, stranger,' she said. 'What's with all the static?'

'It's windy where I am.'

'And where's that?'

'I went for a drive. Where are you?'

She giggled. 'I've gone for drinks with the girls after work.'

'I hope you're having fun!' I said too brightly.

A rustling sound. 'Wait. I'm going somewhere quieter.' The music faded. 'Okay. What's up?'

'Not much.'

'Well, you're lucky I picked up because I'm having a great time and neither you nor Martine is going to ruin my day.' She spoke lightly, but underneath there was a hint of annoyance.

'Martine?' I said.

'She's been calling and calling. It's obviously not an emergency, otherwise she would have left a message and you would've already mentioned it.' She paused. 'It's not, is it?'

'No, no...'

'What's wrong?'

I started to speak but the words caught in my throat. What could I say? *I am in a destructive and co-dependent relationship with a man who is not my husband.* If I gave Jess any indication I was in a bad place she would set things in motion to rescue me, and it was too soon to let that happen. The fear that he knew as much as he implied, that he listened to my conversations or somehow read my messages, had abated – if I believed that was the case, I could have switched phones at any time, I would have written everything down, left more clues.

The awful truth was that, if I couldn't bring Sarah home, I didn't want to go back.

Murray was right – it wasn't purpose I was looking for, but penance, and I was no longer driven by the need to know but the need to destroy. The fear and grief had been replaced by hate. I carried it with me like a grenade. I wouldn't stop until I'd set it off.

Nothing else mattered.

'Everything is fine,' I said. 'I went home to get something and I didn't tell Martine I was coming. You know what she's like.'

Jess was quiet for a moment. 'What for?'

'What? I can't hear you.'

'You said you went home for something. What was it?' A note
of suspicion.

Evidence. Proof.

'Jess, you're breaking up. I've got to go.'

'Abbie, wait –'

'Have a great time tonight, okay?' A well-timed gust of wind cut
her off and I took the opportunity to hang up.

'I love you,' I said to a dead line.

The enormity of the decisions I'd made hit when I saw the sign for
Vale Wreckers and pulled up outside the entrance. The yard was
a riot of junk set in a shallow valley surrounded by shorn golden
fields, which gave the impression that the teetering piles were
poised on the edge of a giant sinkhole, waiting to be sucked down.
There were no immediate neighbours, no life apart from a bored
goat tied to a post in the adjacent paddock.

Without the car I'd be stuck; without my phone I'd be
untraceable. It was the kind of place that made me want to check
my tetanus shots were up to date the second I arrived, but nothing
had happened yet to make me feel as if I'd reached the point of no
return. The yard didn't look open.

I drove beneath a rusted steel arch and along the deeply-rutted
driveway, following an arrow pointing in the direction of the main
office: two raised forty-foot shipping containers set at a ninety-
degree angle. There was a peeling weatherboard house set way
back on the lot, and an enormous sagging shed that appeared to
be an amalgam of mismatched pieces of corrugated iron. The
choking clutter all around was made up of the skeletons of cars,
old farming machinery, warped furniture and nature fighting
back. A feral-looking cat sauntered past, flattening its body to
squeeze through a gap between sheets of iron.

I followed the driveway all the way to the shed. The sliding door was open. I stopped the car just short, unwilling to venture into the murk, and turned off the ignition. I stepped out onto ground thick with sawdust. Inside the shed were the darkened shapes of other cars, parked in neat lines, shrouded in tarpaulins and car covers. In one section, a block and tackle held an engine suspended over an oily pit.

'Hello?'

A middle-aged man in filthy overalls emerged from the path running alongside the shed. I jumped back and swung my handbag in front of me as if for protection. I didn't care what he looked like. I needed to hear his voice.

'Help you?' He looked the car over. 'Nice vehicle. I'm guessing you're not here for wrecking.'

Vee-hickle. Not him.

'Storage,' I said. 'You were recommended.'

He squinted. 'How long?'

'Three months or thereabouts.'

'Twenty-five a week,' he said, chewing.

'Okay.'

'You're not gonna haggle?'

'I don't have time.'

'Most people want to haggle.' He stood back, regarding me with suspicion.

I opened my bag. 'Fine. Twenty per week.'

'Right. You gotta leave a set of keys in case I need to move things around.'

I glanced in the shed at the covered cars, raising my eyebrow. There was sawdust up to the rims – nothing looked as if it had been moved in decades. Vale Wreckers was a hole where vehicles went to die.

He jerked his head. 'I got a dozen or more vintage in that shed.

Yours won't be the one they take, and anyway, I keep the keys in a safe.'

'Fine,' I repeated, dangling the keys. 'Where should I park?'

'I'll do it.' He held out a greasy hand. 'It's a delicate operation.'

I lobbed the keys rather than touch him.

'Let me just get my stuff.'

I kept an eye on him as I grabbed my phone, my water bottle, and the cash from the glove box. I counted out three hundred in fifties and stuffed the rest in my bag.

'Do I need to sign something? How do I get the car back?' I slapped the cash on the bonnet.

'I never forget a face,' he said.

I muttered, 'I'm counting on it,' but he added, 'There's a small matter on account of if you don't come back for it after a year, ownership passes to me.'

'Is that legal?' I sputtered.

He only laughed and reached for the money.

I couldn't get out of there fast enough.

I walked in the trench next to the road. I felt a rush of fear when a couple of semis passed: was that the way I'd go, clipped, spun around, dead in a ditch? Two separate cars stopped to ask if I needed a ride, a youngish guy on his own and a family of four, but I hadn't yet reached the dam where I was meant to dispose of my things. I told them I was fine walking – I lived just down the road.

I felt for Sarah's beads in my pocket, running them between my thumb and forefinger as if saying a rosary. It distracted me from the urge to check my phone for a signal and call Jess back, tell her the truth: that I was headed willingly into danger, that I didn't know who I was anymore, and everything was not fine.

But she'd sounded so carefree and happy. Finally she was living her life. Good for her.

AFTER

Until I had Sarah, I never used to wonder how Jess and I turned out so different from each other. When I was a child, if I was upset I'd crawl away like a wounded animal and nurse my grudges. Jess, on the other hand, was prone to dramatic and public rages, but once she'd cooled off she behaved as if nothing had happened. I was secretive; Jess was too candid and liked to shock. I kept my room tidy, but Jess's was a disaster zone. She cheated at board games, while I was the one who seethed and sought justice. She believed in fate, serendipity, past lives, signs and ghosts. I was tethered to reality. I didn't believe in anything I couldn't see. But some patterns are impossible to see unless you're looking for them.

It was after Sarah started walking and her distinct personality began to emerge that I knew there was something else at work inside us – a legacy of generations, a mysterious potion of genes and blood memory and other factors I'd never truly understand. I'd kept her for myself, but she wasn't all mine. If I thought of Reno, it was only to convince myself she was better off not knowing him. If I was honest, Reno was the main reason I'd avoided contact with Cass for so long.

The older I got, the more I realised I had made decisions – having Sarah, leaving the security of my parents' home – that were simultaneously risky and gave me a feeling of control. That perceived control, however, was an illusion. The decisions I'd made affected the course of my parents' lives and forced Jess to turn into an adult before her time. When our father died I'd made a promise to her that it was my turn – I'd look after Martine, or at least relieve Jess of some of the burden.

My failure in that area added another layer of shame, and I realised that the overwhelming emotion in relation to the women in my life was guilt.

I'd left Kelly to be with Murray. I was in love, and Kelly said she understood. We'd kept in touch – she pretended everything was okay, but her latest agency carer only visited three times a week and I suspected Kelly's life had closed in on her like a one-way tunnel after I moved away. I avoided my mother because she brought out the worst in me, and me in her. And from the moment I told my family I was pregnant, Jess's life had changed – she was pushed from being the centre of her own story to playing a bit part in Sarah's, my and my parents' tragedy.

For a long time I thought my sister kept no secrets from me, but not long before the wedding Jess told me a few things she'd kept to herself. She said she had stopped talking for five days the week after Sarah was born and nobody noticed. She was right: I didn't notice. When I asked her why she did it, she said it was an experiment – she wanted to see if anyone would care if she disappeared.

'But you just stopped talking,' I said. 'It's not the same as disappearing.'

'I know that now. I used to think it was my fault Sarah was taken. This is hard to admit to you, but I resented her at first... not later of course, but when you first brought her home, I wished she wasn't there.'

'You were sixteen,' I said. 'It doesn't count.'

'Yeah, but you know the idea that if you put something out in the universe, it will come to pass? When it actually happened six years later, I thought it had been floating around up there all this time and it eventually fell back down on our family.'

Jess was riddled with guilt too.

I rushed to reassure her. 'It wasn't your fault. It was mine. I should have taken better care of her.'

She shook her head. 'You sound like Martine. Don't let her in your head.'

'She was right. About a lot of things.'

'She was wrong about a lot of things too.' Jess paused, noticeably wary of continuing. 'About a week before you left with Sarah, I heard her talking to someone on the phone. She said you weren't coping. She said she was scared you might hurt the baby.'

My body jerked in shock. 'Who was she talking to?'

'I don't know. Auntie Lira, maybe?'

'Why didn't you say something?'

She flushed. 'It was true. You *weren't* coping. I often heard you crying in the night.'

'I was tired and frustrated. I was nineteen!'

'Well, I didn't say anything because for a long time… I believed her.'

I remembered the time Martine caught me spinning Sarah in circles. Did she really think I'd hurt her? Was that why she kept turning up unannounced over the years, to try to catch me out?

It took everything to keep my anger in check. 'I *never* hurt Sarah. I made some shit life decisions and I didn't protect her the way I should have, but I never so much as smacked her, not *once*.'

I wanted to. Some days she pushed every button and twanged every string, but thoughts and actions were a long way apart, weren't they? I thought about the day she disappeared, how I'd dragged her to the bus stop and hid from her. I'd played mind games with a *six-year-old*.

Maybe Martine sensed I had that in me. She loved Sarah in the way grandparents were supposed to love their grandchildren, completely and without reserve, but I could never escape the feeling that she wanted me to fail.

Jess said, 'Anyway, you're getting married. Let's focus on the wedding.'

But I couldn't let it go. 'Martine still blames me.'

'She blames herself. She thinks if she had helped more, maybe you wouldn't have left.'

'She told you that?' It surprised me. Martine wasn't one for regrets.

'Not in so many words.'

We exchanged wry smiles.

'Do you blame *her*?' Jess asked.

I decided to be honest. 'I don't *not* blame her.'

'You were a good mum, Abbie,' Jess said. 'You couldn't have changed what happened.'

It was easy for Jess to say, but I knew my carelessness was at the root of the guilt I carried; I believed there was no one to blame but myself. Were those five minutes crucial? If I had my time again I would have looked for Sarah straightaway. No, I'd go back further. I wouldn't have let go of her hand at the market. I would have turned left instead of right at the end of the street, caught a different bus. Decided not to go to the market at all and watched a movie. Or stayed with my parents in Athena Bay instead of taking the lease on the Rosewood flat. If time travel was possible, at what point could I still have changed course? Sometimes I'd go as far back as Sarah's conception – but that was where I stopped. She was gone, but I couldn't imagine my life without her in it.

It became an obsession. I'd replay key scenes, like cutting myself with a sharp knife again and again.

NOW

Ten minutes later, I arrived at the dam – it was wide, deep and close to the road, a dying red gum in its centre. Judging by the exposed roots of the trees around the edge, the water level had been much higher in the past; now the dam was barely half-full, its surface scummy and still. A shrieking flock of corellas circled above and came to settle in the tree, drowning out the whine of mosquitoes.

My legs ached, I needed to pee. I looked around before squeezing between the barbed wires of the fence, and I pulled down my jeans behind a bush.

The light was turning, yellows to orange, blues to purple, and the wind had settled to a light breeze. By now Murray would be arriving home, wondering where I was. Judging by the number of missed calls, Martine was at home, calling me every hour. Jess was probably still drunk in a bar, while I was descending into a rural noir nightmare, my pants around my ankles.

I zipped my jeans and stood, twisting my ankle on a tree root. My feet were heavy as I limped forward, my white sneakers caked with an inch of red clay. Insect bites on my bare arms were red and swollen.

This was absurd. The perfect intersection between comedy and tragedy. I laughed, sending the corellas flapping and screaming, and then I cried. When the flock disappeared, there was a hush.

I checked my phone. No signal. I had an hour at most before it was completely dark.

I took the SIM card from my phone and tucked it inside the coin pocket of my jeans. So tiny, so easy to conceal. I split the cash into two bundles, one for each back pocket, and slid my cards from my purse – Visa, Medicare, a couple of memberships to places I visited once and never returned, like the gym – and frisbeed them into the weed, where they floated like tiny log-jammed boats.

I left my purse jammed between the tree roots, with a passport-sized photo of Murray and me on our wedding day inside. From the large compartment in the side of my bag, I took the sheaf of Sarah's sketches, separating the pages, looking at her eerie, unfamiliar face.

This Sarah isn't real. She has never been real.

I scattered the pages among the trees. Last, I heaved my bag into the dam, phone and all, and it sank as if it was filled with stones.

Clues, everywhere. Or maybe this was another one of the dark places, where things disappeared and were never found.

The Maiden Motel was a long, squat building on the exit side of the town, depending which way you were travelling. I'd walked past a pub and several takeaway shops, pausing to wonder whether I was hungry or wanted a stiff drink. Each time the answer was a hard no. I dragged my exhausted body the last hundred metres, my gait rigid, to avoid bursting the blisters on my heels. Again, he was right. I couldn't have driven for another two hours. I couldn't think straight. I needed to rest.

The motel was painted bright white, but the walls were stained yellow in places where rain must have burst through the gutters and eaves. Red and green Christmas lights were strung outside reception as if nobody could be bothered to take them down.

There were a few vehicles in the car park, but no beige Toyota Land Cruiser. Either he hadn't kept up his end of the deal or I was in the wrong place.

I pushed through the door to reception.

A harried-looking woman around my age swivelled on her chair. 'Can I help you?'

'Is there another motel in Maidenvale?'

'This is it,' the woman said. 'Unless you want a room with a shared bathroom in the hotel. Or there are B&Bs.'

'But no other Maiden Motel?'

'That's what I said.'

Headlights illuminated the wall behind her. I jerked around, but it was only a car doing a U-turn in the street.

'I need a room for one night. Room twelve, please.'

She looked me over, somehow managing to appear devoid of curiosity 'You haven't pre-booked?'

'No.'

'You want breakfast?' I hesitated and she added, 'Breakfast in your room – you take a tray with cereal and bread for toast. Milk's in the fridge and there's a toaster and kettle. Sixty for the night and twenty bucks for the breakfast. Fifty deposit held for the minibar.'

I nodded.

She clicked her mouse, printed out a sheet and slid it across the counter. 'Fill out your details and sign at the bottom.' She offered a pen.

For a long time I studied the paper, as if I'd been presented with a complex legal contract. *Sherri Murray*, I wrote. I put Jess's mobile as a contact and her work email. I flipped the paper over and added Murray's name, our address and home phone number on the back of the sheet. Where the sheet asked for a signature, I signed *fuck you* in elaborate cursive.

'What's that you wrote on the back?' she asked.

'Next of kin.' I smiled grimly.

She didn't find it funny either. 'ID?'

I took one bundle of cash from my back pocket and counted three fifties. 'I don't have my driver's licence with me. I can round up?'

She shrugged, grabbed the cash and handed me a key. 'Room twelve is the last on your right. You can claim your deposit back when you check out.'

'Keep it,' I said. 'Do you happen to have a notepad and pen I can borrow?'

'By the phone in the room.'

'What about some envelopes? Say, three?'

Sighing, she reached under the counter. 'Anything else?'

'That's all. Thank you.'

'Wait.' She shuffled out wearing slippers. A few minutes later she came back with a breakfast tray covered with a cloth napkin. 'Here you go. You're all set now?'

'Only if there's a sharp knife under there,' I said.

'What?'

'Never mind.'

On the way to my room, I passed a group of five teenagers sitting under a tree near the car park, their phones lit up in the dark. They were smoking and sharing a bottle of something in a paper bag, giggling. Couldn't have been more than fourteen.

Number twelve was the last room at the far end of the block. A sensor light flickered on outside. I placed the breakfast tray on the ground and unlocked the door. As it swung open, I checked over my shoulder – still no Land Cruiser in the car park. Hardly any guest vehicles.

Cautiously, I picked up the tray and went in.

The room was basic but clean: a double bed, a TV on a chest of drawers, a two-person dining setting, a dull lamp switched on next to the bed, everything in the pilled textures and dirty shades of the seventies. It smelled of dust and bleach, and it made me feel terribly alone.

I set the tray on the table and locked the door. There was a wide window in the bathroom, which had been left open. I peered through the screen: the rear overlooked a narrow laneway. Beyond that, a low mesh fence and a tree-lined paddock. Too exposed.

I wound the window closed, locked the bathroom door and undressed. I needed a quick shower, enough to rinse off the grime and ease my sore muscles, but after a minute the hot water ran cold and the burst blisters on my feet were stinging.

Shivering and damp, I put my dirty clothes back on and turned on the TV to watch the local news. I scanned the banners running across the bottom of the screen, stupidly hoping there might be something –

missing wife
missing sister
missing daughter
missing mother of missing child
mystery deepens: mother of abducted child disappears

– but it was all stock-market prices and the weather.

My stomach cramped. I considered eating my breakfast for dinner. Instead, I reached for the bar fridge, cracked open two mini bottles of Jack Daniels and a Coke, drank a few mouthfuls from the can, poured the spirits in, finished half and poured the rest down the sink. I needed enough to quieten my mind, but not to cloud it.

The headlines at seven o'clock: a train derailment, the driver critical and sixteen injured, a major drug bust, and somewhere in New South Wales a man was holding his wife and three children hostage. Of course there wouldn't be anything. News didn't travel that fast, and it was still possible nobody had realised I was gone.

Help seemed far away.

I needed to sleep, but to do that, to even think about it, seemed obscene. I paced. I picked up the phone next to the bed and listened to the dial tone, but paranoia kicked in. He'd told me to throw my things in that particular dam; he'd made me check in to this motel, this room – all for a reason.

The kids. Their phones.

I unlocked the door and called, 'Hey?'

One of the girls stabbed out her cigarette. 'Oh, for a second I thought you were my mum.'

They laughed in unison, watching warily as I approached.

'Do any of you have an iPhone?'

Four shook their head but the fifth, a boy, tucked his phone under his leg.

'I'll give you five hundred bucks for it right now.'

His eyes lit up but he shook his head. 'I would, but my parents would kill me.'

While I stopped to think they gathered up their things, dusted off their backsides and made to move on.

'Wait,' I said, holding out my hands, pleading. 'Any of you, any phone. Please. I need a mobile. Preferably with a SIM. Come on – a thousand bucks.'

They eyed each other. One guy sniggered and nudged the girl next to him. I could tell they thought I was either drunk or crazy.

'I'm sorry,' I said. 'Forget it.'

As we strode off in opposite directions, the youngest boy yelled, 'Lady, there's a public phone box round the corner.'

I turned around. He pointed, his brow furrowed with concern. The kindness just about did me in.

I dashed back to the room, slammed the door and locked it again.

The TV was too loud. I dialled it down and made toast with margarine and strawberry jam, but let the toast go cold on the table.

Why *three months* in storage for Sherri's car? Was it to buy time before any evidence of my movements popped up? Assuming the guy at the wreckers would report the car unclaimed – it seemed unlikely, given what he'd said about keeping it. And I knew next to nothing about tracing a signal on a mobile phone. Would it be obvious my call to Jess from the lookout was the last call I'd made?

But it wasn't being found that consumed me, it was being understood. I wanted Martine to know I had finally taken responsibility. I needed Jess to know that, for once, I hadn't dragged her down with me. Murray had to know I didn't leave because I didn't love him, that I was driven by my need to know what happened to Sarah. I wanted them all to understand that it was never my intention to hurt anyone, that I had been given a terrible choice.

I couldn't let my family believe I was a liar, a drunk, a thief, if I didn't make it home. But perhaps that was exactly what he wanted them to think. That way it would be easy for him to make me disappear.

It took eight sheets of paper and almost two hours to write a summary of everything that had happened since the wedding, ending with the words: *Tomorrow, I will meet him at Mount Aramus lookout. I don't know what will happen next.*

I wrote letters to Murray, Martine and Jess, and placed them in separate envelopes. I drank the complimentary bottle of water from the bedside table, peed, brushed my teeth using my finger. If the car was there in the morning, I'd take the letters to reception, ask the receptionist to post them the following day, and drive to the lookout. There was nothing more I could do.

I thought about Murray, how fast we'd fallen for each other, how quickly our relationship had fallen apart.

In order to be with Murray there were parts of myself I had to let go: the young Abbie, who took risks and made reckless mistakes; the damaged, fragile Abbie, who locked herself away and kept a growing list of reasons not to live. Even invincible Abbie, who was probably delusional. I hid all of them from him. The new version had been capable, reliable, functional – I became everything Murray wanted and needed.

I stayed awake for as long as I could, keeping watch through the gap in the curtains. At 11 o'clock I lay on the bed, exhausted and numb, aware I should have felt something more – guilt, regret, shame, fear. But I was not the same person who got married a month ago. I had left everything behind; I had been stripped back to the most basic of elements. My fate was out of my hands.

When sleep came, it was deep and unnatural.

AFTER

The day I met Murray, I had taken Kelly to an appointment in the city. When we got home she realised she had forgotten to fill a prescription. The nearest late-night chemist was twenty kilometres away and we needed milk, so I dropped her home and set off again.

It was dusk and I was driving too fast on a winding road. I had the window down, the music up, and I was distracted. I knew better. The first roo, a huge buck, was standing motionless in the middle of the road. There was a steep rocky drop on one side, an impenetrable bank of trees on the other.

I braked hard in a straight line, knowing it was better to swerve late or hit the roo head-on at a reduced speed than lose control and risk leaving the road or hitting a tree. And I managed it – I turned the wheel at the last second, missed the buck and straightened the car without losing traction.

When I checked the rear-view mirror, the buck had ducked the headlights and bounded away, but as I continued to slow down I felt the thump.

I pulled over, put on the hazard lights and got out of the car.

I didn't want to look. Kelly worked with other wildlife carers who took on injured roos and I knew she'd want me to check whether the animal was still alive.

There was a decent dent in the plastic bumper, but it would pop out. Not much blood. About twenty metres behind the car

I found her, a doe, her body twisted and her eyes glassy. She was clearly dead, but there was a rippling bulge in her pouch, similar to Sarah's full-body rolls when she was in my belly. Two quivering hind legs were sticking out.

I felt sick. I sat on the verge with the dead doe's head in my lap, unable to bring myself to put my hands inside her. A couple of cars passed and nobody stopped. Eventually, I dialled Kelly's number.

'You should be able to pull the joey out, feet and tail first. There are pillow cases in the back of the car – put it in one of those. I'll contact some carers and call you back.' She hung up.

No question of whether or not I could do it.

I pulled the doe by the tail and dragged her heavy body to the side of the road. I rolled her onto her back, took hold of the joey's legs and tugged gently. The joey wriggled itself from the pouch – it was old enough to stand, blinking, and fully covered with fine hair. I slipped the pillow case over its head and scooped it up inside.

Kelly called back. 'No carers available right now – I've let Murray at the vet clinic know you'll be bringing it in.' She gave me the address of the clinic.

I drove carefully, the joey on my hip, tucked under my left arm, its heart fluttering against my ribs. I was relieved it wasn't hairless and pink; something that fragile would have brought me undone.

When I pulled into the car park at the clinic, it was dark. The joey hadn't moved in a while. I was terrified it was dead too.

An older man in green scrubs was waiting by the door. 'You're Abbie? Kelly's friend?'

'Yes.' Tears rolled down my cheeks.

He took the pillow case. 'Don't be too hard on yourself – this happens all the time. At least you stopped.' He held the door open and followed me inside, carrying the joey cradled in one arm like a baby. 'Do you want to come into the examination room?'

'I'll wait here.'

He nodded and took the joey through a glass-slatted door. A few minutes later he came back, beckoning me. 'He looks pretty good. No breaks or bruising. He's about six months – another month or so and he'd be ready to leave the pouch.'

'That's great.'

'We can keep him here overnight until there's a carer available. If you don't have to dash off, you could stay and see if he'll feed?'

'Okay,' I said.

That was the first night Murray and I spent together – most of the night, anyway. I curled up on the couch in his office with the joey and fell asleep. I woke around 1 o'clock to find a doggy-smelling blanket had been placed over my legs, a pillow under my head. When he realised I was awake, Murray made tea and gave me other simple tasks to perform for the overnight patients: outside toilet breaks for the dogs, changing soiled bedding, refilling water bowls.

We talked. We laughed. I fell in love with his eyes: bright blue, intense, kind. And his hands. strong, gentle, expressive.

I'd had some experience looking after Kelly's rescue birds, and when I managed to crop-feed a sick cockatiel, Murray said, 'Want a job?'

I shook my head. 'I have a job. I look after Kelly.'

'Breakfast, then?'

The problem with loving Murray was I had nothing to compare it to. I'd never been in a loving, monogamous relationship, not like ours, the kind that fitted the script of a romantic comedy.

There had been the boys from the bay: unrequited crushes, sticky hook-ups and a 'long-term' high-school romance with Devon Christian that lasted a year. I lost my virginity to Eli Beckett at fifteen in the back of his station wagon and we cheated on each other three months later. Typical high-school stuff: all high drama and low stakes.

There was Evan, a friend of Tansy's. Moody and unpredictable, he literally came and went for a period of about six months while I lived in the Rosewood flat, when Sarah was still a baby. No dates, only intoxicated evenings sitting on the couch drinking UDLs and watching DVDs, followed by uncomfortable nights wrestling in my single bed while he tried to please me in increasingly non-missionary ways, as if he had a 'Fifty Ways to Make a Woman Orgasm' checklist in his back pocket. For a while I found Evan interesting; over time I grew bored with his angst. When I stopped trying to fill our silences, I realised we had absolutely nothing to talk about.

The last few times he knocked, I didn't bother answering. Sometimes I came home to notes, passed under the door:

You think you can pretend I don't exist? Call me. Followed by his number.

I scribbled a reply and stuck the paper on the outside of the door:

It's over. Let's be honest — it never started. Please don't come here again. Bitch. Whore. Liar.

I was used to name-calling. I turned off the lights and sat in the dark until he left.

When Sarah was about four years old there was Jonathan, a recently divorced neighbour for whom I developed a kind of loveless fascination. Again, we didn't date, didn't go out for dinners or a movie. When he was feeling horny, he knocked on my door; when I was feeling lonely, I knocked on his. We had a signal: except on rubbish-collection days, if our council bins were parked near our front doors it meant we were up for company. More specifically, it meant his ex-wife and two children weren't on the scene.

My bin stayed near the front door almost permanently. His, maybe twice a week. The only gift Jon ever gave me was his car space — we'd swapped so I didn't have to walk the alley between the units alone late at night. After Sarah came into my bed one morning to find Jon in it, I stopped seeing him – she was so upset. A few months later he moved and I never heard from him again.

Reno was a mistake. They all were, really, but supposedly we learn from mistakes.

For two years after Sarah disappeared, there was no one. My only long-term relationship was with the nameless, faceless people who sent me their hate mail, threats, conspiracy theories and even love letters, who relentlessly tracked me down wherever I went. I could spot a late notice or a letter of demand by the print on the label, and it was the same for the 'fan mail' – I threw the letters in the bin, unopened. If I didn't read them, they ceased to exist.

I became very good at ignoring conflict and unpleasantness until it went away.

When Murray made it his business to court me – dinners, flowers, gifts, moonlit walks on the beach – I didn't know how to react. For weeks, our kisses seemed not to be a prelude to anything, but standalone acts that ended when he saw me to my door. He made no moves without warning; he didn't touch me without asking. I learned I was not expected to pay for or repay anything. Murray had an ex-wife, two almost-grown kids, a meaningful career and a beautiful home. He'd built a life, accumulated assets, could afford to eat out every night of the week if he wanted to. He was twenty years older – steady, financially secure, accomplished.

Sarah and I had lived a different life. I had few possessions and the money I earned barely covered food and rent. When we moved house we could do it in a single car trip.

That Murray had cheated on me with his ex-wife didn't shock me. It hurt, but it didn't change the way I felt about him. He might have thought I had nothing, no skills, nowhere to go; it likely made sense to him that he could do what he did, and that I'd stay.

NOW

Darkness. Fading in, fading out. For the longest time it was like being suspended in deep water, trying to swim to the surface with no air in my lungs and without a source of light to tell me which way was up. I drifted, came back. I heard sounds – a cough, rustling, footsteps – but they were far away.

A touch: clinical.

Underneath was soft and yielding: a mattress.

My name: Abbie Morgan.

The last thing I remembered: the motel. Drinking the bottled water.

Something in my mouth and throat: a tube?

Hospital.

The relief was immense. I was alive. Someone had saved me and I was alive.

Pain brought me up, the agony of pressure on joints that had been still too long. A blinding headache behind my eyes. I tasted bitterness, like foul medicine from childhood.

Heaviness all over my body – real, physical weight.

A blanket.

I opened and closed my eyes but the darkness was the same.

A blindfold.

I tried to call out but my tongue wouldn't work; my mouth was spitless, my throat raw.

A gag, strapped around my jaw, depressing my tongue.

I tried to swallow, couldn't. I panicked, tried to move, but my hands and feet were tied – to a bed.

I heard sounds – movement, breathing, a smothered laugh.

I couldn't see, but I knew he was there.

The next time I woke, I went through the process again: reorientation, remembering who I was, realising I was alive, only this time I wondered if it was possible for an otherwise young and healthy person to will herself to die the way an old, sick person could. Just let go and drift away. But the anchor of hate held me there as physically as the ties around my ankles and wrists, and the voice in my head chanted new instructions:

Hold on.

You are strong.

You can kill him.

You have nothing more to lose.

Some part of me had known it would be like this.

I tried to imagine the space: a room, average-sized, perhaps twenty squares, a stained ceiling, exposed pipes, peeling paint, bloodstains and scratch marks on the walls – the kind of picture a terrified mind paints when it has only imagination and no evidence. The only thing I could do to keep from succumbing to panic was to imagine myself submerged, ration my breath, slow my racing heart.

I took inventory of the sounds. Water running somewhere, but muffled. Maybe the room was underground – no, I could hear birds. Daytime. No traffic noise or voices. A slight echo when I groaned. I smelled something fruity and sweet.

The weight of the blanket was comforting before; now it was infuriating, like a steel band across my body, and too hot. The restraints around my wrists and ankles bit into my skin, and when

I tried to move my tongue past the object pressing down on it, I felt a sharp sting as it sliced the skin underneath. Tasting blood, I turned my head as far as it would go and let bloody spit dribble from the corner of my mouth.

The ache in my joints was excruciating, but the thirst was worse than the pain. My spine felt fused; I arched my back to relieve the pressure and moaned, expecting the laughter I'd heard before, but there was nothing.

Night sounds. Crickets, the far-off cry of an owl and wind rustling through trees. I felt light, cool puffs of air on my skin. I tried to move, but the restraints held me in place. My mouth was parched, but at least I could swallow.

The gag had been removed.

I cleared my throat to test my voice: it came out raspy, as if I had pharyngitis. I tried again.

'Please talk to me,' I whispered.

He wasn't there. I was alone. Perhaps he'd left me there to die. For a long time I cried silently, thinking of everything I'd lost.

NOW

'I know you're here. I can hear you.'

I couldn't, but I could *smell* him – the awful scent of an unseen stranger's body heat and sweat, masked by cologne. I had been awake and reasonably alert for what felt like ten minutes or more and heard no noise coming from inside the room, but the odour was getting stronger.

Nothing.

'What's the point of bringing me here if you're not going to talk to me?'

The door opened and closed. Did he leave? Or enter? For a moment I thought I had been mistaken and he wasn't in the room at all, but being unable to see had left me with a heightened sense for the direction of sound. He'd only pretended to enter the room – he was already here. What game was he playing?

'Where is she?'

A pause. 'There are some things we need to take care of first.'

There it was: the voice.

'You promised. I've done everything you asked.'

'You and I are going to enter into a relationship. It's important that we understand each other,' he said.

So here we were. I knew the risks. The possibility that he would abduct and kill me had been at the back of my mind from the outset, hadn't it? But now he was implying something else.

Repulsed, I tried to curl into myself, but the restraints held me spreadeagled like a sacrifice.

'Are you going to kill me?'

A huff of breath.

'At least tell me where she is before you do it.' My voice shook. 'What time is it?'

'Just after four in the afternoon.'

'Where am I? How long have I been here?'

'Since last night,' he said.

'Then how –' I became aware of discomfort between my legs, but not the ache of a full bladder. Something else. I tried to lift my head, my hips. 'Is that –?'

'A catheter, yes. A simple procedure. I have not violated you.'

My breath whooshed out of me. *This was not violation?*

I clenched my muscles as if I could expel the tube simply by squeezing. I lifted my upper body, but could only rise so far. My stomach muscles cramped and tore; bile came up in my throat. I gagged, swallowed, choked.

Footsteps. He had crossed the room. A clattering sound from beneath the bed.

'A bucket. It's to your right.'

He gripped the back of my neck as I thrashed and retched, but nothing came up. He continued to hold the bucket close in one hand as he felt my forehead with the other. Satisfied, he grunted and peeled my upper lip back, pressing his thumb to my gums and releasing several times.

'You're mildly dehydrated. Here.'

Glass on my bared teeth.

'Drink.'

'No.'

'Drink.'

'We all know how that turned out,' I said, jerking away.

'I want you to be well.'

'Then you drink first.'

He sighed, a perfect reproduction of the sighs I'd heard over the phone. I heard him take a mouthful and swallow. When he brought the glass to my lips again, I drank without stopping until it was empty, and asked for more.

'Not yet. You have to take it slowly until the drug is out of your system.'

'It was the bottle of water.'

'Yes.'

'Why? I would have come anyway.'

'I know,' he said. 'But this way you don't know where we are and you have no idea how long it took to get here.'

He was right. He said we had arrived yesterday, but I could have been out of it for hours.

'How did you get into the motel room?'

'Does it matter?'

'Take off the blindfold.'

'Not yet.'

His finger stroked my hand and I curled it into a fist.

'I have your SIM card. You were instructed to leave everything. I have your letters too. Why must you break the rules, Abbie?'

My heart sank. He'd found the SIM. He'd taken off my clothes, undone my bra, touched my breasts.

'I was scared,' I admitted.

'It doesn't matter now,' he said. 'You're here. Your old life is over – you ended it. Now we start again.'

'You forced me to end it. I hate you. *Hate*. Do you get it? I can't imagine feeling any other way.'

He was quiet for a moment, as if the word troubled him. When he spoke again, it sounded as if he was smiling. 'I made *her* love me. It's not impossible.'

White noise in my head. I strained against the shackles; I screamed and kicked and spat, but the remains of the drug in my system had left me sluggish and disoriented. I ran out of fight quickly and slumped back against the pillows. Nothing but the sound of my ragged breathing.

I felt a warm hand on the freezing skin of my ankle, tightening its grip until the fingers met. The hand ran along my calf muscle to the back of my knee; it travelled to my taut quadriceps and moved lightly across the outer curve of my hip.

When I no longer felt its touch, I exhaled sharply. The strength I'd built in my body was useless while I was tied up. The strength I'd tried to build in my mind might not be enough – I could feel it slipping away.

'You've been working out,' he said.

'I'm a swimmer. You should know that. You know everything.'

'These are not a swimmer's muscles. The structure and definition are from lifting weights. Why do you lie?'

I went still. He'd been watching me somehow. It was the only explanation.

'I haven't been watching you,' he said, as if he could read my mind. 'You're just predictable, but most people are. I'm disappointed, though.'

'What did you expect? That I'd be pleased to wake up somewhere else, tied to a bed? That I wouldn't try to save my own life?'

'You came,' he said, as if it was a choice.

'I came to find out where she is!'

I kicked out, but the shackles only wrenched me back. I cowered, expecting some kind of punishment, but he only sighed – that awful, disappointed sigh I remembered from the phone calls.

'It will take time. I'm a patient man. Once you stop this behaviour, I'll untie you,' he said, as if I was a rude guest.

'Yes, untie me.'

'When you demonstrate that you trust me,' he said. 'Not before.'

The strangeness of his perspective was beginning to sink in; surely it would be the other way around – when he could trust *me*?

'I don't even know you.'

'But you do, Abbie.' He waited.

'Take this thing off. Let me see your face.'

'Not yet.'

Behind the blindfold, I stared towards the ceiling. Tears had made damp patches near my cheeks. I was glad he couldn't see them.

'I'm going to make you something to eat. Then you're going to eat it, and following that you're going to talk.'

'About what?'

Did he shake his head?

'I don't know what you want from me,' I whispered.

Exhaustion, so deep in my bones I could barely move.

'Perhaps you need some more time by yourself to think.'

'No, please –'

He was gone again.

I measured time passing by the sounds outside and the increasing warmth on my skin. After several hours the heat had intensified. I could feel the sun burning my forehead and scalp, and there was still a faint breeze coming from somewhere near my face, but the noises were muffled and the air movement was not enough to mean a fully open window. A slight gap, maybe.

He hadn't returned with food. I couldn't have eaten anyway. Isolated aches and pains had merged into a wave of agony that seemed to build, peak and retreat, like the pain of labour only not limited to my lower body. I lay as still as I could, but the muscle spasms were increasing in frequency. Despite the catheter, my bladder felt so full I could burst.

I had to think rationally, otherwise what little strength I had would be depleted by thrashing and crying. It was useless – whatever his motivation, I couldn't do anything until he untied me. I was beginning to suspect it was a brutal punishment for something I had done, only I didn't know what it could be.

When the door eventually opened, I sobbed with relief.

'Shall we try again?' he asked.

I nodded.

'Are you hungry?'

I shook my head.

'Are you in pain?'

I groaned. 'All over.'

I heard a familiar sound: pills being popped from their blisters.

'What is that?'

'Pain relief. They'll help you sleep.'

'I don't want to sleep. What time is it?'

'Seven-thirty. Night.'

I tried something else. 'I need the toilet.'

'No, you don't. There's nothing left in your body.' He put his hand beneath my head. 'Take the pills, Abbie. I won't bring food until we start making progress.'

A catheter and *an enema*? My empty stomach revolted. I turned my face away, moaning. Perhaps the plan was simply to break my will. Maybe I should stop fighting?

'Here.' He pressed the pills into my mouth. 'Water.'

I swished and swallowed and showed him under my tongue. 'Okay, I took the pills. But if you don't untie me, I'll die here.' I fell back onto the pillow. 'I can't last much longer.'

He patted my arm. 'I think I know your limits, and mine.'

'You don't know anything about me.'

240

He got up and moved across the room. A door opened – not the main door but one that came unstuck with a creak. There was a faint tinkle of metal on metal before it was shut again.

'What are you doing?' I craned my neck even though I couldn't see anything.

The bed sagged under his weight. 'I have something for you.'

'What is it?'

'You know, you could leave right now if you wanted,' he said. 'Just tell me to let you go.'

I didn't dare hope. *All of this just to let me go? What was the catch?*

'I don't understand.'

'You would sleep for a while and wake up exactly where you were before – in a motel room.' He cleared his throat. 'In fact, you could have made this decision earlier and saved me the trouble.'

'Yes,' I groaned. 'Please.'

'What could I do to change your mind?'

'Nothing. Let me go.'

'There's this.' He took one of my hands.

Automatically I curled it into a fist, but he straightened my fingers one by one. He lifted my arm and ran my palm across a piece of rough material. My breath caught and both my hands moved of their own volition – it was a skirt, tulle by the texture of it, gathered in stiff folds. My fingers travelled up to find the softer section of bodice.

'Is it pink?' I choked out.

'Yes.'

'Is it hers?'

'Yes.'

He brought the material to my face. It smelled faintly of lavender, but not her.

Breath in my ear. 'Leave or stay, Abbie? It's your call.' Slowly, I shook my head.

'That's what I thought,' he said.

Even if I was allowed to leave, or if somehow I was given the opportunity to kill him – by knife, by heavy object, or simply by pressing my fingers into his eyeballs, into his brain – I couldn't do it until I knew everything. I wanted to know it all. Only then could this be over.

That was my weakness and he knew it all along.

NOW

I woke to the heat and scent of his armpit. He reached across my body to flick a switch – a lamp, maybe. The heavy scent of a spiced, woody aftershave filled my nose and throat and I tried not to gag.

'Good morning, Abbie. Did you sleep well?'

The blindfold kept me in the dark; a light made no difference in my world. The aftershave couldn't mask the smell of my own sweat, and I could feel stickiness between my thighs. I hadn't taken the pill in a couple of days. Was it my period?

He touched my cheek and I writhed in agony and mortification.

'Let me go. *Please.*'

'Tell me what you're thinking.'

I wanted to scratch and spit, but I tried to lie still. 'I'll do whatever you want.'

In response he slid a second pillow behind my head and pressed something cold to my lips.

'What is it?'

'Food. Eat.'

I turned my head. 'What kind of food? Is it drugged?'

'No more drugs if you behave. Eat and I'll take the blindfold off.'

He spoon-fed me what tasted like lukewarm oats. I tried to chew and swallow, but a lump remained in my throat.

'Water.'

'Slowly.'

When I'd finished, I said, 'Take it off.'

'Soon.'

'Now.'

'Later.'

He left and I howled.

I slipped in and out of delirious dreams. I didn't know how much time had passed before he came back, chiding me about the marks on my ankles and wrists.

'Stop fighting. You're only making it worse.'

'Okay.' I forced myself to keep still.

'Okay,' he said.

He released a tie from beneath my chin and the pressure of the blindfold was gone. That's why I couldn't get it off. It was more like a mask. The gag had been uncomfortable but the blindfold was worse – without knowing what was around me, I'd felt even more lost and vulnerable.

The sudden flash of light felt like a skewer. Too bright. I closed my eyes, squinted, let the light through in increments. Gradually the shapes around me came into focus, and I turned my head towards the movement across the room.

This is what he looked like: a person I sensed I had seen before, but not memorable or distinctive enough for me to recall his name or remember where we'd met. Medium height, slim build, brown eyes. Mid to late thirties. Dark hair a shade on the lighter side of black, cut short around the nape and ears but longer on top, a gelled wave in the front. Wearing an open-collared blue shirt and loose denim jeans, no shoes or socks. Dressed up – and down. Trying too hard. His chest was hairy, his jaw clean-shaven but shadowed. He seemed mildly self-conscious standing there: thumbs hooked through empty belt loops, an obscenely bare foot turned to one side. Overinflated chest, paunchy around the middle. Sucking in his gut.

He was unremarkable – forgettable in every way. Not a man I'd be drawn to or repulsed by; someone my eyes would not settle upon in a room full of people, or a person who'd attract my attention without speaking. This man could have passed in and out of my life many times and I would not have noticed.

I turned my head to the side to focus on the space and the objects in it – everything but him. It was still daytime. I lay on a single bed with a white mosquito net hanging above, pulled to the side. The walls were papered, a print with delicate yellow flowers and sage-green leaves; the floors were polished timber the colour of honey, scarred beneath the finish with old cracks and grooves. An old-style ceramic bowl and pitcher and several books were on a white dresser that stood against one wall. There was a wardrobe the same colour as the floor, with panels of blue and yellow stained glass, high ceilings with an intricate plaster cornice and a swaying brass pendant beneath a ceiling rose. Behind my head, a narrow sash window with a metal grate on the outside.

Something about the room was surreal, as if it had been taken from an illustration in a children's picture book. He didn't look like a monster; the room was not the torture chamber I had imagined. If it wasn't for the fact I was shackled to the bed, I could have been lying in a charming guest room in a quaint bed-and-breakfast.

Slowly, I swung my gaze back to him. His only movement was to shift his weight to the other foot. He stayed near the door, watching me carefully, as if I might be dangerous. His hands were square with stumpy fingers; those fingers had touched me, pushed a tube into my urethra. For some reason, the most unsettling thing about him was his bare feet.

I wanted to scream.

'Do you remember, Abbie?'

I'd met him, perhaps more than once. I knew I was expected to remember.

He turned his head to give me his profile. Hooked nose. Full lips. Slight underbite.

'Do you see?'

Despite the fear and the pain, I had the odd urge to be polite and play along until it came to me, the way people do when they meet an old acquaintance. It was not a madness in his eyes that made my blood run cold, but an intentness, as if the game had begun, it was my move, and my life depended on it.

I don't know you.

I don't remember you.

You're a stranger.

I gave a slight nod.

'Then you know why we're finally here,' he said.

'Not… everything. Tell me.'

He slouched and let out a long breath, his gut straining against the shirt. 'You'll do the talking. I want to know your side. *Why?*'

I strained at the ties. 'I want to know where she is. You told me if I came you'd tell me where she *is!*'

He gave me an exasperated look. 'It looks like we're at an impasse. *Six years*, Abbie. Perhaps you need some more time to think about that.'

Confusion clouded my head. Why was he so angry with *me*?

Again he left the room, closing the door behind him and turning a key in the lock on the other side.

Now that I could see, I felt more in control. I lifted my head as far as it would go – only a few inches before my neck started to burn, but I could see the leather ties binding me by the ankles and wrists to the bed. They were worn and well-used, but tough enough to leave my skin raw. The only way to get out of them would be to amputate a limb, or convince him to untie them.

He wasn't gone for long. When he came back, he was carrying a glass of orange juice and a sandwich on a plate.

'Can I get up?' I asked. 'We can't talk like this. I'm in pain. My kidneys hurt – I might be developing a UTI.' It wasn't a lie. The ache in my lower pelvis and back was excruciating. 'And I need a shower. I think I have my period.'

He set the plate and cup on the dresser, pulling a face halfway between concern and disgust. He made a move towards the bed.

'What are you doing?'

'I'll check you,' he said.

I shrank away. 'Don't touch me.'

Sighing, he sat on the end of the bed. 'I think it's time you knew how committed I am.' He started undoing the buttons on his shirt.

I blocked him out. Tears squeezed from the corners of my eyes as I twisted my head from side to side. 'No, no, *no*.'

'Look.'

'No.'

Nothing happened. He didn't touch me.

'Abbie, look.'

I opened my eyes. He was facing away. I gaped at his bare back – hairy across the shoulder blades, gone to fat under his arms – and my daughter's image stared back, her face more lifelike than any sketch.

'What's your name?'

He spun around, eyes dark with hurt.

'Tell me your name!'

I thought I'd hyperventilate and stop breathing, until I realised it was the opposite: it wasn't that I couldn't get enough air, I just kept sucking it in without letting any go. The sound I made was horrible – a grating wheeze, like a broken whistle – and he panicked.

In seconds he'd untied the wrist restraints and I could sit up. He tried to push my head between my knees and I fought him, slapping and biting, forcing him to retreat. When I'd caught my breath, I reached for the buckles around my ankles.

Groaning, he slipped away through the door, locking it behind him again.

He was right to be afraid. I *was* dangerous.

I stayed on the bed for long minutes, frozen. I couldn't hear any sounds coming from inside the house. Outside, the birds sang and the sky was a perfect cerulean blue.

Lizard brain, Murray called it, when a person stopped thinking of the past, the future or the consequences, and acted purely in the moment. I'd forgotten why I was here – I only wanted not to be here anymore. Knowing was suddenly less important than getting away, and this most recent development only made me more desperate.

It was the tattoo, a mirror image of mine, with Sarah's face and the cherub's wings. The detail was extraordinary. The work had to be Steve's. *But how?* My tattoo had been a spontaneous original, improvised in sections over weeks. If it was Steve's, it seemed unlikely that he could have remembered every detail. Did they know each other? Had Steve been part of it?

There were too many pieces and none fitted.

I massaged the raw skin on my wrists and flexed my muscles, testing them. With an eye on the door, I hunched over to check inside my underwear. No blood, just leakage from the catheter. It dawned on me that he must have medical expertise. A doctor?

Wincing, I reached between my legs, exhaled and pulled the catheter tube out. Too quickly. There was lingering discomfort and the urge to pee. Dark urine spilled and beaded on the white sheet.

I stretched each limb carefully, working some blood back into the muscles. When I'd regained some strength, I stood slowly. Weak, but not too dizzy. The urine bag was hanging on the underside of the bed frame from an S-shaped steel hook – I detached it and jammed the hook between my middle finger and forefinger, the way women carry keys at night as a weapon. It wasn't particularly sharp but it was better than nothing.

I burst into action, circling the room like a wild animal. I checked the window and door for a way out: the grate was immovable and the door was locked. Apart from more dusty books in a drawer, the dresser was empty; the wardrobe contained a garment inside a dry cleaner's plastic bag and a stale bag of lavender potpourri. Sarah's dress was not there.

If I called through the window it might set him off, so I pressed my face to the glass, trying to get the widest field of vision.

A narrow stony path lead to an orchard. I recognised apple trees, maybe plum and almond too. Beyond the orchard, a row of tall pines bordered either a fence line or a driveway, but it didn't appear wide enough to be a road. Were there neighbours nearby? None that I could see through the small window. The grass in the yard was tall and wild, the tips browning off under the sun, but the fruit trees, covered with white netting, looked well-tended and recently pruned. A brightly coloured lorikeet had found its way inside the net – I watched it flap crazily then flutter to the ground, panting and distressed.

To the left of the orchard I could just glimpse the corner of an aluminium shed and the rear of a red ride-on mower. To the right there was an old Hills hoist set in a diamond of patchy grass. Four cheerful tea towels hung on the line, the kind people buy as souvenirs, but they were too far away to read the print.

This was not an abandoned place. It was a home.

Warily, I put down the hook. I sniffed the sandwich and pulled the bread slices apart to check the contents. Ham, tomato and some kind of pickled relish. I scraped off the relish, ate the sandwich and drank the juice, my back pressed against the door.

The chafed skin on my wrists and ankles was less livid, but my lower back still ached and the urge to pee was getting stronger. For lack of anything else, I squatted over the pitcher – on inspection my urine was a strange dark colour, possibly tainted with blood. The juice had taken the edge off my thirst but I craved fresh, cold water.

I picked up the hook. 'Hello? Are you there?' I said through the door.

I held my breath and waited.

No reply.

I crossed the room, pulled the curtain aside and tested the bars with a shake: they were solid. I could smash the window, but that wouldn't take care of the grate. The bars were pitted and corroding, speckled with rust, but they'd probably been there for at least fifty years.

In the furthest corner of the room, nearest the door, I spotted an irregularity in the floorboards. It looked as if they had been cut to make an opening around half a metre square. The gaps had been refilled and smoothed.

I bent down and pressed my fingernail into it. Putty. Fairly soft.

How much time did I have?

I used the hook to scratch. The putty came away easily, but the sound it made was horribly loud in the quiet. I stopped once I'd completed one section, slid the hook into the gap I'd made and turned it sideways to lift a single piece of wood. The floorboard creaked, popped and gave way.

As I set it aside a rush of foul air escaped; I coughed and drew back, my hand across my nose and mouth. The space under the board was dark, but I knew the smell.

Death.

The full horror of what I might discover hit and I scuttled

backwards, trembling all over. This was my nightmare and I'd walked willingly into it. Sour orange juice burned my throat. I couldn't think, couldn't reason – it was like trying to work a thousand thoughts through a pinhole, but I kept coming back to this: my baby – my baby, buried under the house.

This was what you wanted. You wanted to know.

Outside, I heard the awful flapping as the lorikeet continued its futile attempts to escape, launching itself at the net, only to fall again – lured by the fruit, imprisoned in a cage.

Breathe.

In and out. In and out.

Sarah has been gone for six years. It can't be.

But he brought me here to find her. It could be.

I had no idea how much time had passed. I stared at the hole in the floor, my arms wrapped around my knees. If this was knowing, I didn't want it, but I didn't want to die. I wanted to go back and undo everything I'd done, to hold the people I loved again.

Flap, flap, flap.

There were fruit trees in my parents' backyard too. When my father was alive, he'd stand in the yard in his pyjamas and scare the birds away from the fruit by blasting a ridiculous air horn. I missed him. I missed the shape of him in his old chair, and the oily patch inside his ute where his flyaway hair had rubbed against the roof. I grieved him when he died, I did, but I wondered where this fresh pain was coming from, emerging like a living thing that had been put on ice.

I sobbed. And I raged. It wasn't fair. This stupid, stinking life wasn't fair. I wasn't a terrible person; I never hurt anybody. I never took somebody's child away from them.

The hole in the floor beckoned. I inched closer to it.

My parents' house had similar sections of cut floorboards. It might not be sinister at all. It could be a termite inspection point, a place to spray the poison. Maybe an animal had crawled under the house and died.

I got to work again with the hook. *Scrape, scrape.* A second board popped out. Shaking, I leaned down to peer in: dirt, stones, pillars of wood, and the foul, fruity odour, which didn't smell as bad as it had at first. The hole was no deeper than two feet, maybe less. The crawlspace extended another three or four feet before the shadows took over. Enough room to crawl under the house on my belly – but where would I end up? Was there a way out?

I reached in, leaning my head and shoulder into the space. When I turned to face the outside wall of the room, stripes of dim light appeared: cracks between the outer boards. But no exit.

A dull thud echoed through the floor.

I jumped, hitting my head. I scrambled out, brushing the clumps of putty into the hole and the dust from my clothes – *his clothes* – and dropped the floorboards back into position as quietly as I could. If he looked, it would be obvious they'd been tampered with, but it was another thing I couldn't undo.

A door slammed. I felt the vibration through my feet. Terrified, I moved towards the door, changed my mind, darted to the bed. I sat, drawing my knees to my chest. I kept my eyes on the door handle.

Tap, tap.

'Open the window.'

I spun around. He had his face and one hand to the glass. I thought about jabbing the hook between the bars, taking out his eye, or using my nails if the hook didn't work.

He tapped again. 'We don't have a lot of time. We need to get things moving.'

'Just let me go,' I begged. 'People will be looking for me.'

'I need to be able to trust you first.' He gave a sad smile. 'They're not looking for you. Even if they were, they wouldn't know where to start. Open the window.'

I turned wild eyes to the hole in the floor. If I could push the wardrobe or dresser in front of the door, there still wasn't enough time to make the opening wide enough to crawl through. I turned the latch and slid up the sash – just a few inches and no further – and moved to the foot of the bed.

He smiled. 'I don't want to hurt you. I just need you to stop fighting so I can make you understand.'

'So talk.'

'You must have questions –'

'Oh, you have no fucking idea.' I noticed my tongue was thickening, my mouth getting dry.

'Ask me one,' he said. 'One question. Then I have some of my own.'

'Did you drug me again?' My words were getting slow. 'You said you wouldn't.'

'I'm guessing that's not your question.'

I had a thousand questions but my limbs were growing heavy, a familiar fog drifting in.

Where is she?

What did you do to her?

How did she die?

Did she fight?

Did she call for me? How do I know you?

What is your name?

Where am I did you drug me again why can't you just tell me what happened tell me where she is tell me where she is tell me where she is –

But all I could manage was, 'Why?'

The fog was taking over. I felt drunk. Suddenly he seemed ridiculous, hiding behind the bars.

'You're pathetic,' I slurred.

He changed. His eyes flashed dark and he disappeared from the window.

Maybe he would hit me, or worse. I wouldn't know if he did – I was already drifting away. He was pathetic, but he was capable of kidnap and murder too. I'd have to remember that for later.

NOW

When I came to I was lying on the bed, still unrestrained. The light outside the window had faded; the crickets were chirping. It felt as if I'd been here for weeks, but there was so much missing time it could have been just hours. I woke feeling less disoriented than before – maybe he'd given me a lower dose of sedative, or it was a different kind. I checked for evidence that he'd been in the room or done something to me – I seemed to be untouched, but the lamp was on, illuminating the ceiling and casting the corners of the room into deep shadow.

I smelled the rank odour of sweat, piss and stale human and knew it was me.

A scratching at the door.

'Move to the bed, Abbie,' he called.

'I'm here,' I said.

'Stay there, otherwise we'll be back to square one.'

He came in carrying a tray of food and left the door open as he placed the tray on the dresser. He picked up the empty glass and plate, his eyes hooded and anxious. 'It's getting late. Eat, sleep. Tomorrow we'll try again.'

'Try what, exactly?' I said.

He ignored the question and moved to block the open door. 'Eat.'

I eyed the tray. Bottled water. Bread, soup, some kind of pudding with custard and a plastic spoon. Prison food.

'No more drugs. I can't function. You can't expect me to do whatever it is you want if I'm out of it all the time.'

'Then stop resisting.'

'Then let me go.'

He glanced at the corner where I'd lifted the floorboards. I held my breath, but he swooped forward to pick up the urine bag lying half under the bed. 'I'll let you out when you stop behaving like an animal.'

'Stop treating me like one. Let me use the bathroom at least.'

His nose twitched like a rabbit.

My gaze snapped to the dresser. 'I pissed in the jug.'

He emitted a soft groan of anguish, his eyes darting from place to place as if he'd been presented with too many tasks at once; if his hands weren't already full I would have expected them to start flapping. Decision made, he rushed for the door and set the glass, plate and bag outside.

I made my move. By the time he turned around again I was off the bed, swaying from the sudden rush of blood to my head. There was nothing I could use as a weapon apart from the hook, and I couldn't find it. For lack of anything else I grabbed the jug.

He backed away as if it was acid, his nostrils flared like a frightened animal. 'Don't do it, Abbie.'

'Fuck you.' I raised the jug as if to fling the contents at him. Urine splashed on the floor.

There was a moment of contained violence on both sides as we squared off, then he did something unexpected: he gave a sweet, sad smile and said, 'You're not the same, Abbie. What's happened to you? It doesn't have to be like this.'

I froze. He had me mixed up with someone else.

'Leave the jug by the door and I'll dispose of it. Good night.'

I wasn't fast enough to react – he was gone. The lock clicked.

Still shaking, I twisted the top off the litre bottle of water and heard the satisfying crack of an unbroken seal. I gulped almost half of it, then realised I should ration the rest. Blobs of grease were beginning to form in the soup, but I was starving. I ate it all. The bread and pudding, too.

For the first time in days I felt better, but I would not be grateful. I wouldn't. I kept the jug of piss next to the bed and the plastic cutlery under the pillow.

Breakfast came via another tray in the morning. He opened the door without warning, slid the tray across the floor and left again. There was bran cereal, stewed fruit with cream and a mug of lukewarm tea. Again I ate everything. I craved calories and I was now less concerned that the food or drink might be drugged – at least while I was sedated I couldn't think or feel.

An hour after eating, there had been no effect. My head was clear. Stretching had relieved my sore muscles, and the pain in my lower back and kidneys had eased. I paced a hundred or more laps, to and fro across the room, to take my mind off my aching bladder.

When he finally knocked and peered around the door, he said I could use the toilet. I could have cried with relief.

'First, stack both trays and return the cutlery. Bring everything including the jug and leave them here.' He pointed to the spot where he stood and stepped back.

Red-faced, I took the spoons from under the pillow. I did as he asked and meekly placed the trays on the floor.

'All the doors are locked. You can't get out, so don't bother trying.'

I nodded. He had no weapon, only his hands. But I had none either.

He shuffled sideways, beckoning me to follow.

For the first time, I got a sense of the layout of the house. At one end of the long, central hallway there was a solid-looking front door; at the other, an archway leading to what looked like a kitchen and the only source of light. The floorboards were polished and the walls were bare; the hallway was airless and dark. We passed six closed doors, three on each side, including the one he opened on the right. Inside was a toilet and a small basin with a hand towel hanging from a metal ring.

'There's soap, a toothbrush and toothpaste on the basin,' he said. 'I'll wait.'

'I need some privacy.'

'I'll wait,' he repeated. 'Don't drink from the tap. There's fresh water in the cup.'

I locked the hook and eye on the inside of the door and felt safer, but it wasn't as if I could stay there for any length of time with him waiting outside. The window was no bigger than a cat flap; even if I managed to squeeze through, it would take too long.

For now I'd just do as he asked.

I peed loudly without holding back. Despite my churning stomach there was nothing more. I cleaned my face and hands, under my armpits, and soaped up the hand towel to wipe between my legs. These small courtesies made me feel absurdly grateful – like when he brought the trays of food – but I reminded myself he was manipulating me, wheedling me into compliance.

I brushed my teeth. The moment I rinsed and spat, he knocked.

'Finished?'

I unlatched the hook.

'Get your shoes and come with me,' he said, leading me back to the bedroom.

I put on my sneakers. 'Where are we going?'

'You'll see.' He lifted a lightweight rain jacket from a hook near the front door and handed it to me. 'It's misty out. Put this on, but back to front.'

Outside. He unlocked the front door simply by turning the deadbolt. *No key.*

I slipped my arm inside one sleeve. I broke into a sweat at the thought of being out in the open. First chance I got I'd run.

'I said back to front. Like this.'

He turned the jacket around and zipped it at my back. I was confused until we were outside and he pulled the rain hood over my face. I felt his fingers at my nape, tying the string. Immediately everything was dark and my breath steamed the inside of the hood.

'Is this necessary?'

'Yes,' he said, and tugged me forward by the elbow. 'Three steps. Ready?'

One, two, three.

Slippery gravel, then something soft, like mulch. We were climbing a gentle slope; the ground was uneven, my progress unsteady. I heard wind in the trees above. The air was pine-scented. No bird sounds. When I stumbled, he put an arm around my waist. I didn't want him touching me but there was no other choice.

We reached a crest and descended, but not far. I had counted my steps from the house to where we stopped: almost a hundred and fifty, so we were probably more than a hundred metres from the house.

He untied the hood.

We were in a clearing, set in a circle of straggly pines. There was a campfire pit and four rough seats made from pine stumps. I could not see the house, or any other signs of habitation or life.

'What is this?'

'Have a seat.' He gestured to a stump.

'I'd rather stand if you don't mind.'

'I mind.'

I sat, shivering.

The ground was covered with a layer of pine needles, undisturbed but for our footprints on the path. Weak shafts of sunlight made it through the canopy of the trees, only to disappear in drifts of mist. The air was thin and I found it hard to breathe – or maybe it was rising panic that made my throat tighter and my chest constrict. The way he stood with his head bowed and his fingers steepled gave me the sense that he was about to perform some kind of ceremony.

The dread I'd felt when he pulled the hood over my face grew stronger.

'I can't begin unless you close your eyes.'

I pretended to shut them, leaving the faintest slit, praying my fluttering eyelashes wouldn't give me away. My muscles were rigid, poised for flight. One step towards me and I would run, but he moved in the opposite direction to reach behind a tree.

He was holding something. A weapon of some kind? No. A guitar.

He sat, clearing his throat, then played a chord. A brief hush before he started singing a familiar song, and a whisper of memory returned. I remembered the song, but not the circumstances. Wait – a house, a girl. It was Cass, dancing, her arms swaying above her head. Or was the girl me?

When I opened my eyes properly, I saw his were half-closed, and he was smiling as he played. I was yanked from the memory to a disturbing realisation: this was a courtship ritual. The song was a serenade.

He finished on an off-key chord and set the guitar aside.

'Do you remember?'

'I'm trying,' I said, but I was too tense, too afraid. All I had were faded images from another time and a strong feeling of déjà vu. Nothing was making sense.

He approached to squat in front of me and took my hands,

turning them over and tracing a finger across the paler skin where my wedding ring had been.

'This will fade,' he said.

I struck out.

My fist connected with his temple, a sickening impact that sent jarring pain through my wrist, a twanging vibration into my shoulder. All the frustration and hopelessness of the past months in one moment of blind, fluid, unthinking reaction, and it worked. He went down with a groan as if he'd been hit with a bat to the knees, his body limp, one leg bent at an awkward angle.

I took off, running blind.

There was no trail where I was headed, only thick pine needles and fallen branches. I went up because we had come down, but when I made out the shape of a white house in the distance I had to assume it was his house.

I made a sharp turn. I wasn't going back there. I'd rather be lost in the woods.

My head pounded and my eyes were streaming; I could barely see in front of me. Branches whipped my face. I gasped for breath, willing my weakened muscles to move faster. I shook off the burn in my calves and powered to the crest of a hill – from the top there was nothing but pine trees, thousands in rows, rising and falling across the hills and valleys, like a painting.

I glanced back. The mist swirled, closing in around me. I skidded down an embankment and climbed over a platform of granite rock. Through a strip of tall grass and across a dry creek, up a steep incline and into a newer section of pines spread more widely apart.

The forest seemed to stretch forever. I could see no end to it.

Now I heard him coming, crashing through the trees, calling my name.

A stitch caught in my side; I kept running, bent sideways,

pressing my fist into it. The ground flattened out and the going was easier, but I was getting short of breath. I stopped to wipe the sweat from my eyes — my wrist came away streaked with watery blood. I couldn't see him behind me, but there was smoke in the distance, a thin spiral rising above the distant tree line.

I headed towards it, crawling on all fours when I lost my balance. Beyond a row of gum trees, I ducked between the wires of a fence to find a dirt road on the other side, fresh tyre tracks in the mud.

People, this close the whole time.

A sprawling modern log home set in the side of a hill, and two people on horseback cantering figure-eights in a sandy ring, one a lean teenage boy, the other a younger-looking girl with a blonde ponytail rippling down her back. The house was less than a kilometre from the one I'd escaped. It was like believing I was stranded in the middle of an ocean and diving from a sinking boat, only to find all along the water was scarcely a foot deep.

I stumbled along the last fifty-metre stretch of driveway. Before I could regain enough breath to scream for help, a woman emerged from behind a nearby shed, wiping her hands on a dirty rag. She took in my appearance, my wild hair and scratched cheeks.

'Can I help you?'

'I need to use your phone,' I gasped.

'Where did you come from? What's going on?'

'*Please*, it's an emergency.'

Abruptly she called out, 'That's enough for today. Head down to the stables. Make sure you walk those horses down.' She reached out and led me to a bench seat on the porch. 'Put your head between your knees. I'll make a call.'

'The police, please,' I begged. 'Tell them where I am. I don't know where I am.'

262

She nodded, her mouth pinched, and went inside through a screen door. I did as she said and lowered my head between my knees. I'd forgotten to tell her my name.

Minutes later she came back out carrying a glass of water. 'Here.' I drank.

'Would you like some more?'

She seemed nervous. I supposed anyone would if a deranged stranger had burst out of the forest near their house, screaming for help. But there was something not right about her.

'No, but thank you.' I handed her the empty glass. My heart wouldn't slow down. 'How long did they say they'd be?'

Instead of answering, she stuck out her hand. 'I'm Daniella. Dani for short.' She smiled and it didn't reach her eyes. 'Abbie?'

Stunned, I couldn't reply.

'It is Abbie, isn't it?' She said it gently, but there was fear there too.

'How did you know that?'

My vision narrowed to a tunnel. A car was making its way up the driveway.

'Look, I don't know what's going on, but –' Her head snapped up. 'That was fast.'

'You didn't call the police, did you?' I said flatly.

She shook her head. 'I know detox is hard, but you should let him look after you.'

Detox? What the *fuck*?

I groaned. 'You have no idea what you've done, do you?'

'Well!' She put a hand to her throat. 'I'm just trying to help.'

The car pulled up and he leaped out. In quick strides he was on the porch and grabbing me by the elbow.

'I just called you and left a message,' the woman said, rattled.

'I'm so sorry this has happened. You know she hasn't been well.' For the first time his composure was slipping.

'I thought we were set for tomorrow?'

His fingers dug into the soft flesh around my tricep. 'An unexpected change of plans. It's taking longer than I thought.'

'Given what's happened, do you want me to –'

He cut her off. 'Another day will be good, Dani, if it's not too much trouble.'

'Okay, that's fine,' she said, but clearly it wasn't. 'You have a good night.'

I wanted to scream at her, but it would have done no good. I knew she wouldn't help. Whatever he'd told her, it must have been bad enough for her to throw a woman in trouble to the sharks.

He steered me around and dug a knuckle in the small of my back.

'No, no, no,' I whimpered, pulling away. I glanced back.

Dani was still standing there, watching us.

He hissed, 'Stop this now, or you'll ruin everything.'

I shrugged off his hand and turned to face him. 'I don't know you. If we've met, I don't recall the circumstances. I don't remember that stupid song and I've only been pretending to know you because that's what you seem to expect. So if there's something you want to say to me, you'd better say it – all of it – because you have one move left. I'm tired of being afraid. I don't care if I die,' I said, and his face lost all colour. 'Or maybe it will be you.'

NOW

He gripped my arm as we entered through a door that led straight into the kitchen. Once inside, he toed his shoes off on the mat near the door and lined them up neatly, frowning when I left mine on. There were four other pairs – sneakers, thongs, thick-soled leather boots and a pair of white sandals.

I looked around. The cupboards were painted eggshell blue; much of the space was taken up by an enormous wooden country table and a sideboard. I counted ten chairs. The objects in the room were unnervingly feminine: ruffled curtains, floral-patterned crockery, delicate doilies and ornate silverware.

He seemed calm but I could smell his agitation, the pungency of fresh sweat. The kitchen was roomy enough, but the space felt cramped. I moved to the opposite side of the huge table, positioning it like a shield.

'Does your family live here too?' I asked. 'When you're not abducting people?'

He paused for a moment, his lips twisting. 'It's a rental. I needed somewhere close and private.'

'Isolated, you mean.'

He gestured. 'Please, have a seat.'

Without turning his back to me, he switched on a kettle and spooned tea leaves into a pot. He took two cups from the cupboard above his head and set them on a tray with a bowl of sugar, along with a square of something wrapped in a tea towel, then opened a drawer and drew out a blunt-looking butter knife.

Waving the knife, he said, 'This is not exactly how things were supposed to be, you know.'

My legs were shaking. I couldn't make them stop. 'I really don't know,' I said as dispassionately as I could manage.

'I hoped you would remember.' He placed the tray in the middle of the table. 'Or have you told so many lies you don't know what's true anymore?'

We were in an alternate dimension: this pretty country kitchen with its gauzy curtains, dappled sunshine making patterns on the floor, the kettle emitting a low whistle – and a psychopath unwrapping a fruitcake and preparing a pot of Earl Grey tea.

He was insane.

He filled the teapot with boiling water, waiting until I sat down before pulling out a chair for himself.

I could pour the hot tea all over him. I could gouge out his eye with the teaspoon, or flip the table and run.

'Allow me,' I said, and reached for the handle.

He eyed me for a moment before settling back in his chair. 'Don't do anything you'll regret, Abbie.'

'Oh, I won't have regrets.' I smiled.

He ran his eyes over my face and body. 'You're still beautiful.' I snatched my hand back and crossed my arms over my chest, trying to hide a shiver of revulsion. Strangely, I no longer felt threatened. I sensed he didn't want to hurt me – it would only happen if I pushed him too far. It was as if I was another pretty thing in the kitchen, something to be admired, adored.

'Are you going to pour the tea? It'll get cold.'

I lifted the teapot. He watched my movements carefully as I poured the tea into his cup, then into my own. I stirred, fingers trembling, and dropped the teaspoon onto the saucer with a clink. 'You need to talk.'

'But Abbie,' he said, giving a helpless shrug. 'That's all I've ever wanted.' He got up. 'Wait here.'

He left the kitchen. I heard his footsteps in the hall, the creak of a door, something heavy falling to the floor. I felt my racing pulse, the stiff patches of dried sweat under my arms – if there was time enough to escape again it was fast ticking away – and he was back.

'I want you to see these.'

He placed an album on the table in front of me. It was almost two inches thick. The way he leaned forward to watch my reaction, his eyes hungry as if he was feeding on my fear, made me recoil from it. I pressed my hands on the edge of the table and pushed back, the chair legs scraping against the floor.

'Look inside.'

'No.'

He sighed and, before I could close my eyes, flipped the cover.

Paralysed, I braced myself for something horrific.

Adrenaline shot through my body before I could take in the first image: a close-up of Sarah asleep, around four months old, her face squashed against someone's shoulder.

I pulled the chair closer.

Another, this time taken from a distance. The person holding Sarah was me, striding along a street, my hand visible at the nape of her neck. More of her as a baby, wearing the second-hand clothes I'd bought for her from the op shop, lying in her pram outside the fruit-and-vegetable market. In one photo, I recognised my own feet in my favourite pink thongs. Sarah, sitting on a rug in the park, smiling, drool stringing from her chin. More close-ups: a rare, full-faced smile, directed at the camera, followed by a sideways grin with a glimmer of a top tooth.

I took a shaky breath and exhaled slowly. I turned another page.

Sarah again, just over twelve months old, at the beach, her chubby legs buried in the sand. Standing, feeding the ducks by the lake, a bag of bread clutched in her fist. Eating a biscuit, her cheeks smeared with chocolate. Despite the strangeness of the images, they were familiar, and my first thought was that he'd stolen my photos, or possibly Martine's, or Jess's. But there were so *many*. Maybe he had made copies and returned them before we knew they were missing.

It took several pages before I worked it out: these were all images from my life – *our* life – but there was something different about them. I had not taken these photos. Nor had anyone I knew. Some were real memories brought to life, but as far as I recalled, photos had not been taken at the time. In others, the places were familiar and I had similar images at home in my boxes, but in these the perspective was altered.

The next page revealed what my muddled mind already knew, but couldn't accept: the perspective was that of a voyeur.

There was a photo of me lying on a towel in the backyard of the Rosewood flat, topless. Sarah was sitting in her paddling pool, a metre away. Three more of the same scene, but from different angles, followed by a close-up of my tattoo. Another zoomed in on the curve of my breasts, pressed against the towel. Yet another of my face in profile, head resting on my folded arms, my eyes closed.

The tension in my body reached breaking point. My breath was ragged. I turned the pages faster, faster, tearing at the plastic sheets, scattering the photos across the table. He tried to gather them up, but I stood and lunged at the picture of my breasts, yanking it from his hands and ripping it in half.

'Abbie, *stop*.'

I flung the pieces at him and shook my head, tearing at my hair. 'I don't understand. I mean, seriously. What the *fuck*?'

He was breathing hard, the whites of his eyes showing. 'These aren't yours to destroy,' he said coldly, still gathering up the photos one by one. 'I'm shocked. This is awful behaviour.'

'Why are you shocked? Are you telling me you followed us since she was a baby – are you out of your fucking mind?'

I picked up the album and threw it across the table, where it landed open on the last double-page spread. I flew at him, slapping and kicking. He moved swiftly aside and twisted my arm behind my back, wrenching it so hard it took my breath away. As he shoved me against the wall with one hand, the fingers of his other hand dug into the straining tendons of my neck.

My vision started to go black.

'Stop it,' he muttered in my ear.

I went limp – not by choice, but because my legs wouldn't hold me up.

He took my full weight, dragging me across the floor to my chair. 'Please. Sit down and we can try again to talk about it. I don't want to hurt you but I'm not sure I have much patience left.'

I slumped into the chair, all the fight gone out of me. My head throbbed and my throat was sore. In the scuffle, I'd gouged him with my fingernails – a trickle of blood ran down his forearm in a perfectly straight line and dripped from his middle finger.

He wet a tissue under the tap and dabbed at the blood. 'I know how it looks. I expected the police would find me quickly, to be honest, but they didn't. And that's your fault, isn't it?'

'How is it my fault?' I said dully. 'I didn't know you were stalking us.'

'They didn't find me because you didn't tell them about me. You didn't tell *anyone* about me. How could they find a suspect who doesn't *exist*?'

I smacked the table to punctuate every word. 'I. Don't. Know. Who. You. Are.'

His intake of breath made me look up. My words had enraged him. His hands were fists, his lips bloodless, his entire body rigid with the effort of trying to control himself.

'Why can't you just admit what you did?' His voice was low and hoarse, pleading.

'Why can't *you*!' I screeched. I reached across the table intending to throw the nearest object, but my eye was caught by Sarah's face. I pulled the album to me. 'Wait.' I ran my fingers over the images. 'Is this –?'

He hissed, 'Now do you see?'

In the first photo Sarah was in the back seat of a car, asleep, her mouth open, half her face in deep shadow. The delicate skin beneath her closed eyes was puffy, bruised-looking, and outside the car window was a white portico leading to the front door of a house. In the next photo she was staring at the horizon as if looking for something or someone, her skin glowing with the colours of the sunset. It was the kind of candid shot taken without the subject knowing – they all were – but it wasn't her sadness I found unsettling.

These photos had been taken in places I didn't recognise. I barely recognised Sarah – her hair was shorter and several shades lighter. Her ears were pierced and her front teeth had grown. It was like looking at the police sketches, an altered reality, except this time I didn't feel a disconnect.

This was what she should have looked like.

I gagged, hit with a fresh wave of horror. The drawing on the wedding card – it *was* hers? The lines were cleaner, the writing clearer, because she was older when she'd drawn it? The only thing that had kept me sane some days was knowing the statistics: it was likely Sarah hadn't lived long after the abduction. My family and I had to endure the aftermath, but her suffering was over.

'You kept her?' I whispered.

He nodded.

I imagined her gagged, tied up, locked in a room, without the resilience or strength of an adult and with all the confusion and distress of a six-year-old girl. Was it months? Years? Did she hate me when she called and I didn't come?

I sobbed openly, aghast that his only response was to smile as if this was all coming to a predetermined and satisfying end.

'*How long did you keep her?*'

'You know how long, Abbie.' He leaned close. '*Six years.*'

NOW

'Tell me from the beginning,' I said. 'Tell me everything.'

He'd finished putting the photos away. Now he was preparing another pot of tea. Watching him go through his rituals was maddening, but I didn't want to break the slowly tightening thread that pulled my story towards his.

'But, Abbie, you were there. Don't you remember?' he said.

My mind was a queue of responses, none of them wise or rational. I didn't remember. Had he mistaken me for someone else? How could I keep him talking without making him angry?

'It was a long time ago,' I said carefully. 'I don't know what happened *before*.'

He sat down. 'Well, now we're going way back.'

He grew up on a four-hundred-acre property, over ten kilometres from the nearest neighbour. His parents ran sheep and a few hundred head of beef cattle. His mother was Spanish and for forty years had refused to speak a word of English; his father flew a light plane, seeding and crop-dusting, and ferrying locals to regional airports for cash on the side. From a young age he knew the farm was doomed – lack of feed, ongoing drought, low beef and wool prices – and by the age of nine he was already dead-eyed about putting starving stock out of its misery.

He worked hard towards his tertiary admission score, earning a three-year scholarship at university. At the time, his ambition was to leave the failing farm forever, finish his degree, start his own business, marry a nice girl.

He picked up a spoon, sugared and stirred his tea. 'But you weren't a nice girl, were you, Abbie?'

It seemed best not to answer the question, but to throw vague questions like a Magic 8-ball.

'What happened next?'

He was twenty-one, an IT student, musician (guitar, bass guitar), gamer and one of four tenants sharing a house at number seven, Gordon Road – a complete dive but it was close to the city and all they could afford. He drew the shortest straw and took the smallest room, a converted sunroom at the rear of the house. It was quieter back there, except for the clanging of the copper pipes sticking out of the wall. The previous tenants had left behind a red Holden motor in the dining room, a shed full of hydroponic gear, a Commodore on bricks in the middle of the front lawn, a flea infestation and a cat.

'Fleas?' I said. 'A cat?'

An old memory surfaced. *Itching, burning. A trail of insect bites.*

He went on, describing himself as gifted and brilliant. He was also lonely. He didn't particularly enjoy the company of his sharehouse mates but occasionally he would make an effort: dust off his guitar, down a few beers in the backyard, pretend he found them entertaining.

The first time they all got drunk together they taped him to the streetlight pole in front of the house, but more fool them because electrical tape stretched dead easy. He waited until they'd passed out and let down Andy's tyres. The next day he locked the cat in Leroy's room until it pissed and shat everywhere, and the following weekend he sold Mike a bag of cocaine cut with laundry powder – just enough to make him feel like crap for a couple of days. He was doing time, working in a bar, selling weed on the side, studying hard and waiting for the two-year lease to run out. On weekends he only left his bedroom and the gaming console to use the bathroom.

'Then everything changed,' he said.

A shiver ran along my spine. 'How did it change?'

'You came.'

He had been strumming away, trying to find the rhythm of a song, while Leroy and Andy wrestled and yelled over the top of him. He thought he'd lose it right there, pack his stuff and leave, regardless of whether or not he had a place to sleep that night. He remembered Andy's expression when the screen door opened and a girl wearing heels fell down the back steps – astonishment, as if he thought his housemates had organised a stripper for his birthday. Except they hadn't: the girl wasn't a stripper – in fact there were two of them – and it was all a big mistake. Wrong party.

The first girl was all in for a few drinks, but the second one wanted to leave. Someone convinced them to stay. He mustered the courage to sing again because the silence was awkward. At first he couldn't tell them apart. They were both beautiful: long-legged, sparkly-eyed, high on something.

Abbie and Cass.

'I couldn't look at you, you were so beautiful,' he said softly.

I was trying to conjure images. Faces, events. I pictured his fingers, strumming. Heard his pitchy voice.

'You were shy,' I said.

He didn't drink much that night, maybe two beers. The others were intoxicated, including the girls. Midnight came and went. He hadn't spoken more than two words to either of them, but he'd wanted to. He had stayed up late two nights running and could barely keep his eyes open, so when the other guests left, he saw them out and sneaked away to bed.

His father used to say the singer/guitarist always got the girl, and he was right. Around 2 o'clock, the bedroom door opened. A figure slipped inside and closed the door again. He heard the whisper of clothing as it fell to the floor. The sheets were pulled back; cool air rushed in.

'You smelled of cigarettes and perfume,' he said. 'I've never forgotten it. But when I woke, you were standing there with your shoes in your hand. What did you say, Abbie?' he asked in a voice like silk.

'Thanks for everything,' I choked out. 'It's been lovely.'

I thought I knew what was coming, and it made me feel ill.

He had no idea how to find Abbie. He found the red poncho on the couch where her flatmate Cass had slept, and contemplated going house to house with it, like Cinderella's slipper.

Only it wasn't Cass on the couch. It was me. But when he woke, I was the one in the bedroom holding Cass's shoes; it had been Cass in his bed, but it was my face he saw and remembered.

For almost two weeks he left the poncho swinging on a hanger on the front porch – he figured Cass might come back for it, and she'd lead him to Abbie. He'd left a note in the pocket in case he wasn't there when she came.

She never came.

He found Abbie by accident while he was working at the bar. He glanced up from serving a four-deep line of customers to see her, the girl he'd been looking for, caught in the cage like a frightened bird. Moments after she came down there was a fight with her friends. When he saw her go, he left without finishing his shift and followed her home.

I covered my face with my hands. *It was him.*

'I tried to do things properly,' he said.

The night he followed her he didn't introduce himself – he made sure she got home safely and went back to the unit and knocked on the door the following day. Nobody answered, so he went back again several days later. This time the flatmate was there. She looked different – shorter, bright red hair – and she gave no indication that she recognised him. She told him nobody called Cass or Abbie lived there and closed the door.

Oh, Cass.

He left a note in the letterbox but nobody called. He started to worry he really had knocked on the wrong unit, so he kept watch over a few days. One Saturday night, three girls came back to the unit. In the darkness he couldn't be sure if one of them was her. They closed the blinds and he wasn't able to see through the window, so he went around to the adjoining property and climbed the fence into the backyard.

I gasped.

I heard a thud, as if someone or something had dropped softly to the ground.

My fear was beginning to make sense now.

A white, shocked face appeared at the window. It was her. It was Abbie. He knew he'd scared her – he didn't want her to know the intruder was him, so he left it even longer before he tried to contact her again. This time he found out where she worked by following her onto a bus. He booked a lane at the swimming centre that day, and for the following four Wednesdays, in the hope that he might find a way to renew their relationship. If only she could see him again, talk to him, she'd remember.

But Abbie rarely had a moment between classes. He settled for watching her with the kids as he swam slow laps, waiting for his chance. One day she'd even smiled at him and said hello. Someone else was watching Abbie too – a big guy, another instructor. A few times she'd got into his car after her classes. He was there when the instructor followed Abbie into the change room, and when the instructor emerged minutes later, white-faced and guilty, he knew something was wrong. He'd raised the alarm, and waited when they strapped Abbie to the gurney and took her to hospital. He'd left flowers on the porch for when she came home.

'It was the last time I saw you for almost a year,' he said, close to tears.

I was at the point of hyperventilation. It took everything in me to leave space for him to continue.

He went back to the unit. The red-haired girl was rarely home, and when he finally spoke to her she looked at him strangely, made him feel uncomfortable. She told him Abbie didn't live there anymore. The second time she slammed the door in his face. The third time she gave him a number and an address to make him go away.

Logistically it was difficult to travel to Athena Bay – he had classes and work and some weekends he was expected to travel home to help his parents out on the farm – but on a rare weekend off he hired a car and drove to the address.

A woman answered. She looked enough like Abbie for him to assume it was her mother. When he asked to see Abbie, she rudely told him to leave her alone, she had terminated the pregnancy. She was living somewhere else now. She was sorry – Abbie should have told him herself.

He was devastated. He didn't know Abbie was pregnant. He didn't suspect her mother had lied. When the lease ran out on the share house, he packed his things and moved into his own place.

Life returned to normal for a while, but he thought about Abbie all the time. He was still lonely. He still had the red poncho hanging in his wardrobe. On a whim, he called Abbie's parents' number. It was easy: pretend he was calling from her previous place of employment and ask for a current phone number and forwarding address to arrange transfer of superannuation funds.

People were so trusting.

When he found Abbie she had been living in a flat in Rosewood for a few months, above a tattoo parlour. Abbie came down a flight of steps, then turned around and went back up as if she'd forgotten something. She looked different. She'd changed her hair – it was blonde and curly, not dark and bobbed. She'd gained weight. It suited her.

When she came back down everything changed again.

Abbie had a baby.

The baby looked just like him.

He fell in love for the second time.

'I tried to do things properly, I really did,' he said urgently, still on the verge of tears.

I couldn't keep quiet anymore. 'This is a mess,' I growled. 'You have no idea what you've done.'

He put up a hand. 'You wanted me to tell you everything.'

For a while he was content to observe from a distance. Something made him hold back from confronting Abbie – he knew he had a temper and he didn't want to give her grounds to keep him from seeing his daughter when the time was right. He wanted her to come to him, but she was always surrounded by people. It hurt his heart to see the squalor his child lived in – she was being dragged up by an extended family of druggies and degenerates, and the owner of the Snakepit made his skin crawl.

But he was patient. He took photos to look at when he couldn't be near Sarah. She looked like him – nothing like Abbie. He left gifts; he cleaned up the backyard so his daughter would have somewhere to play. When he summoned the courage to knock on her door, Abbie wouldn't answer, but she finally responded to one of his messages.

It's over. Let's be honest – it never really started. Please don't come here again.

After the fire, keeping track of Abbie and Sarah's whereabouts was almost a full-time job. He struggled to keep up with his classes.

A year shy of completing his degree, he dropped out. He took a government job in cybersecurity because it gave him access to the personal information he needed, but Abbie was as irresponsible with updating her details as she was with bringing up their child. He ran into dead ends and false information – there was a period when he didn't see his daughter for over two years.

He suspected Abbie was being calculated about her movements. She moved frequently and each time he got close, she packed up and disappeared.

'You're wrong,' I interrupted. 'I didn't know you were looking – I had no reason to hide!'

'Let me *finish*.'

Eventually Abbie got careless: when Sarah started school her name popped up in the system. He resumed his surveillance when he could, watching them, noticing the way they interacted, like opposing forces.

Abbie wasn't happy.

Sarah wasn't happy.

He wasn't happy.

He could have gone the way of the family court, he knew, but a brief and unexpected conversation with Sarah had changed his mind. He'd gone to the school, as he often did on his days off – she'd spoken to him through the fence, asking if he was waiting for a bus. He'd replied that he was looking for his daughter.

We look alike, he said. *Maybe she's you?*

I don't think so, she replied. *My daddy is dead.*

'You pushed me over the edge, Abbie,' he said now. 'I'm not insane. I'm not a monster. I'm a father. Do you see?'

NOW

My emotions had run the full spectrum from hope to despair to hope again. I struggled to make sense of some of the things he said, but I began to understand as more pieces clicked into place. Oh yes, I had been careless and egocentric and irresponsible and all the other things Martine had ever accused me of, but the sheer magnitude of a story that ran parallel to mine, occasionally crossing over and spanning almost *thirteen* years, was too much to take in.

How had I never noticed him hovering at the edges of our lives? Was everything he said true? Had he set the fire? I had a thousand questions – the biggest one was a fist, squeezing my heart.

Sarah had asked about her father several times – three that I could remember clearly, the first time on Christmas Day when she was around four years old, the second after she had started school. I never spoke of him unless she brought it up. I figured it was a conversation to be had when she was old enough to understand.

'Ava's daddy dresses up as Santa to deliver the presents,' she told me when she'd finished opening her own. Uncharacteristically, she had made a neat pile of her gifts and was patiently deciding which one to play with first. 'Why don't I have a daddy?'

'Everyone has a daddy, but some of them just aren't around,' I said.

'Did he see me come out of your tummy?'

'No, he wasn't there.'

Her face lit up with morbid fascination. 'Was it because of all the blood?'

'He wasn't there because he didn't want to be there,' I told her.

It was a response meant to shut down the topic of conversation, and it felt true at the time.

She dropped the subject and I was grateful.

The next time was different. I had been dreading the inevitable family-tree assignment or the Father's Day card-making project, but in the end it was a far more sinister occurrence that prompted her to ask. All parents had received a letter from the principal advising that a man had been reported frequenting the bus stop near the school – never catching a bus, just sitting there. Attached to the email were a number of links to resources to help parents talk to their children about the dangers of trusting people they didn't know.

'Promise me you'll go to a teacher if you see anyone hanging around the school,' I said. 'Don't approach them, just tell a teacher.'

Sarah shrugged. 'Maybe he was just a daddy looking for his kid.'

'No, he wasn't, Sarah. Do you understand what I'm telling you about safe adults and unsafe adults?'

She nodded, then asked, 'Does my daddy look for me?'

'I don't know where he is,' I said. 'If he came looking for you we would talk about it.'

'Do I look like him?'

'Yes,' I admitted. 'Sometimes I think you do.'

'Does he know where I am?'

It was my turn to shrug. 'There are lots of kids without dads, but you have me and Poppa and Nanna Martine and Auntie Jess.'

Once Sarah got hold of an idea she hung onto it like a pit bull. She shook her head. 'We have to tell him.'

'But what if he turned out to be a bad dad – wouldn't you be better off without him?' I said.

She stuck out her bottom lip. 'What if you're a bad mum?'

I was on the verge of losing control. 'I'm sorry you feel that way. Go to your room.'

She went, but only because she wanted to.

The third time Sarah brought up her father, she asked Martine. They were doing a puzzle together and I heard them talking – in whispers, as they so often did, like co-conspirators – and I crept closer to listen.

'Do you know my daddy, Nanna?'

'I met him one time,' Martine said.

'Do you think I'll ever meet him?'

Martine stopped what she was doing to stroke Sarah's hair. 'Oh, honey, he died.' Then she went back to what she was doing.

I stepped back in shock. This was something that would be difficult to explain and impossible to undo, if I wanted to undo it.

'Why did you say that?' I hissed, after Sarah had left the room.

'Because, unlike some people, I never do things by halves,' Martine said. 'She deserved to know. You're welcome, by the way.'

Martine had been mistaken about meeting Sarah's real father – it wasn't Reno who'd knocked on my parents' door. When Martine told Sarah her father was dead, it was the truth, a truth she had learned before I did. She must have heard about Reno's death – through the Athena Bay grapevine, via Cass's mother, and ultimately via the source, Cass – but after what she told me about Reno on the day of my father's funeral, she never mentioned him again.

How long did Cass say Reno had been gone? *Years.* How many? Too many? If I had asked, I might have realised the person claiming to be Sarah's father wasn't Reno, but someone else.

Him.

Despite the stuffiness of the room, my skin was clammy with cold sweat. I shivered from the effort of paying attention, keeping still. I would not interrupt – once he stopped talking he'd find out how quickly things could change again. I held the pieces that *he* was missing, but I had to keep them in my hand until the right time.

He sipped cold tea and grimaced. 'You might as well cut the act now, Abbie.'

'Why didn't you contact me if you believed she was your child?' My voice rasped, my throat tight with tears.

'I *did* contact you,' he said, banging his fist on the table. 'The letters, Abbie, the notes. I sent her gifts. Every time I got close, you moved again.'

Letters, notes, gifts – my habit of throwing away mail, unopened, went as far back as when I'd lived in the unit with Cass, and only got worse after Sarah was taken. How many letters had I missed? The notes I'd thought were from Evan. The swing set, in a box, by the gate. *Click*.

'I don't understand why you didn't just *talk* to me!'

He gave a helpless shrug. 'I tried. I knocked on your door you wouldn't answer. I tried to speak to you more than once – you walked away like you didn't know me, as if I made you uncomfortable.' He squirmed. 'I didn't want an ugly confrontation. I wanted everything to be perfect, including this reunion, so don't pretend you didn't hide her existence from me and don't deny you told her I was dead.'

I clapped my hands over my mouth. If only I had been paying attention, if only I had looked around instead of straight ahead.

'That's not what happened. It isn't that simple.'

Reno. Cass. The missing pieces.

'Why do you *lie*?'

'Tell me everything. That day in the market – you just took her?'

'I didn't plan it.' He glared at me. 'I took her to teach you a lesson, but she came willingly enough. She recognised me. She *knew* me. It was only meant to be a couple of hours. I just wanted to spend time with her, but she fell asleep in the car – before I knew it I was driving. I kept on driving, and then I couldn't let her go.'

I'd tried to teach Sarah a lesson. Oh god oh god oh god.

I hit my forehead with my palm. 'What did you tell her? How could she not know she was missing?'

'She wasn't missing. She knew where she was – with her father.'

I locked onto his words. The hairs on my arms stood up.

'My job takes me all over. We lived overseas for a while. We moved around a lot – like you, Abbie. Do you see the irony here?'

For all my heightened emotion and the unpredictability of a still-dangerous situation, with every passing minute I was growing lighter; with each new revelation I was becoming surer of the greatest revelation of all.

He couldn't have killed her. He loves her.

'Why didn't she look for *me*?'

His silence was telling. I knew.

'You told her I didn't want her.'

'I told her you needed time to get better.'

Detox.

'You told her I was a drug addict? For *six years*?'

He nodded. 'And now we're even.'

'You can't just take somebody's child!'

He gave a sad smile. 'You took mine.'

I shook my head. 'No. No, this is all wrong.'

'It was never an abduction – at worst it's a custody case, Abbie, but you know that. You knew all along. What I can't figure out is why you didn't confess to the police and make me their number one suspect. Now there's a mystery that needs solving.'

'Because I didn't *know*...'

He was on a roll. 'You thought I was filming you, listening to your conversations. I didn't have to – I knew everything I needed to know about you from years of observation. I'm an anomaly. I may even be an aberration, but I am *not* a monster. Everything I've done I did for her, and for me, and now I'm doing it for you. This is your one chance to get back everything you thought you'd lost.'

'What do you want from me?' My tone was bleak.

'For us to be the family we should have been,' he said calmly.

I shuddered at the thought of his hands on my body. I felt sick knowing those hands had touched Sarah, even if it was only in the way a father would touch a child.

'You abducted *me*,' I said. 'Even if a court agreed it was a custody matter, they'd never let you near her again.'

I regretted saying it as soon as the words left my mouth, but again he wasn't fazed.

'You came here of your own volition. I have copies of every letter I sent. You've been moving around to avoid me for years.'

I shook my head. 'Until you took off the blindfold, I didn't know you existed. You're crazy.'

'I'm far from crazy,' he said. 'But on paper, you are.' He held up both hands and began flicking up his fingers. 'Depression. Drug abuse. Drinking. Risk-taking behaviour. Promiscuity. Unresolved anger and public aggression. Dishonesty and theft. Shall I go on?'

I knew I should stop but I couldn't – I ticked off my fingers too. 'You stole my child. You gaslighted me and drugged me, you gagged me and tied me to a bed and you let me think my daughter was dead for six years. No court would accept that was within the bounds of normal behaviour.'

He shrugged. 'They can charge me for kidnapping but it won't stick. Six years you weren't a mother, yes. I was not a father for the same time. Like I said, we're even.'

'There will be evidence somewhere and they'll find it.'

He folded his arms. 'Who's *they*, Abbie? The same people who can't find missing kids? I didn't even have to change her first name.' He leaned forward. 'I've been waiting for *them*. I was ready for *them*. In the end I had to find *you*, except I left it too late – you got married. What, you just found a new family?'

'You're delusional.'

'I'm meticulous,' he said. 'I've thought of everything.'

Except the possibility that the entire premise for his actions over the past thirteen years was based on a delusion.

My face was streaked with snot and tears. 'Where is she? I need to see her *right now*.'

'She's not here.' He patted my shaking hand as if I was a child. 'Give up, Abbie. You have no control over anything anymore. It's *our* family, or it's nothing.'

He handed me a tissue. He'd gone through several trying to remove every trace of blood from his arm, obsessively dabbing at the scratch when it oozed. With his other hand he had been moving the objects on the table one by one – teacups, spoons, salt and pepper shakers, coasters – to form a perfectly straight line in front of him. As he assessed the objects, he made tiny adjustments; when the salt shaker fell over, he repeatedly licked his finger and picked up every grain, flicking them over his left shoulder.

I thought I knew hate before, but I didn't. Now my monster had a face.

Think, Abbie, think. Pull the pin on the grenade.

My eyes were drawn to the line of shoes by the door.

Martine had similar habits – not exactly a form of compulsion in her case, but a way to exercise control, to impose order in a house she had shared with three noisy, lazy, disorderly personalities. And one of the reasons she and I had clashed so often was because, as she said, I had a talent for chaos.

I wanted everything to be perfect, he said.

I removed a spoon from the line and stirred my tea. When I set it on the saucer he took it, wiped it clean and replaced it in the line. I reached for the salt shaker and poured a pile on the table, pinching the grains to form a pyramid. His shoulders were drawn high and tense, his fingers twitching.

'And if I reject your proposal?' I said, pushing the salt around with my finger. 'If I get up right now and walk out of here?'

'I told you – we'll disappear. By the time you return we'll be gone. You'll never see her again.'

The grains were clogging the holes in the shaker. I twisted off the lid. 'That's assuming you've covered your tracks properly. Also assuming she never wants to find me herself.'

He inclined his head. Apparently he'd thought of that, too. 'That's another six years away. If it nearly killed you not knowing if she was dead, what will it do to you knowing she's alive and out there somewhere?'

'Knowing would be worse,' I said.

She's out there somewhere. Alive.

He seemed pleased with my response. 'I'm not so arrogant as to think nobody will take you seriously when you show up claiming you found her. But it won't matter by then – we'll be gone.'

I tipped the remaining salt onto the table and took the bread knife from the line of utensils. I used it to spread the salt into an even layer, drawing slow and deliberate shapes in the grains, idly flicking the excess across the table and onto the floor.

'So – it was all about revenge in the end. It wasn't about her at all.'

One hand shot out to grip my wrist. 'Stop.' His pupils were dilated. He was blowing hard through his nose, like a bull.

I gripped the knife hard. We arm-wrestled. I was stronger than him – I could feel it.

'What are you doing, Abbie?' he asked softly.

'Leaving,' I said.

With Sarah, I was going to add, but there was a shadow at the window. A tinkling sound, outside, followed by scraping and scuffing. The air changed.

His reaction was violent: he let go of my arm, shot to his feet and upended his chair.

The back door flew open. As the handle hit the wall, sending plaster chips flying, the rope that tethered me to reality was cut. I was left spinning in space. Here was my nightmare *and* my dream – my missing child. Years older, but undeniably, unmistakably *her*.

My mind scattered, in pieces, but my heart expanded to fill the spaces that had been left empty for so long.

I recognised her: she had been one of the figures on a horse. Both the police sketches and my imagination had been wrong: at twelve she was taller, thinner, with lighter hair, cut short as a boy's. I knew her from the set of her spine, the curve of her chin. Her eyes, grey and startling. I knew her because a mother *knows* and none of the details I thought I'd forgotten over time mattered – my body remembered.

She was mine.

'S –' Her name caught in my throat.

'I know you said tomorrow, but I couldn't wait,' she said breathlessly, her eyes darting between us.

'Bad timing,' he muttered through white lips. 'This is very bad timing. You should have stuck to the plan.'

I felt the need to shout a warning, but she wasn't afraid of him. She was dismissive – the way she brushed her hair from her eyes and settled her hands on her hips.

'I heard what she said. Is it true? She's leaving me again?' Her question was directed at him, not me, her expression a mixture of despair and defiance.

'I can't –' Again I couldn't speak. My vision was dark at the edges. I was paralysed. I thought I'd pass out.

'I told you.' Her eyes fixed on me, her pupils black. 'I *told* you not to make her come!' She stabbed at him with a finger. 'She doesn't want us!'

'It's not over yet,' he said. 'Let's make the best of the situation.'

I reached for Sarah but she reared away. It was only when he nodded that she moved forward, took the furthest chair at the head of the table, and slid into it as if it was hot metal.

My arms ached to hold her. My mind couldn't cope.

I sought out their expressions – his, hers – to give me direction, something to hold onto. Was it *smugness* on his face? No, he looked expectant, as if he'd given me a gift and he was waiting for me to react. But the previous days had taught me *not* to react without thinking, so I didn't. And if Sarah had displayed a single emotion I could have fixed on it, but, like me, she seemed to be swinging from one to the next.

I froze, my hand still gripping the bread knife.

'Is she still sick?' Sarah asked him. 'She looks sick.'

'I thought you were dead.' It came out like a moan.

He laughed. It was loud, incongruous and deliberate. He threw me a warning look. 'She knows you haven't been well, Abbie. I've told her everything but she's willing to give you another shot. Are you going to waste it?'

I had to say something. 'I'm – sorry.'

To Sarah he said, 'I've given your mother the option to stay, but we won't stop her if she wants to leave.' He had the upper hand again. 'Now you see, Abbie?' He waved a hand. 'It's not how things were supposed to go, but here we are. Your family.'

Here we were.

I retched so violently I lurched off the chair and landed on my knees.

Sarah shot to her feet. 'What's wrong with her? She's still sick, isn't she? You said she was better.'

I tried to shake my head, but my body was determined to expel everything in my stomach. I convulsed, spitting up sour bile, knowing it wasn't so much residual drugs or bad food that made me like this, but a poisonous cocktail of emotion:

– shock, confusion, fear

'Do something, Dad! Help her!'

Don't help me so you can be the hero, you sick, twisted, lying fuck.
He hauled me up by the armpits and shoved me towards the kitchen sink, running the tap, pushing my head into the basin

– bitterness, resentment, rage

he held my hair back

Don't touch me

– humiliation, shame, guilt

he wiped my mouth with a wet cloth

I hate you – I'll kill you

– exhaustion, powerlessness, resignation

Let me go

– optimism, jubilation, peace

She's alive, she's right here – it's over

until all that was left was love.

NOW

It was early when he unlocked the bedroom door and told me I could take a shower. He was dressed in a navy shirt, dusty jeans and steel-capped work boots. He gave a slight bow, then placed a bathrobe, a clean folded towel and an individually wrapped soap on the end of the bed, as if I was a guest in a hotel. It was another surreal moment that kept me wondering whether this was all part of a lucid dream.

I crawled out of bed, bleary-eyed and shaking. Knowing Sarah was near had left me sleepless and jittery. Knowing she was alive changed everything. It wasn't knowledge I craved now, but opportunity.

I followed him down the hall. He opened the door next to the toilet.

'You have about ten minutes,' he said. 'It's a small tank and Sarah has already used half of it.'

I peered past him to see if she was in the kitchen.

'You'll see her for breakfast,' he said, shaking his head. 'Knock when you're ready to come out.'

I waited until he closed the door to run the water, not fully intending to get in, but to use the sound to buy time to think, then decided I could do both. I undressed, keeping an eye on the door because there was no lock on the inside. The hot water was barely a trickle, but it felt blissful on my aching body. I gently rubbed the marks on my ankles and wrists. They were chapped, but fading.

I needed to get Sarah alone but he wouldn't allow it, not for a second. I had to tell her things weren't as they seemed.

I'm not sick.

He isn't your father.

I never left you.

I wasn't sure she would let it happen either: to her I was the enemy. She seemed to have no idea how afraid I was; she didn't appear curious as to why he had locked me in the room. She didn't once ask me any questions, as if she was confident she already had all the answers she needed.

I had to see things from every angle.

Sarah had been told I didn't want her, that I couldn't look after her, that I was sick. She thought she'd been abandoned and he'd *saved* her. She had never tried to find me because she didn't know she was missing, and she believed I'd never tried to make contact until now. As far as she knew, this was supposed to be a family reconciliation, but instead of finding me sane, well and overjoyed to see her again, she'd overheard me say I was leaving. Then I'd thrashed and screamed and thrown up – making me look like a detoxing drug addict – and Sarah had run off into the night.

He believed Sarah was his child, and that my family had conspired to keep him from her. Martine had told him I hadn't kept the baby; it was only by chance that he learned he was a father, and he had tried to make contact for years, but I had deliberately moved around to prevent him finding out where we lived. Access to his 'daughter' had been denied, and Sarah was told her father was dead.

And now, after six years of me believing Sarah had been murdered, her bones crumbling away in some dark and lonely place, apparently we were even.

The truth: Sarah was abducted by a stranger who believed he was her father, a stranger who kept her, moved her from place to place for six years, and brainwashed her to punish me – a woman who'd repeatedly and unknowingly rejected a man I had no recollection of knowing. He thought it was a *custody* case. He'd terrorised, gaslighted and abducted me. He'd tried to break me, then woo me, so that when he gave my daughter back I'd be grateful and, presumably, choose to leave my destroyed life behind. All out of some whacked-out idea that he was owed six years of time with his child before we could be a real family.

I never saw it coming – I had a gift for remembering details, but I was clueless when it came to the bigger picture.

You're careless, Abbie. There's a picture of you under the word 'egocentric'.

I felt sick. All those missing pieces. What if Martine hadn't lied about my pregnancy? What if I'd answered the door, just once, when he'd knocked? What if I'd opened my mail like a responsible adult, or paid more attention to the faces in the background?

It was him in the change room, I was sure of it. He was there when I fell and hit my head. He'd been in my bedroom, lain between my sheets, stolen paperwork with my personal details, delivered the flowers to the unit. He was the one who knocked on my parents' door, not Reno, and he'd left the gifts and the note at the Rosewood flat. He'd cleaned up the backyard so his 'daughter' could play there and, when I rejected him again, he'd lost it – the free tickets in the letterbox were to ensure we weren't home when he set fire to the Snakepit, and I was reasonably sure he was there to watch the place burn. He was the guy at the bus stop, at Sarah's school. And when he'd finally made his move, taken Sarah, he'd gone to my parents' house to leave evidence for a time *six years* in the future.

He was clever, methodical and completely insane. But he was not Sarah's father. If he'd bothered with a DNA test, he would have known. I didn't sleep with him, Cass did. I only went back for her shoes. Reno was Sarah's father and Reno was dead.

I knew if I told him, or Sarah, that he wasn't her biological father, this fantasy life he'd so carefully engineered would fall apart. As long as he still believed Sarah to be his child, he wouldn't hurt her — and maybe, if I let him continue to believe the fantasy, he wouldn't hurt me.

The only way to keep Sarah safe was to keep the truth from both of them. Now the thought of seeing her again made me both happy and sad. There was so much damage to undo.

I was rinsing my hair when the water ran cold. Shivering, I left it slimy with conditioner, turned off the taps and towelled myself dry. I wrapped my hair in a towel, put on the bathrobe and knocked on the door.

It opened almost immediately.

'There are clean clothes in your room,' he said. 'When you've changed you can join us in the kitchen.'

I checked the door handle in the bedroom when he'd gone: he had left it unlocked. I wondered if it was a test. He didn't know me as well as he believed if he thought I'd leave her again.

The jeans and T-shirt he'd left on the bed were well-worn, but clean. There was a new packet of three pairs of cotton underwear and a bra as well — both a size too big, but they'd do. I opened the wardrobe door to hang up the bathrobe and my hand brushed against the dry cleaner's bag — I'd seen it before, only now I was clear-headed enough to recognise it.

I lifted the plastic to feel the material, as soft as the day she'd bought it, with a docket still attached to the collar. He'd kept it all this time: Cass's red poncho.

How would he react if I told him it belonged to the girl who'd been in his bed that night, and that girl wasn't me?

I entered the kitchen as he was serving bacon, eggs and thick slices of toast. He turned with a spatula in his hand and gestured for me to sit.

'She's not here,' I said.

He shrugged. 'She'll come when she smells the bacon.'

'Where has she gone?'

I tried to keep my tone even but he heard the catch in my voice.

'Sometimes she runs. Or there's a place she goes to think.'

'Where?'

'Eat first.' He put a full plate in front of me.

I wasn't hungry. I had a burning ache near my sternum and reflux in my throat, as if a peptic ulcer had developed overnight. The bacon was fatty and undercooked. I poked the eggs with a fork and they slid greasily around the plate.

'Thank you,' I said. 'It looks delicious.'

When he'd prepared his own plate, he sat across from me. 'How are you feeling this morning, Abbie?'

He cut three even rectangles of bacon, egg and toast, layered them on top of each other and trimmed the edges of the stack before forking it into his mouth.

I stared, letting my own food go cold. I oozed loathing, but he was oblivious.

'Fine.'

He glanced up. 'If you're up to it, we'll show you around today.'

'That would be nice.'

My docility obviously wasn't convincing enough. 'Don't do anything stupid,' he warned. 'I'm your ally, not your enemy. I want you to strengthen your relationship with our daughter, don't you see?'

I shook my head. 'So I should lie?'

'The only thing she doesn't know is the nature of how you arrived here,' he said. 'Sarah thinks you wanted to see her. She's twelve years old – we can spare her the details, don't you agree?'

It wasn't the only thing. 'She doesn't know you abducted her.'

'That's a matter of perspective.'

'She needs to know I never stopped looking for her.'

'One revelation at a time,' he conceded. 'It's too much. Give her some space.'

I took a risk. 'I'd like to call my family, please. I want to let them know I'm okay.'

Cut, stack, trim, chew, swallow. 'We are your family, Abbie.'

'Just a quick phone call. I won't tell them where I am,' I pleaded.

A quizzical look. 'But you don't know where you are.'

Involuntarily, my head jerked toward the window.

He rapped the table for attention. 'Daniella will protect Sarah. She knows she was abused and neglected under your care. She won't help you.'

'Abuse?' I spat. '*Neglect?*'

'This is your chance to be her mother again. If you want to leave, go, but we'll be gone. Look around you. We don't even need to pack.'

It was true: everything in the house looked as if it had been there for decades. The glimpses I'd seen of other rooms revealed them to be spare, lacking in belongings and personal touches.

'I've thought of –'

'– everything,' I finished. 'I know.' I waited a beat and flashed him a smile.

Flustered, he finished cutting the last perfect rectangle and scraped the trimmings into a neat pile on the side of his plate. He didn't eat them.

'I'll clean up.' I stood and reached for his plate.

'Well. Thank you, Abbie.'

He held onto the plate for seconds too long, his dark eyes fixed on mine, reminding me that in spite of his apparent calm and good manners, his true nature could be violent and unpredictable.

But he hadn't thought of everything.

The docket attached to Cass's poncho was dated recently,

and I had recognised the dry cleaner's address. His fastidious nature might be his undoing – we weren't as far from home and civilisation as he'd had me believe.

NOW

I took my time washing the greasy dishes, acutely aware of him sitting behind me, watching, and grateful to have something to do with my hands. Anything to avoid eye contact and conversation. He was relaxed when I played along with the charade, but even his mildest expression was unnerving. Perhaps, like me, he only appeared calm.

I dried the cutlery and put it away in the drawer. There were knives in there. The one I wanted – chunky, deadly sharp – was too large to hide. With my back to him, I grabbed a smaller paring knife and tucked it with the blade pointing up inside the waistband of my jeans, pulling my T-shirt down to conceal it. There was a ballpoint pen lying on the counter. I took that too, slipping it into my back pocket.

As I let the dishwater out of the sink, Sarah flew inside. Again the door hit the wall, deepening the divot in the plaster and rebounding so hard and fast it closed behind her. She dashed into the kitchen and shot down the hall, throwing me an unreadable look on her way.

I experienced a fresh wave of joy.

Alive.

I remembered this, the way she had always entered a room and left it like a half-tamed horse bolting from a gate. I also remembered how often I'd yelled at her – her exuberance had been a near-constant source of irritation. *Calm down, be quiet, knock it off, put a sock in it, put your toys away, because I said so, don't make me pull over, close the door, were you born in a barn?* Everything Martine had ever shouted at me and Jess, all bar the five o'clock warning: *just wait til your father gets home.*

I swore then that I'd never say those things again.

He didn't react to Sarah's dramatic entrance and exit. A mobile phone had appeared in his hand and he was busy typing.

My stillness made him look up. 'Sarah doesn't have a phone, if you're wondering. She won't be getting one until her fourteenth birthday.' He turned the phone off and slipped it into his shirt pocket. 'The money you brought will be deposited in her trust account as soon as I'm able. Let's call it back-paid maintenance.'

I didn't have the chance to reply. Sarah came back, entering the kitchen the same way she left it. We both froze and she glanced up, returning my beseeching look with an accusing one. But her hostility triggered a hard-learned response to an old piece of advice: *always smile when your child enters the room frowning.*

I gave that smile everything – wonder, elation, love – and Sarah was rattled. Her eyes welled; she blinked rapidly and wiped her nose with a shaking hand. She broke eye contact and burst into action again – it hurt, but at the same time I understood her need for perpetual motion as a way of regaining control.

The tea towel was wrapped so tightly around my hand it had cut off my circulation – I unwound it and the blood rushed back. I stepped aside as Sarah reached for a glass from an overhead cupboard and filled it with water from the tap. Frowning, she stared at the residue in the bottom of the sink, then held the glass to the light from the window, scrutinising it with the intensity of a scientist.

'The bore pipe has come off again.'

He looked up. 'Are you sure?'

'Mud's coming through.' She showed him the glass of water.

He pulled a face. 'Have you been down there? What's the level like?'

'Deep,' she said. 'Still over half.'

I barely registered what they were saying – my only thought was that my lost child was standing less than three feet away, flesh and blood, her skin flushed and smelling woodsy and sweet.

'So what's that –'

'About three or four metres,' she said.

'It's the weekend. The scuba guy won't come out.'

'Rainwater tank's nearly empty too.'

'Do you think –?'

Sarah nodded. 'We can do it.'

It was all riddles to me.

I'd noticed the water from the tap was cloudy, but I hadn't mentioned it. Now he came to look, running his finger through the silty layer that had settled on the bottom of the sink. He turned on the tap. It sputtered and spat brown water.

He and Sarah looked at each other. He shrugged and she nodded.

'Why is it doing that?' I asked.

'The pipe has come loose from the float. It's sucking mud,' he said. 'Lucky you got a shower in time.'

'That happened to me once,' Sarah said. 'I came out dirtier than I went in.'

She smiled and my heart swelled.

I saw Martine in the crinkles at the corners of her eyes; her left dimple was just like Jess's; the way her hand flew up to cover her teeth was all me. No police sketch could ever have caught these features and mannerisms. She looked like us.

'Put on your shoes, Abbie,' he said. 'We're going for a walk.'

I nodded. 'They're in the bedroom. I'll just be a minute.'

He didn't follow. I sighed with relief and pushed the door to, but didn't close it.

If I had the chance to run, would Sarah run with me? I couldn't be sure. I didn't think she would. When I'd taken the pen it was to write Sarah a letter, slip it to her when he wasn't looking. Now there wasn't enough time.

I looked around. Could I write on the wall?

The books on the dresser. The hole in the floor.

I chose a book and wrote quickly. When I lifted the section of floorboards a nail tore, leaving a smear of blood across the cover of the book. The boards dropped into place with a loud clunk.

'Abbie, let's go!' he called.

Panting, I pulled on my shoes and adjusted the knife in my jeans. 'I'm coming. I'm ready.'

We walked in single file. Sarah strode ahead, gangly but graceful. She seemed to know exactly where to place her feet. I stumbled along in the middle, finding every pothole, and he followed close behind, occasionally putting his hand in the small of my back when I tripped.

Yesterday I had run blindly without taking much notice of the landscape; now I mapped our progress, committing landmarks to memory and trying to get a sense of where we were.

The house was as quaint on the outside as in, a neat weatherboard cottage, painted white with dove-grey trim and three wooden steps leading to a wide front porch. A large area around the building had been cleared, possibly as a defence against bushfire. Beyond the perimeter, the land was densely wooded with thickets of pines in various stages of growth. The air was fresh, pine-scented, suggesting a higher altitude than the vast plains I'd passed along the way. A thick layer of dead pine needles crackled under our feet.

Here was the fire pit and the circle of stumps. The woman, Daniella, and the log home, were somewhere over the hill, past the older section of trees to our left. A gravel driveway wound down the hillside behind us, disappearing from view around a bend. The property seemed isolated but I wasn't convinced. Typically, a driveway led to a road.

In the distance I thought I heard an engine revving.

Every so often Sarah glanced back at me the same way I looked at her, as if she was trying to drink me in without him noticing. I didn't bother hiding it any more – I was starving to touch her, but her body held the tension of a coiled snake. It killed me to know that it was not *him* who made her feel this way, but me.

The tangle of lies – that I'd given her up, that I didn't want her – would be hard to unravel, but surely a smart kid like her didn't get to be twelve years old without questioning if everything he'd told her was true. I had to find the chink in her belief, a way to solidify any doubts, if she had them. My own lies and omissions were part of the reason we were here: if she had known Reno was her biological father, she wouldn't have trusted this man, she wouldn't have believed his version of the truth. She might have screamed and tried to escape.

'How long will we stay here?' I asked.

Sarah turned, hands on hips. 'Oh, does that mean –?'

He cut her off. 'I told you, Abbie. It's rented. What happens after this very much depends on you.'

I stopped listening. The familiarity of Sarah's stance and expression took my breath away – how could I ever have thought she didn't look like me, like us?

My family would be frantic by now. They wouldn't know if I was alive or dead, and I knew exactly how that felt. How strange to be so far from them, living another life, experiencing the joy and wonder of knowing none of my worst nightmares had been real.

I wasn't afraid anymore. I was *hopeful*. Sarah was alive and this would come to an end.

'I like it here,' Sarah said. 'It's better than the last place.'

'It's only temporary,' he said tightly. 'You know that. We can't stay.'

She rolled her eyes. 'I don't know why we can't just be normal at least *some* of the time.' She stomped on ahead, leaving us to trail after her.

Maybe she did have doubts.

Last night I had lain awake for hours, torturing myself about what happened to her during those missing years. Was she scared, lost, lonely and abused? Did she cry herself to sleep? How many days, weeks, months before she stopped calling for me? How long before she couldn't picture my face, the way I couldn't picture hers?

I'd been thinking of Sarah as damaged. Stolen, brainwashed, taken too far and gone for too long to ever be whole again. But less than a minute ago she had been standing with her hips slouched forward in a wide stance, like mine, wearing a combative expression like Jess's, her mouth twisted just like Martine's, her grey eyes so like my father's – and I came to a different, stunning realisation. Was it possible she could be this fierce, unbroken, complete? Despite the circumstances, had she been safe all this time? Had she *thrived*?

I sped up. I didn't want to let Sarah out of my sight – I had to get her alone, talk to her. This charade couldn't go on much longer.

'Not far now,' he said.

We emerged from the trees to a stunning panoramic view of a deep valley, open to the sky but for the plantation pines framing the edges. A large dam sparkled at the bottom, brown with a hint of green. The narrow path merged with a dirt track, wide enough for a single vehicle. The track ran around the rim of the dam and doubled back on itself.

Sarah had reached the point where the track ended alongside the dam. She rolled up her jeans, took off her shoes and stepped into the murky water up to her knees, only pausing when he called out to her.

'Sarah, wait!'

Again, I heard the sound of an engine. I looked around. The source appeared to be a green shed at the edge of the water. A black pipe snaked its way from the rear of the shed, up the hill and over the ridge – leading, I assumed, back to the house and the tanks.

I moved to join Sarah, but he caught me by the elbow.

'We could be good together if you give it a chance.'

I shuddered, and he felt it. His expression turned blank and his eyes were bottomless. I tried to pull back but he held on, digging his fingers into my flesh.

'You think you've left enough clues?' he said. 'Nobody knows where you are. Your things in the dam, the car at the wreckers – your clues lead hundreds of kilometres in the wrong direction. You're the only other person who knows Sarah is alive, and we won't spend another second looking over our shoulders.'

Dully, I understood: we did not include me.

'You get it now? I can't have you out there, searching. If you try to leave, I'll kill you. If you try to take Sarah away from me again, I'll kill you.' He swept a hand to suggest the vastness of the pine forest. 'I'll bury your body so deep, no one will find it. Your family will never read your letters – they'll spend a lifetime wondering.'

He let go.

The thought of my family not knowing, of Sarah motherless, living her life with him and not knowing the truth, doubled me over. Paralysed, I pressed my palm against the knife hidden in my waistband. I no longer felt hopeful; anything I did might make the situation worse.

'I won't do anything,' I said. 'I won't move.'

When we reached Sarah at the edge of the dam, he pulled her aside and said something in her ear. She frowned and nodded. She went to the green shed, opened the door and stepped inside.

He pinched the tender skin of my upper arm and leaned close. 'Don't use Sarah for your own agenda, Abbie. I told her not to believe anything you say.'

I pulled away, rubbing my arm. A moment later the motor sputtered and stopped.

Sarah stuck her head out. 'Okay. The pump's off.'

He untied his boots and stripped out of his shirt and pants. His forearms, lower legs and the V of his neck were deeply tanned, but the rest of his body was pale, covered with a mat of coarse, dark hair. There was strength in his thick arms and broad chest, but how athletic was he? If I waited, I'd have a head start. Could he catch me if I ran again?

We watched as he waded in until the water was up to his chest; then he pushed away. He was an awkward swimmer – too much effort in the arms, dragging his legs like weights. About thirty metres out, he reached the float, a white plastic container with a blue screw-top lid, and duck-dived under.

Sarah sat on the slope of the dam and pulled her knees to her chest. She was silent but fidgety, snapping sticks into pieces and flinging them into the water.

I dropped down next to her. Near, but not too close. 'What does he have to do?'

'Find the end of the pipe and reattach it to the float. Simple.'

'How deep is it?'

'Only about three metres.'

More, I thought, judging by the steep angle of the bank. And the water was muddy. It would have made more sense to follow the pipe's end coming from the shed. But I didn't say anything – I was lost in a fantasy where he emerged from the water and I stepped forward to gut him like a fish. Or I could go in after him, wrap my legs around his neck and hold him under, except this might be my only chance to speak to Sarah alone.

'There are things you don't know,' I said in a low voice.

She stared stubbornly ahead.

'I'm not sick. I never was. He took you without permission.'

'He told me you'd say that.'

'Because it's true.'

She glared. 'And anyway, you don't need permission to see your own kid. He said I had to tell him if you try to get in my head.'

'Please don't do that.' I ached to touch her. 'Just listen – we don't have much time.'

She inched away, but didn't get up.

'Sarah, whatever happens, I love you. I always have. I never left you and I've never stopped looking for you. Okay?'

Still she stared ahead, but she appeared to be listening.

'If something happens and I have to leave, I promise it's not because I'm leaving *you*.' I turned sideways to face her. 'In the bedroom, under the floor, there's a book. You have to lift the floorboards in the corner –'

Sarah was rigid. 'Something's wrong.'

'*Please*,' I begged. 'Don't forget. Under the floor, Sarah. It's –'

'Look!' She pointed.

I checked the surface of the dam. A faint ripple and swirl. He surfaced briefly, hand in the air as if he'd tried to grab onto the half-submerged float, before slipping back under.

Sarah's mouth was slack with worry, her body tense and shivering.

I grabbed her shaking hand. 'He's fine.'

I lied. He was struggling.

He made it back to the surface to drag in another breath, his head thrown back, lips sucking languidly, like a goldfish. There

306

was no yelling, no thrashing. I watched his body roll and go down again; the passive way he went under was a warning sign.

A shiver of anticipation passed over me. I said I wouldn't do anything – at this rate I wouldn't have to. I could picture what was happening under the water: *in active drowning, a conscious victim will struggle, often silently, moving their arms and legs in a motion like climbing a ladder. This is the danger point in a rescue – the will to live is strong and a drowning person can easily drag the rescuer under in order to save themselves.*

All that mattered was taking Sarah home. I wanted him gone, because whatever happened after this, she would think of him as her father and I couldn't have that. It wouldn't be *fair*.

'He's not coming up,' Sarah said. 'We have to do something.'

'No.' I squeezed her hand tighter so she couldn't get away. 'He'll come back up. Wait a bit longer.'

As the head sinks lower and the body submerges, the victim begins to hyperventilate, expelling air and using up more oxygen as they resist the urge to breathe. The struggle could last a minute or more, and they may experience excruciating pain in the muscles and pressure in the head.

I wanted him to suffer. I promised him I wouldn't move. So I didn't. I wouldn't.

Next, the breathing reflex is triggered by a high concentration of carbon dioxide combined with a low concentration of oxygen in the blood, and the victim will take a breath underwater – a deep one that draws water into the airway and prompts the larynx to close. At this point the victim will often lose consciousness. The larynx spasm relaxes and water enters the lungs, causing the alveoli to collapse and preventing oxygen from entering the bloodstream to reach vital organs.

Sarah launched to her feet, tugging on my hand.

I got up and hung on.

Her breathing was fast and tortured. I found myself matching it, except I wasn't experiencing fear, but elation. This was the way it was meant to be. It was the universe, setting things right.

Breathing ceases. Without immediate assistance the victim will die. The heart beats a little while longer at an accelerated rate and progresses to fibrillation.

Sarah was sobbing now. I wrapped my arms around her waist and pulled her close to me. The knife blade sliced into my stomach, but I didn't let go.

'Wait,' I whispered. 'Everything will be okay.'

The heart stops.

It was for the best. This way he'd be gone. The truth would come out and there'd be a funeral. Sarah could grieve and say goodbye, which was more than I ever had.

NOW

The last ripples on the surface smoothed and settled. His last breath was over a minute ago but it felt like aeons. How long before I could be sure? *Five minutes?* Surely I owed him that.

Sarah struggled until I couldn't hold her any longer. She wrenched herself away, sobbing. She ran to the water's edge and stood poised, as if to dive in, and I went after her immediately but there was no danger of her going after him: she was afraid, hugging herself and shaking all over. She was still so young, a child.

I saw it all as if I was outside my body. Sarah's disappearance had been the most traumatic event of my life and this, most likely, would be hers. But what seemed like justice to me was unfair to her. My beginning was her ending. Letting him die wasn't for her, but for myself.

This time I'm right here and I have done nothing. I am the monster.

'*Please*, Mum.'

When she turned, I had my shoes off and my jeans pulled down to my knees. My underwear was pink with blood from the cut, but it wasn't a deep one; the knife fell, hit the water and sank.

'Don't follow me.'

I hoped that if there was one true thing she remembered, it was that I could swim like a dolphin and float like a cork. But this wasn't the ocean – there was zero visibility. I had carried the weight of an unconscious swimmer before, heavy as an anchor, but he had been a teenager weighing at least twenty kilos less.

I waded out. Just metres in, the bottom dropped away sharply; the water was lukewarm on top and freezing from the waist down. I freestyled to the middle, the place where he'd disappeared, and caught hold of the handle on the float. I took a breath and dived, measuring the depth until my fingers touched mud. I guessed the water was about four metres deep, so cloudy I could only feel my way around. I brushed the nylon rope attached to the float and grabbed it to bring myself up.

I sucked in more air, slowly releasing some as I descended.

There was no current; he couldn't have floated far. This time I swam in a widening spiral with the float and the rope in the centre, and on my third rotation my foot hit a solid object.

There. I spun around.

He was hovering midway in the space between the surface and the bottom, a couple of metres down, motionless. I found his head and wrapped one arm around his neck, propelling us both towards the surface with the other arm and strong flipper kicks. When we broke the surface his body was a dead weight; I slogged to get him back to the bank, repeatedly going under in the process. There was no point expending too much energy trying to keep his head up – the water was already in his lungs.

My feet touched down on the mud. 'Help,' I gurgled to Sarah, who was already standing thigh-deep.

She grabbed one arm. Between the two of us we dragged him onto the muddy bank.

His lips were blue. I checked his breathing and pulse: nothing. I looked at his eyes: his pupils were not dilated, but he was unconscious and unresponsive.

I had performed dozens of water rescues. I had even saved a life, a toddler who'd convulsed and stopped breathing, at the local park when I was sixteen. But the toddler had been nowhere near the water, and I was straight out of a lifesaving First Aid refresher

– I was calm and methodical about it, following a process, and the ambulance had arrived within minutes.

This was different. I was dizzy, exhausted and trembling. There would be no immediate assistance.

I tilted his head and lifted his tongue. After two breaths and thirty compressions there was no change. I performed two more cycles and asked Sarah to take over until I could regain some strength in my dead arms.

'You have to help. Okay? Here.' I took her cold hands and showed her the midway point of the sternum, the way my hands folded over each other. 'Like this. Don't be afraid to press hard, okay?'

Sarah shook all over, her teeth chattering. She gave it everything, counting aloud, her lips pursed in concentration. 'Twenty-four, twenty-five... is this right?'

'You're doing great. Stop now.'

Two more breaths, sickened by the feel of his mouth on mine, resenting every breath I gave him. After, I jiggled my arms and rubbed some feeling back into them.

'It's not working,' Sarah cried. Tremors shook her thin body; as she bent over him I could see each vulnerable bump of her spine through her wet T-shirt.

'It can take a while. While we do this, his blood is still pumping oxygen.'

A cloud passed over the sun. He was so still. There was a quiet and terrible moment when I knew it was too late – *I* had been too late. Sarah knew it too. I could have stopped then and it would have been enough.

'Switch,' I said. 'Two breaths, whenever I say. You can do it.'

I gave another twenty or so compressions, so tired I kept losing count. 'Now.'

She breathed into his mouth. 'There's water coming out!'

'That's good.' *Fifteen, sixteen, seventeen.* 'Where's his phone?' *Twenty, twenty-one.*

Sarah looked around. 'I don't know. At the house?'

'Breathe now.' *One, two.* 'Sarah, go check his jeans.'

She rummaged through his pockets. 'Not here.'

I blew again. One, two, three compressions. 'How far are we from – anything?'

'Not far,' she said, her eyes bloodshot from crying. 'About three kays.'

Five more compressions. Two more breaths.

'I need you to run to the house. Find a phone and call an ambulance.' I wiped sweat from my eyes and resumed counting. 'If you can't find one, go to Dani's.'

She nodded, apparently relieved to have something else to do. 'But don't stop. Please don't stop.'

'I won't.' I bent to exhale another breath. More water bubbled up in his throat. 'Sarah, go!'

She slipped her shoes on, sprinted to the path, and disappeared over the hill.

Long minutes passed with only the sound of my ragged breathing. Almost certainly I'd broken one of his ribs, but a rib would heal. The muscles in my shoulders and my core burned. I'd promised Sarah I wouldn't stop, but it was beginning to seem futile. Had the rib punctured a lung? Or, worse, was I keeping alive a body whose brain would never function normally again?

Suddenly his back arched. There – was it a gag reflex?

I twisted his head to the side. A weak dribble of water came out, and I scooped the back of his throat with two fingers. I turned his head back. Two breaths, several more compressions, and the dribble welled into a gush – black water spewed from his mouth and nose, and his lips drew back in a grimace.

I rolled him onto his side and scrabbled backwards, heaving with exertion. There was nothing more to do but monitor his progress as he gagged and coughed. I listened to the awful sound of air and water battling for space in his lungs, and kept counting. At least four minutes in the water. Easily more than fifteen minutes of CPR. And now, after long minutes of coughing and retching, it still seemed as if it would never stop. He was semiconscious, clearly aware of nothing but the desperate need to breathe.

A violent heave and he was still.

I thought I'd lost him again. I knew I didn't have the strength or the will to continue, but seconds later he drew a whooping breath and flipped onto his back. His chest began to rise and fall in a constant rhythm. The death rattle resumed.

'On your side.' I crawled towards him and pushed his shoulder. 'You have to stay on your side.'

He was still in danger of cardiac arrest. There could be after-effects: possible brain injury, respiratory-distress syndrome, pulmonary oedema.

'The ambulance is coming but you need to keep still. Don't –' I was cut off by another bout of violent coughing. The blood vessels in his eyes had burst. He brought up more water and stringy bile, but his grey skin had brightened to pink, and he now had enough motor control to wipe his mouth.

The coughing eventually eased. He was unable to speak.

'I pulled you out. I could have left you there, but I didn't,' I said. 'Do you understand?'

He blinked rapidly, his mouth working around his tongue as if it couldn't move. I could tell he knew I was there, that he understood what I was saying.

I shook the mud from my jeans. I shimmied into them lying down, pulled up the zipper and stood.

'You'll be taken to hospital. There can be serious after-effects following drowning. It might take a while to recover.'

Another spasm of coughing.

I waited until he was quiet again and told him, 'I'm leaving when they get here.'

His eyes rolled.

'I'm taking her with me. But you already know that, right?'

He groaned and tried to sit up.

He was weak as a baby, and I pinned him down with one hand. 'If it was just between you and me I would have left you to die, but it's not – it's about Sarah and what's best for her.'

I let go. He rolled onto his back, clutching at my face and neck. I batted his hands away. There was nothing he could do to hurt me. I'd lived with fear for so long, but I realised it was gone now, as if a malignant tumour had been excised from my body.

'What's your name anyway? Your real one, I mean.' Despite everything, I couldn't recall it. He had disappeared from my memory like smoke.

His jaw clenched. Silence.

The wail of a siren broke the stillness and I heard my daughter, calling for me some distance away.

He heard it too. His arm reached out; his fingers encircled my ankle. He tried to speak.

I kicked him lightly. 'Shut up. It doesn't matter anymore.'

Suddenly, viciously, I leaned in to pinch his nose and cover his mouth.

'If I tell you Sarah isn't your child, will you still love her? Will you kill for her now?'

I stifled his breath a little longer before letting go.

Everything happened fast.

The ambulance came into view. It bumped carefully along the fire track, led by Sarah, who loped ahead of it. Daniella and her blonde-haired daughter, who must have made their way through the forest rather than by road, appeared from the opposite direction. They clutched at each other like extras in a dramatic scene, mouthing reassurances. The paramedics, an older man and a young woman, strapped him to a gurney and he was soon breathing oxygen. Sarah hovered next to him, her eyes bright, oblivious to anything else. He raised his head and tried to say something to her but, still blessedly incapable of speech, settled for pressing a palm to her cheek.

I stood back, impatient. It was taking too long. I let out a sigh and Dani shot me a look of suspicion. When he'd started breathing on his own, I had it in my head that it was over – he'd be taken to hospital and Sarah would go home with me.

The ambulance doors closed. When Dani stepped forward to put a protective arm around Sarah's shoulder, the gesture prompted such a visceral reaction in my gut that I had to turn away.

'Are you the wife?' the male paramedic asked.

I shook my head.

'She's the mother,' Dani said. 'But she doesn't have custody. They're estranged.'

'You don't know anything,' I snapped. 'You have no idea what's been going on.'

She lifted her chin. 'I know enough.'

'Well, can you both sort this out quickly because we need to take him *now*.' The paramedic waved a hand.

'She'll stay with me.' Dani tightened her grip on Sarah's shoulder. 'I'll drive her to the hospital.'

'I want to go in the ambulance,' Sarah begged.

'You can't,' Dani said. 'I'll take you.'

I reached for Sarah's hand. 'She's coming with me.'

Sarah squinted against the afternoon sun. 'Where are you going?'

'Home. We're going home.'

She leaned ever so slightly in Dani's direction, and the pain of it made me double over.

'Sarah, you're coming with *me*,' I said, my voice too sharp.

Alarmed, she tried to yank her hand away, but I held on.

Dani hung on too, shifting her arm from Sarah's shoulder to her chest.

The tears poised on Sarah's lower lashes spilled over, and I had a flashback to the day she was abducted: me pulling her along the pavement, her screaming.

She was already terrified. I was making it worse.

'I'm leaving,' I told her. 'I won't make you come with me, but — things will happen when I go back. I won't be able to stop it.'

'What things?' she asked.

What things. If she knew, why would she ever come home willingly? Hadn't we been through enough? I had to be the one to tell her. Nobody else. And not here.

'Go,' I choked out. 'I'll be waiting for you.'

The ambulance set off along the fire track and, as Dani led her in the opposite direction, Sarah looked back.

Thank you, she mouthed.

I stood watching their figures grow smaller, until they disappeared over the rise.

I was strangely calm. The final piece was in place and it was as if the box, the place where I'd kept everything that hurt, had burst open: the agony of not knowing was gone and my mind was clear. Memories came flooding back, and I let them.

After the fire at the Rosewood Flat, Sarah had continued to sleep with me. The second bedroom of our new place was only used as a playroom and we shared my double bed, each becoming used to the twitches, the kicks, the sleep-talking of the other. I told myself it was for her, but the truth was I couldn't drift off without the shape of her next to me, in the dark. Sometimes I'd hold the back of my hand near her mouth – not out of fear, to check if she was still alive the way I did when she was a baby, but to experience love that was at its most intense when she was sleeping, the burst of wonder at her warm puffs of breath.

I made you. You were cells – now you are mind, heart, lungs, blood, flesh. You are perfect.

You are love.

It happened slowly.

One night she was on the floor – she'd dragged the pillow and sheet down with her. Another time I heard her get up in the night; I assumed she'd gone to the toilet, but when she didn't return I started checking every room, trying to quell my rising panic. I found her asleep in the lounge room, on the couch. When she turned four, she still went to bed with me as if she knew I needed her there, but as soon as she thought I was sleeping she'd sneak into the playroom and curl up in her nest of soft toys in the corner.

For her fifth birthday she had requested a Nerf gun, a sleigh bed and her own room.

Oh yes, I thought, as I watched my daughter disappear again. *Martine warned me of this – the pulling away. All I can do is hold on.*

NOW

The driveway led to a road. The road led to a town, the town led to a main street, and it was there I returned to the land of the living.

It was not a perfect ending, but if anyone had stopped when I was walking along the side of the road, crying, I'd have told them I was happy and it would have been true. It was only when I approached the police station that I was hit by the full realisation of what would happen next. I had been interrogated before; they'd tell me to start at the beginning. But I knew the first thing they'd ask:

How did you find her?

That would mean beginning at the end.

I lingered outside the police station, in filthy clothes that weren't my own, leaking blood from a cut on my stomach, going over and over the tiniest details. Those details were crucial – a person could go mad thinking about how every moment that came before had led to this. For years I had been living like a rat in a maze – I'd escaped, but to step inside the station would be to hand over any last shred of control.

I crossed the street and entered the hotel. The interior was all cave-like booths and dark wood panelling, prints of Arthur Sarnoff's dogs playing pool hanging on the walls. I found the bathroom and saw my face for what seemed like the first time in weeks: washed-out complexion, hollow eyes, ratty hair and a yellowing bruise on my cheekbone. My clothes were stiff with dried mud, emanating the scummy smell of stagnant water. Blackened blood around my cuticles, under my nails. I pulled the T-shirt away from the cut: it was long, but not deep.

I asked to use the phone. When I explained I had no money and no ID, the bartender offered me a drink on the house and listened as I made the call. Afterwards, I sat in a corner booth, nursing a tall vodka, lime and soda, picking at my torn fingernail.

I knew it would appear irrational to have walked away from the house, leaving Sarah with strangers. Horrific, even. To her, however, *I* was the stranger. But I was alive. *She* was alive. It was all that mattered now.

The dirt, the blood, the bruises – that was on the outside. Inside I was changed. I felt savage, yet fragile, incapable of making further decisions. I needed my family. I had been somewhere they couldn't follow, but I couldn't do the next part on my own.

I needed my mother. I needed her to tell me the worst was over and this could be fixed.

Martine showed up almost two hours later, her expression inscrutable. She wore a pair of torn cargo pants, a stained T-shirt and dirty sneakers, just her keys in her hand. I guessed she'd been working in the garden when I'd called, and left straightaway without bothering to change. She'd made good time.

She looked around, spotted me in the corner.

I raised my hand and she approached warily, as if I was a bomb that might go off. I wondered what had been going through her head during the long drive; I braced for accusation or recrimination, but she only put her keys on the table and slid into the seat opposite.

'Thank you for coming,' I said. 'You're probably confused.'

Her hand inched across the table to take mine. 'You're okay. That's all I need to know.'

I was transfixed by the dirt under her fingernails, the blood under mine.

'Let me take you back home,' she said.

'Not yet.' I shook my aching head. 'There are things that need to be done and Murray isn't... *we* aren't good together right now.'

Martine frowned. 'I meant *home*, Abbie.'

I pulled away. 'No, you don't understand. When I tell you what has happened, I'm asking you not to interrupt and I need you to believe me. Can you do that?'

Martine squeezed my hand. 'I've been looking for you. I haven't stopped. You would know that better than anybody.'

I cried then, loud, awful sobs that shook my whole body. It took some time before I could compose myself. When I could speak, I said, 'I'm not sure where to begin.'

'Just tell me.'

Begin at the end. It's the only thing that matters. You can always go back.

I took a shuddering breath. 'I found Sarah.'

Martine was quiet until I finished, her only movement the jerky, repetitive twisting of her wedding ring. Tears had collected in the skin folds of her neck and travelled all the way to the hollow in her clavicle. Still, underneath the raw emotion she looked frighteningly fierce, and I had been counting on that.

She let loose with rapid-fire questions.

'Where is she?'

'With him. With the neighbour, at the hospital.'

'Is she in danger?'

I didn't have to think about it. I shook my head. 'He loves her. He would have hurt me, but never her.'

'Is he crazy?'

I nodded. 'In a calm, methodical, reasonable way – which is to say, most people wouldn't see him as crazy at all.'

'Doesn't matter. He's going to prison one way or the other. Why did you wait so long to tell him she isn't his?'

'You don't know what he's like,' I said. 'He would have had nothing to live for.'

'Right. Okay. So we go to the house and call the police. Could you find your way back there?'

'Yes.'

Her mouth twisted. 'But you don't want to do that.'

'I don't want a scene.'

Martine laughed – a short, humourless sound. 'A scene? You don't want a *scene*? She's a *child*.'

'She's almost a teenager,' I said. 'She's so grown up. You should see her.'

Martine swiped at her drying tears. 'Will he try to take her away again?'

'I don't know,' I sobbed. 'He's in no state to leave the hospital anytime soon. I think we have time.'

'Time to do what?'

'To do it right.'

Martine checked her watch. 'Jess should be here.'

'She's coming?'

'Of course,' she said. 'But tell me this – you got away around three. It's almost six and there's a police station right across the road, Abbie.'

'I know.'

'What have you been waiting for?'

I gave a helpless shrug. It should have been more clear-cut than this. If I hadn't gone in after him it would have been easier. It took everything I had to bring him up, to breathe life back into him.

'You don't understand.' I punched my chest. 'It can't be *me*.'

Martine sighed – not the kind of sigh that conveyed exasperation, or defeat, but release. 'Okay. I know. I do understand.' She blinked rapidly several times. 'She'll come back to you. I know she will.'

She stopped short of saying that I came back to her. I knew that's what she was thinking. I recognised the agony in her eyes – not the pain of a single betrayal, but the accumulation of little hurts she'd had to bear every day.

We sat in silence for a while. Martine downed a beer and I watched as her agitation slowly turned to resignation. I knew what was happening – she was processing the facts, connecting the dots, only to arrive at the same place I had already been for several hours. It was far from over.

When the glass double doors flew open and Jess entered, looking like a train wreck, we shot to our feet.

'You tell her,' I said.

Martine shook her head. 'I think she already knows.'

Jess had her phone pressed to her chest. When she spotted us, she rushed at me and held it out. 'It's some woman. She's asking for you – she says she has Sarah. She's not lying, is she? Is it a joke? Oh God, is it true?'

The book, under the floorboards. There had been no time to write anything but the phone numbers I could remember. Jess's had been the first on the list.

Martine pulled into the multistorey hospital car park and drove along the rows, looking for a space. Jess had left her car behind at the hotel.

'Just park in a loading zone,' Jess said.

Martine shook her head. 'I'll get a fine.'

Jess yelled, '*Jesus*, I'll pay the fine!'

'Wait. This one's coming out.' Martine flicked on the indicator.

It took forever. I drummed my feet on the floor. In the back, Jess was doing the same thing. Once Martine had parked, things sped up and they both flew into action, but for me everything slowed down.

'Did she say to meet at the main entrance?'

I told her yes. But when she and Jess strode away I couldn't get out of the car, couldn't find the words to explain why I was just sitting there.

Jess gestured wildly for me to hurry.

Martine yelled, 'Abbie, come *on*.'

'Wait,' I said.

Martine returned to the car and yanked the passenger-side door open. 'Get it together. Clean your face – it's filthy. There are wipes in here.' She opened the glove box, rummaged through bits and pieces that had accumulated over the years, scattering them on the floor. She found the wipes and pulled a couple from the packet. 'Here.'

Like a robot, I complied.

'That's better. Now let's go.'

I picked up a sheaf of papers from the footwell and shuffled through the pages. They were copies of the Missing posters I had carried around with me for years. I knew Jess had always carried them with her too, but Martine – she was a realist. I thought she'd given up hope long ago.

I looked up. I recognised the desperation in their eyes. Together they were a force: it would be too much for Sarah. It felt as if I was headed out onto a frozen lake – one wrong move, an uneven distribution of weight, the ice would give way and I'd never reach her. She'd disappear again.

'You need to know this won't go the way you're hoping,' I told them. 'She hates me.'

Martine kneeled on the concrete and tugged at my hand. 'That's what you think, but it isn't true.'

I shook my head. 'She only knows the bad stuff. That's all he told her. That's all she can remember.'

Martine glanced at Jess, who stood behind her. 'We'll tell her the truth.'

I closed the glove box and got out of the car, still clutching the posters. 'Not we. Just me.'

Jess hissed her frustration through her teeth, but Martine surprised me by putting her hand on Jess's arm.

'Whatever you think is best. We'll wait here.'

I gave them both a brief, hard hug. Jess was hysterical. Martine felt boneless in my arms. For the first time I felt like the strong one, the rock, the glue.

We're all connected. We're tied together, even when we're falling apart.

I took the lift to the ground floor. When I exited, the main entrance was obscured by a taxi rank and for a sick moment I thought Sarah had changed her mind. But the first taxi moved along, then the second, and there she was.

She looked small and scared, sitting next to Dani, who seemed reluctant to let her go. I knew Dani was right to be wary, but I couldn't find it in me to feel sympathy for the last person standing between me and my child. I stopped several metres short, lingering awkwardly at the edge of the path, my heart like Jess's baby bird, so close to my skin I was sure they could see it beating.

Sarah clung to Dani's hand, a small bag on the ground between her feet. She was caked with dried mud, like me, and pale with exhaustion.

'I don't know if I'm doing the right thing,' Dani said. 'He asked me not to – it doesn't feel right to me, but she wanted you, so –'

They stood.

Dani let go of Sarah's hand and it fell limply to her side.

'They said he'll be kept in for a few days,' she said. 'You'll bring her back then?'

I couldn't lie. 'I'll take her home where she belongs.'

'Maybe the police should be involved so there's some record of the handover?'

'No police. Please.' I stepped forward and thrust the sheaf of posters at her chest. I had folded them in half so the images weren't visible. 'It's the right thing,' I assured her. 'You'll know how right very soon.'

She took them. 'What is this?'

'Paperwork,' I said. 'Not now. After we've gone.'

Dani nodded and tucked the papers under her arm. She handed me Sarah's bag. 'I told her to pack enough things for a couple of days. I hope she's got everything.'

'We'll be fine,' I said.

Distractedly, I checked the contents: a jumble of clothes, a toiletry bag, a pair of shoes, the blood-streaked book – and a bundle of cash held by a rubber band. At a guess, just under eleven thousand dollars.

My eyes shot to Sarah, but she was staring at her feet. She must have taken the money when she went back for the book – did it mean she had doubts now? Questions?

'Are you sure?' Dani asked her.

Sarah nodded and took tentative steps in my direction. 'Bye,' she said to Dani, her voice low and tremulous.

I offered my hand, but she wouldn't take it. She shuffled alongside as we headed towards the lift, her movements sluggish.

Things weren't happening quickly enough. It felt like a ransom exchange; my instincts were telling me to run for it, as if I was the criminal on the verge of payoff and something could go wrong at any moment. We approached the lift, where there was a long queue. I beckoned Sarah toward the escalator and we rode up, standing on the same step, miles apart. Just as we reached the top, I heard the shout.

Sarah spun around in alarm and I looked back: Dani and a

security guard, sprinting after us. Dani was clutching her handbag and waving the posters, yelling. People were turning to stare and point in accusation.

Adrenaline shot through my body. I resisted the overwhelming urge to howl, to let out the hot fury I'd been holding inside for so long. These strangers were already judging me, making assumptions – what did any of them ever do to help, apart from read the papers and shake their heads and think, *thank God it wasn't my child*?

I wasn't taking her. I was taking her back. 'Keep going, Sarah.'

I put my hand between her shoulder blades and propelled her forward. At the top, I reached for the emergency stop button and hit it with a closed fist. The escalator slowed to a halt.

I grabbed Sarah's hand and pulled her along with me, weaving between cars. It wasn't that she was fighting to get away from me; she was oddly passive, probably suffering some kind of delayed shock. When we reached the start of the lane where Martine had parked, Sarah's legs went from under her. She slumped sideways onto the concrete floor. Her eyes were glazed, her bottom lip juddering as if she was trying to speak.

I had heard of mothers being able to lift cars from their trapped children in a display of superhuman strength, but it wasn't like that now. I put one arm around her waist, the other under her legs; I tried to get up and couldn't.

'Please, Sarah. Please try.'

Sarah curled into herself, her body vibrating with fear.

Then there were voices, a hot press of bodies, hands pulling at Sarah. Everything was black, spinning. It was always going to end here, at the vortex. But I wasn't afraid. My mother and sister were there, holding on to us both. It was safe to let go.

NOW

Martine and Jess stared ahead, rigid and silent. Martine paid for the ticket and exited the car park so nonchalantly I had to question if any of this was real. I kept my back hunched and my head down until we reached wider roads, more free-flowing traffic, while Jess flicked between radio stations, searching for music to break the terrible quiet.

Martine indicated and turned onto the freeway. 'Where?' she said.

I hesitated before I spoke. 'The nearest police station.' We couldn't risk anything else going wrong.

I glanced at Sarah to see her reaction, but there was none. She'd angled her body away from me to stare resolutely out her window – she was right there, but somehow not, lost in thoughts of her own. It was killing me not to embrace her, smell her hair, feel her skin, make sure she was whole.

Once I contacted the police, it would begin: the media circus, the conspiracy theories, the endless telling and retelling of truth to people whose job it was to be suspicious. I'd been through it and it nearly killed me, but Sarah was a child. She'd be questioned and interviewed until her reality blurred at the edges. They'd stick cameras in her face. She'd be deprogrammed, reprogrammed, and we wouldn't have the time we needed to get to know each other again. She stood to lose the only father she knew; she'd have to relive everything, but see it through a different lens. Strangers would have control over our lives until it was over.

It could be a long time before she heard our story.

It wasn't the way he told you

there were good times

I loved you

you loved me back

we had fun together

when I covered myself with red Texta dots to match your chickenpox and we painted each other's spots with calamine lotion using paintbrushes and when

we watched Shrek four times in one day and when

you accidentally swallowed your first lost tooth after days of poking it with your tongue and I asked Martine for one of mine and we pretended it was yours so you wouldn't miss the Tooth Fairy and whenever

we heard a P!nk song no matter where we were even if we were in the supermarket we had to stop and dance and when

you tried cauliflower rice for the first time — your face! — and when

you put make-up on me and I had to go out like that and when

you learned to swear in German because it didn't count and when

we rode on a train and you hung your head out the window like a joyful puppy and when

I taught you to swim like a fish like a dolphin like a mermaid and when

the moonlight hit the sea in a certain way you said it looked like a staircase to the moon

and when you were gone I was lost

but I have found you

and I have to remember remember

remember

my mother kept my teeth

she is a good mother

and

I am a good mother too.

But there was protocol to follow, a proper way to move forward. A good mother should do the right thing. A good wife should call her husband. As we drove on, daylight fading, I knew a kind stranger was waiting to deliver a message written on a napkin, and a nameless monster lay on a hospital bed, awaiting his fate. There was a long list of things I should do, many other decisions to be made.

Where would we go? How would we live now? Would we find each other again?

I pictured Sarah sleeping in my childhood bedroom; I imagined her as a teenager, laughing with friends in the corner booth at the kiosk, surfing at the beach. I saw us living with Kelly, sharing a loft bedroom with a window like a changing postcard – *my home is yours*, Kelly always said, if I ever wanted to return. And I left a blank space, an unfinished portrait of a combined family, in the event that Murray and I might find a way back to each other.

Across the water, pinpricks of light flickered on the peninsula; in between, pockets of blackness. There would always be dark spaces, but there were safe places too. When this was over we would find one, together. We just needed a place to begin.

Lulled by the rhythm of the car, I dozed.

When I woke, the car had stopped. Jess and Martine sat motionless in the front, their hands laced together and resting on the centre console.

I stretched my stiff neck. 'What's happening?'

Sarah was asleep, her body slipped sideways, her head on my lap, warm breath on my thigh. I heard the familiar hypnotic slap of waves against a shore and recognised the pale crescent of the beach below.

Martine switched off the ignition and the headlights. 'We're home.'

'But we should be –'

She turned around in the driver's seat. Her eyes glinted in the semi-dark. 'There's a storm coming.'

I peered through the window at the sky. It was darkening but clear, not a cloud, a bright almost-full moon risen above the sea. Where the bay waves normally pounded the seashells to grit, there was only a peaceful rolling-in, rolling-out – an unusual calm for this time of year.

In my lap, Sarah stirred.

'We can't stop it, but we can sit tight until morning,' Martine said. 'You should go for a walk along the beach while I make dinner. Wander back in your own time. Before the weather hits, I mean.'

Jess chose that moment to take Martine's side. 'I agree. We should wait it out.'

My mother and sister, united against me.

I gave Jess a wry smile and stroked a wisp of hair from Sarah's cheek, swallowing at the lump in my throat. Tomorrow might bring change, but for now it was just us.

I woke Sarah the way I used to when she was small, by blowing gently on her face.

Her eyelids fluttered and opened.

We slipped off our shoes and left them at the start of the path through the dunes. I led Sarah through the softer sand, still warm from the sun, along the clean hard crust left by the ebb tide, down to the ribbon of foam at the water's edge.

I looked back, but she was gone. Only one set of footprints marked the hard sand.

I twirled around in a moment of blind panic – no, just behind where I stood, my set of prints diverged into two. Here she was next to me, digging her toes in the sand, studying the way the moonlight reflected on the ocean.

I pointed right, showing Sarah the rocks where we had once explored natural caves and tidal pools; to the left, the jetty where she had caught her first fish. The kiosk, its fairy lights glowing iridescent blue in the coming dark, the grassy slope for rolling down, the car park where the ice-cream van waited for us to return sunburnt and salty from the sea.

When I'd finished, I reached out to her.

She left my hand hanging there for what seemed like forever.

Was there ever a more painful silence, a more gut-wrenching absence?

Yes. There had been, and we'd lived through it.

We would survive this, too.

ACKNOWLEDGMENTS

This story is as much about relationships between women as it is about a terrible crime. Shout-out to the incredible women in my life – my cheer squad, my team, my unruly gang of bad mothers. Thank you for the laughter, tears, wine and confessions, and for the light you bring.

Without the team at Text Publishing, who champion everything I write, this book may have stayed tucked away in the 'someday' folder, unfinished. Thank you, Penny Hueston – brilliant editor and now partner-in-crime. Thank you, Michael Heyward, for saying something (long ago) that made all the difference to the way I approach writing. Thank you to W. H. Chong for this sublime cover-in-blue.

This newbie is forever grateful for the support of the crime-writing community: Sisters in Crime, Emma Viskic, Mark Brandi, Lucy Christopher, Josh Pomare, Sarah Bailey, Anna Downes, Leah Swann, Loraine Peck and Amy Suiter Clarke. Thank you for your generosity and thoughtful words.

To Allayne – you have a gift for making people feel like rock stars. We all need that. Thank you, my friend.

Thank you to my parents, Brian and Julie, who never told me to put down my book and go and play outside, and to Michelle, my Stepmonster, who gives me time to write (and who rightly believes dogs are the best people).

To Russ, Mia and Roan – I know I'm in another world a lot of the time, but I'll never take it for granted that you're there when I return. A special mention to Bowie and Ziggy, the latest in a line of canine muses, who remind me (frequently) to look up from the page and go for a walk.

And finally, vale and thank you, Sheila Drummond. This is the first book I have written without your guidance and friendship. You are missed.

Vikki Wakefield writes fiction for young adults and adults. Her books explore family, class and relationships in a contemporary setting. Her novels *All I Ever Wanted*, *Friday Brown*, *Inbetween Days* and *Ballad for a Mad Girl* have been shortlisted for numerous awards. *This Is How We Change The Ending* won Book of the Year: Older Readers, Children's Book Council Awards, 2020. *After You Were Gone*, a psychological thriller, is her first novel for adults. She is working on her second one.

vikkiwakefield.com

Bedford Square Publishers

Bedford Square Publishers is an independent publisher of fiction and non-fiction, founded in 2022 in the historic streets of Bedford Square London and the sea mist shrouded green of Bedford Square Brighton.

Our goal is to discover irresistible stories and voices that illuminate our world.

We are passionate about connecting our authors to readers across the globe and our independence allows us to do this in original and nimble ways.

The team at Bedford Square Publishers has years of experience and we aim to use that knowledge and creative insight, alongside evolving technology, to reach the right readers for our books. From the ones who read a lot, to the ones who don't consider themselves readers, we aim to find those who will love our books and talk about them as much as we do.

We are hunting for vital new voices from all backgrounds – with books that take the reader to new places and transform perceptions of the world we live in.

Follow us on social media for the latest Bedford Square Publishers news.

🐦 @bedsqpublishers
f facebook.com/bedfordsq.publishers/
📷 @bedfordsq.publishers

https://bedfordsquarepublishers.co.uk/